**image**® comics presents

# Wayward

## Volume One: String Theory



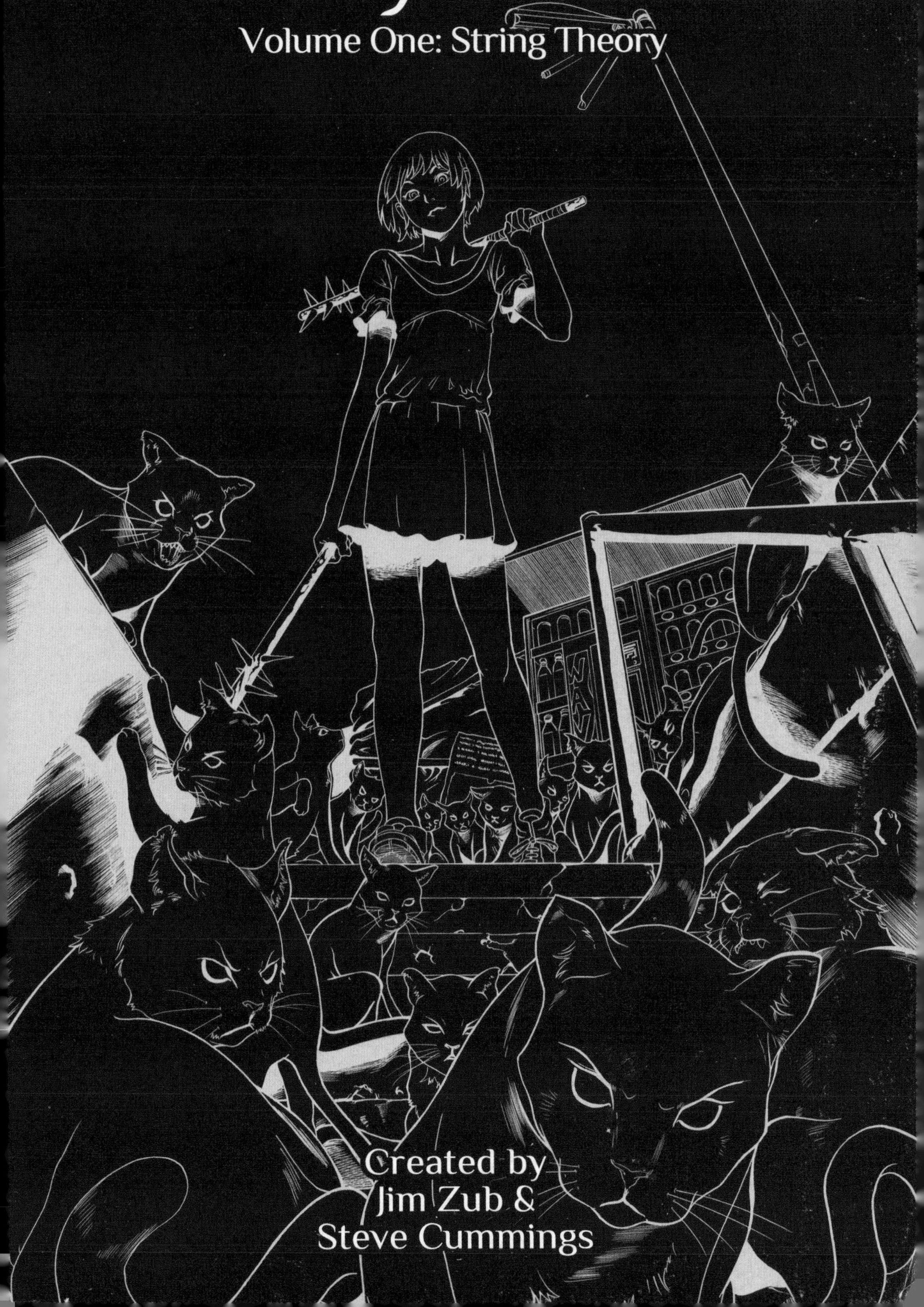

Created by
Jim Zub &
Steve Cummings

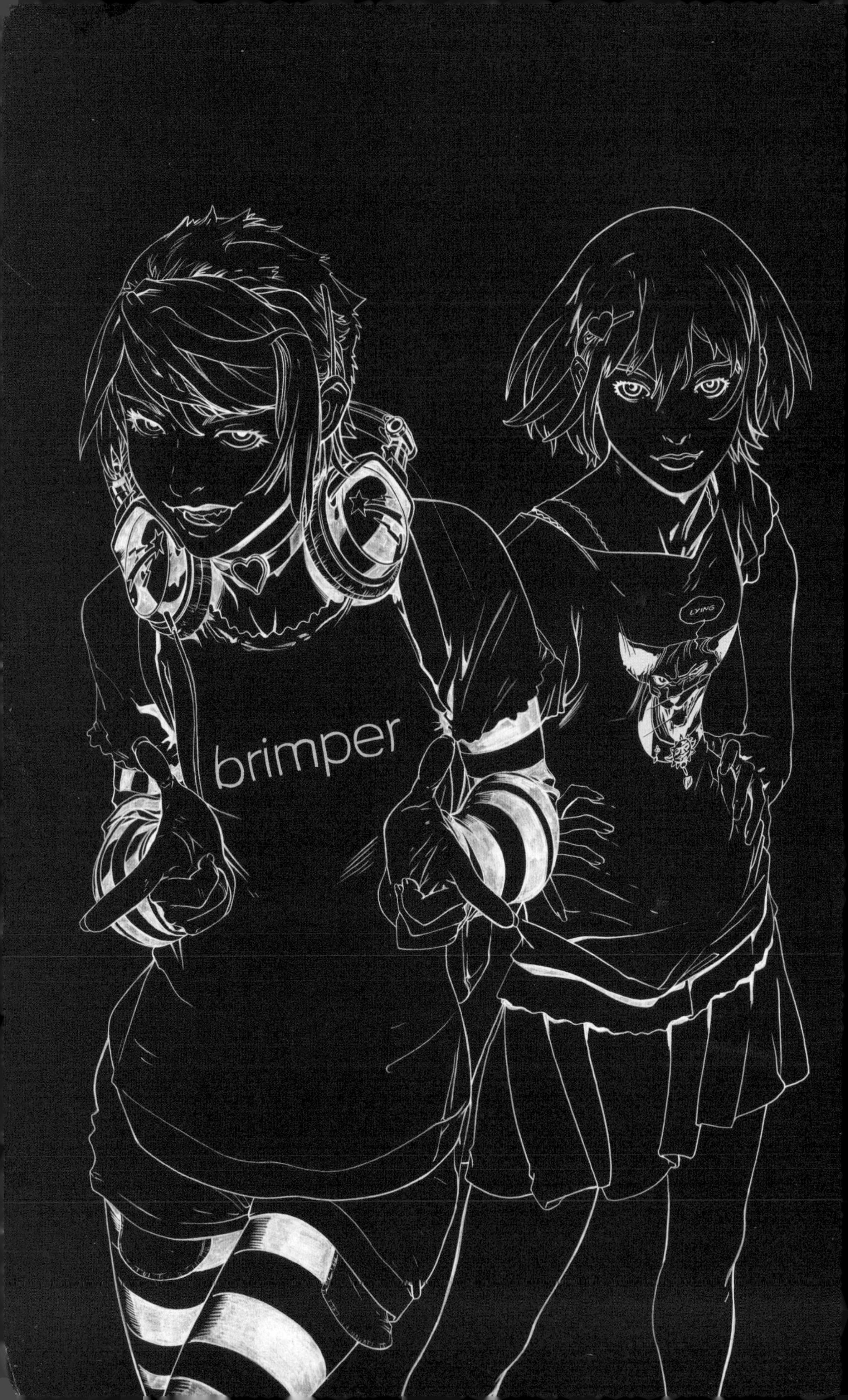
brimper
LYING

story
Jim Zub

line art
Steve Cummings

color art
Tamra Bonvillain
Ross A. Campbell
Josh Perez
John Rauch
Jim Zub

color flats
Ludwig Olimba

letters
Marshall Dillon

back matter
Zack Davisson

**IMAGE COMICS, INC.**
Robert Kirkman – Chief Operating Officer
Erik Larsen – Chief Financial Officer
Todd McFarlane – President
Marc Silvestri – Chief Executive Officer
Jim Valentino – Vice-President

Eric Stephenson – Publisher
Ron Richards – Director of Business Development
Jennifer de Guzman – Director of Trade Book Sales
Kat Salazar – Director of PR & Marketing
Corey Murphy – Director of Retail Sales
Jeremy Sullivan – Director of Digital Sales
Emilio Bautista – Sales Assistant
Branwyn Bigglestone – Senior Accounts Manager
Emily Miller – Accounts Manager
Jessica Ambriz – Administrative Assistant
Tyler Shainline – Events Coordinator
David Brothers – Content Manager
Jonathan Chan – Production Manager
Drew Gill – Art Director
Meredith Wallace – Print Manager
Addison Duke – Production Artist
Vincent Kukua – Production Artist
Tricia Ramos – Production Assistant
IMAGECOMICS.COM

special thanks
Kalman Andrasofszky
Jeff "Chamba" Cruz
Erik Ko
Nishi Makoto
Ron Richards
Brandon Seifert
Charles Soule
Eric Stephenson
Adam Warren

# Welcome To Real Japan

True confession time: When Jim Zub contacted me about *Wayward*, I was trepidatious. I didn't know Jim or his work aside from Skullkickers. We'd been introduced by mutual friend Brandon Seifert (writer for the wonderfully brilliant *Witch Doctor*), and I agreed to give *Wayward* a look and write an essay for the first issue. But I wasn't confident. I'd had bad experiences working on "Japan-themed comics" before...

Then I read the script.

I was hooked. I immediately signed on for the duration, and threatened to cry salty tears if Jim wouldn't let me write backup Yōkai Files as well. It was clear from the beginning that something magical was brewing. Because not only is *Wayward* an excellent story—and it is—but just as important to me, it got Japan right.

One of my pet peeves is what I call "Japan as Decoration." Creators treat Japan as if it were a fictitious fantasyland, with all the reality of one of the kingdoms of Westeros. They pepper comics with ninja and samurai, geisha and Godzilla, sword-wielding schoolgirls and giant robots, trying to add a dash of exoticism to their story. It's the comic book equivalent of a bad kanji tattoo; somehow people feel they are adding depth by writing in a language they don't understand—about a culture they don't understand—just because it looks pretty. (Word of advice kids! No kanji tattoos!)

The academic term for this is Orientalism. It's not a new phenomenon—Japan has been treated as a fairy tale as far back as 1889, when Oscar Wilde declared *"The whole of Japan is a pure invention. There is no such country, there are no such people."*

But for those of us who lived in Japan, we know that there is such a country; there are such people. (I'm married to one.) We know Japan is often no more exotic than Spokane, Washington or Fullerton, California. It's where you wake up, have breakfast, go to work, and do all the things you do anywhere else. Of course, it's equally wonderful—full of inexhaustible charm and mystery. But it's a real place with real people.

And that's exactly how Jim and Steve Cummings portray it.

Steve, of course, lives in Yokohama. His magnificent, detailed, and oh-so-pretty linework anchors Wayward in the physical—if you hopped off a plane in Narita International Airport, you would find Tokyo looking just as Rori does in the opening pages. (Another true confession: When I got the proofs, I scoured the first issue hunting for kanji mistakes. I didn't find a single one. Just the opposite, Steve adds clever bits and clues to the story in the background kanji, a little present for Japanese speakers.)

This isn't limited to the backgrounds. Rori is real. Ayane, Shirai, and Nikaido are real. They dress and act like students I would recognize from my years in Japan's school system. (Magic powers aside.) The scenes with the principal are shockingly authentic. And the monsters are real too.

Japan is the most haunted country on earth—the folklore is immense, and rich and varied. With *Wayward*, Jim and Steve have mined this past and unearthed its treasures. From Nurarihyon to the turtle-shelled kappa, every yōkai has wandered directly from folklore. Japan's monster menagerie has never been so well-portrayed in an American comic.

That said, *Wayward* is very much Jim and Steve's story. From this bedrock of authenticity, they weave their own fantasy, adding to the mythology with original elements seamlessly blended. There is magic and wonder and horror, and an intricate story of the clash of tradition and modernity, of cultural blending and dilution, of beginnings and endings. I am as much a fan of Wayward as anyone, getting ridiculously excited every time I see a new script in my inbox. Knowing the destination, I still am breathless to see the journey.

If this is your first time diving into *Wayward*, know that this is fantastic Japan the way it is supposed to be. A country that embraces the weird—but a country regular people live in. And die in. A very real world. Prepare to be amazed.

- **Zack Davisson**
  January 2015

Zack Davisson is a translator, writer, and scholar of Japanese folklore, ghosts, and manga. He is the author of YŪREI - THE JAPANESE GHOST, the translator of Satoshi Kon's OPUS and Shigeru Mizuki's Eisner and Harvey-nominated SHOWA: A HISTORY OF JAPAN, and creator of the popular Japanese folklore site **hyakumonogatari.com**

# Chapter One

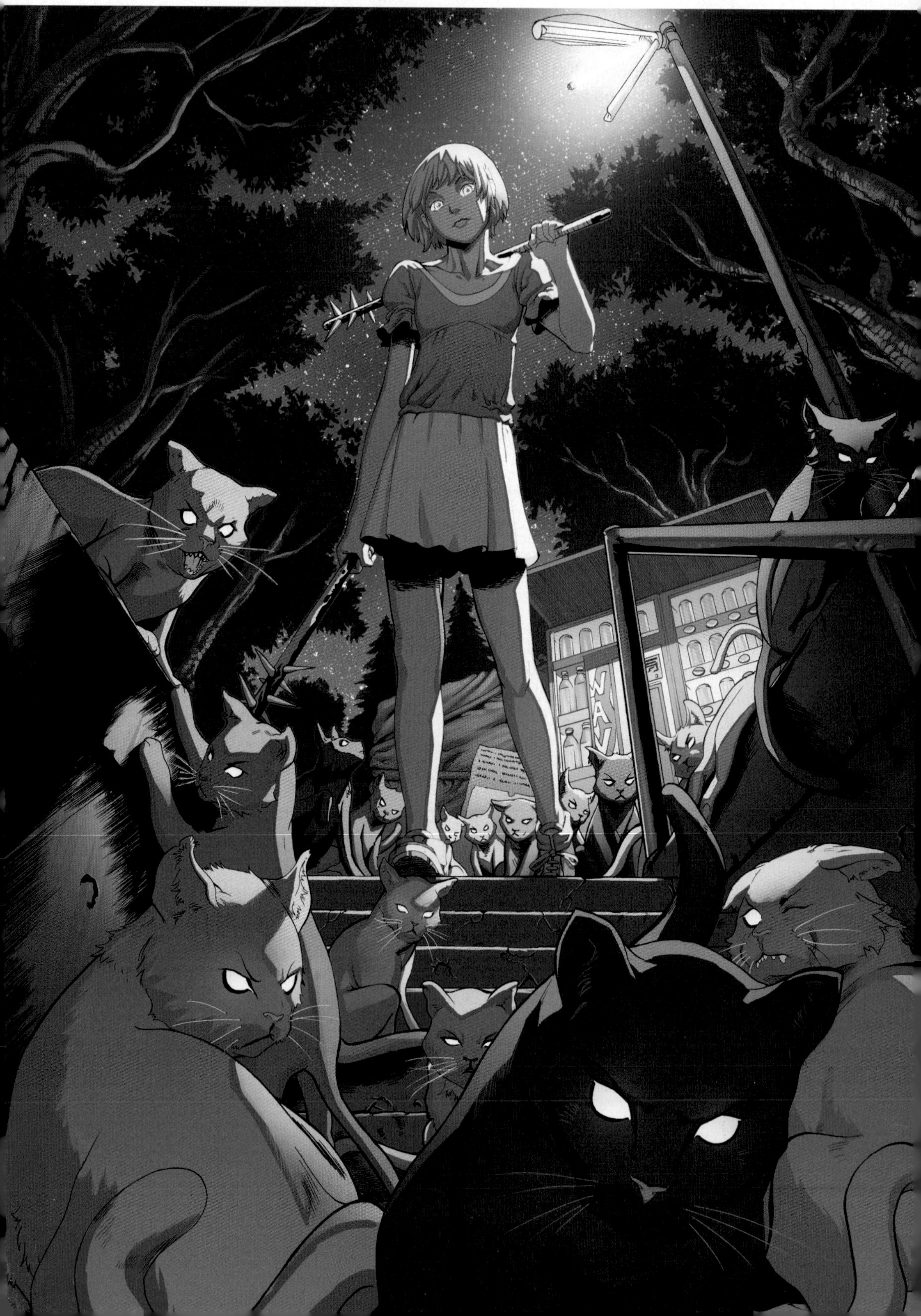

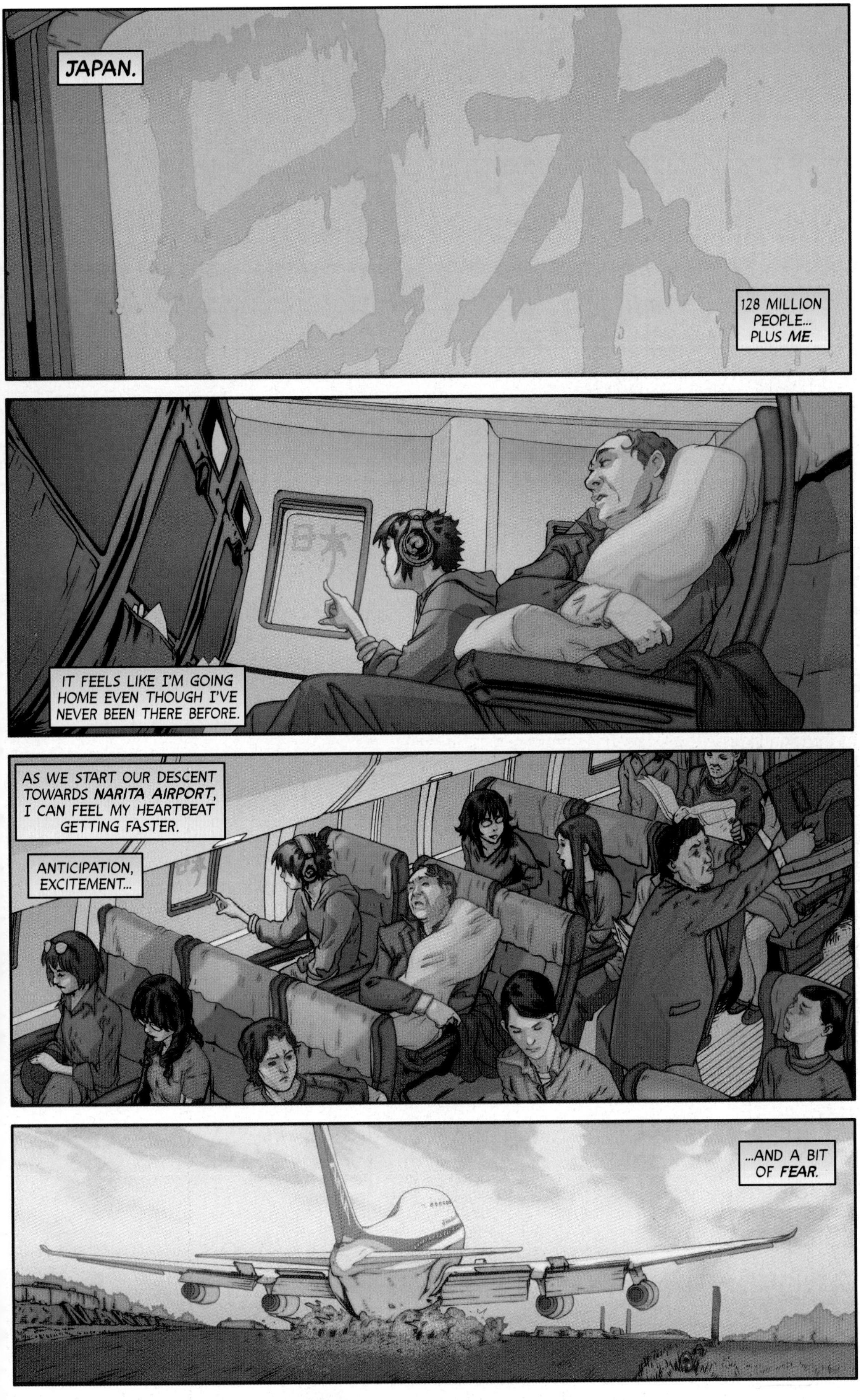
JAPAN.
日本
128 MILLION PEOPLE... PLUS ME.
日本
IT FEELS LIKE I'M GOING HOME EVEN THOUGH I'VE NEVER BEEN THERE BEFORE.
AS WE START OUR DESCENT TOWARDS NARITA AIRPORT, I CAN FEEL MY HEARTBEAT GETTING FASTER.
ANTICIPATION, EXCITEMENT...
...AND A BIT OF FEAR.

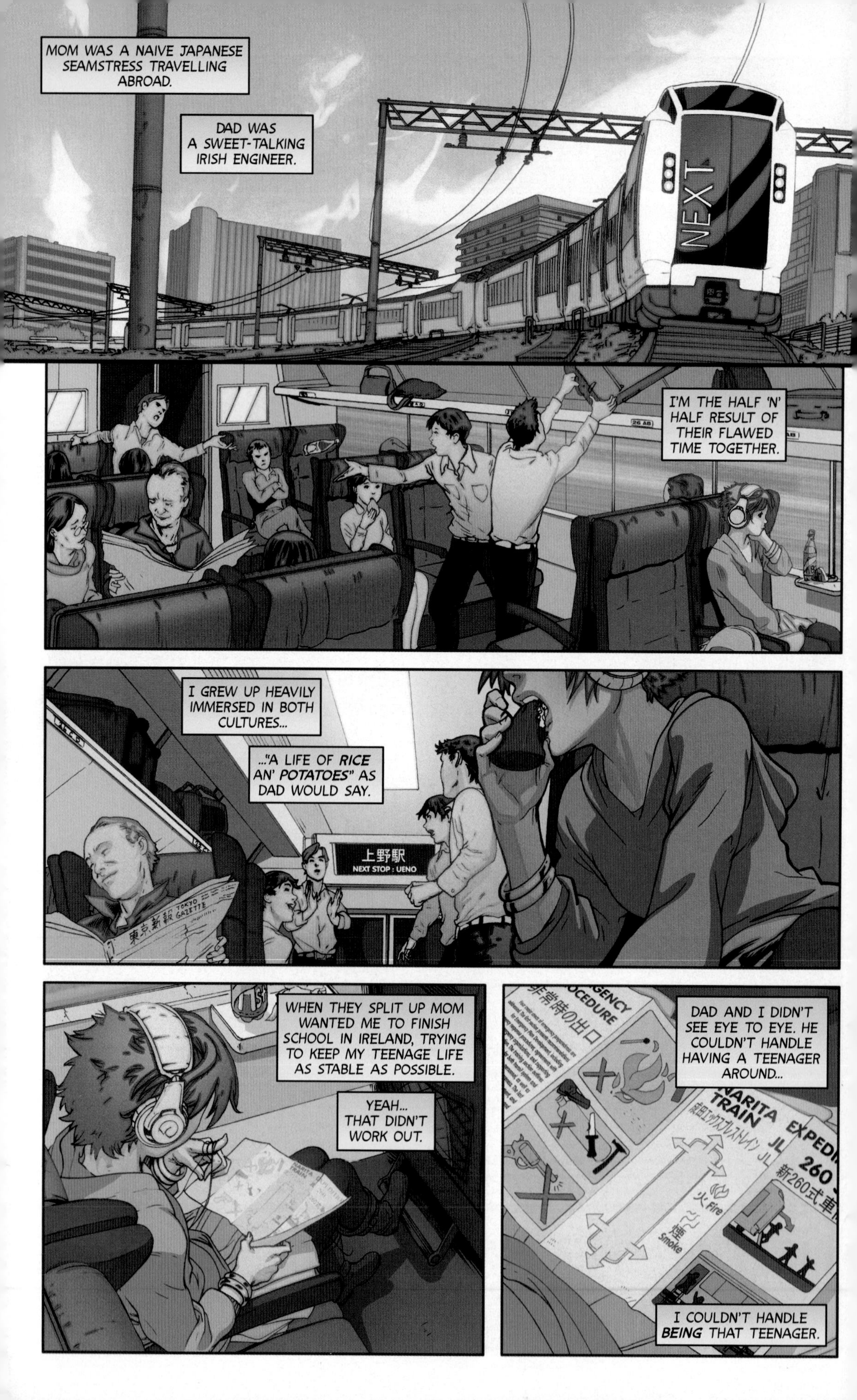
MOM WAS A NAIVE JAPANESE SEAMSTRESS TRAVELLING ABROAD.
DAD WAS A SWEET-TALKING IRISH ENGINEER.
NEXT
I'M THE HALF 'N' HALF RESULT OF THEIR FLAWED TIME TOGETHER.
I GREW UP HEAVILY IMMERSED IN BOTH CULTURES...
..."A LIFE OF *RICE* AN' *POTATOES*" AS DAD WOULD SAY.
上野駅
NEXT STOP : UENO
東京新報 TOKYO GAZETTE
WHEN THEY SPLIT UP MOM WANTED ME TO FINISH SCHOOL IN IRELAND, TRYING TO KEEP MY TEENAGE LIFE AS STABLE AS POSSIBLE.
YEAH... THAT DIDN'T WORK OUT.
DAD AND I DIDN'T SEE EYE TO EYE. HE COULDN'T HANDLE HAVING A TEENAGER AROUND...
非常時の出口
NARITA TRAIN
火 Fire
煙 Smoke
I COULDN'T HANDLE *BEING* THAT TEENAGER.

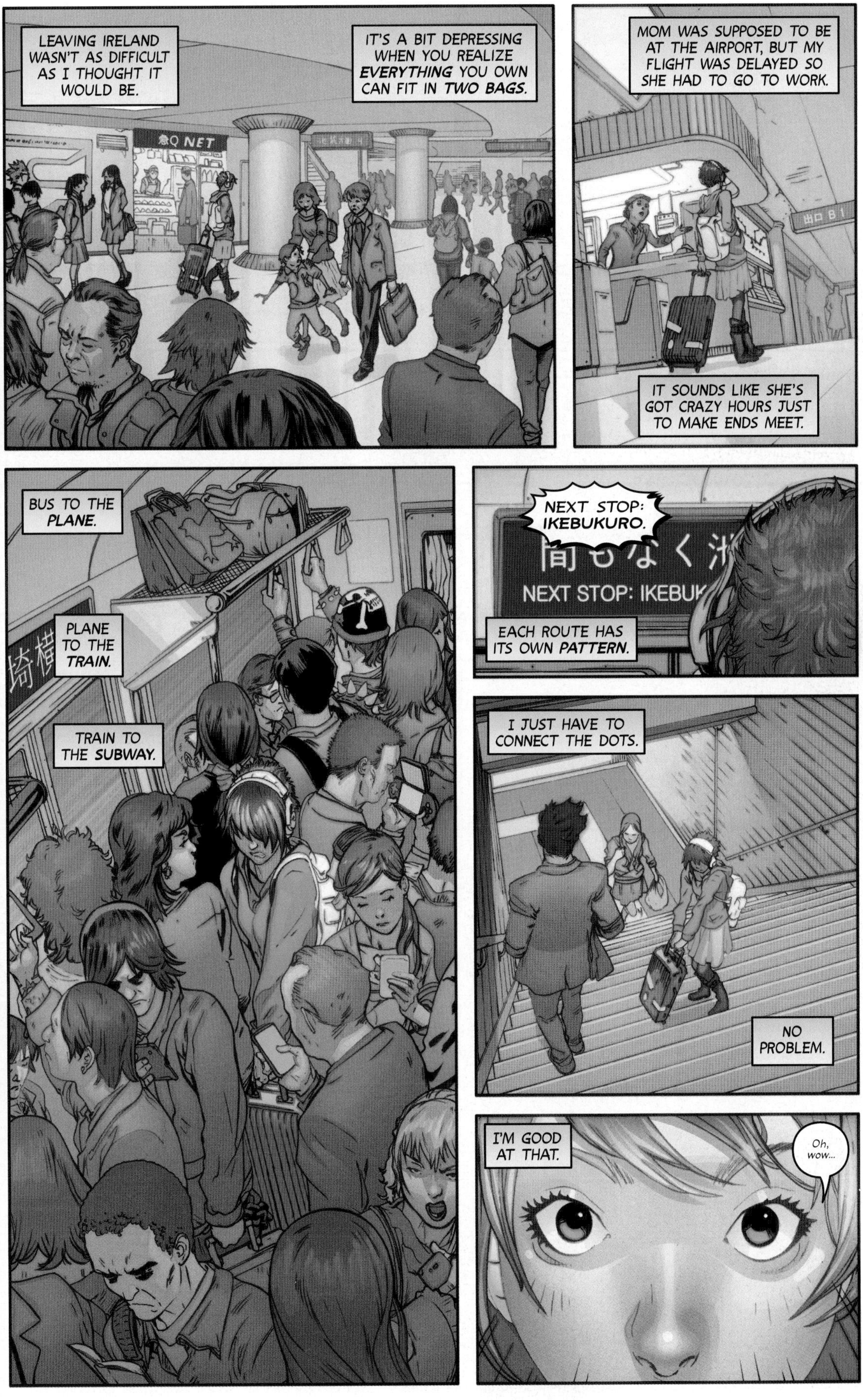
LEAVING IRELAND WASN'T AS DIFFICULT AS I THOUGHT IT WOULD BE.
IT'S A BIT DEPRESSING WHEN YOU REALIZE ***EVERYTHING*** YOU OWN CAN FIT IN ***TWO BAGS.***
急Q NET
MOM WAS SUPPOSED TO BE AT THE AIRPORT, BUT MY FLIGHT WAS DELAYED SO SHE HAD TO GO TO WORK.
出口 B1
IT SOUNDS LIKE SHE'S GOT CRAZY HOURS JUST TO MAKE ENDS MEET.
BUS TO THE ***PLANE.***
PLANE TO THE ***TRAIN.***
TRAIN TO THE **SUBWAY.**
NEXT STOP: **IKEBUKURO.**
NEXT STOP: IKEBUK
EACH ROUTE HAS ITS OWN ***PATTERN.***
I JUST HAVE TO CONNECT THE DOTS.
NO PROBLEM.
I'M GOOD AT THAT.
*Oh, wow...*

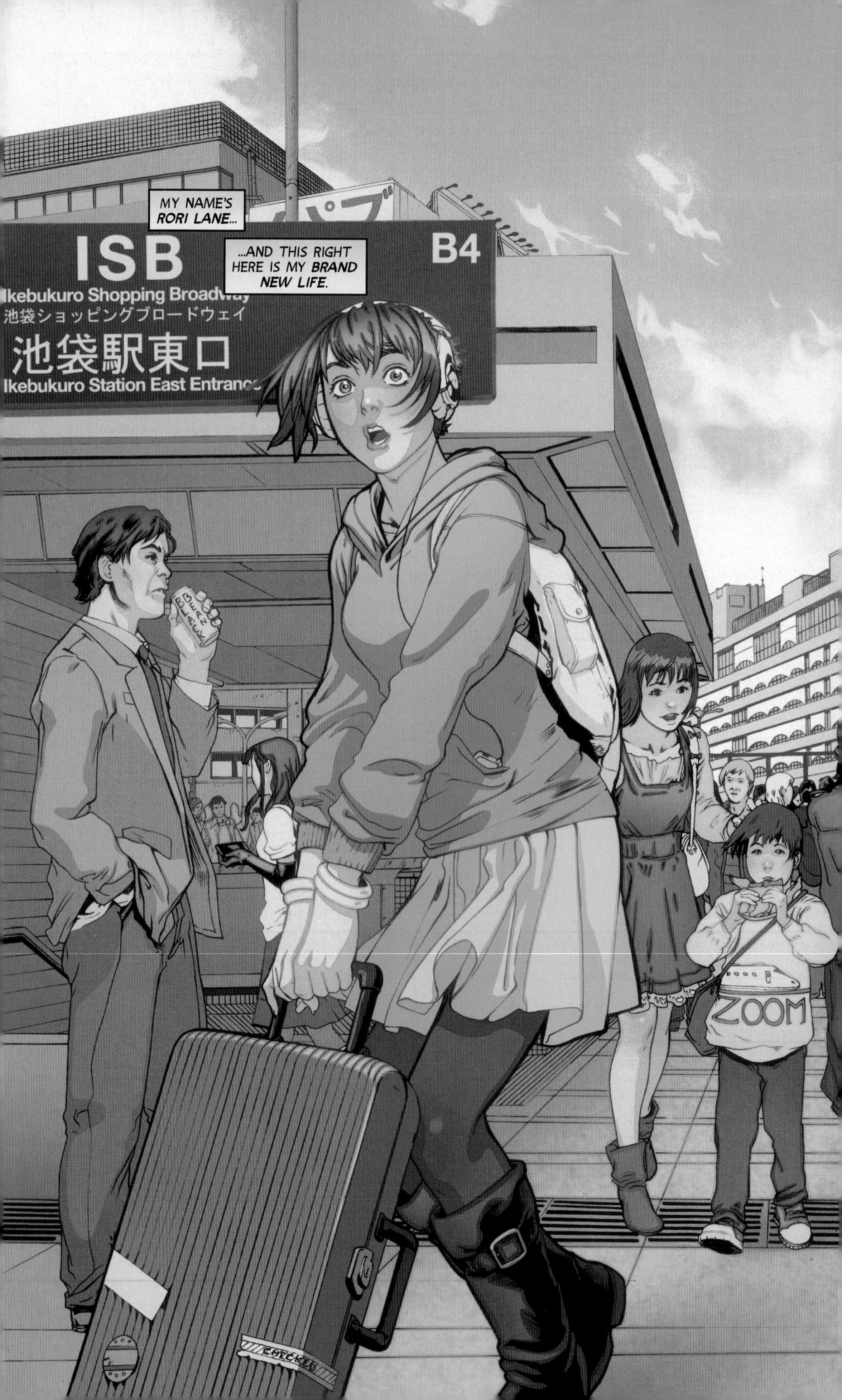

MY NAME'S RORI LANE...
...AND THIS RIGHT HERE IS MY BRAND NEW LIFE.
ISB
B4
Ikebukuro Shopping Broadway
池袋ショッピングブロードウェイ
池袋駅東口
Ikebukuro Station East Entrance
ZOOM
CHECKED

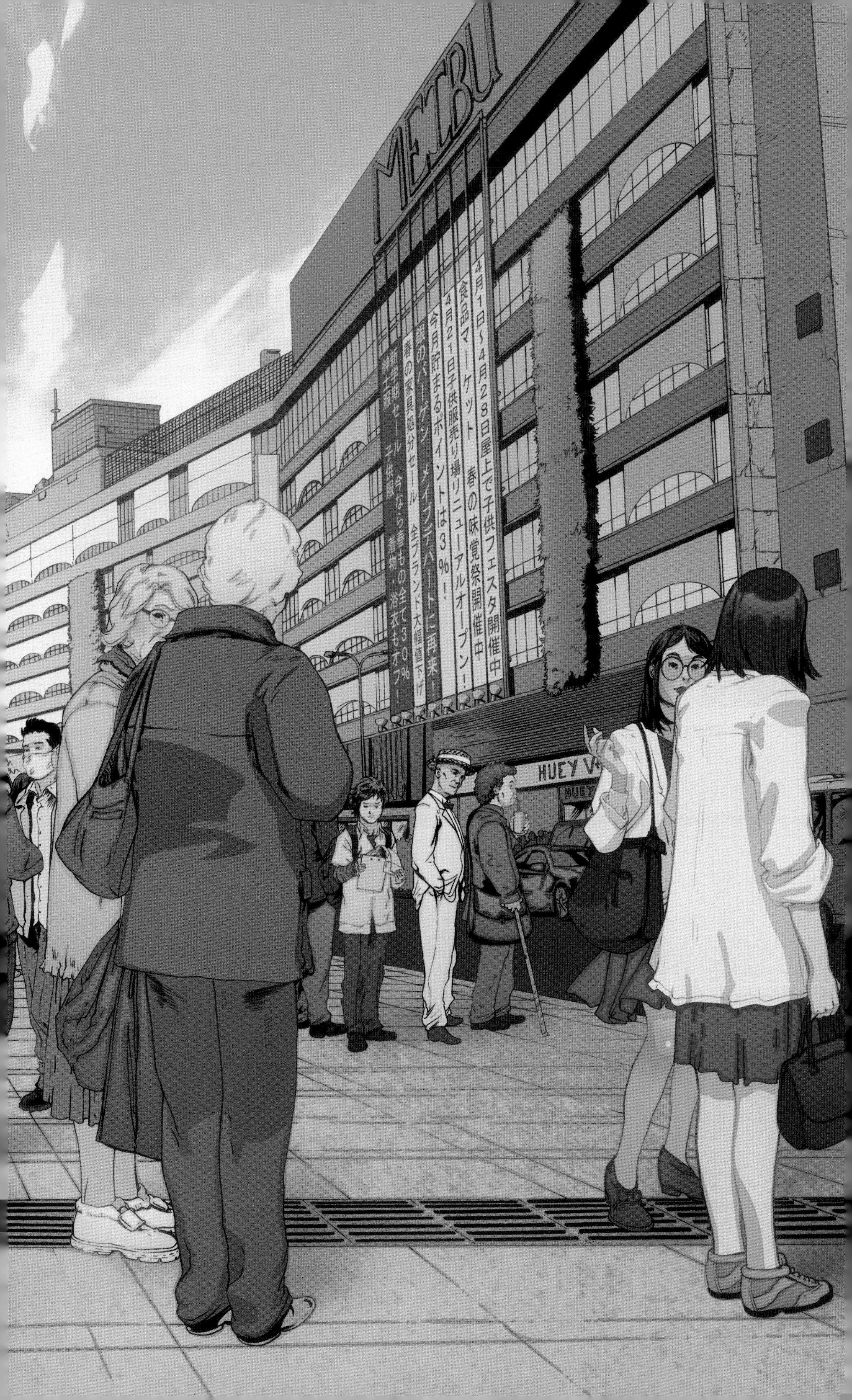
METBU
4月1日～4月28日屋上で子供フェスタ開催中
食品マーケット　春の味覚祭開催中
4月21日子供服売り場リニューアルオープン！
今月貯まるポイントは3%！
銀のバーゲン　メイブデパートに再来！
春の家具処分セール　全ブランド大幅値下げ
新学期セール　今なら春もの全て30%
紳士服　子供服　着物・浴衣もオフ！
HUEY V

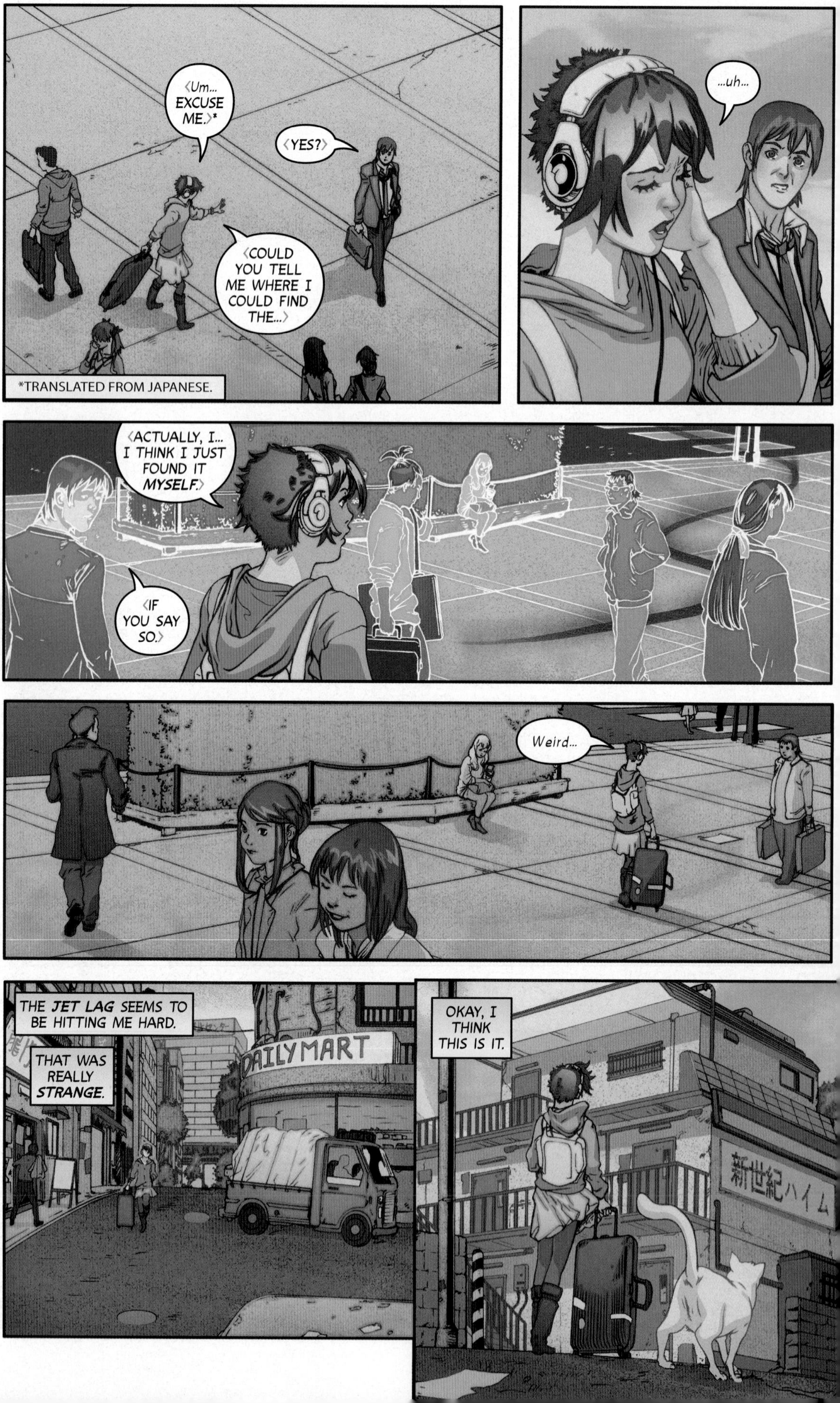
‹Um... EXCUSE ME.›*
‹YES?›
‹COULD YOU TELL ME WHERE I COULD FIND THE...›
*TRANSLATED FROM JAPANESE.
...uh...
‹ACTUALLY, I... I THINK I JUST FOUND IT *MYSELF*.›
‹IF YOU SAY SO.›
Weird...
THE *JET LAG* SEEMS TO BE HITTING ME HARD.
THAT WAS REALLY *STRANGE*.
DAILYMART
OKAY, I THINK THIS IS IT.
新世紀ハイム

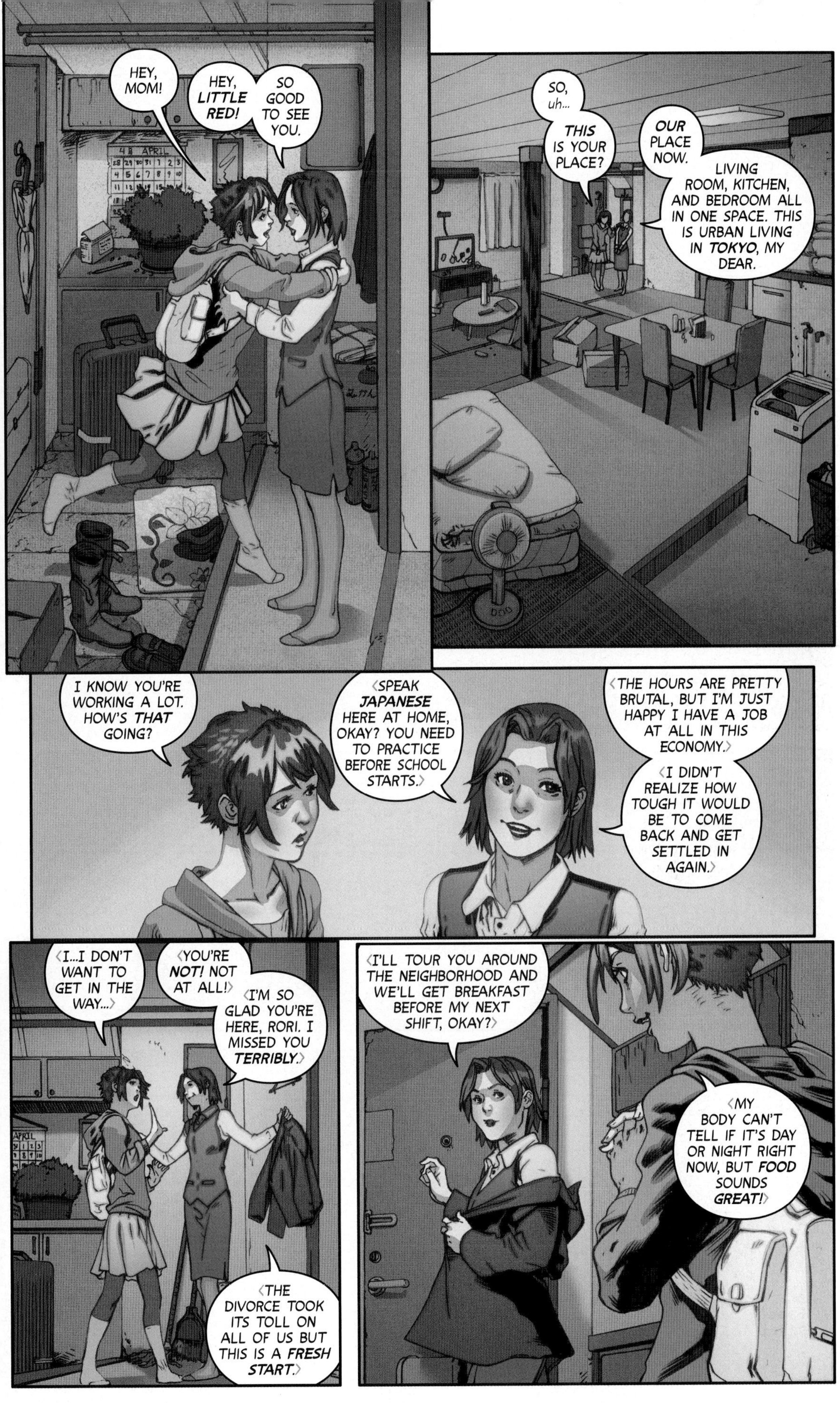
HEY, MOM!
HEY, LITTLE RED!
SO GOOD TO SEE YOU.
SO, uh... THIS IS YOUR PLACE?
OUR PLACE NOW.
LIVING ROOM, KITCHEN, AND BEDROOM ALL IN ONE SPACE. THIS IS URBAN LIVING IN TOKYO, MY DEAR.
I KNOW YOU'RE WORKING A LOT. HOW'S THAT GOING?
<SPEAK JAPANESE HERE AT HOME, OKAY? YOU NEED TO PRACTICE BEFORE SCHOOL STARTS.>
<THE HOURS ARE PRETTY BRUTAL, BUT I'M JUST HAPPY I HAVE A JOB AT ALL IN THIS ECONOMY.>
<I DIDN'T REALIZE HOW TOUGH IT WOULD BE TO COME BACK AND GET SETTLED IN AGAIN.>
<I...I DON'T WANT TO GET IN THE WAY...>
<YOU'RE NOT! NOT AT ALL!>
<I'M SO GLAD YOU'RE HERE, RORI. I MISSED YOU TERRIBLY.>
<THE DIVORCE TOOK ITS TOLL ON ALL OF US BUT THIS IS A FRESH START.>
<I'LL TOUR YOU AROUND THE NEIGHBORHOOD AND WE'LL GET BREAKFAST BEFORE MY NEXT SHIFT, OKAY?>
<MY BODY CAN'T TELL IF IT'S DAY OR NIGHT RIGHT NOW, BUT FOOD SOUNDS GREAT!>

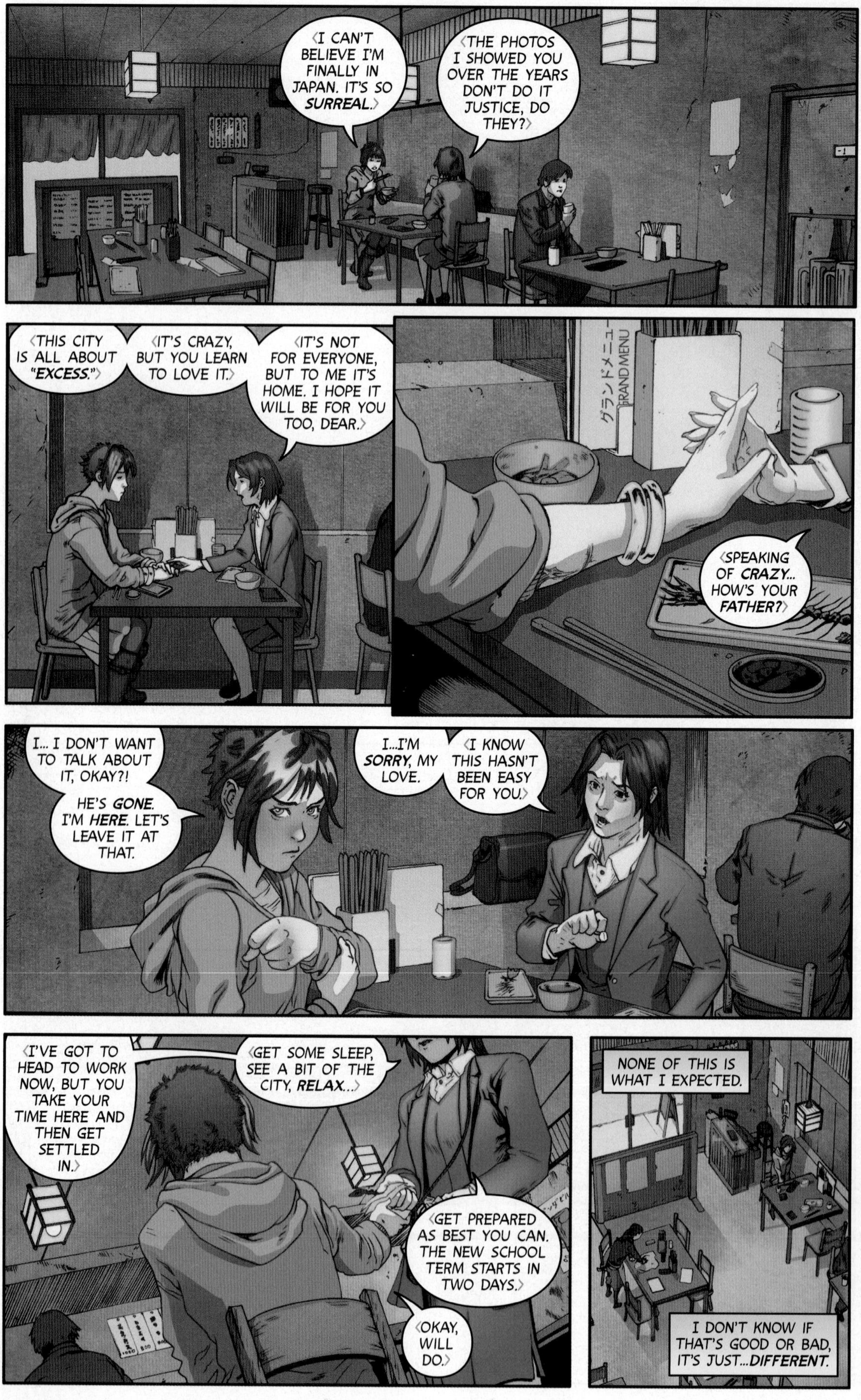
‹I CAN'T BELIEVE I'M FINALLY IN JAPAN. IT'S SO **SURREAL.**›
‹THE PHOTOS I SHOWED YOU OVER THE YEARS DON'T DO IT JUSTICE, DO THEY?›
‹THIS CITY IS ALL ABOUT "**EXCESS.**"›
‹IT'S CRAZY, BUT YOU LEARN TO LOVE IT.›
‹IT'S NOT FOR EVERYONE, BUT TO ME IT'S HOME. I HOPE IT WILL BE FOR YOU TOO, DEAR.›
グランドメニュー
‹SPEAKING OF **CRAZY**... HOW'S YOUR **FATHER?**›
I... I DON'T WANT TO TALK ABOUT IT, OKAY?!
HE'S **GONE**. I'M **HERE**. LET'S LEAVE IT AT THAT.
I...I'M **SORRY**, MY LOVE.
‹I KNOW THIS HASN'T BEEN EASY FOR YOU.›
‹I'VE GOT TO HEAD TO WORK NOW, BUT YOU TAKE YOUR TIME HERE AND THEN GET SETTLED IN.›
‹GET SOME SLEEP, SEE A BIT OF THE CITY, **RELAX**...›
‹GET PREPARED AS BEST YOU CAN. THE NEW SCHOOL TERM STARTS IN TWO DAYS.›
‹OKAY, WILL DO.›
NONE OF THIS IS WHAT I EXPECTED.
I DON'T KNOW IF THAT'S GOOD OR BAD, IT'S JUST...**DIFFERENT**.

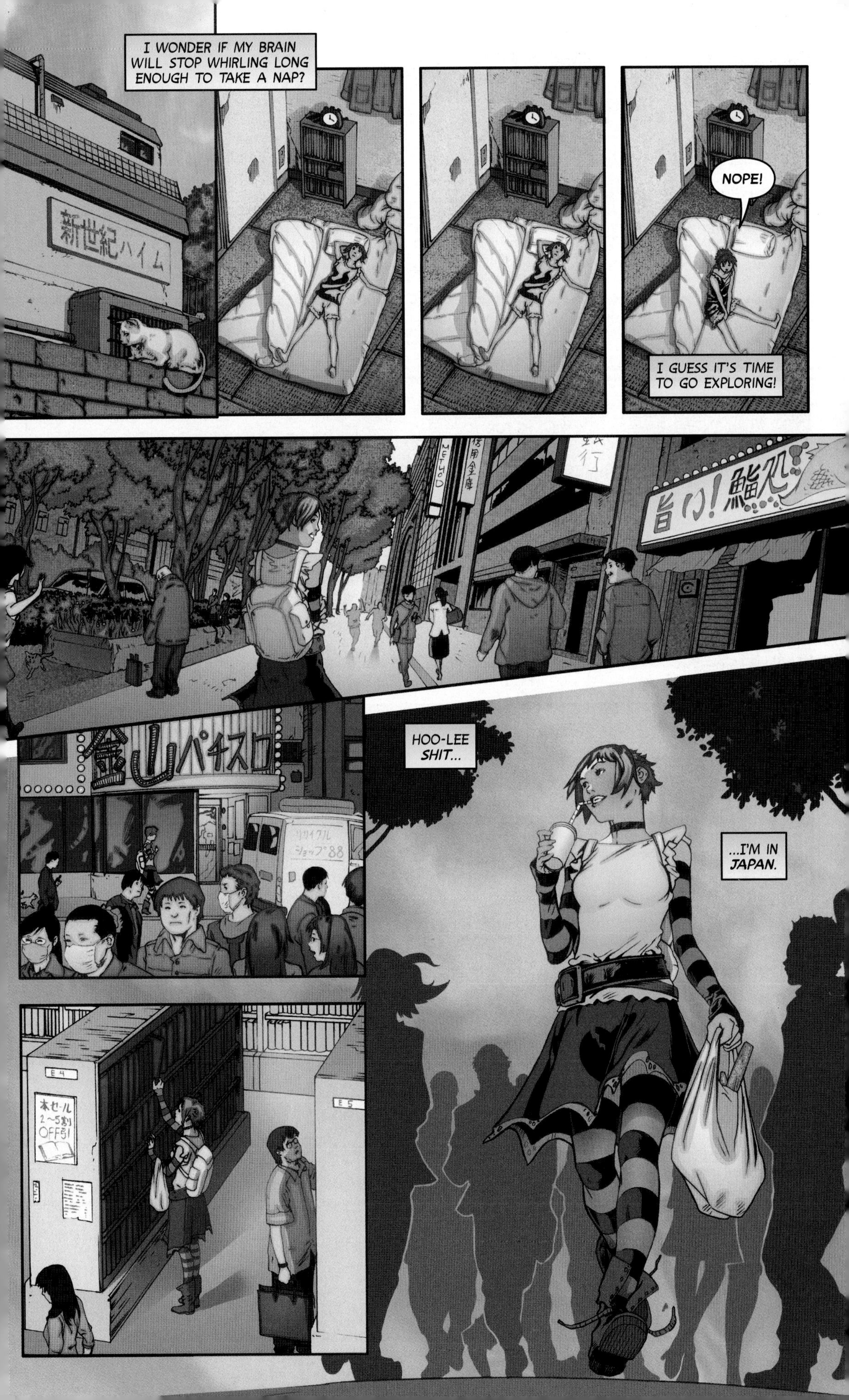
I WONDER IF MY BRAIN WILL STOP WHIRLING LONG ENOUGH TO TAKE A NAP?
新世紀ハイム
NOPE!
I GUESS IT'S TIME TO GO EXPLORING!
HOO-LEE *SHIT*...
...I'M IN *JAPAN*.

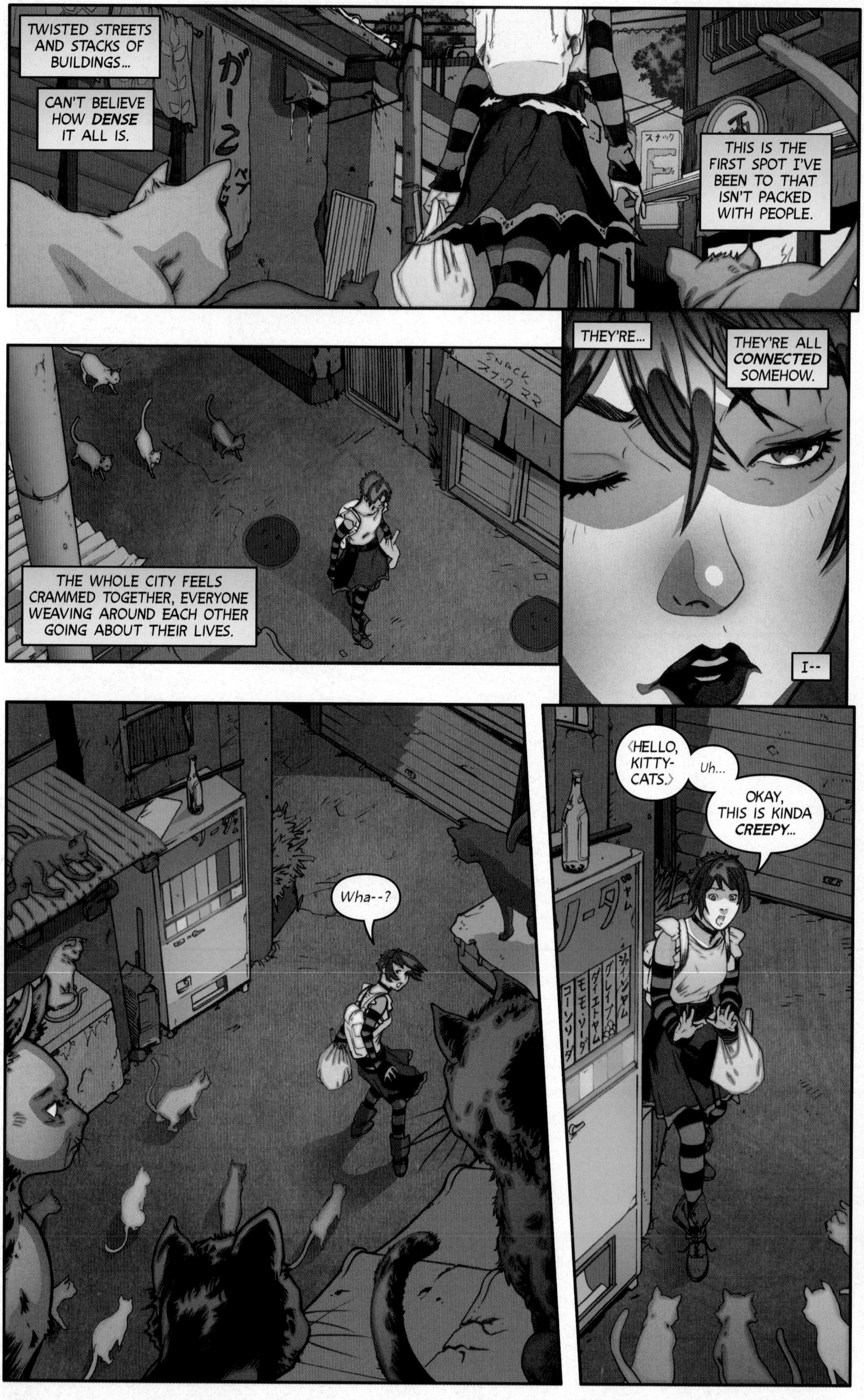
TWISTED STREETS AND STACKS OF BUILDINGS...
CAN'T BELIEVE HOW *DENSE* IT ALL IS.
THIS IS THE FIRST SPOT I'VE BEEN TO THAT ISN'T PACKED WITH PEOPLE.
THE WHOLE CITY FEELS CRAMMED TOGETHER, EVERYONE WEAVING AROUND EACH OTHER GOING ABOUT THEIR LIVES.
SNACK
THEY'RE...
THEY'RE ALL *CONNECTED* SOMEHOW.
I--
Wha--?
⟨HELLO, KITTY-CATS.⟩
Uh...
OKAY, THIS IS KINDA *CREEPY*...

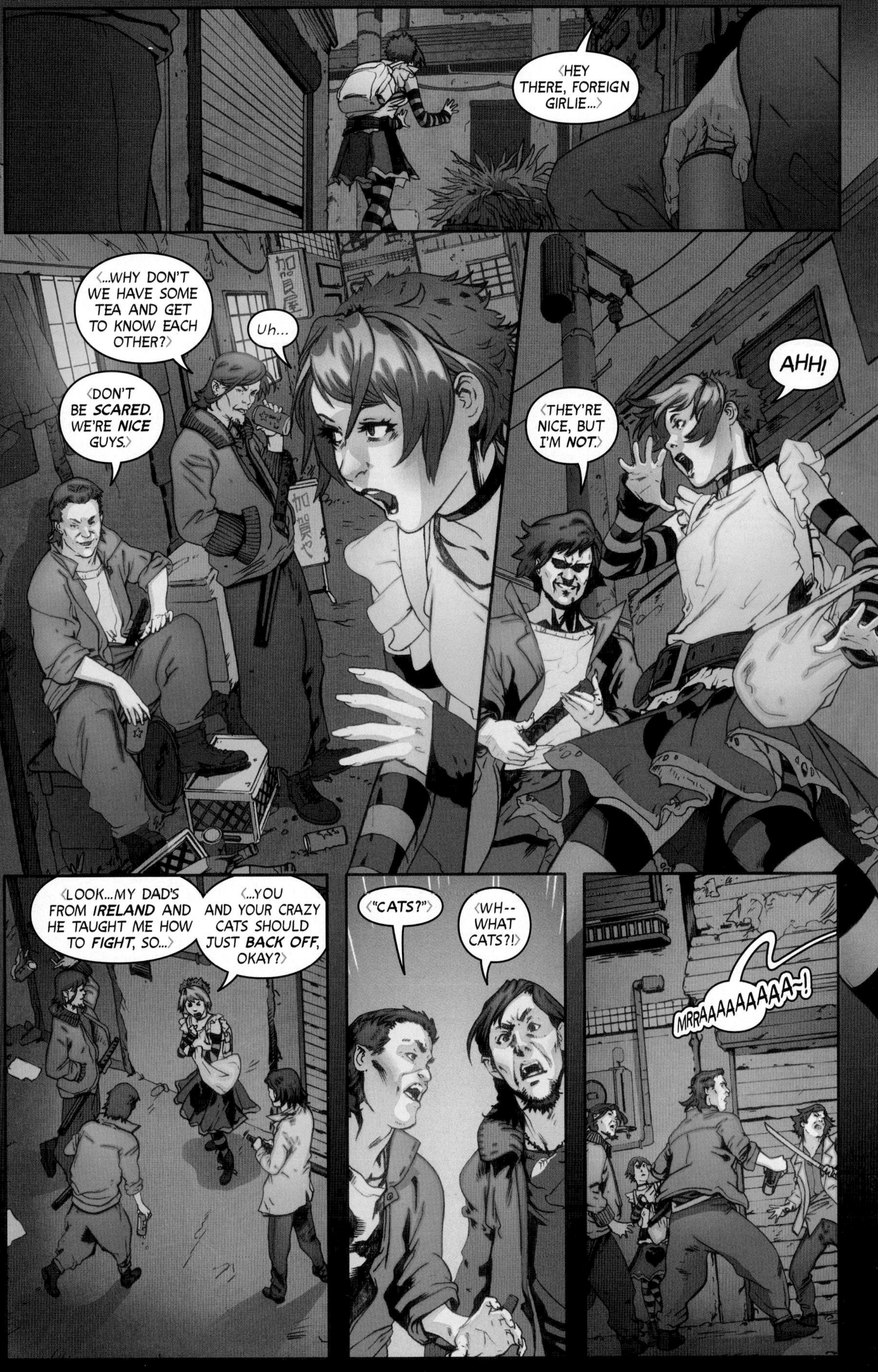

‹HEY THERE, FOREIGN GIRLIE...›
‹...WHY DON'T WE HAVE SOME TEA AND GET TO KNOW EACH OTHER?›
Uh...
‹DON'T BE SCARED. WE'RE NICE GUYS.›
‹THEY'RE NICE, BUT I'M NOT.›
AHH!
‹LOOK...MY DAD'S FROM IRELAND AND HE TAUGHT ME HOW TO FIGHT, SO...›
‹...YOU AND YOUR CRAZY CATS SHOULD JUST BACK OFF, OKAY?›
‹"CATS?"›
‹WH-- WHAT CATS?!›
MRRAAAAAAAAA-!

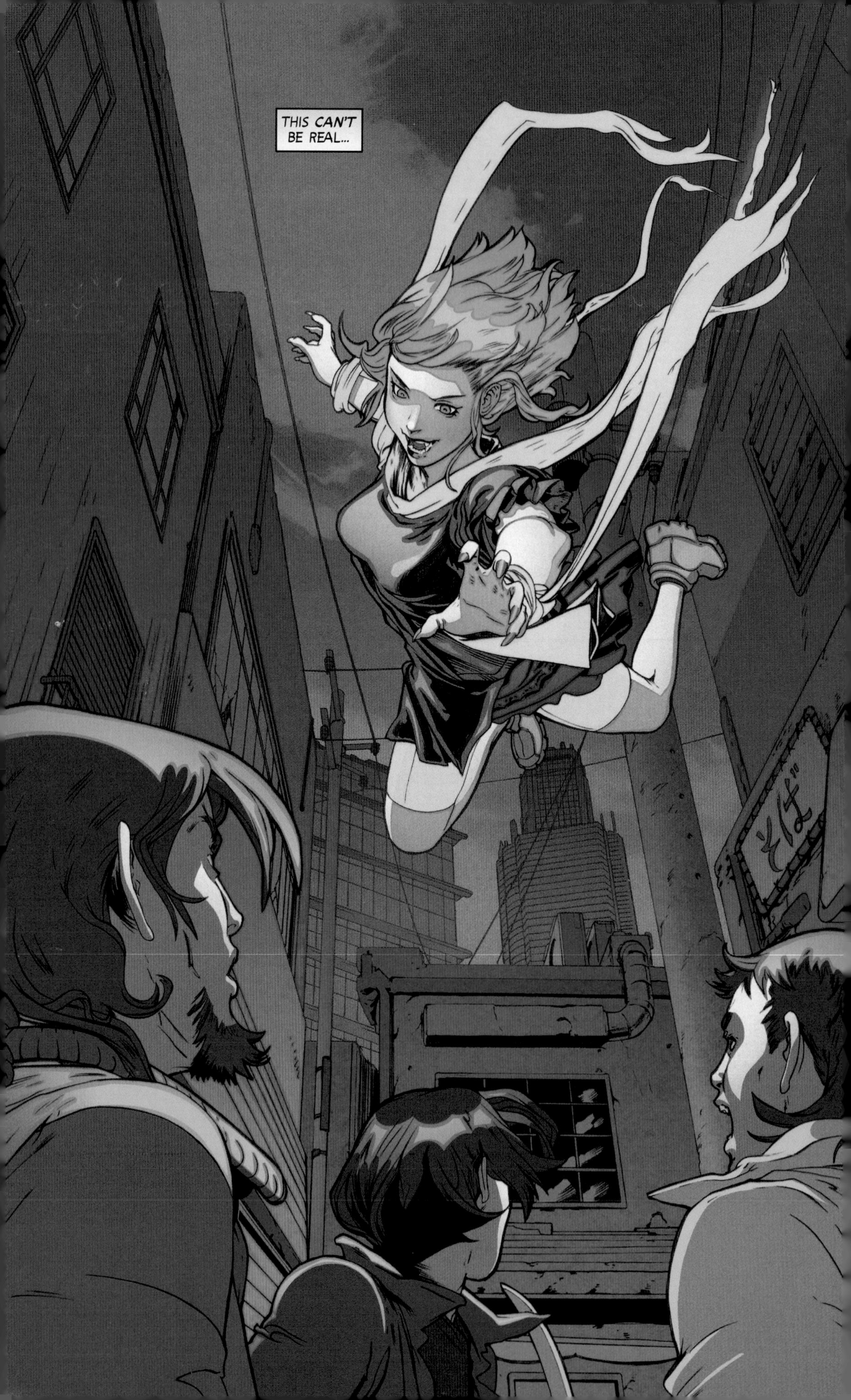
THIS CAN'T BE REAL...

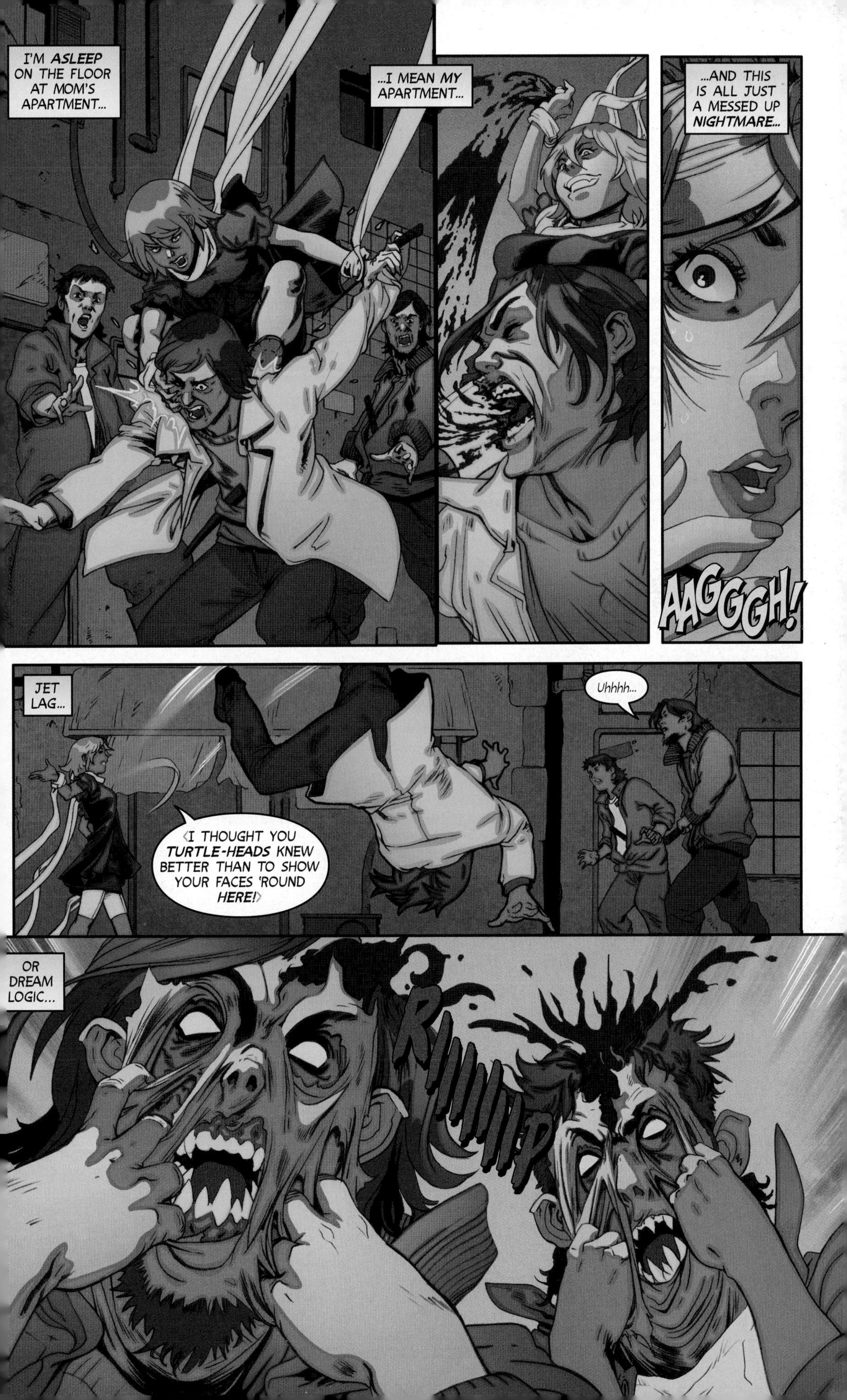

I'M ASLEEP ON THE FLOOR AT MOM'S APARTMENT...
...I MEAN MY APARTMENT...
...AND THIS IS ALL JUST A MESSED UP NIGHTMARE...
AAGGGH!
JET LAG...
Uhhhh...
‹I THOUGHT YOU TURTLE-HEADS KNEW BETTER THAN TO SHOW YOUR FACES 'ROUND HERE!›
OR DREAM LOGIC...
RIIIIIIP

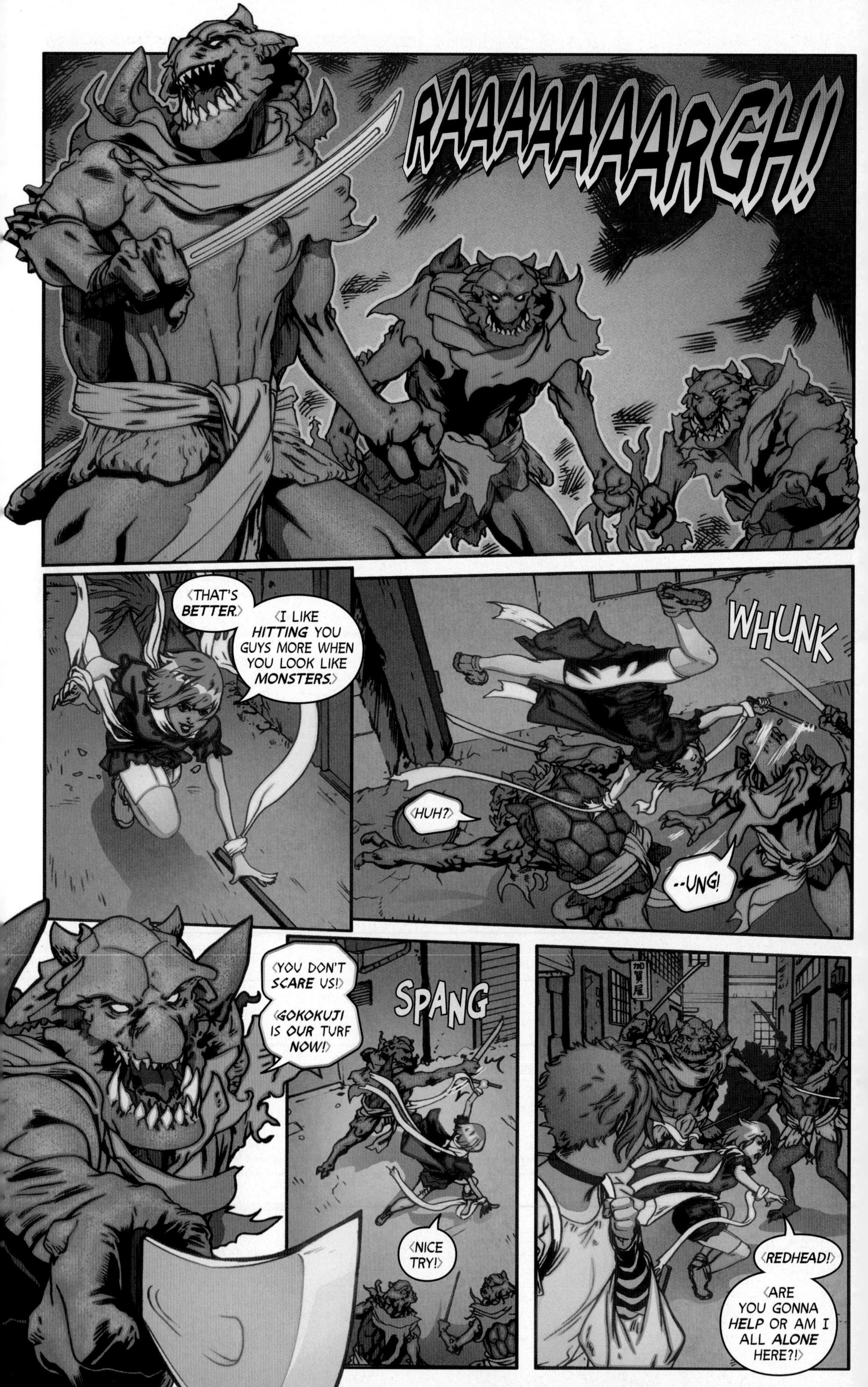
RAAAAAAARGH!
⟨THAT'S BETTER.⟩
⟨I LIKE HITTING YOU GUYS MORE WHEN YOU LOOK LIKE MONSTERS.⟩
WHUNK
⟨HUH?⟩
--UNG!
⟨YOU DON'T SCARE US!⟩
⟨GOKOKUJI IS OUR TURF NOW!⟩
SPANG
⟨NICE TRY!⟩
⟨REDHEAD!⟩
⟨ARE YOU GONNA HELP OR AM I ALL ALONE HERE?!⟩

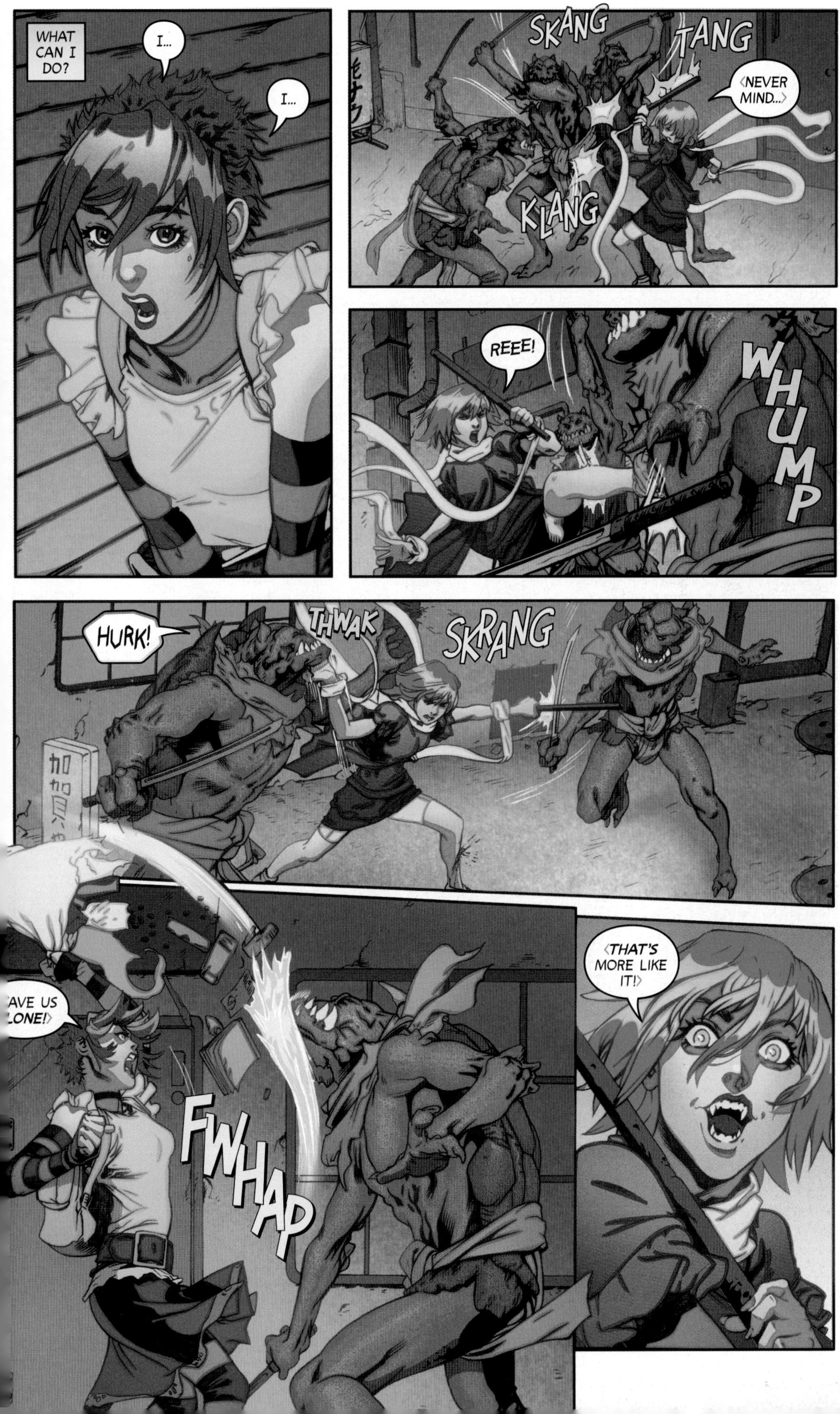
WHAT CAN I DO?
I...
I...
SKANG
TANG
<NEVER MIND...>
KLANG
REEE!
WHUMP
HURK!
THWAK
SKRANG
AVE US LONE!>
FWHAP
<THAT'S MORE LIKE IT!>

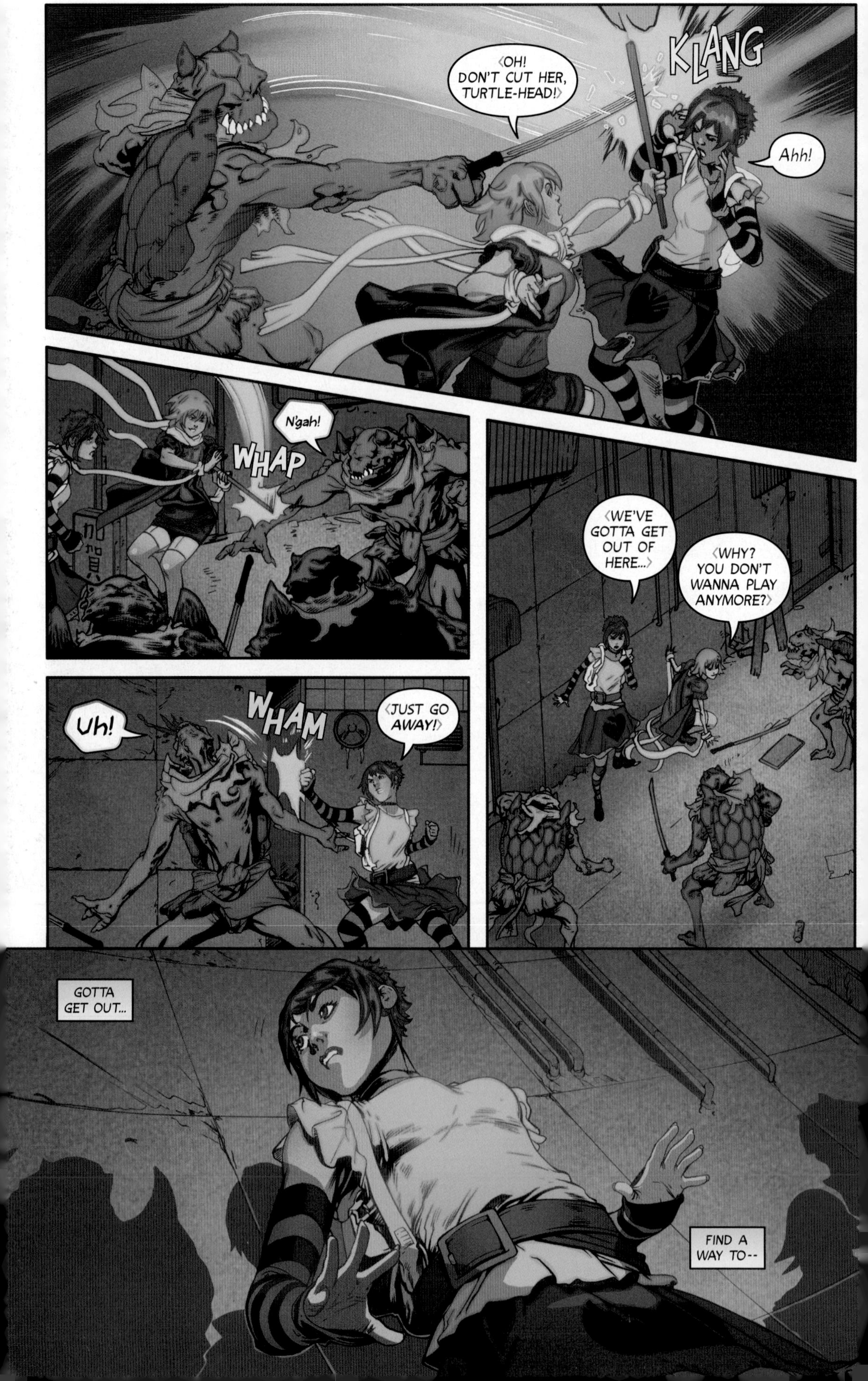

KLANG
‹OH! DON'T CUT HER, TURTLE-HEAD!›
Ahh!
N'gah!
WHAP
‹WE'VE GOTTA GET OUT OF HERE...›
‹WHY? YOU DON'T WANNA PLAY ANYMORE?›
Uh!
WHAM
‹JUST GO AWAY!›
GOTTA GET OUT...
FIND A WAY TO--

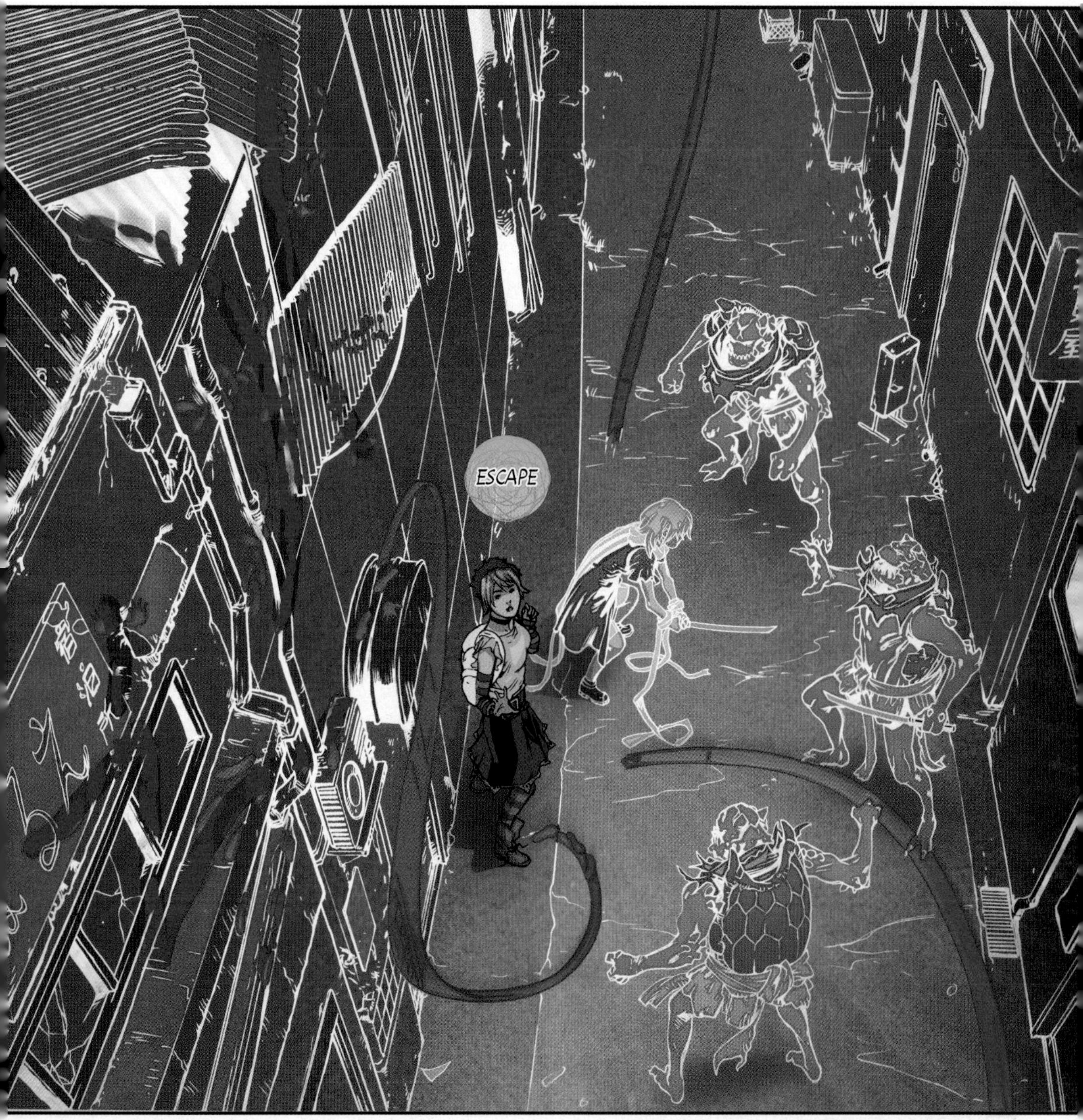
ESCAPE

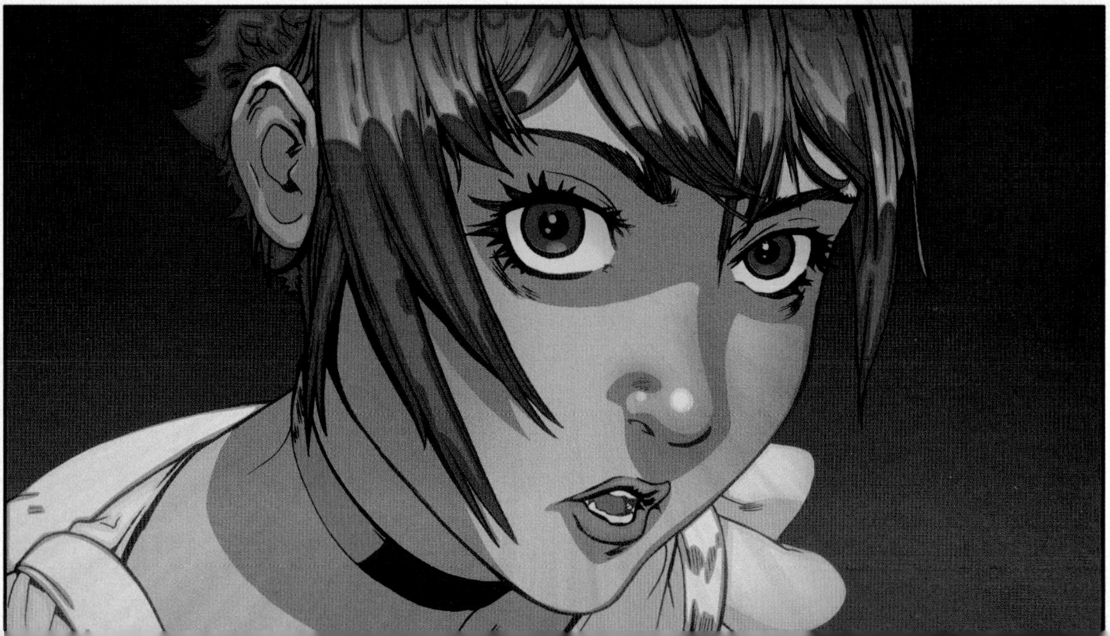

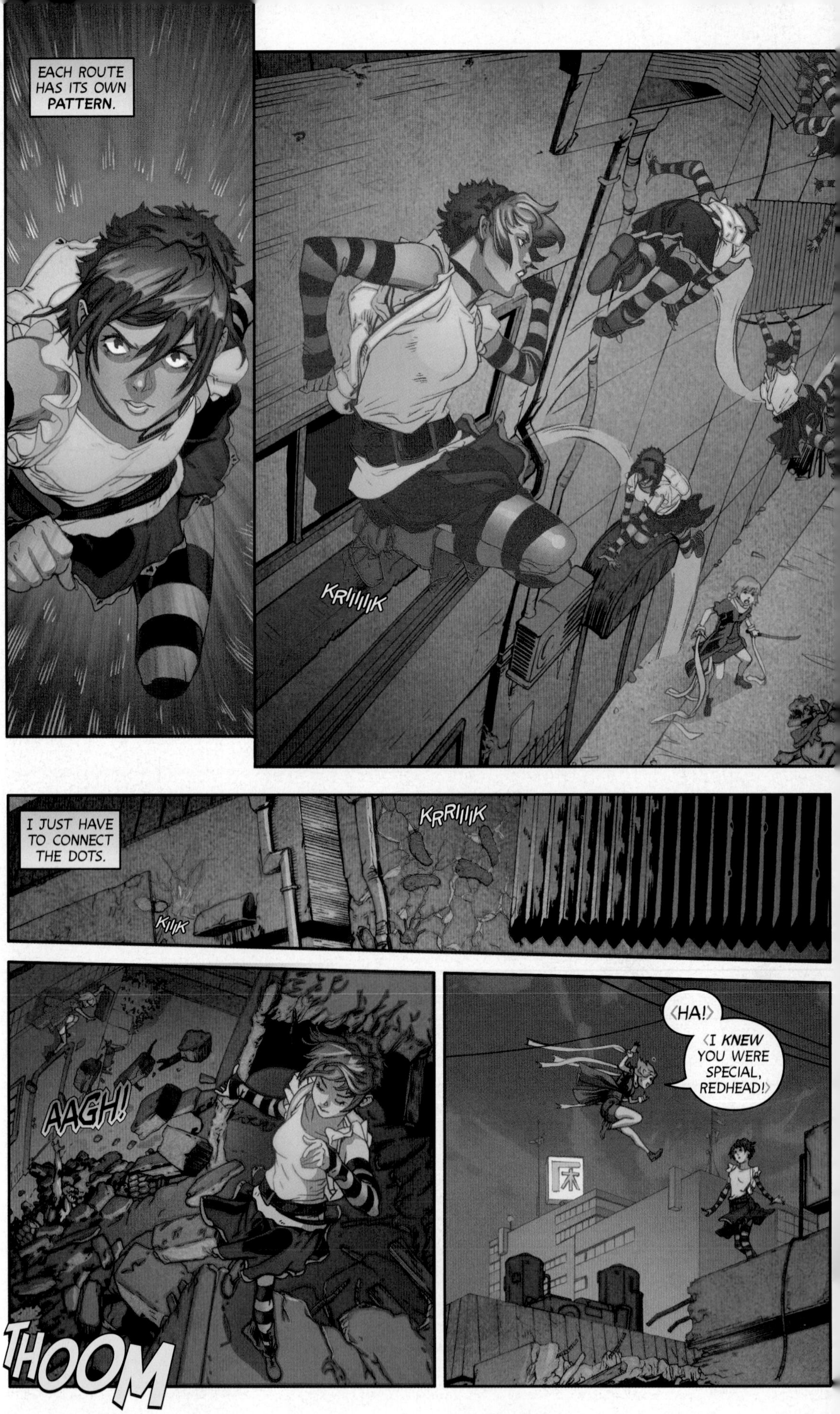
EACH ROUTE HAS ITS OWN PATTERN.
KRIIIIIK
I JUST HAVE TO CONNECT THE DOTS.
KRRIIIIK
KIIIK
AAGH!
THOOM
‹HA!›
‹I KNEW YOU WERE SPECIAL, REDHEAD!›

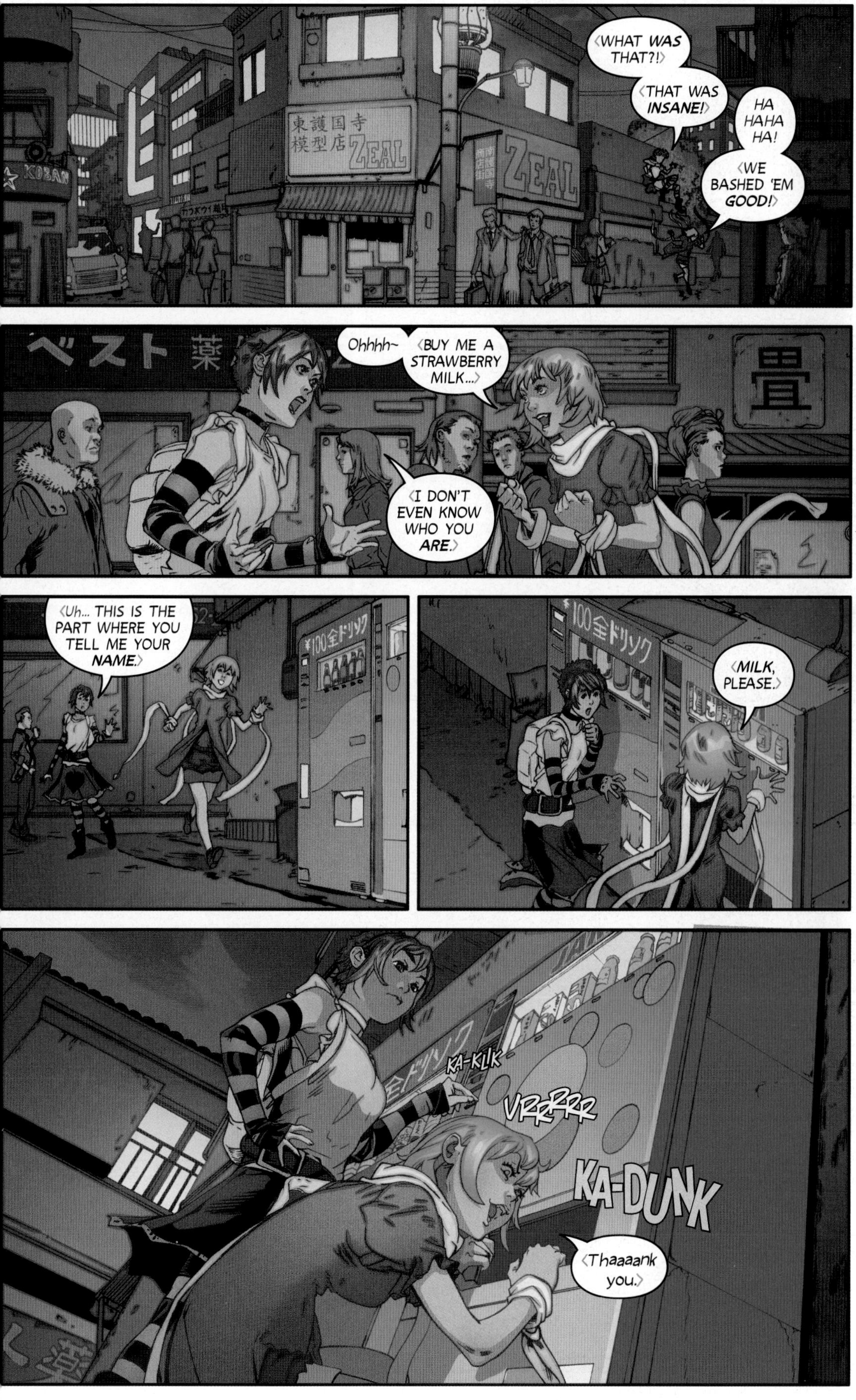

東護国寺
模型店
ZEAL
KOBAN
ZEAL
⟨WHAT WAS THAT?!⟩
⟨THAT WAS INSANE!⟩
HA HAHA HA!
⟨WE BASHED 'EM GOOD!⟩
ベスト 薬
畳
Ohhhh~
⟨BUY ME A STRAWBERRY MILK...⟩
⟨I DON'T EVEN KNOW WHO YOU ARE.⟩
⟨Uh... THIS IS THE PART WHERE YOU TELL ME YOUR NAME.⟩
⟨MILK, PLEASE.⟩
KA-KLIK
VRRRRR
KA-DUNK
⟨Thaaaank you.⟩

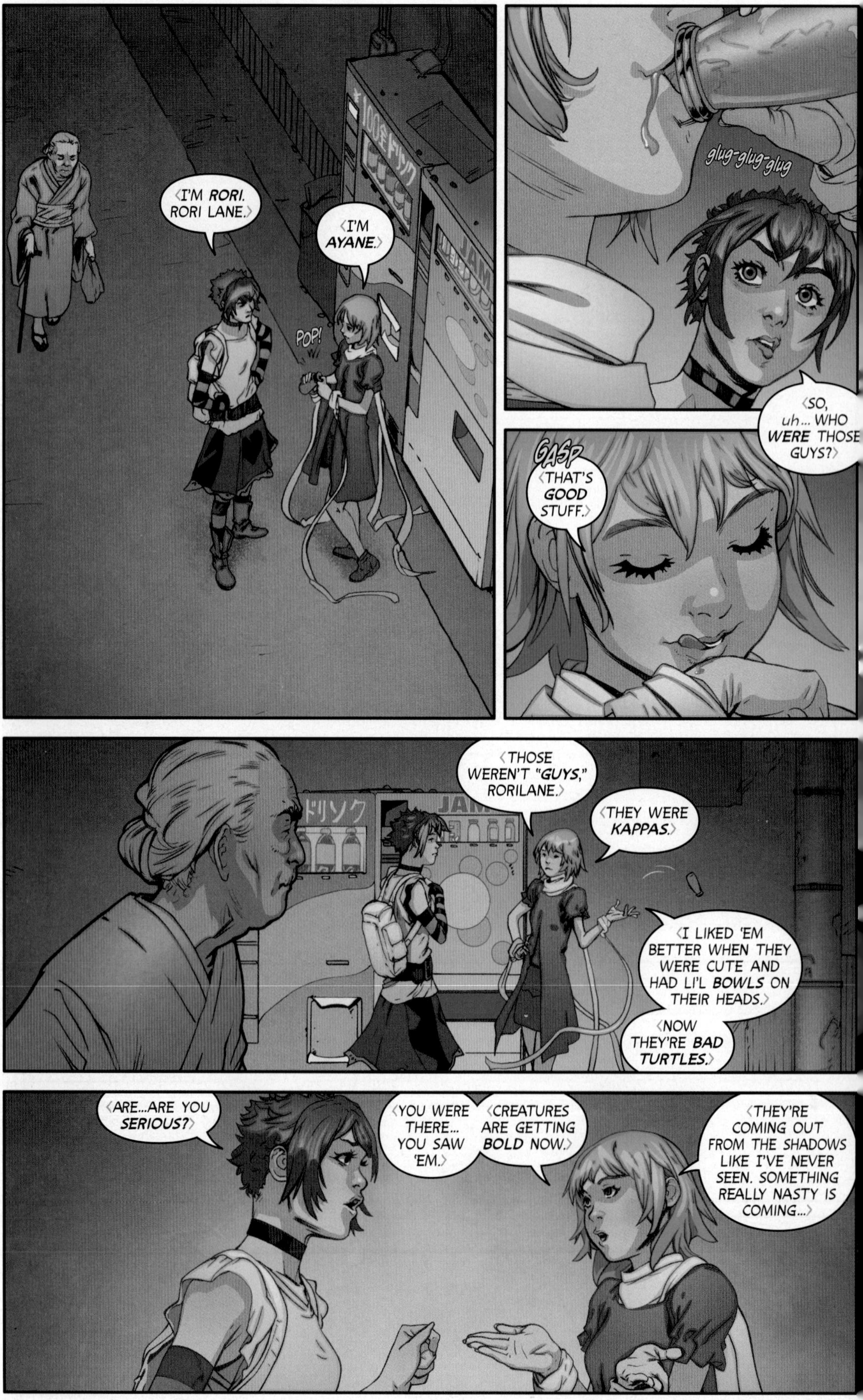

‹I'M RORI. RORI LANE.›
‹I'M AYANE.›
POP!
glug-glug-glug
‹SO, uh... WHO WERE THOSE GUYS?›
GASP
‹THAT'S GOOD STUFF.›
‹THOSE WEREN'T "GUYS," RORILANE.›
‹THEY WERE KAPPAS.›
‹I LIKED 'EM BETTER WHEN THEY WERE CUTE AND HAD LI'L BOWLS ON THEIR HEADS.›
‹NOW THEY'RE BAD TURTLES.›
‹ARE...ARE YOU SERIOUS?›
‹YOU WERE THERE... YOU SAW 'EM.›
‹CREATURES ARE GETTING BOLD NOW.›
‹THEY'RE COMING OUT FROM THE SHADOWS LIKE I'VE NEVER SEEN. SOMETHING REALLY NASTY IS COMING...›

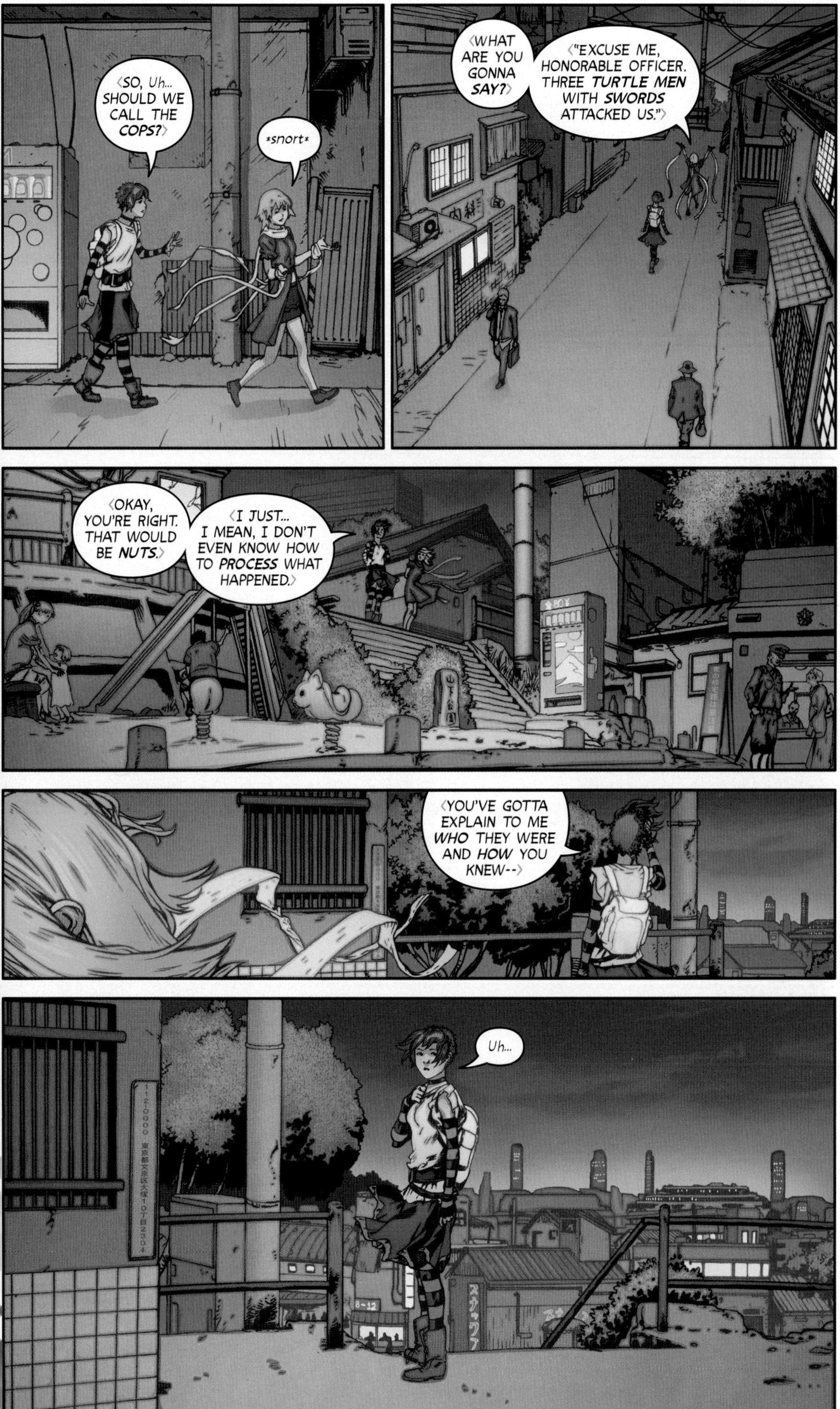
‹SO, Uh... SHOULD WE CALL THE *COPS?*›
*snort*
‹WHAT ARE YOU GONNA *SAY?*›
‹"EXCUSE ME, HONORABLE OFFICER. THREE *TURTLE MEN* WITH *SWORDS* ATTACKED US."›
‹OKAY, YOU'RE RIGHT. THAT WOULD BE *NUTS.*›
‹I JUST... I MEAN, I DON'T EVEN KNOW HOW TO *PROCESS* WHAT HAPPENED.›
‹YOU'VE GOTTA EXPLAIN TO ME *WHO* THEY WERE AND *HOW* YOU KNEW--›
Uh...
8-12

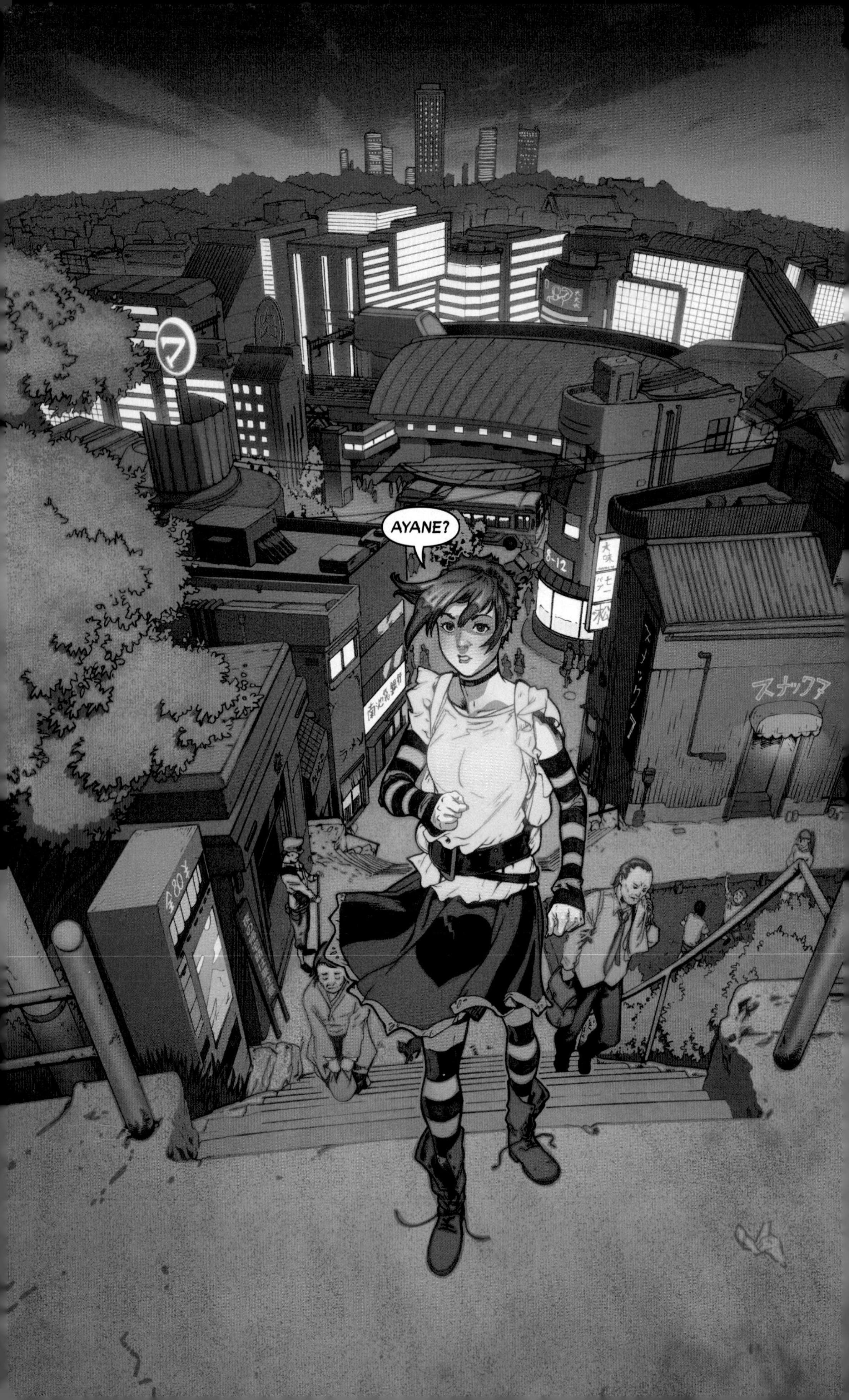
AYANE?
8-12
スナックア

# Chapter Two

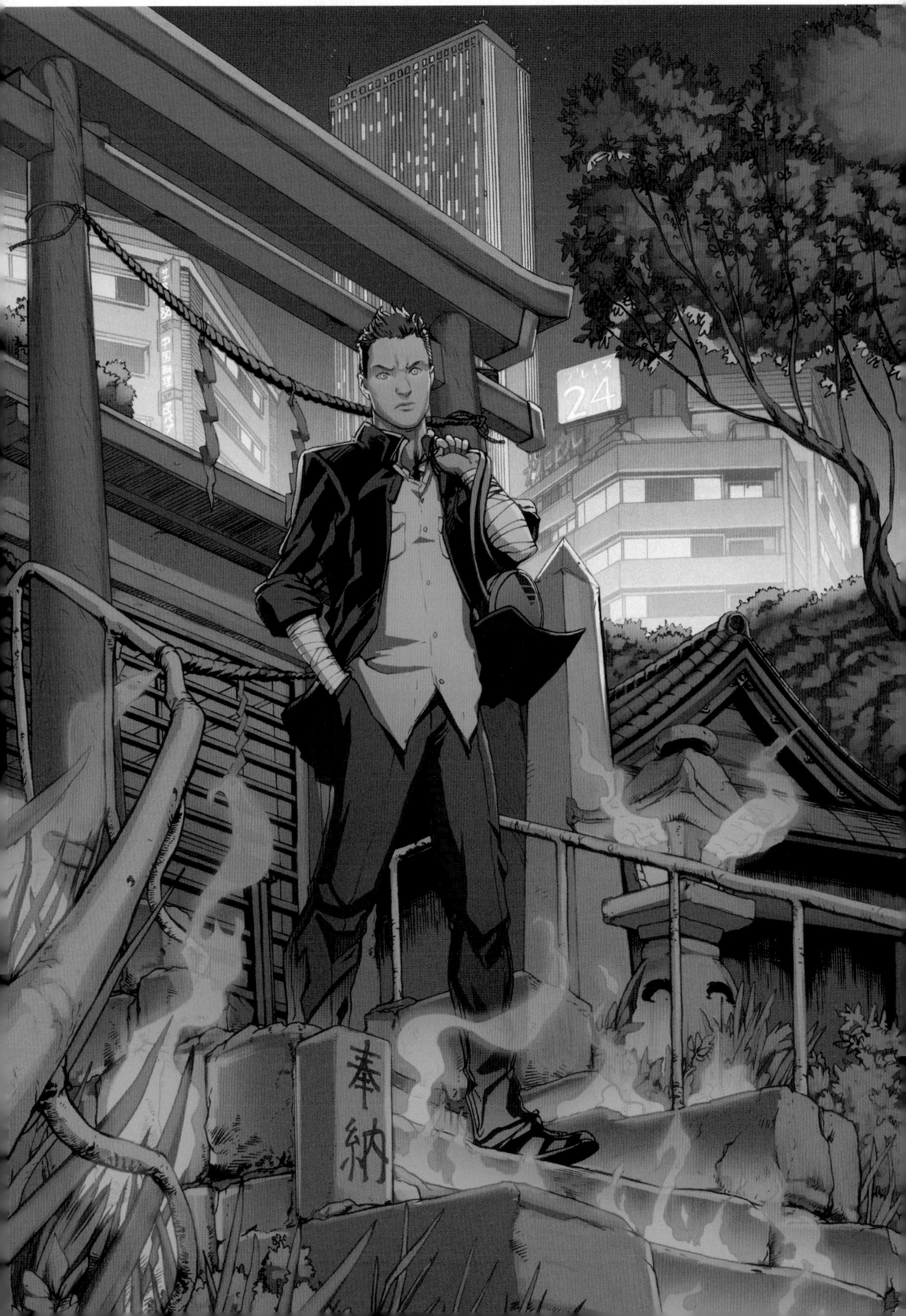
中国料理
プレイズ
24
奉納

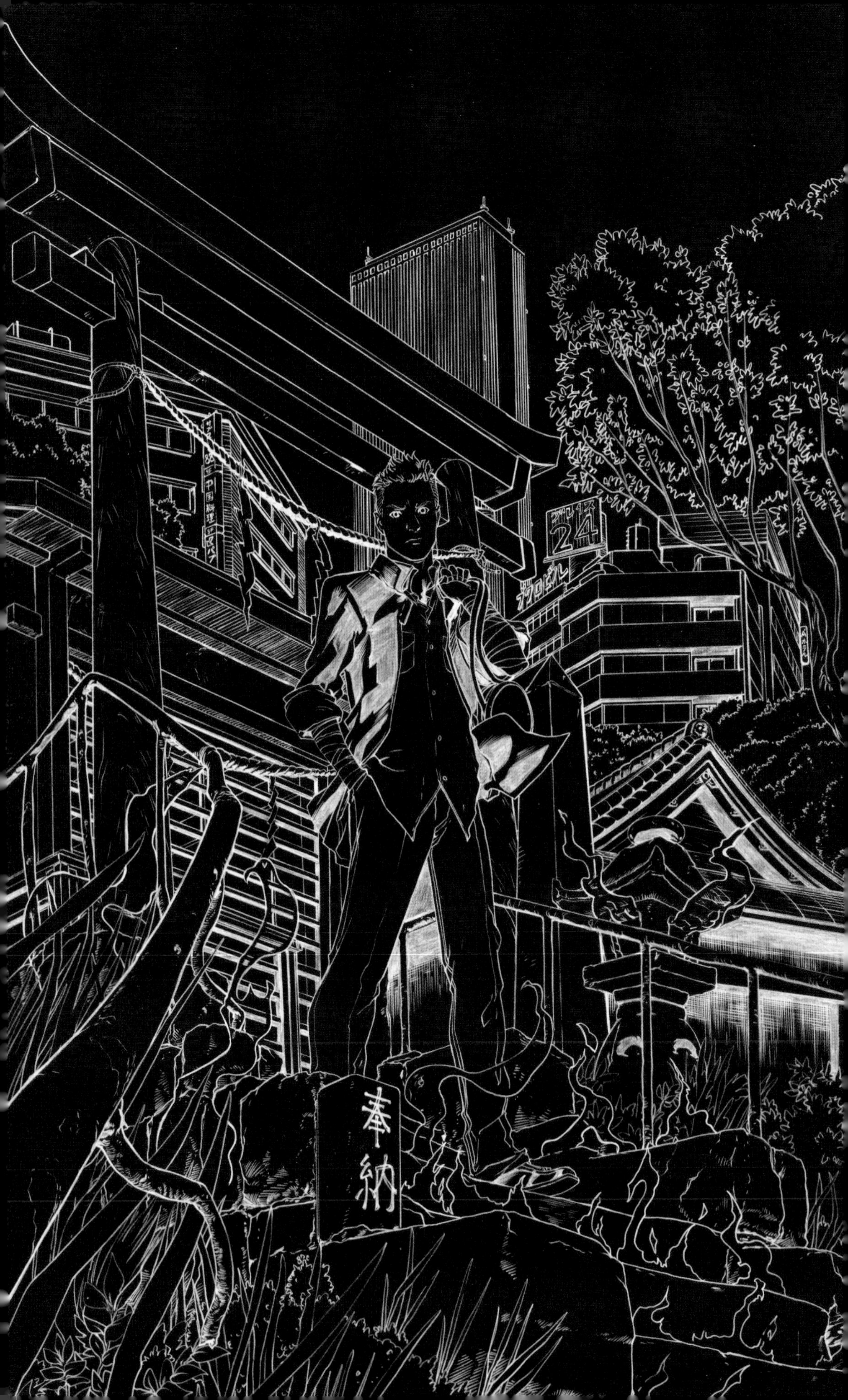
24
奉納

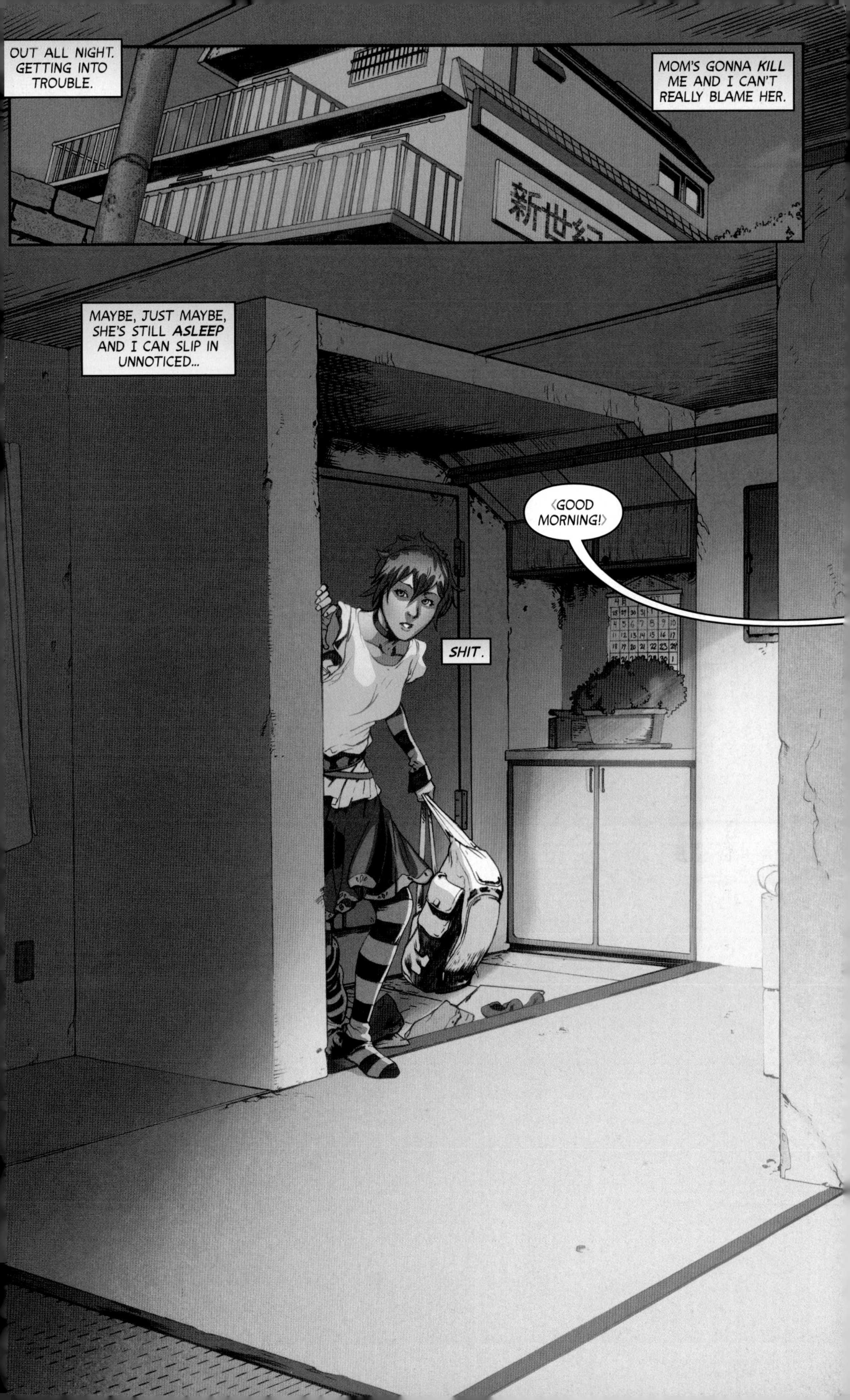
OUT ALL NIGHT. GETTING INTO TROUBLE.
MOM'S GONNA KILL ME AND I CAN'T REALLY BLAME HER.
新世紀
MAYBE, JUST MAYBE, SHE'S STILL ASLEEP AND I CAN SLIP IN UNNOTICED...
‹GOOD MORNING!›
SHIT.

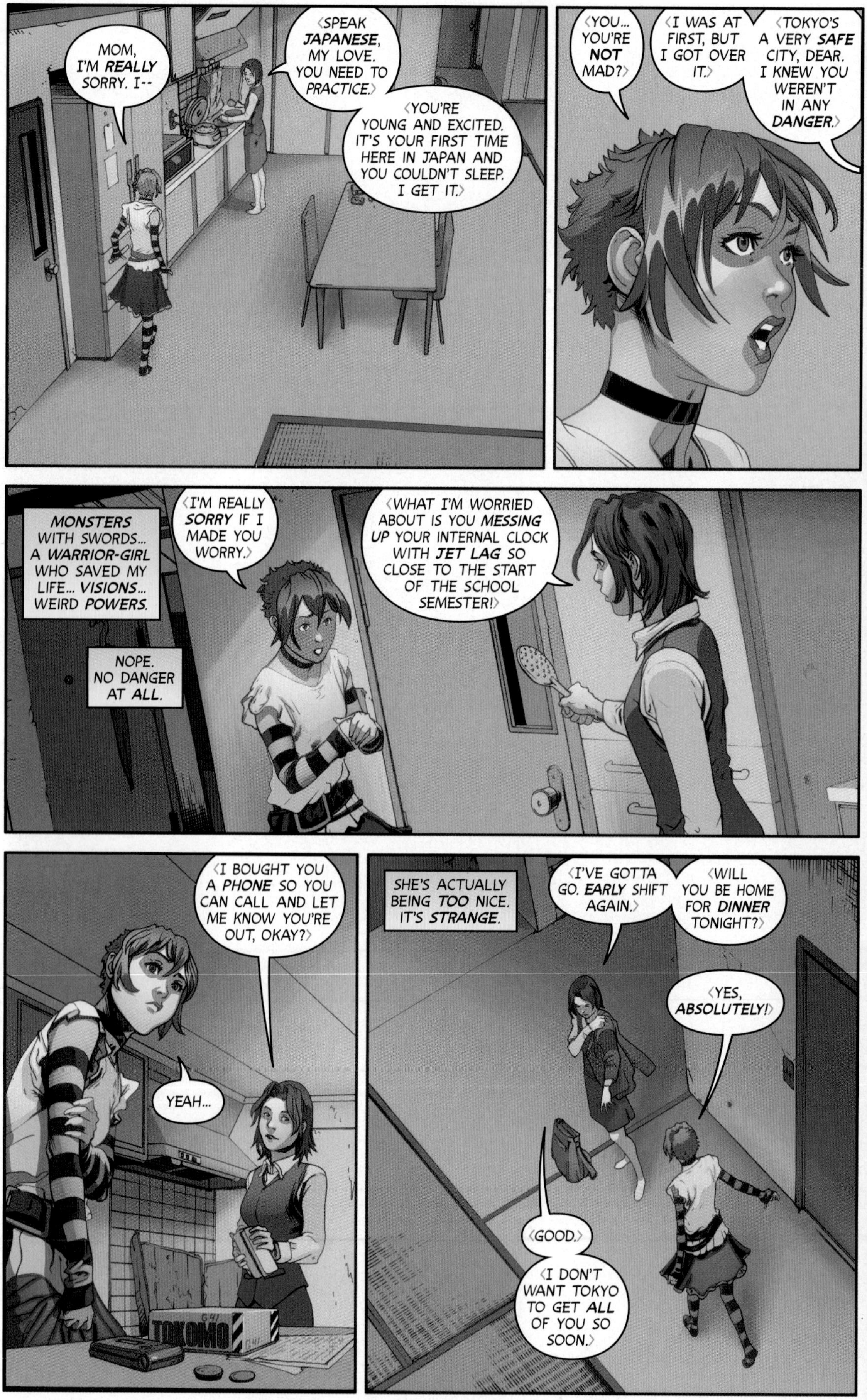
MOM, I'M REALLY SORRY. I--
<SPEAK JAPANESE, MY LOVE. YOU NEED TO PRACTICE.>
<YOU'RE YOUNG AND EXCITED. IT'S YOUR FIRST TIME HERE IN JAPAN AND YOU COULDN'T SLEEP. I GET IT.>
<YOU... YOU'RE NOT MAD?>
<I WAS AT FIRST, BUT I GOT OVER IT.>
<TOKYO'S A VERY SAFE CITY, DEAR. I KNEW YOU WEREN'T IN ANY DANGER.>
MONSTERS WITH SWORDS... A WARRIOR-GIRL WHO SAVED MY LIFE... VISIONS... WEIRD POWERS.
NOPE. NO DANGER AT ALL.
<I'M REALLY SORRY IF I MADE YOU WORRY.>
<WHAT I'M WORRIED ABOUT IS YOU MESSING UP YOUR INTERNAL CLOCK WITH JET LAG SO CLOSE TO THE START OF THE SCHOOL SEMESTER!>
<I BOUGHT YOU A PHONE SO YOU CAN CALL AND LET ME KNOW YOU'RE OUT, OKAY?>
YEAH...
TOKOMO
SHE'S ACTUALLY BEING TOO NICE. IT'S STRANGE.
<I'VE GOTTA GO. EARLY SHIFT AGAIN.>
<WILL YOU BE HOME FOR DINNER TONIGHT?>
<YES, ABSOLUTELY!>
<GOOD.>
<I DON'T WANT TOKYO TO GET ALL OF YOU SO SOON.>

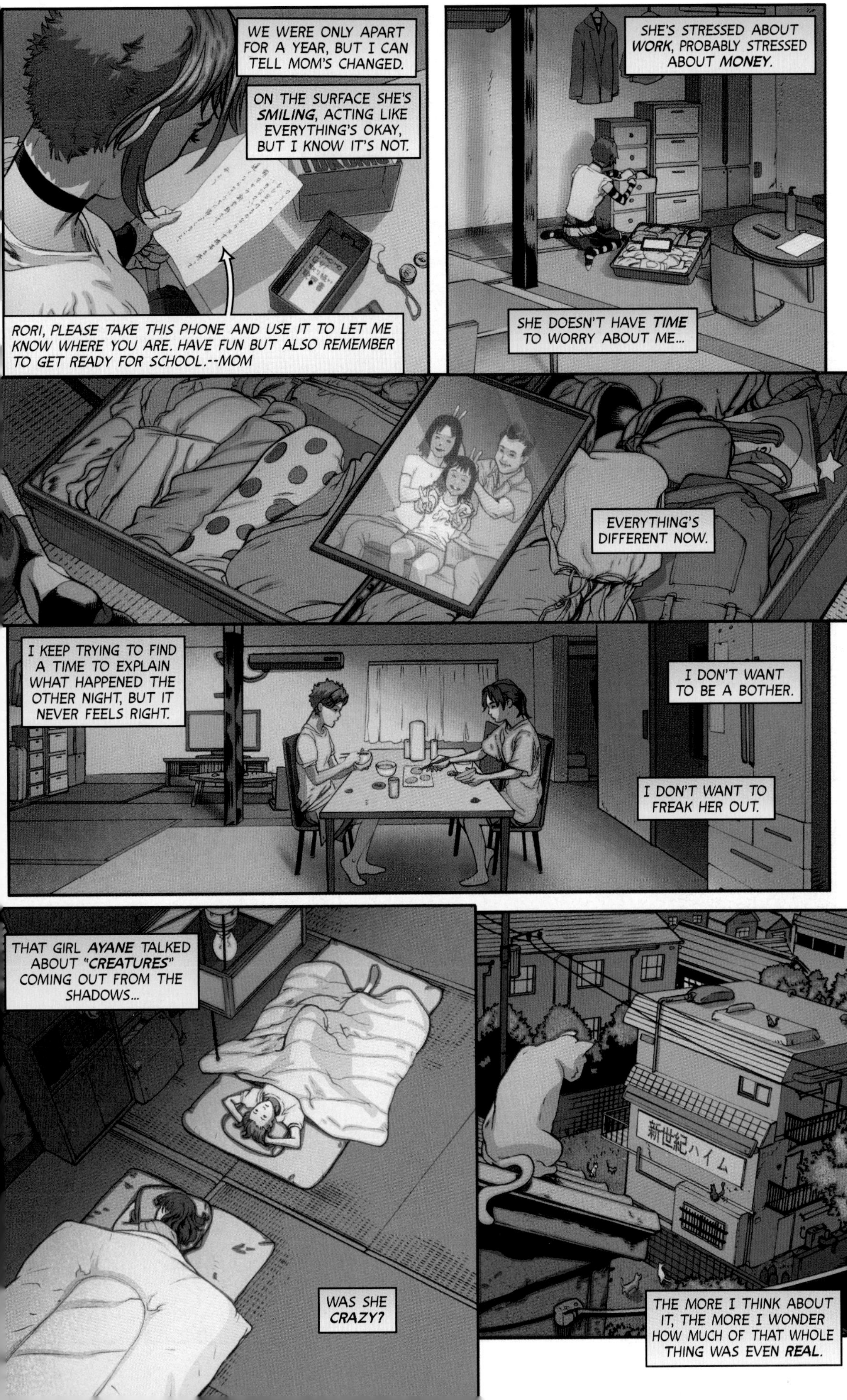
WE WERE ONLY APART FOR A YEAR, BUT I CAN TELL MOM'S CHANGED.
ON THE SURFACE SHE'S *SMILING*, ACTING LIKE EVERYTHING'S OKAY, BUT I KNOW IT'S NOT.
RORI, PLEASE TAKE THIS PHONE AND USE IT TO LET ME KNOW WHERE YOU ARE. HAVE FUN BUT ALSO REMEMBER TO GET READY FOR SCHOOL.--MOM
SHE'S STRESSED ABOUT *WORK*, PROBABLY STRESSED ABOUT *MONEY*.
SHE DOESN'T HAVE *TIME* TO WORRY ABOUT ME...
EVERYTHING'S DIFFERENT NOW.
I KEEP TRYING TO FIND A TIME TO EXPLAIN WHAT HAPPENED THE OTHER NIGHT, BUT IT NEVER FEELS RIGHT.
I DON'T WANT TO BE A BOTHER.
I DON'T WANT TO FREAK HER OUT.
THAT GIRL *AYANE* TALKED ABOUT *"CREATURES"* COMING OUT FROM THE SHADOWS...
WAS SHE *CRAZY?*
新世紀ハイム
THE MORE I THINK ABOUT IT, THE MORE I WONDER HOW MUCH OF THAT WHOLE THING WAS EVEN *REAL*.

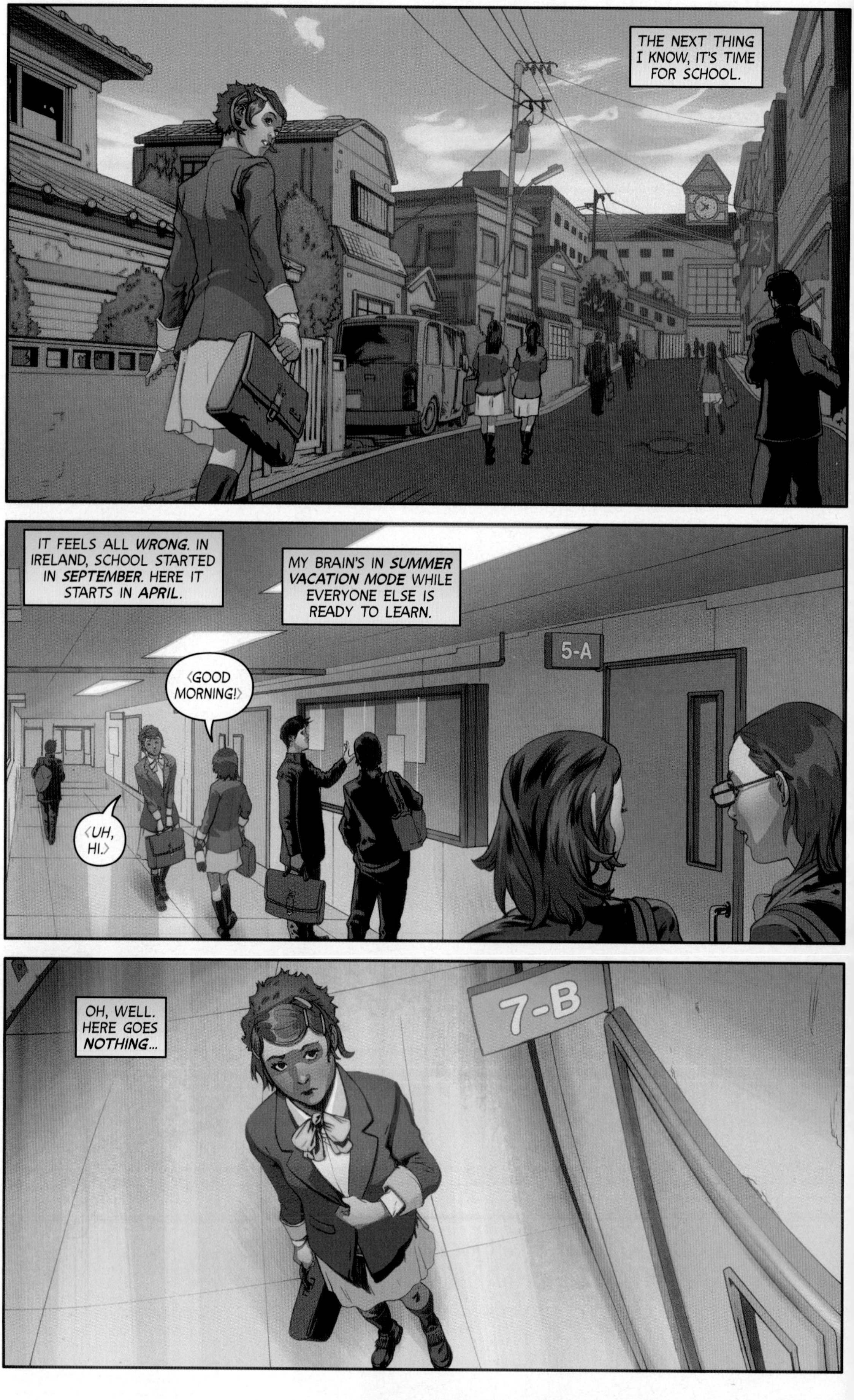
THE NEXT THING I KNOW, IT'S TIME FOR SCHOOL.
IT FEELS ALL *WRONG*. IN IRELAND, SCHOOL STARTED IN *SEPTEMBER*. HERE IT STARTS IN *APRIL*.
MY BRAIN'S IN *SUMMER VACATION MODE* WHILE EVERYONE ELSE IS READY TO LEARN.
5-A
〈GOOD MORNING!〉
〈UH, HI.〉
OH, WELL. HERE GOES *NOTHING*...
7-B

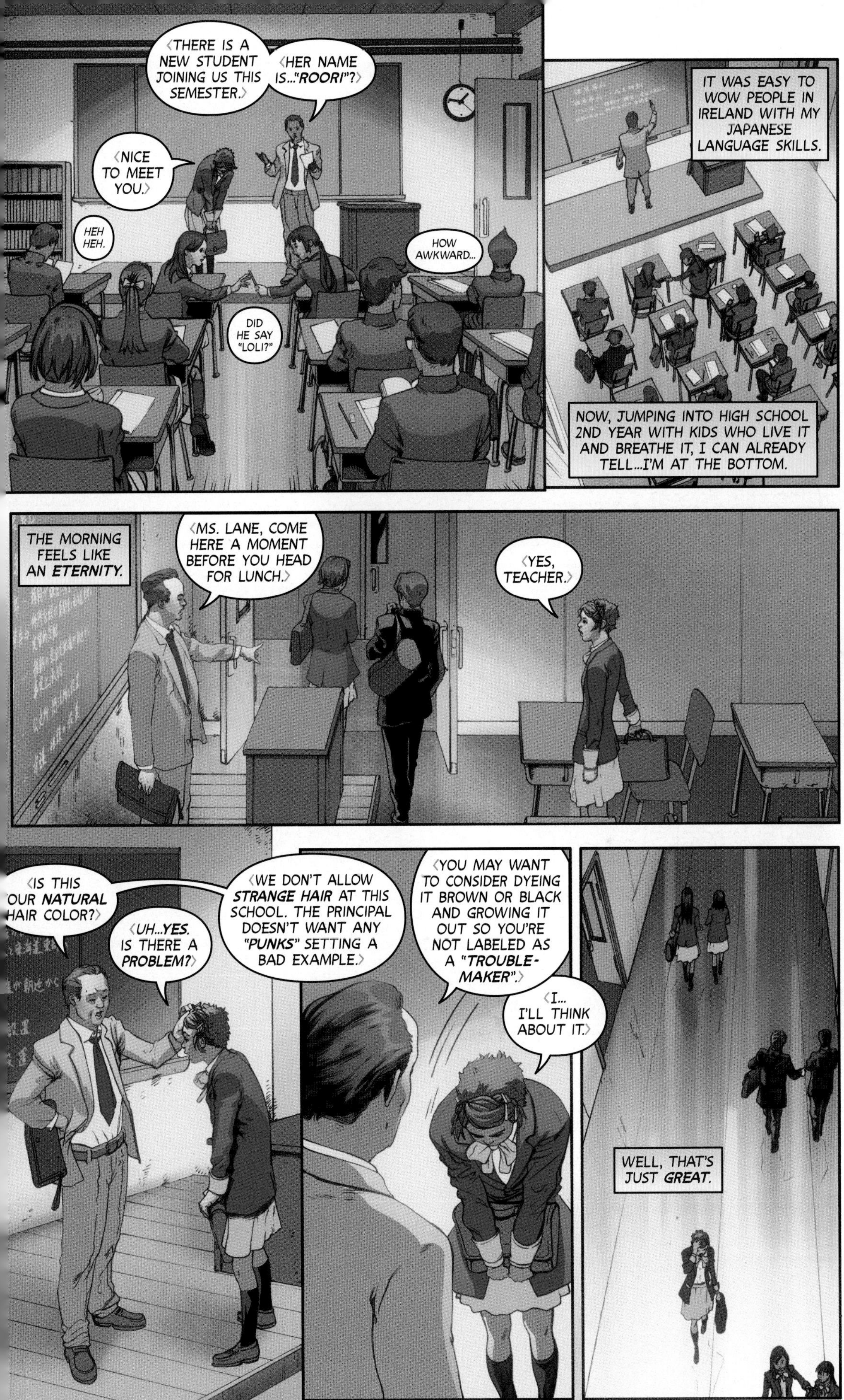

‹THERE IS A NEW STUDENT JOINING US THIS SEMESTER.›
‹HER NAME IS..."ROORI"?›
‹NICE TO MEET YOU.›
HEH HEH.
HOW AWKWARD...
DID HE SAY "LOLI?"
IT WAS EASY TO WOW PEOPLE IN IRELAND WITH MY JAPANESE LANGUAGE SKILLS.
NOW, JUMPING INTO HIGH SCHOOL 2ND YEAR WITH KIDS WHO LIVE IT AND BREATHE IT, I CAN ALREADY TELL...I'M AT THE BOTTOM.
THE MORNING FEELS LIKE AN ETERNITY.
‹MS. LANE, COME HERE A MOMENT BEFORE YOU HEAD FOR LUNCH.›
‹YES, TEACHER.›
‹IS THIS OUR NATURAL HAIR COLOR?›
‹UH...YES. IS THERE A PROBLEM?›
‹WE DON'T ALLOW STRANGE HAIR AT THIS SCHOOL. THE PRINCIPAL DOESN'T WANT ANY "PUNKS" SETTING A BAD EXAMPLE.›
‹YOU MAY WANT TO CONSIDER DYEING IT BROWN OR BLACK AND GROWING IT OUT SO YOU'RE NOT LABELED AS A "TROUBLE-MAKER".›
‹I... I'LL THINK ABOUT IT.›
WELL, THAT'S JUST GREAT.

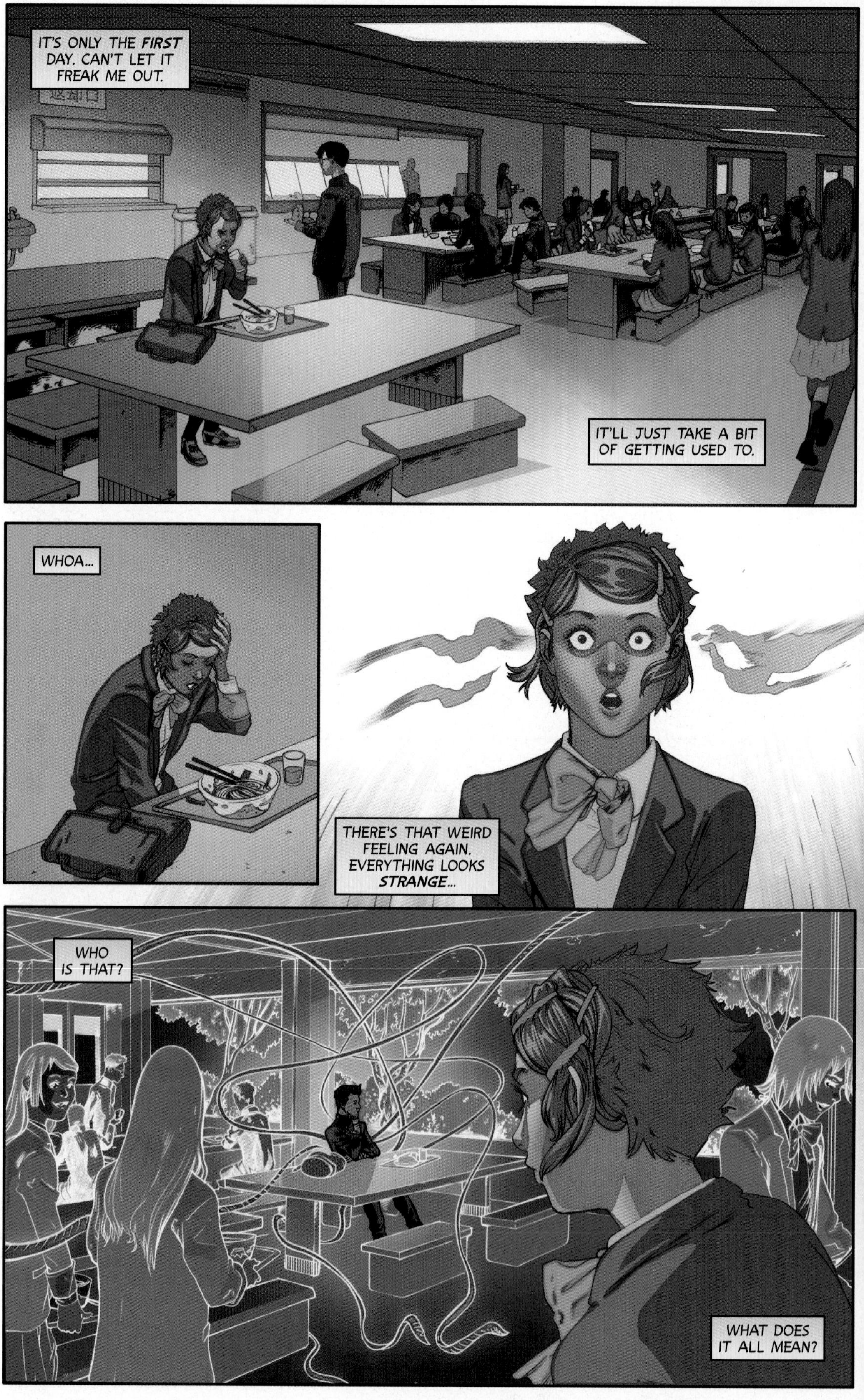
IT'S ONLY THE *FIRST* DAY. CAN'T LET IT FREAK ME OUT.
IT'LL JUST TAKE A BIT OF GETTING USED TO.
WHOA...
THERE'S THAT WEIRD FEELING AGAIN. EVERYTHING LOOKS *STRANGE*...
WHO IS THAT?
WHAT DOES IT ALL MEAN?

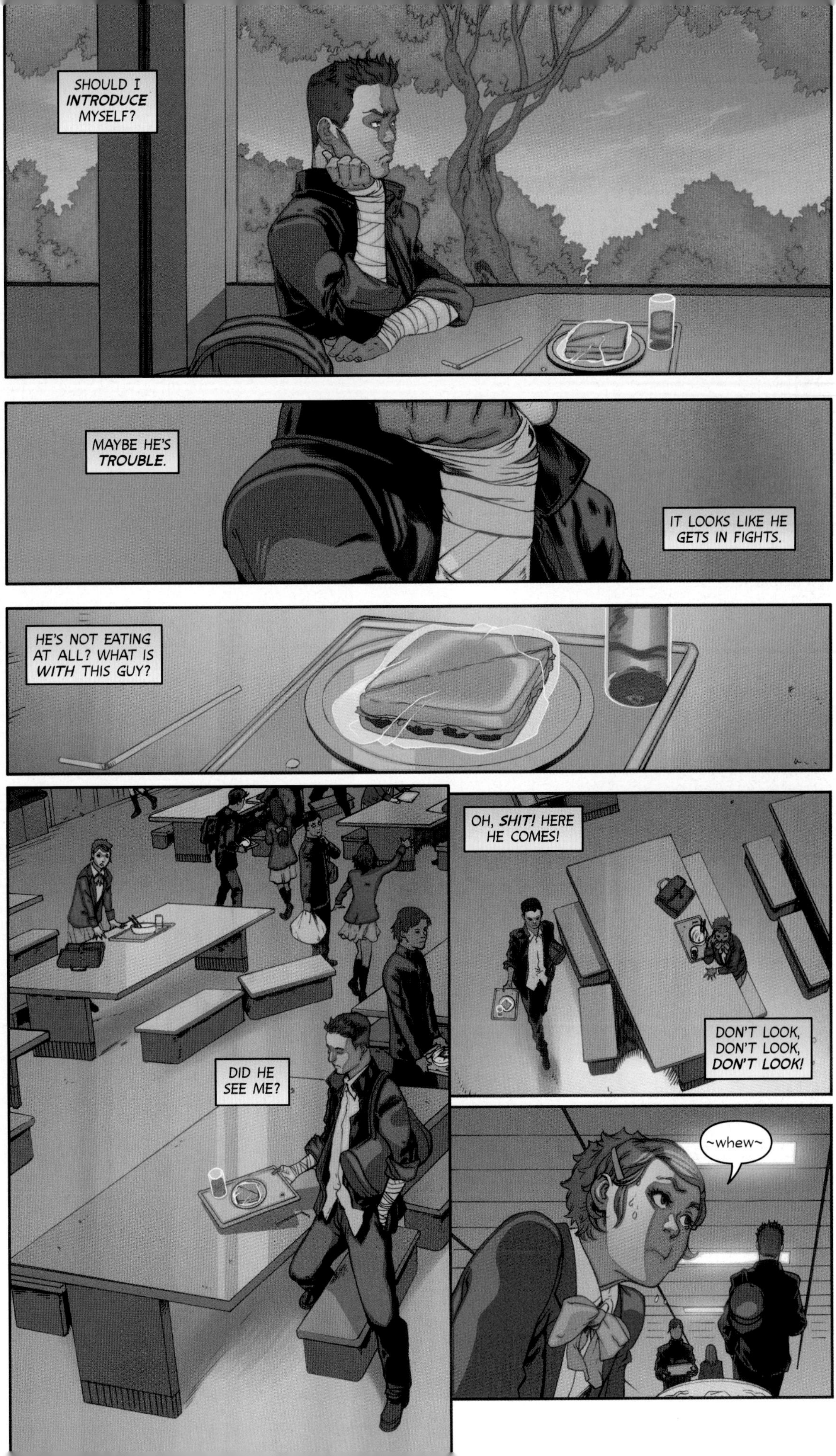
SHOULD I INTRODUCE MYSELF?
MAYBE HE'S TROUBLE.
IT LOOKS LIKE HE GETS IN FIGHTS.
HE'S NOT EATING AT ALL? WHAT IS WITH THIS GUY?
DID HE SEE ME?
OH, SHIT! HERE HE COMES!
DON'T LOOK, DON'T LOOK, DON'T LOOK!
~whew~

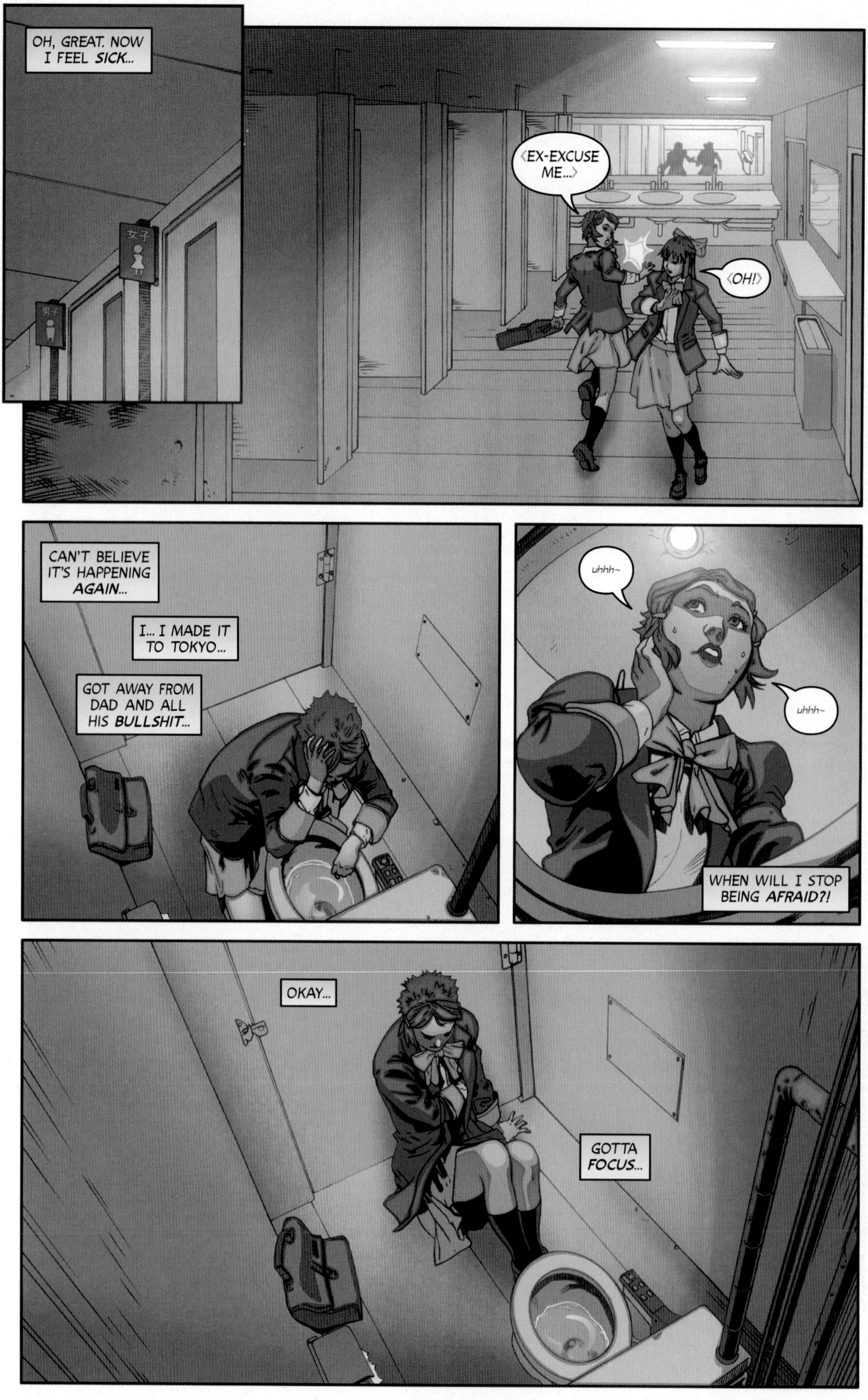
OH, GREAT. NOW I FEEL *SICK*...
女子
男子
⟨EX-EXCUSE ME...⟩
⟨OH!⟩
CAN'T BELIEVE IT'S HAPPENING *AGAIN*...
I... I MADE IT TO TOKYO...
GOT AWAY FROM DAD AND ALL HIS *BULLSHIT*...
uhhh~
uhhh~
WHEN WILL I STOP BEING *AFRAID?!*
OKAY...
GOTTA *FOCUS*...

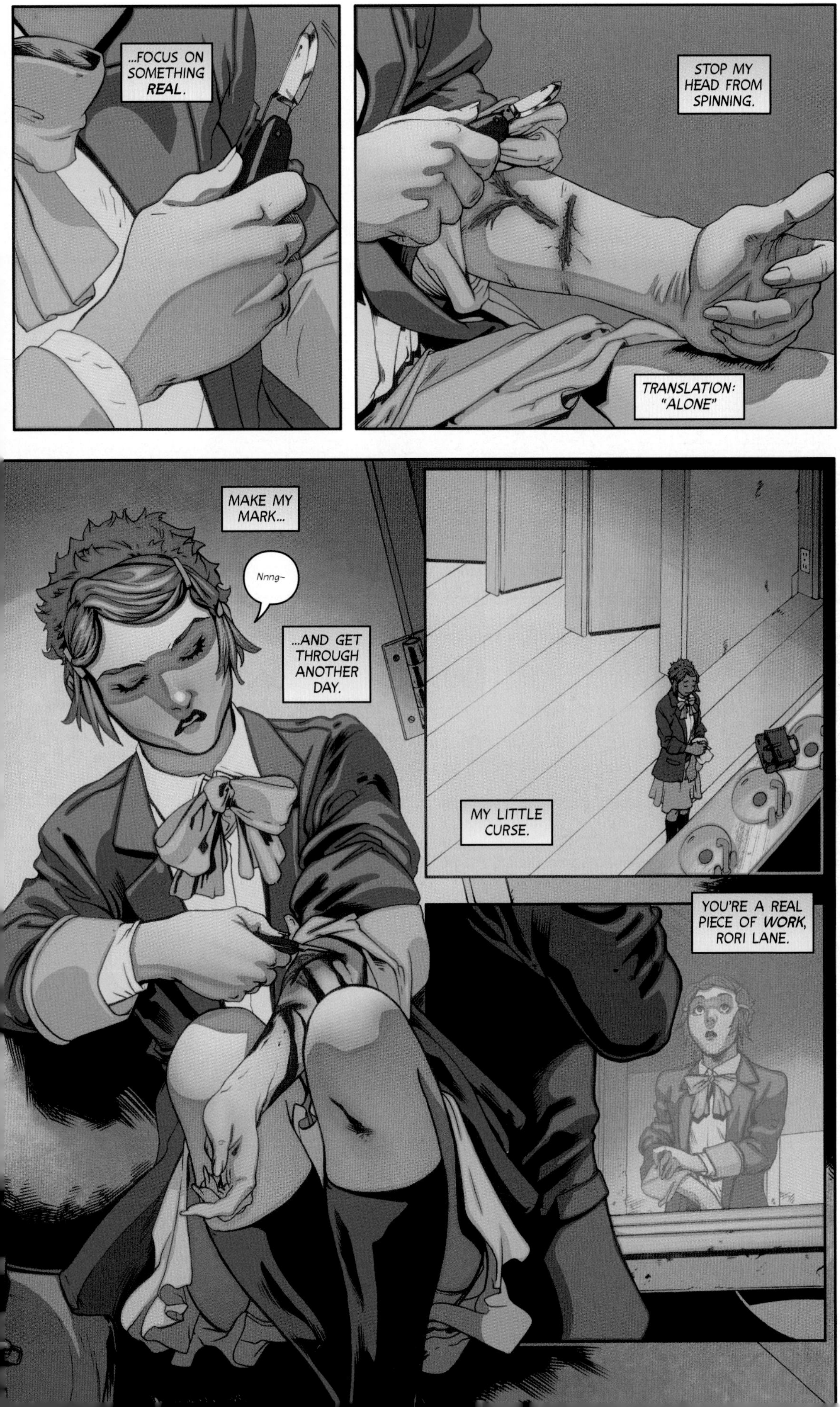
...FOCUS ON SOMETHING *REAL*.
STOP MY HEAD FROM SPINNING.
TRANSLATION: "ALONE"
MAKE MY MARK...
Nnng~
...AND GET THROUGH ANOTHER DAY.
MY LITTLE CURSE.
YOU'RE A REAL PIECE OF *WORK*, RORI LANE.

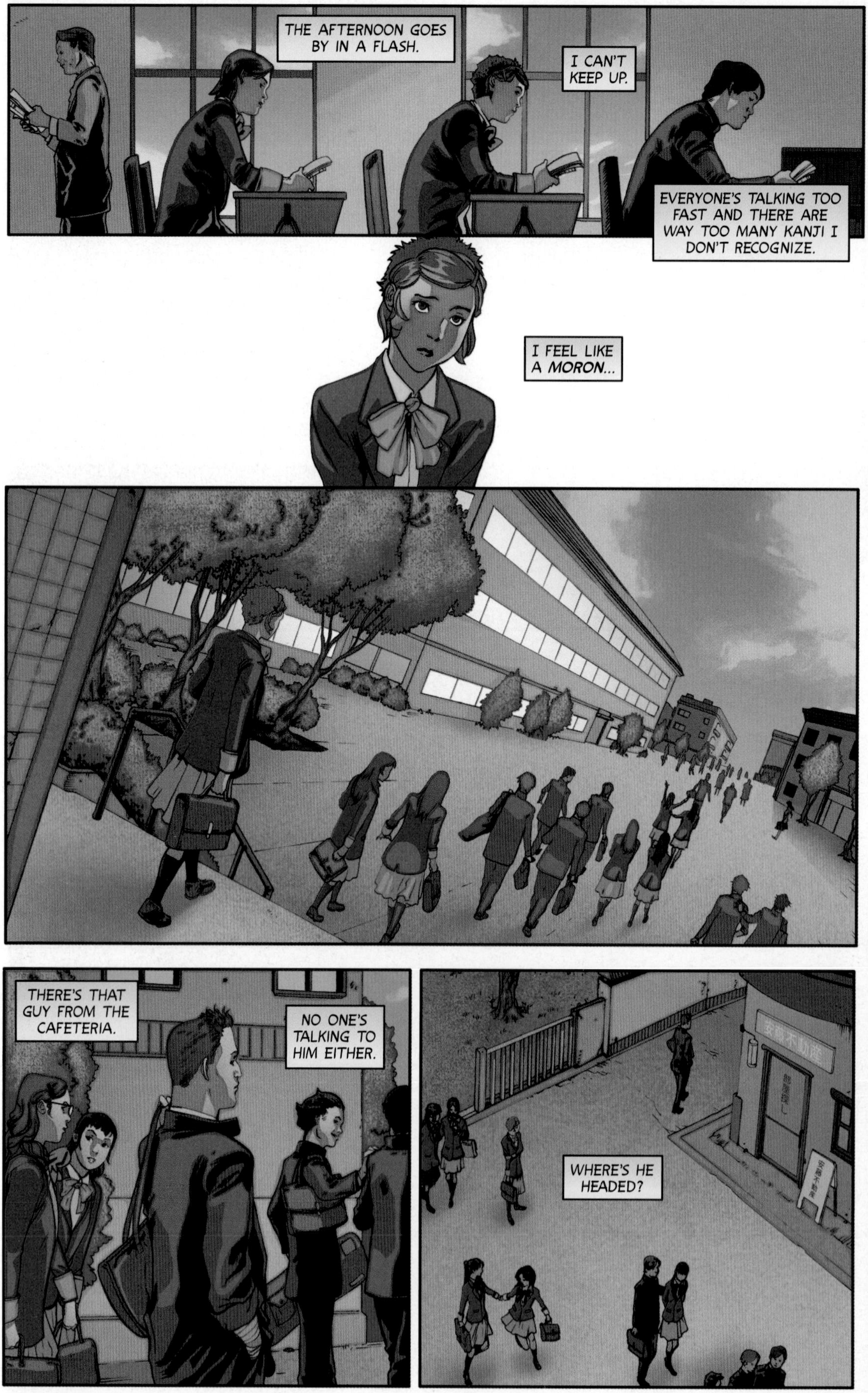
THE AFTERNOON GOES BY IN A FLASH.
I CAN'T KEEP UP.
EVERYONE'S TALKING TOO FAST AND THERE ARE WAY TOO MANY KANJI I DON'T RECOGNIZE.
I FEEL LIKE A *MORON*...
THERE'S THAT GUY FROM THE CAFETERIA.
NO ONE'S TALKING TO HIM EITHER.
WHERE'S HE HEADED?

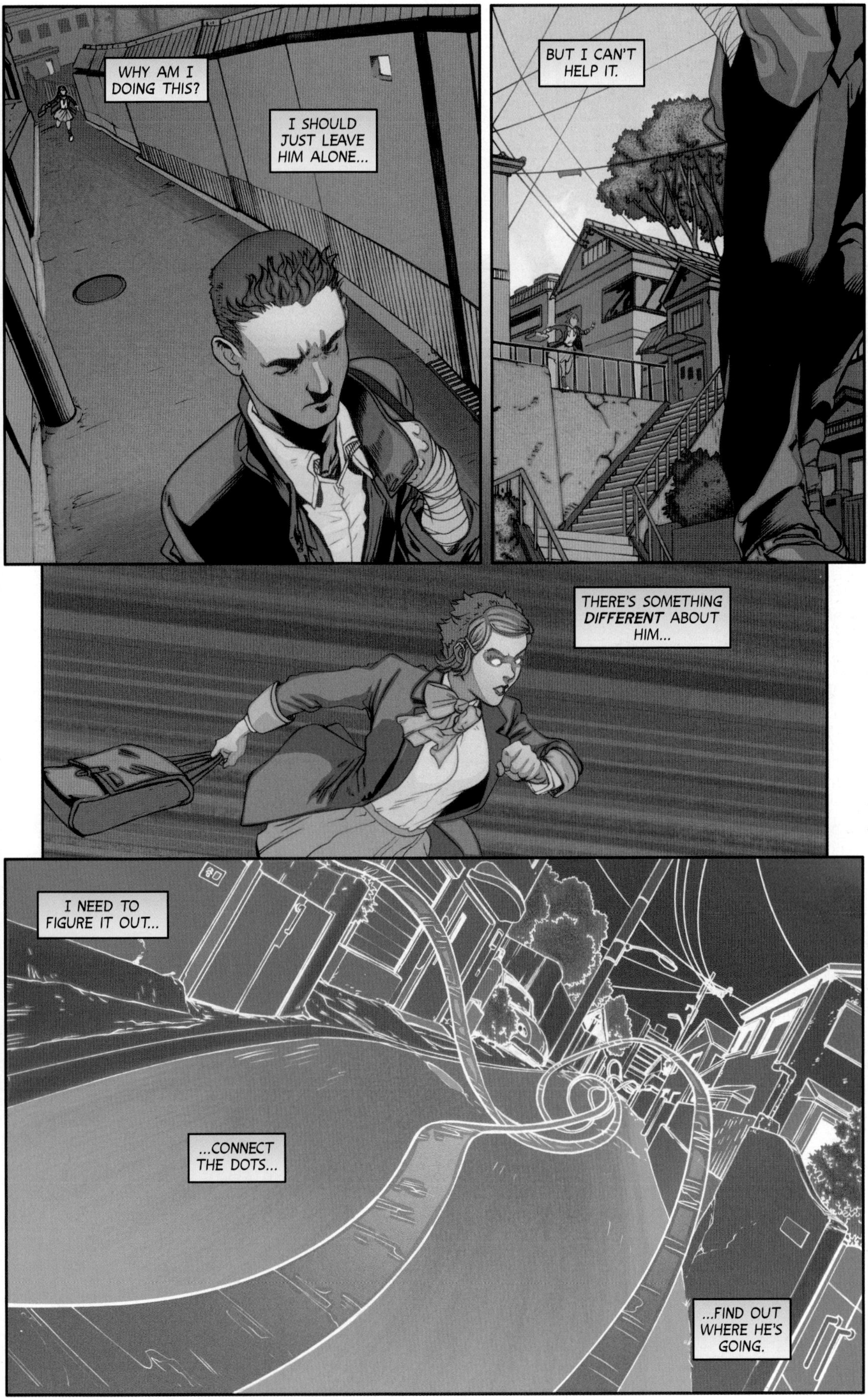
WHY AM I DOING THIS?
I SHOULD JUST LEAVE HIM ALONE...
BUT I CAN'T HELP IT.
THERE'S SOMETHING *DIFFERENT* ABOUT HIM...
I NEED TO FIGURE IT OUT...
...CONNECT THE DOTS...
...FIND OUT WHERE HE'S GOING.

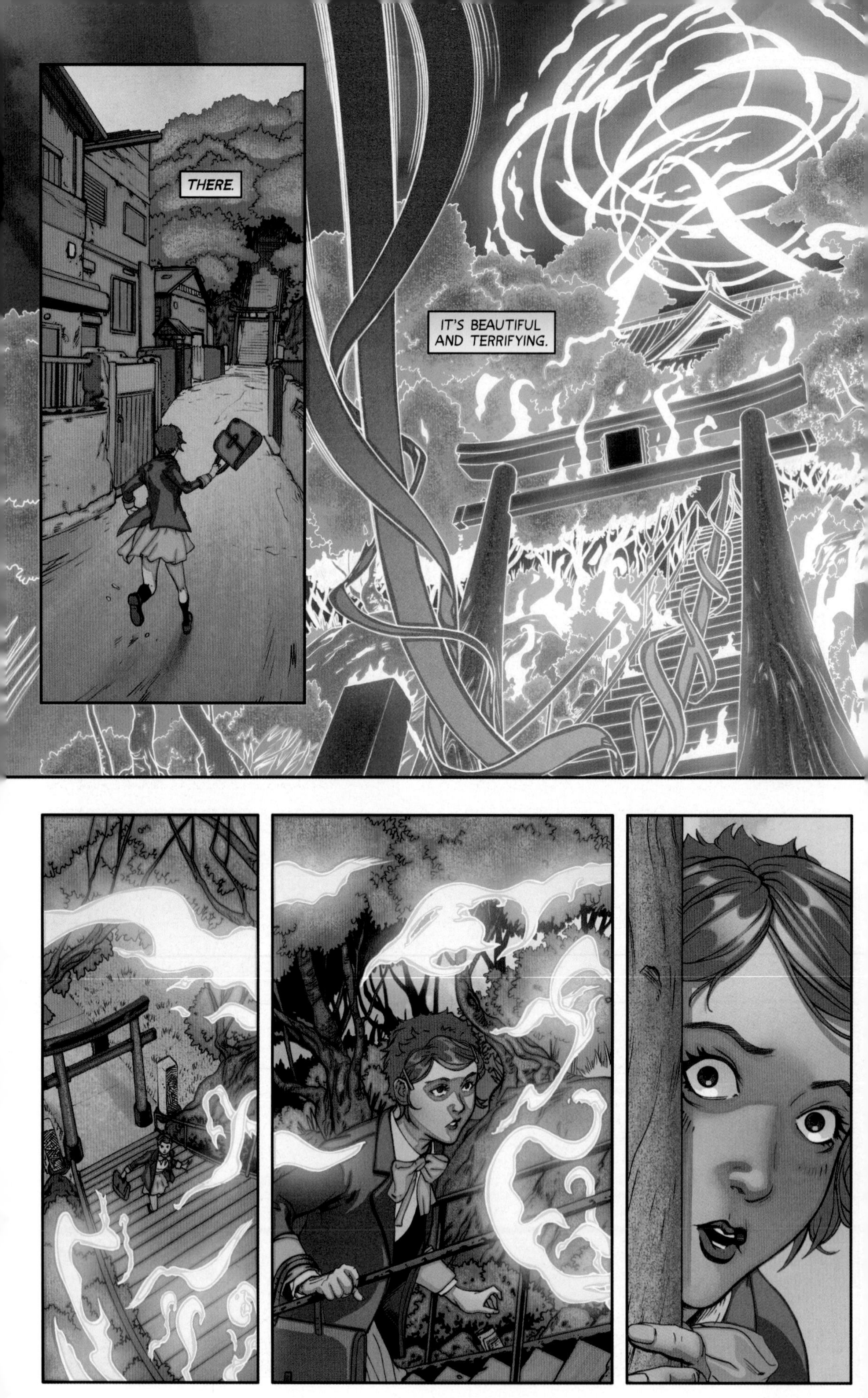
THERE.
IT'S BEAUTIFUL AND TERRIFYING.

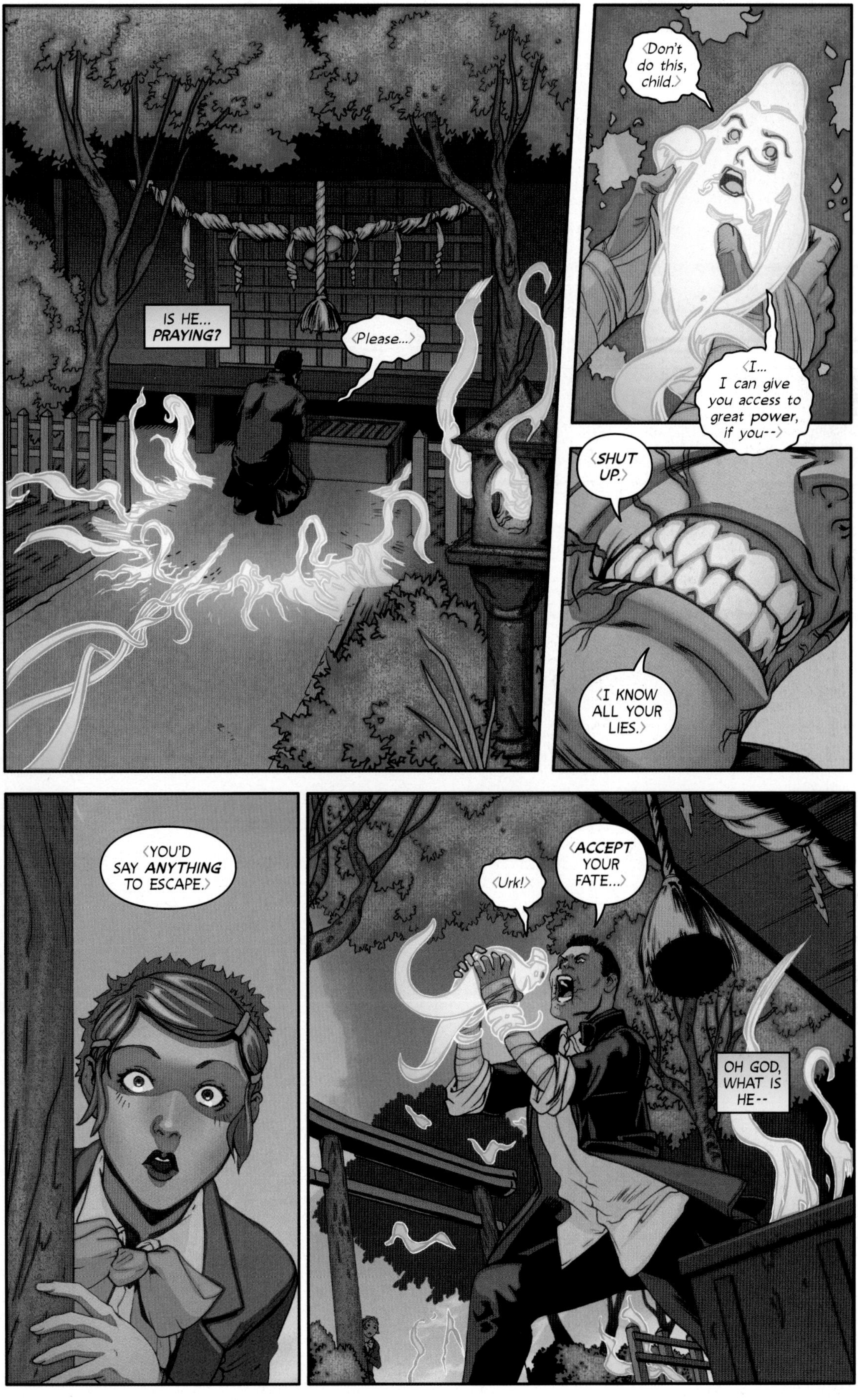
IS HE... PRAYING?
⟨Please...⟩
⟨Don't do this, child.⟩
⟨I... I can give you access to great power, if you--⟩
⟨SHUT UP.⟩
⟨I KNOW ALL YOUR LIES.⟩
⟨YOU'D SAY ANYTHING TO ESCAPE.⟩
⟨Urk!⟩
⟨ACCEPT YOUR FATE...⟩
OH GOD, WHAT IS HE--

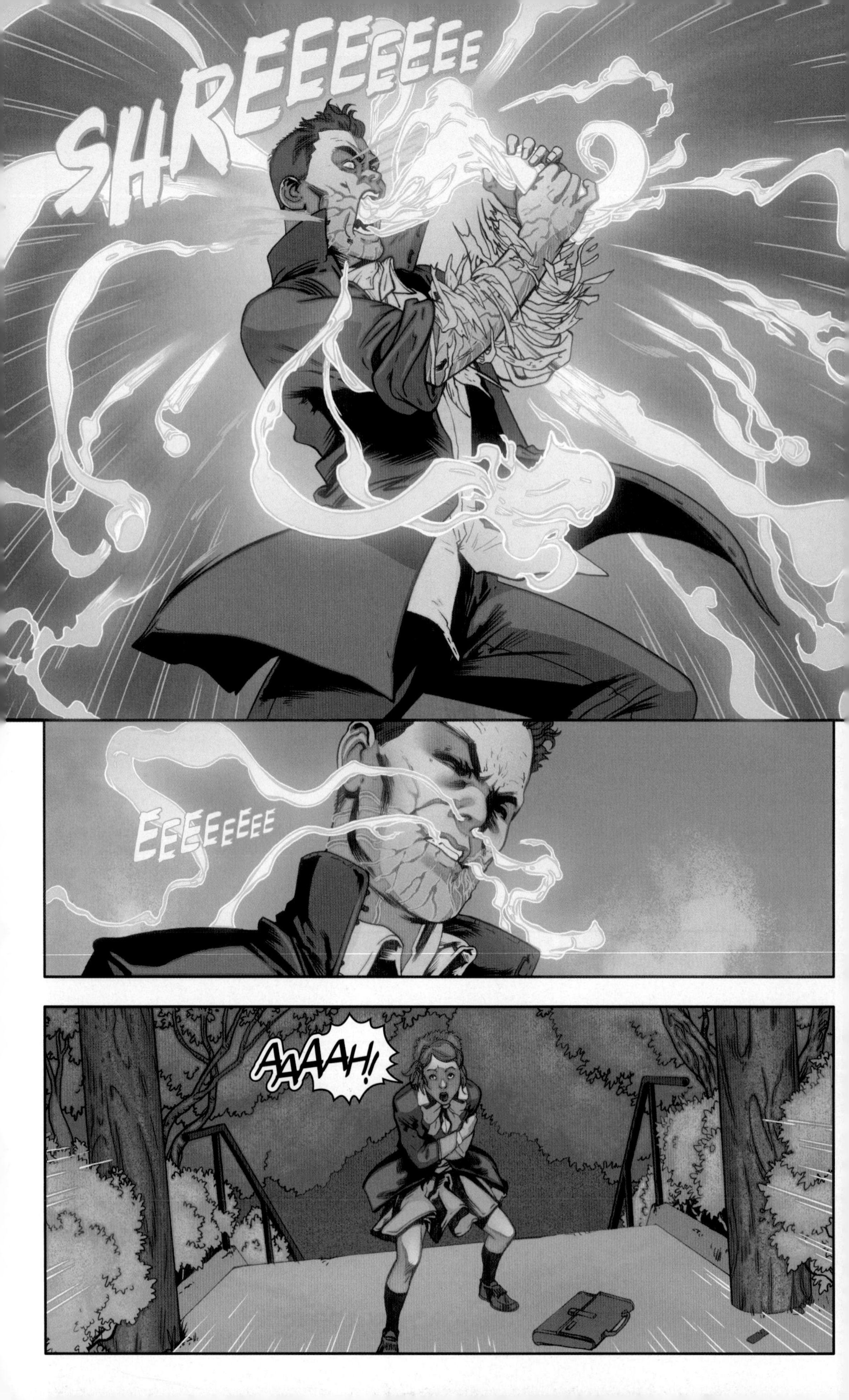
SHREEEEEEEE
EEEEEEE
AAAAH!

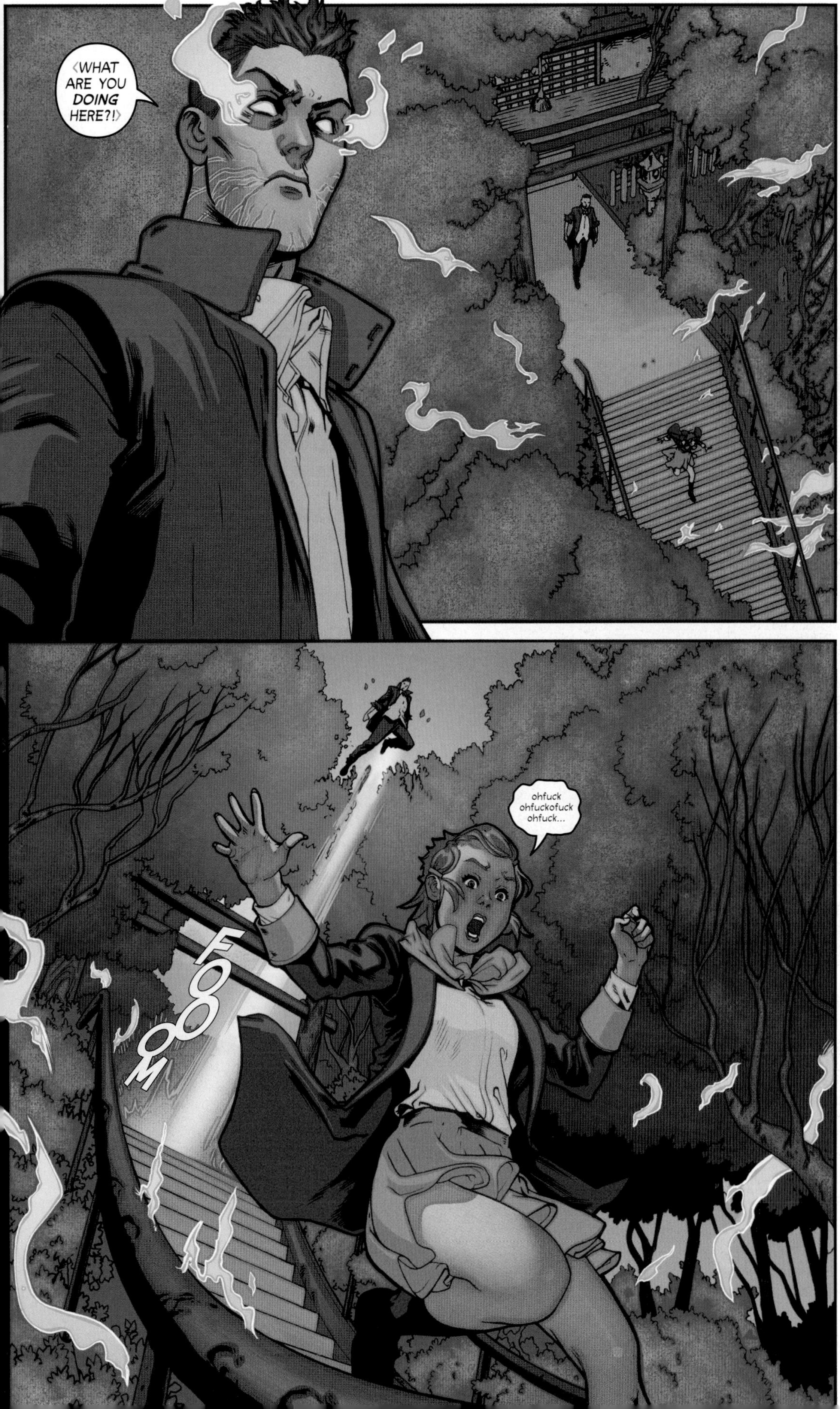
‹WHAT ARE YOU *DOING* HERE?!›
ohfuck ohfuckofuck ohfuck...
FOOOOM

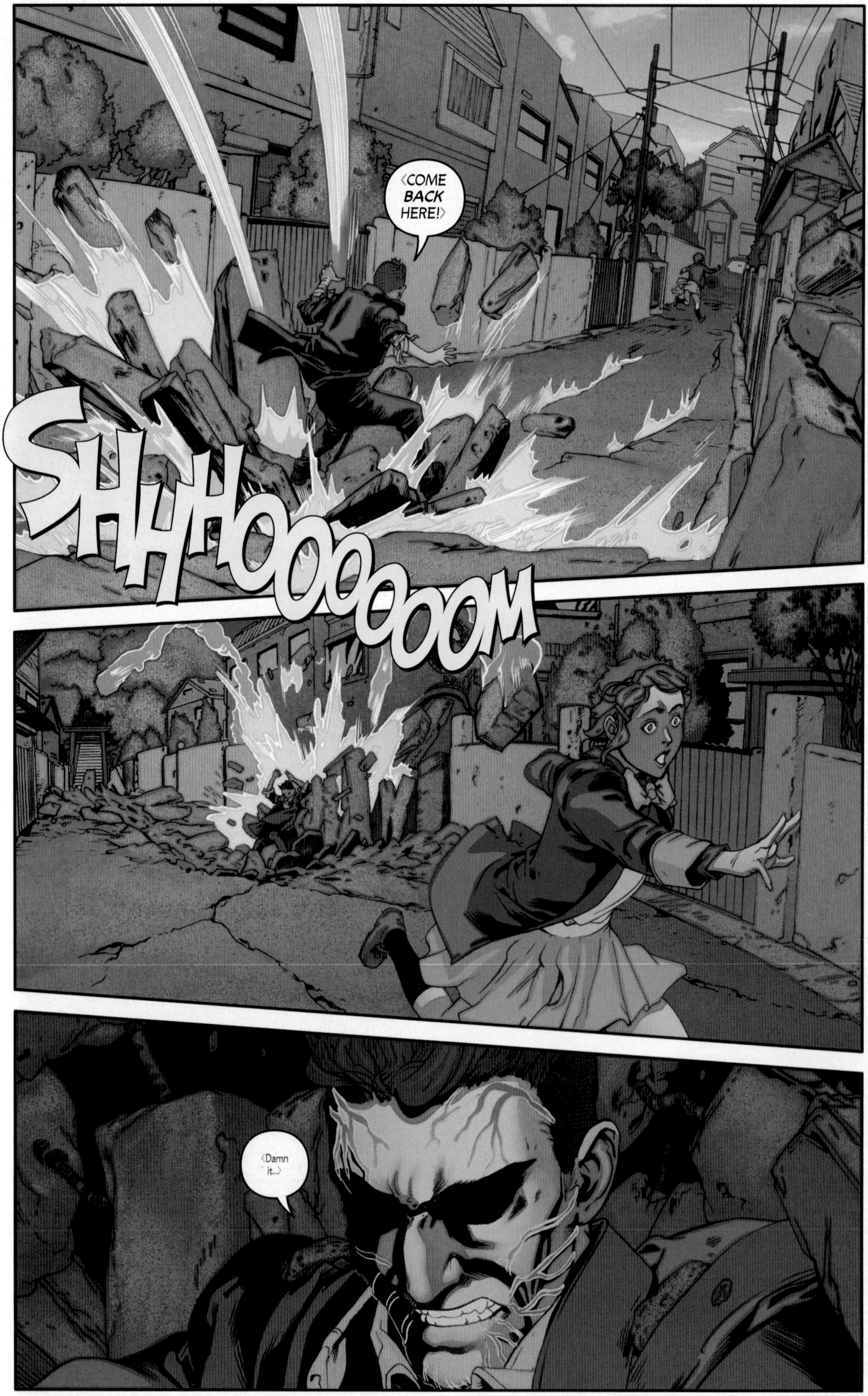

<COME BACK HERE!>
SHHHOOOOOOOM
<Damn it...>

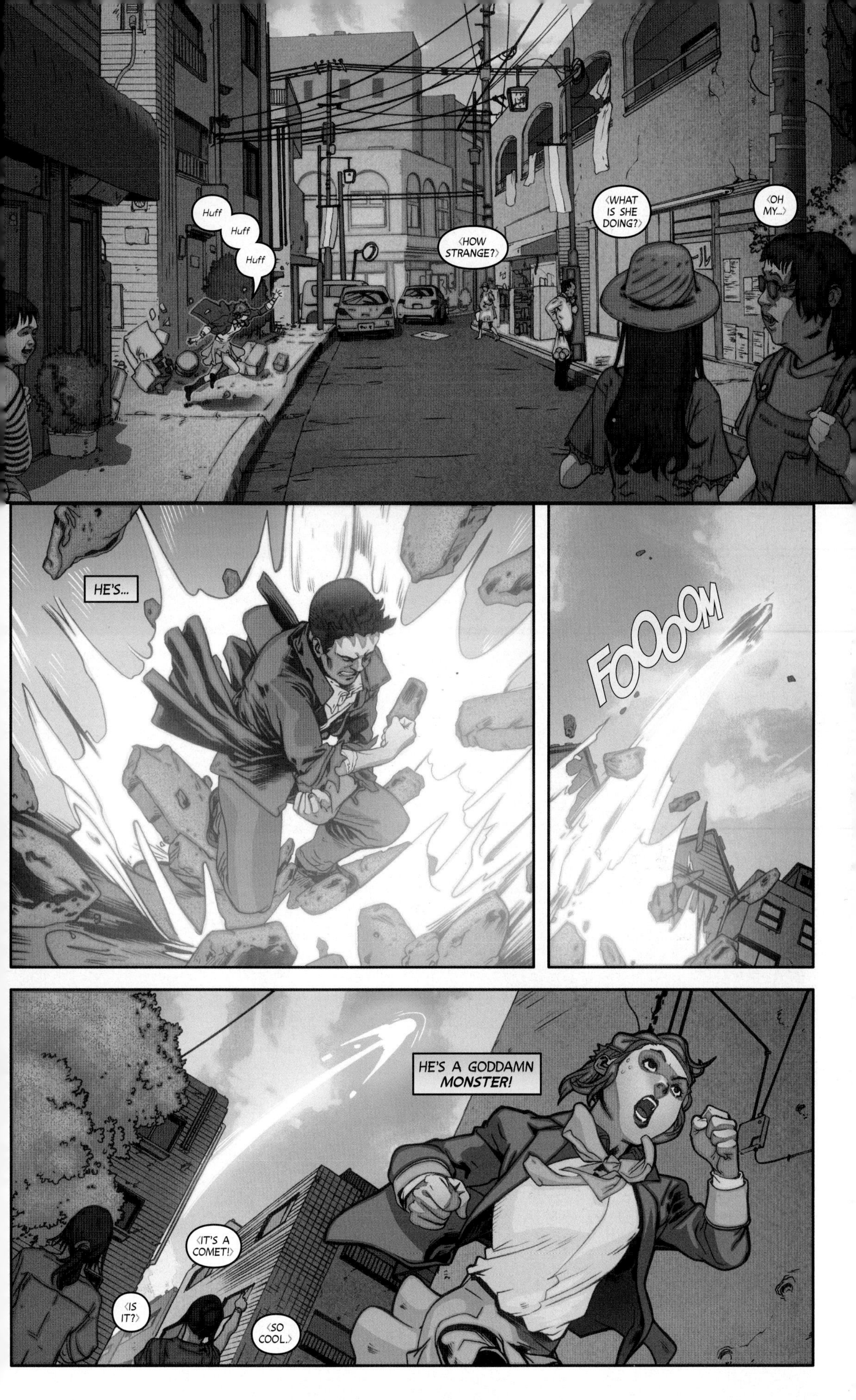
Huff
Huff
Huff
‹HOW STRANGE?›
‹WHAT IS SHE DOING?›
‹OH MY...›
HE'S...
FOOOOOM
HE'S A GODDAMN *MONSTER!*
‹IT'S A COMET!›
‹IS IT?›
‹SO COOL.›

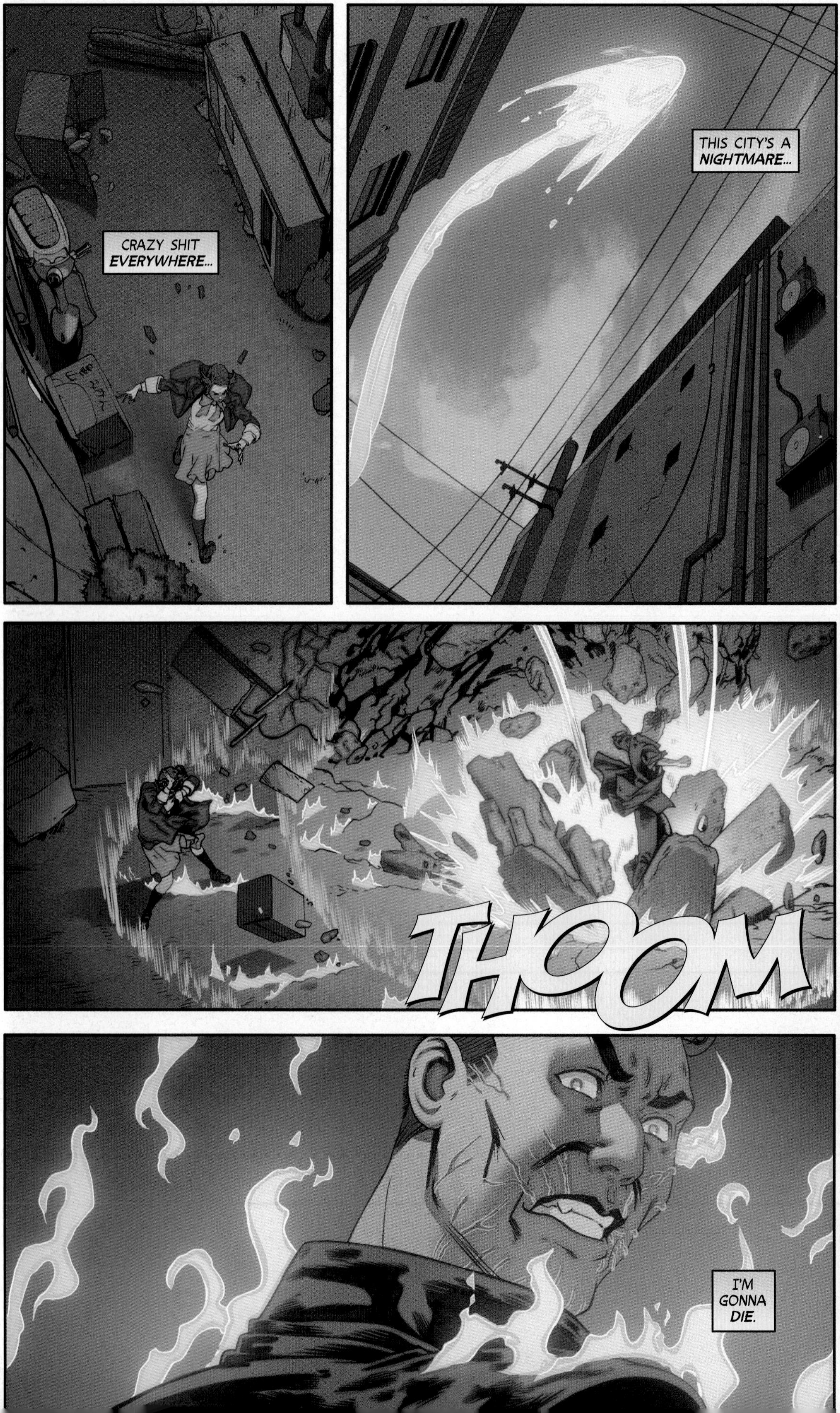
CRAZY SHIT
EVERYWHERE...
THIS CITY'S A
NIGHTMARE...
THOOM
I'M
GONNA
DIE.

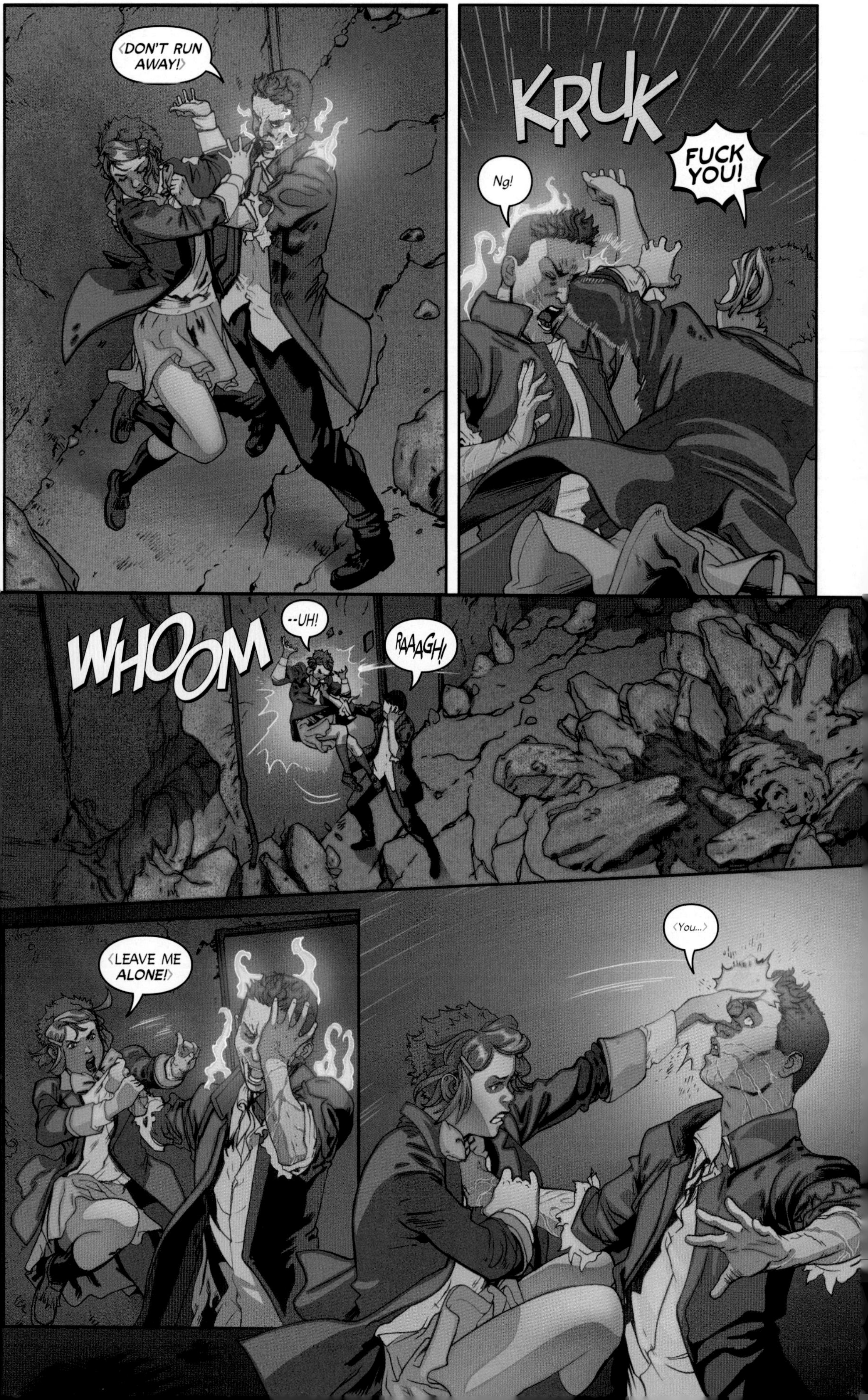
‹DON'T RUN AWAY!›
KRUK
Ng!
FUCK YOU!
WHOOM
--UH!
RAAAGH!
‹LEAVE ME ALONE!›
‹You...›

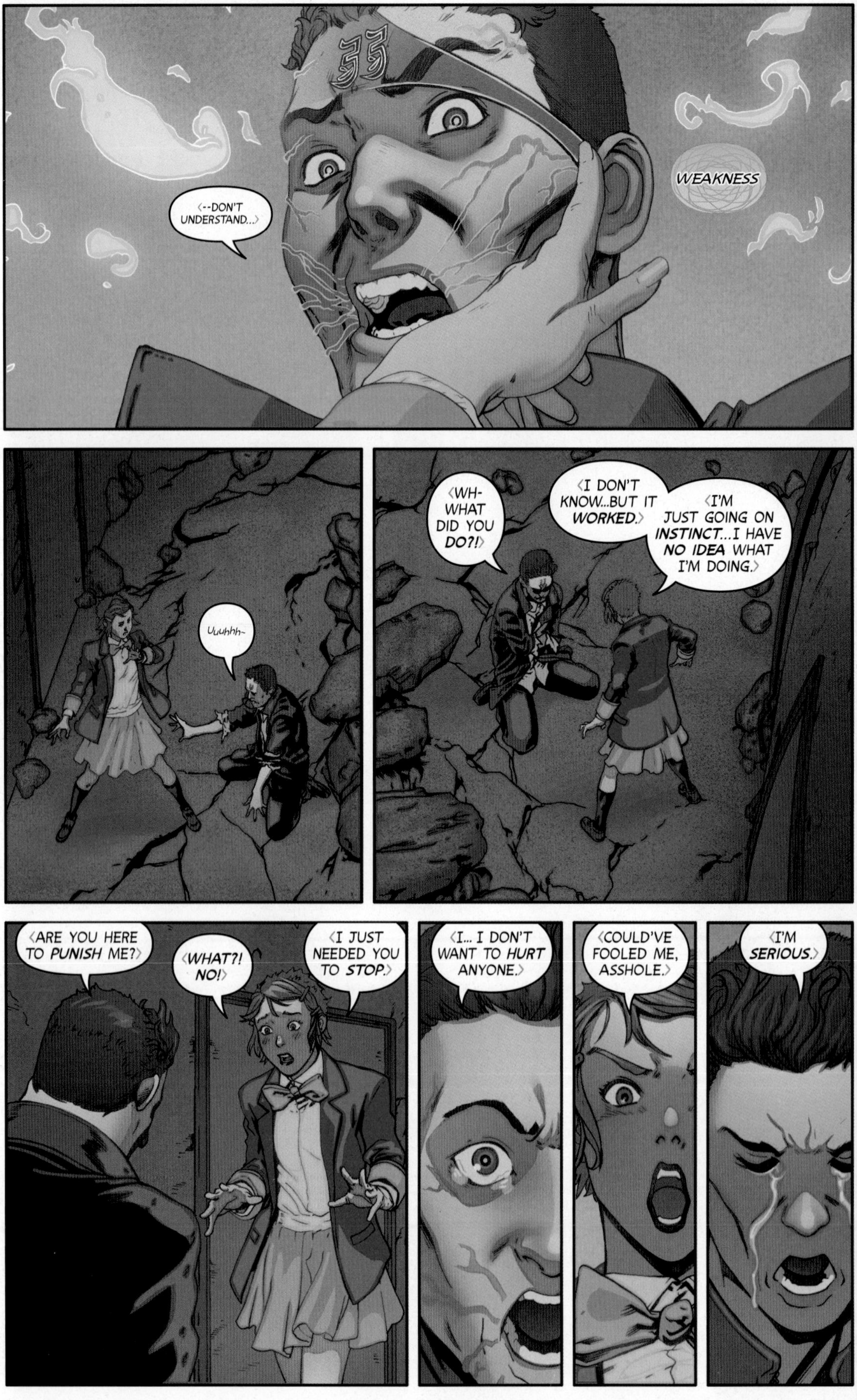

‹--DON'T UNDERSTAND...›
WEAKNESS
Uuuhhh~
‹WH- WHAT DID YOU DO?!›
‹I DON'T KNOW...BUT IT WORKED.›
‹I'M JUST GOING ON INSTINCT...I HAVE NO IDEA WHAT I'M DOING.›
‹ARE YOU HERE TO PUNISH ME?›
‹WHAT?! NO!›
‹I JUST NEEDED YOU TO STOP.›
‹I... I DON'T WANT TO HURT ANYONE.›
‹COULD'VE FOOLED ME, ASSHOLE.›
‹I'M SERIOUS.›

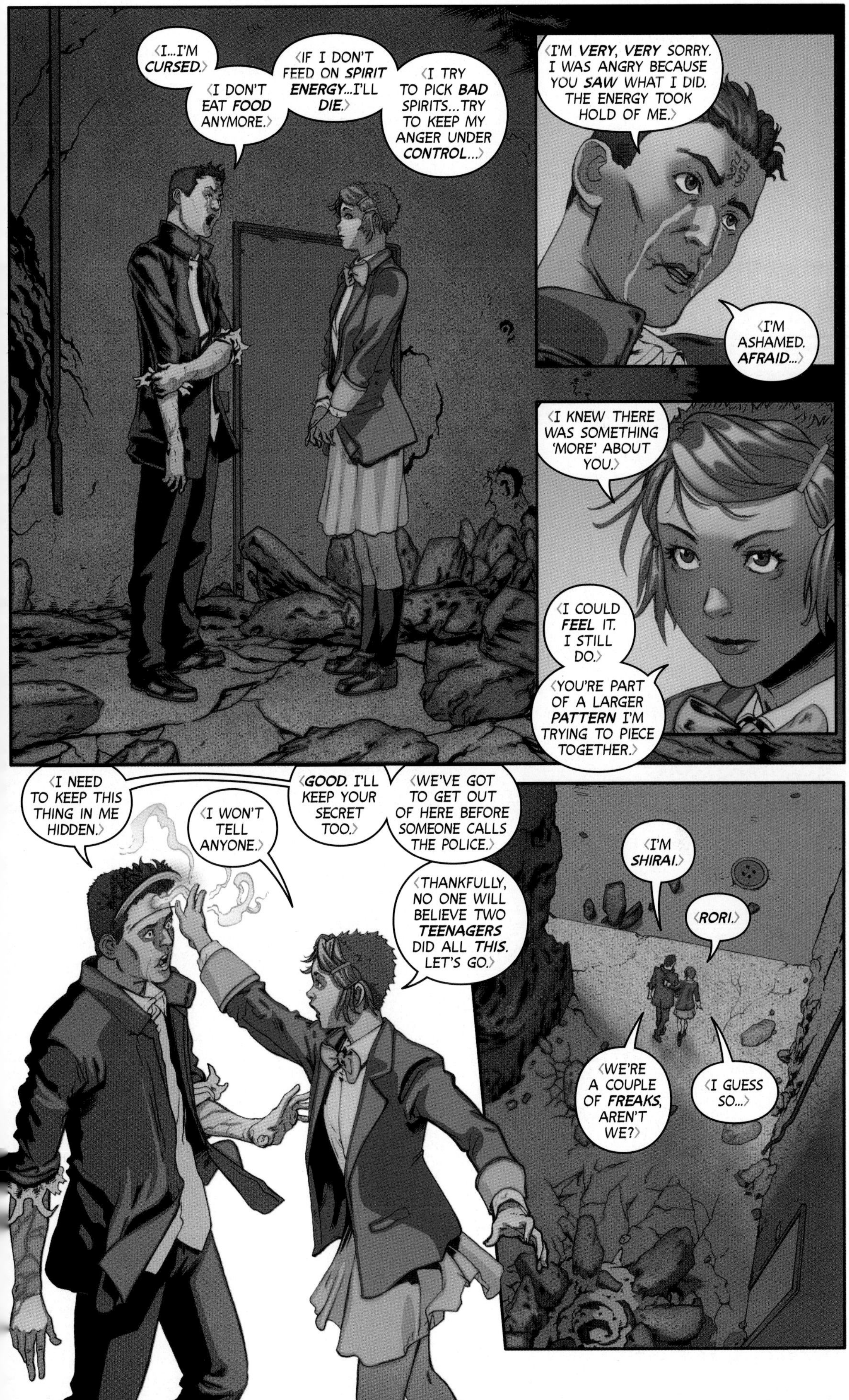

‹I...I'M CURSED.›
‹I DON'T EAT FOOD ANYMORE.›
‹IF I DON'T FEED ON SPIRIT ENERGY...I'LL DIE.›
‹I TRY TO PICK BAD SPIRITS...TRY TO KEEP MY ANGER UNDER CONTROL...›
‹I'M VERY, VERY SORRY. I WAS ANGRY BECAUSE YOU SAW WHAT I DID. THE ENERGY TOOK HOLD OF ME.›
‹I'M ASHAMED. AFRAID...›
‹I KNEW THERE WAS SOMETHING 'MORE' ABOUT YOU.›
‹I COULD FEEL IT. I STILL DO.›
‹YOU'RE PART OF A LARGER PATTERN I'M TRYING TO PIECE TOGETHER.›
‹I NEED TO KEEP THIS THING IN ME HIDDEN.›
‹I WON'T TELL ANYONE.›
‹GOOD. I'LL KEEP YOUR SECRET TOO.›
‹WE'VE GOT TO GET OUT OF HERE BEFORE SOMEONE CALLS THE POLICE.›
‹THANKFULLY, NO ONE WILL BELIEVE TWO TEENAGERS DID ALL THIS. LET'S GO.›
‹I'M SHIRAI.›
‹RORI.›
‹WE'RE A COUPLE OF FREAKS, AREN'T WE?›
‹I GUESS SO...›

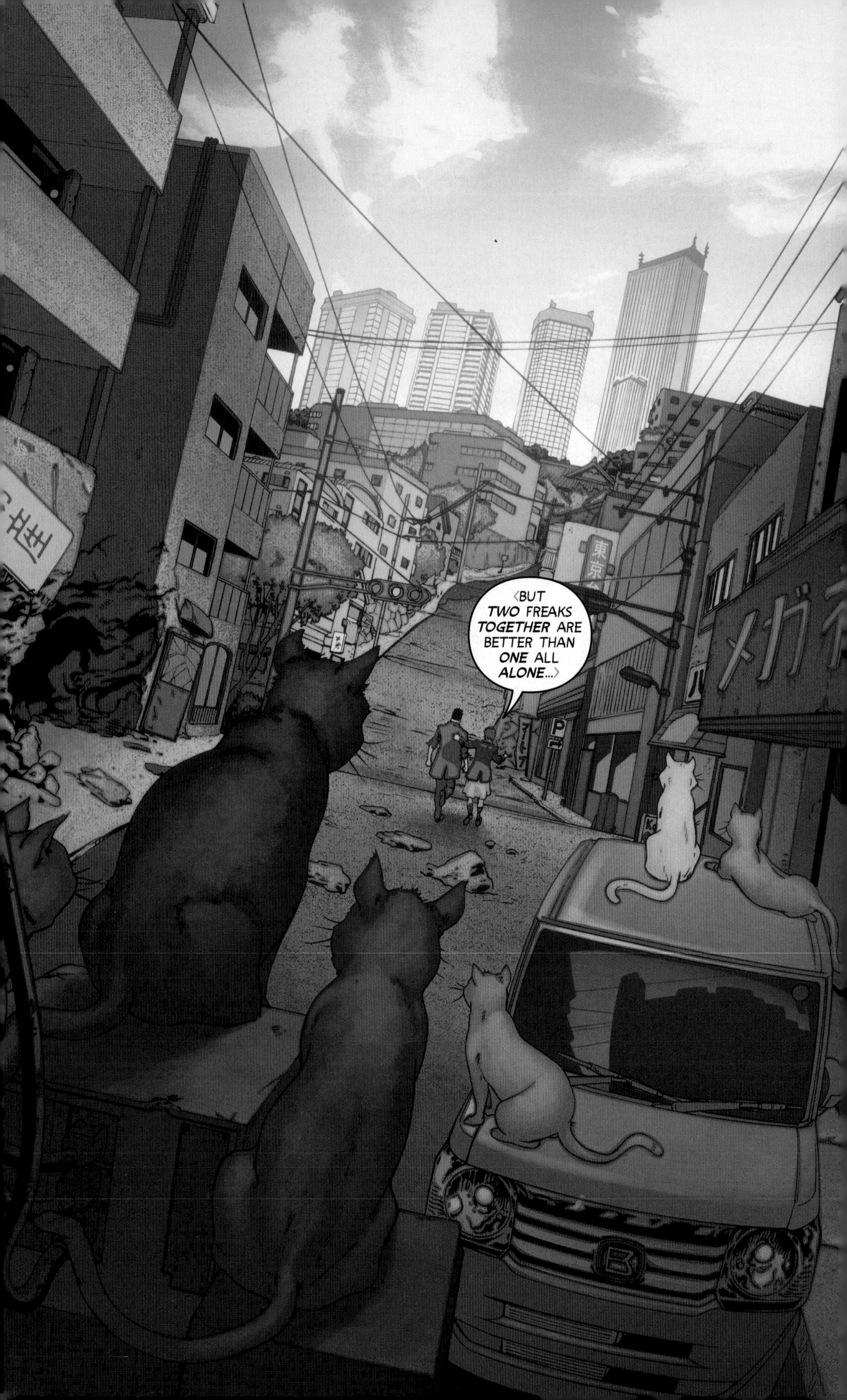
‹BUT TWO FREAKS TOGETHER ARE BETTER THAN ONE ALL ALONE...›

# Chapter Three

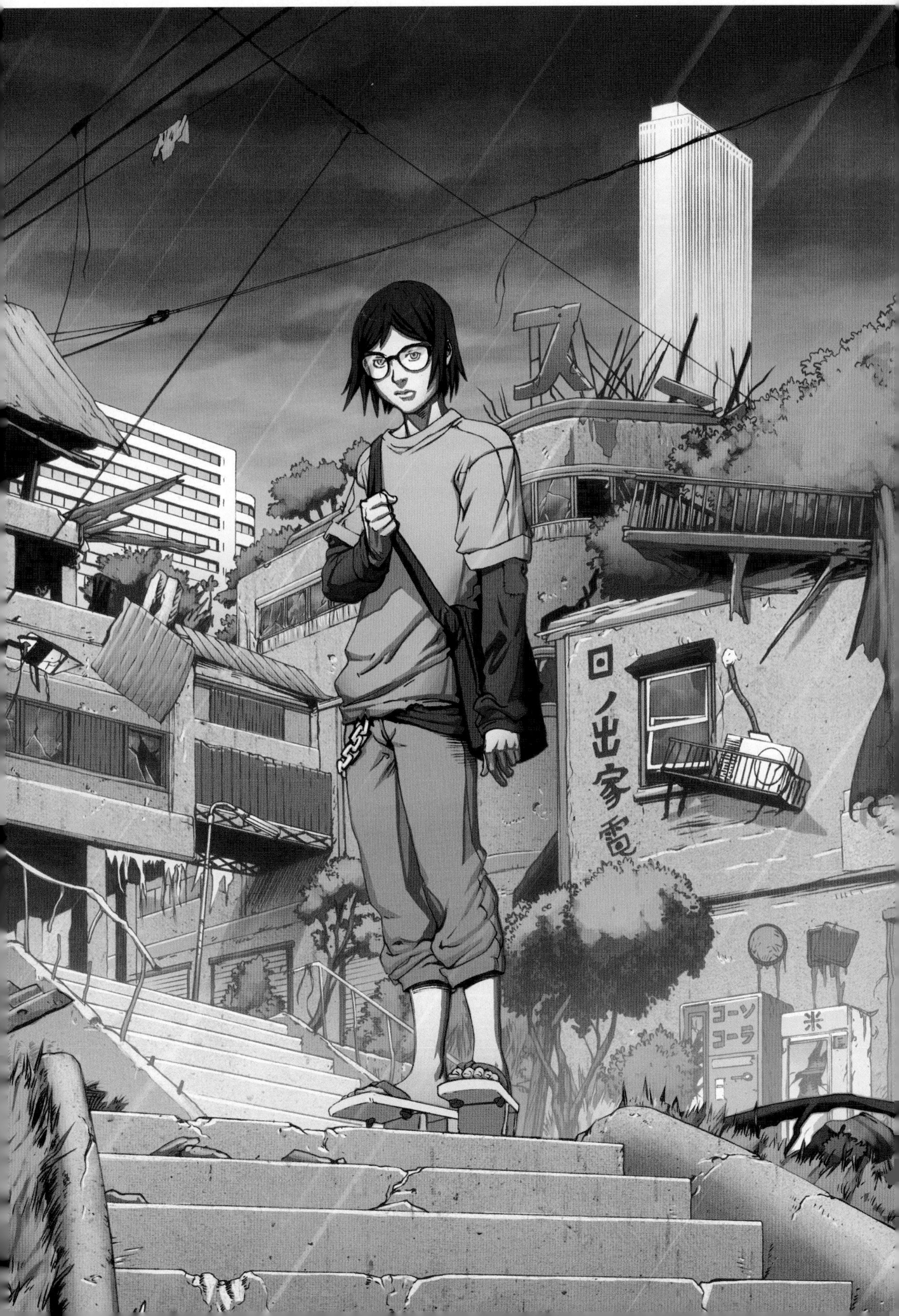
口ノ出家電
コーソ
コーラ
米

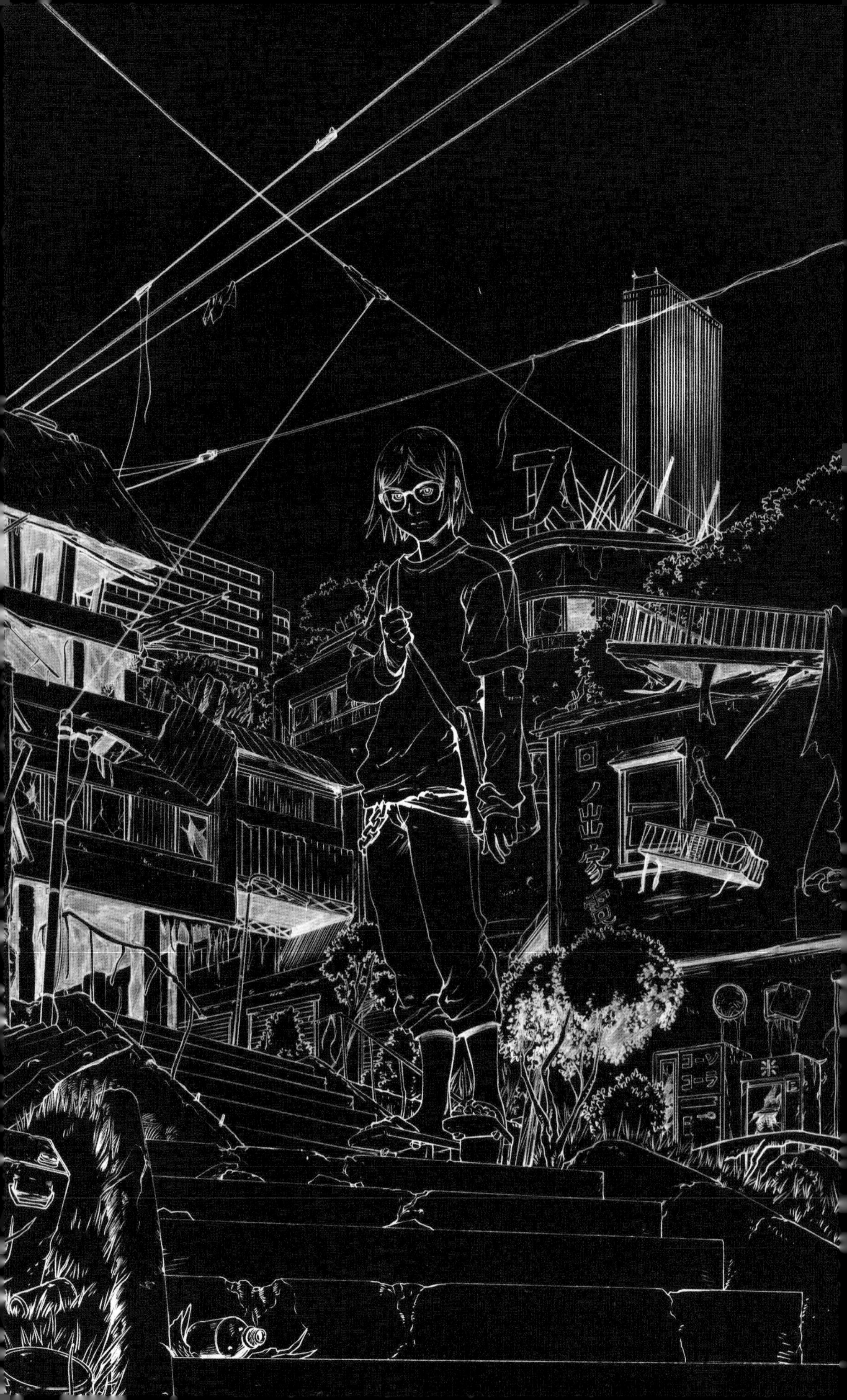
ノ出家電
コーラ
米

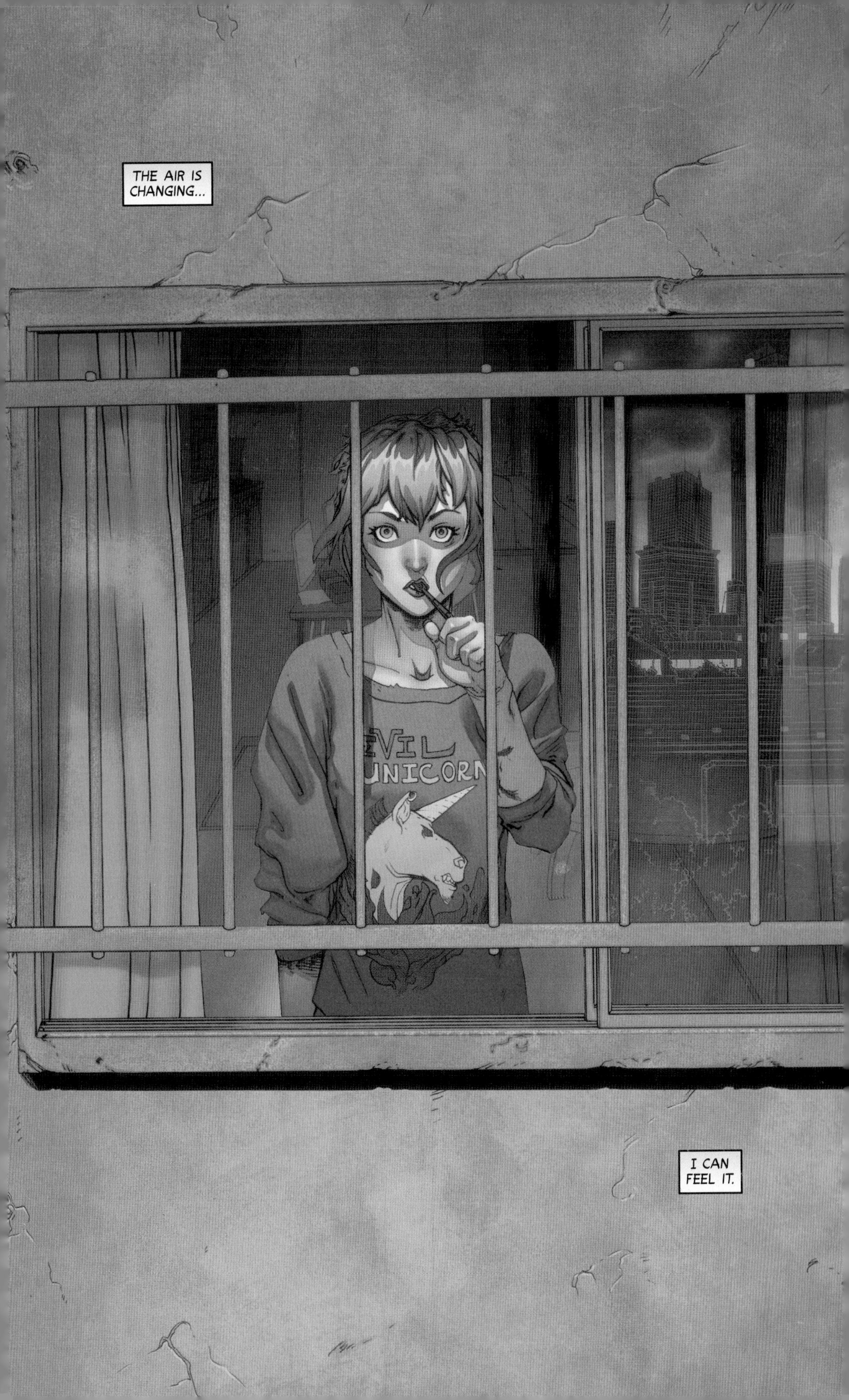

THE AIR IS CHANGING...
I CAN FEEL IT.

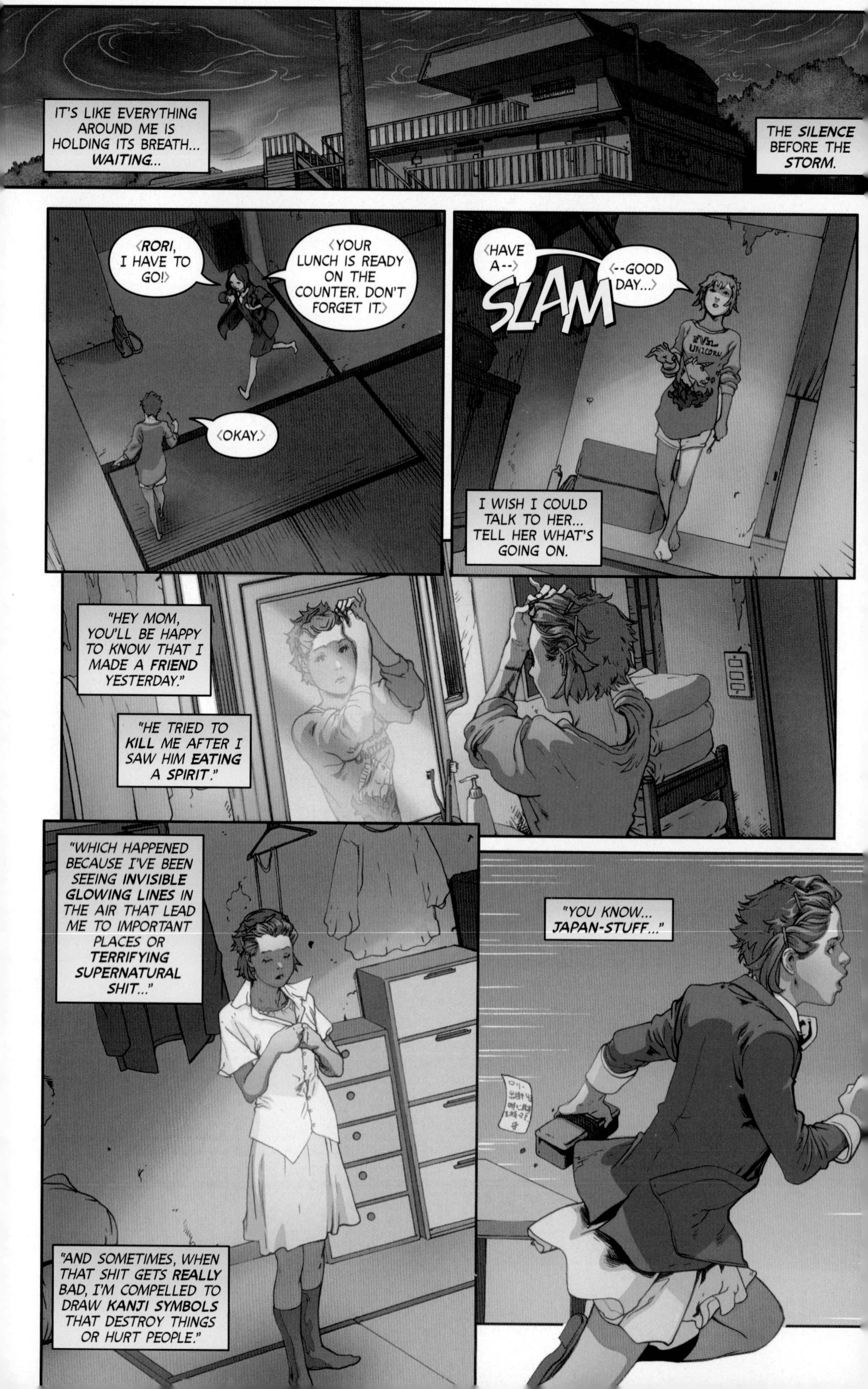

IT'S LIKE EVERYTHING AROUND ME IS HOLDING ITS BREATH... WAITING...
THE SILENCE BEFORE THE STORM.
‹RORI, I HAVE TO GO!›
‹YOUR LUNCH IS READY ON THE COUNTER. DON'T FORGET IT.›
‹OKAY.›
‹HAVE A--›
SLAM
‹--GOOD DAY...›
I WISH I COULD TALK TO HER... TELL HER WHAT'S GOING ON.
"HEY MOM, YOU'LL BE HAPPY TO KNOW THAT I MADE A FRIEND YESTERDAY."
"HE TRIED TO KILL ME AFTER I SAW HIM EATING A SPIRIT."
"WHICH HAPPENED BECAUSE I'VE BEEN SEEING INVISIBLE GLOWING LINES IN THE AIR THAT LEAD ME TO IMPORTANT PLACES OR TERRIFYING SUPERNATURAL SHIT..."
"AND SOMETIMES, WHEN THAT SHIT GETS REALLY BAD, I'M COMPELLED TO DRAW KANJI SYMBOLS THAT DESTROY THINGS OR HURT PEOPLE."
"YOU KNOW... JAPAN-STUFF..."

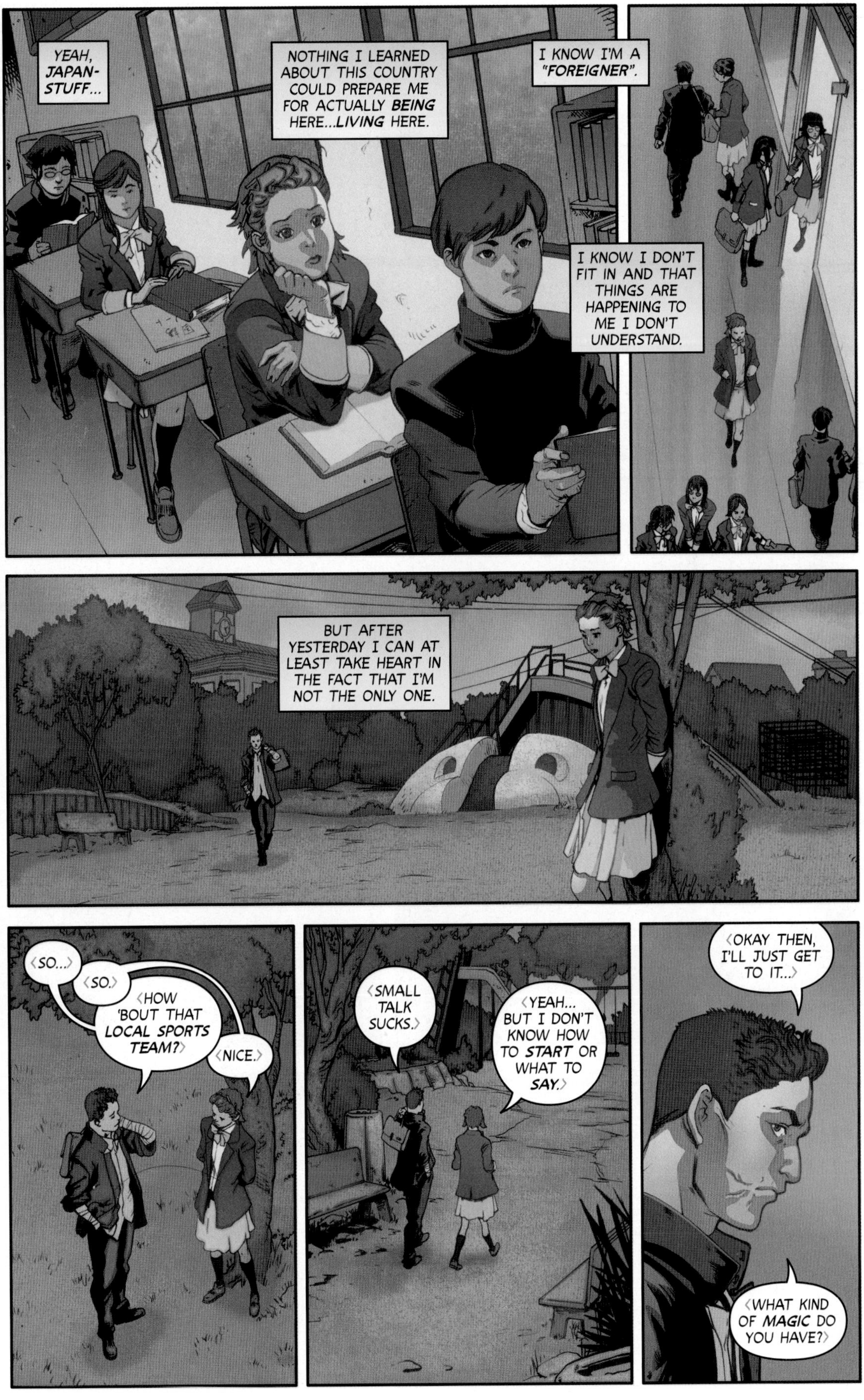
YEAH, JAPAN-STUFF...
NOTHING I LEARNED ABOUT THIS COUNTRY COULD PREPARE ME FOR ACTUALLY BEING HERE...LIVING HERE.
I KNOW I'M A "FOREIGNER".
I KNOW I DON'T FIT IN AND THAT THINGS ARE HAPPENING TO ME I DON'T UNDERSTAND.
BUT AFTER YESTERDAY I CAN AT LEAST TAKE HEART IN THE FACT THAT I'M NOT THE ONLY ONE.
〈SO...〉
〈SO.〉
〈HOW 'BOUT THAT LOCAL SPORTS TEAM?〉
〈NICE.〉
〈SMALL TALK SUCKS.〉
〈YEAH... BUT I DON'T KNOW HOW TO START OR WHAT TO SAY.〉
〈OKAY THEN, I'LL JUST GET TO IT...〉
〈WHAT KIND OF MAGIC DO YOU HAVE?〉

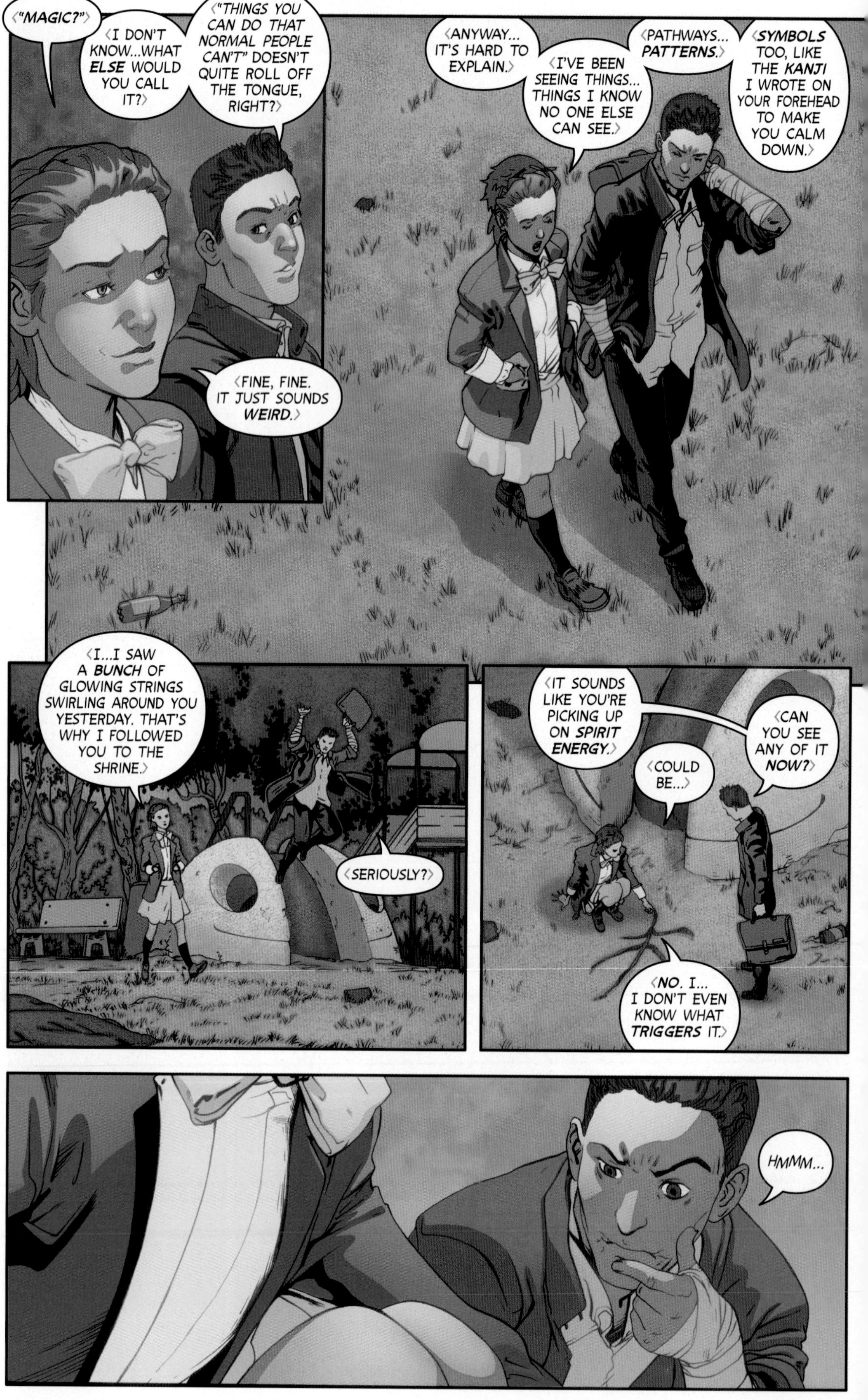

⟨"MAGIC?"⟩
⟨I DON'T KNOW...WHAT ELSE WOULD YOU CALL IT?⟩
⟨"THINGS YOU CAN DO THAT NORMAL PEOPLE CAN'T" DOESN'T QUITE ROLL OFF THE TONGUE, RIGHT?⟩
⟨FINE, FINE. IT JUST SOUNDS WEIRD.⟩
⟨ANYWAY... IT'S HARD TO EXPLAIN.⟩
⟨I'VE BEEN SEEING THINGS... THINGS I KNOW NO ONE ELSE CAN SEE.⟩
⟨PATHWAYS... PATTERNS.⟩
⟨SYMBOLS TOO, LIKE THE KANJI I WROTE ON YOUR FOREHEAD TO MAKE YOU CALM DOWN.⟩
⟨I...I SAW A BUNCH OF GLOWING STRINGS SWIRLING AROUND YOU YESTERDAY. THAT'S WHY I FOLLOWED YOU TO THE SHRINE.⟩
⟨SERIOUSLY?⟩
⟨IT SOUNDS LIKE YOU'RE PICKING UP ON SPIRIT ENERGY.⟩
⟨COULD BE...⟩
⟨CAN YOU SEE ANY OF IT NOW?⟩
⟨NO. I... I DON'T EVEN KNOW WHAT TRIGGERS IT.⟩
HMMM...

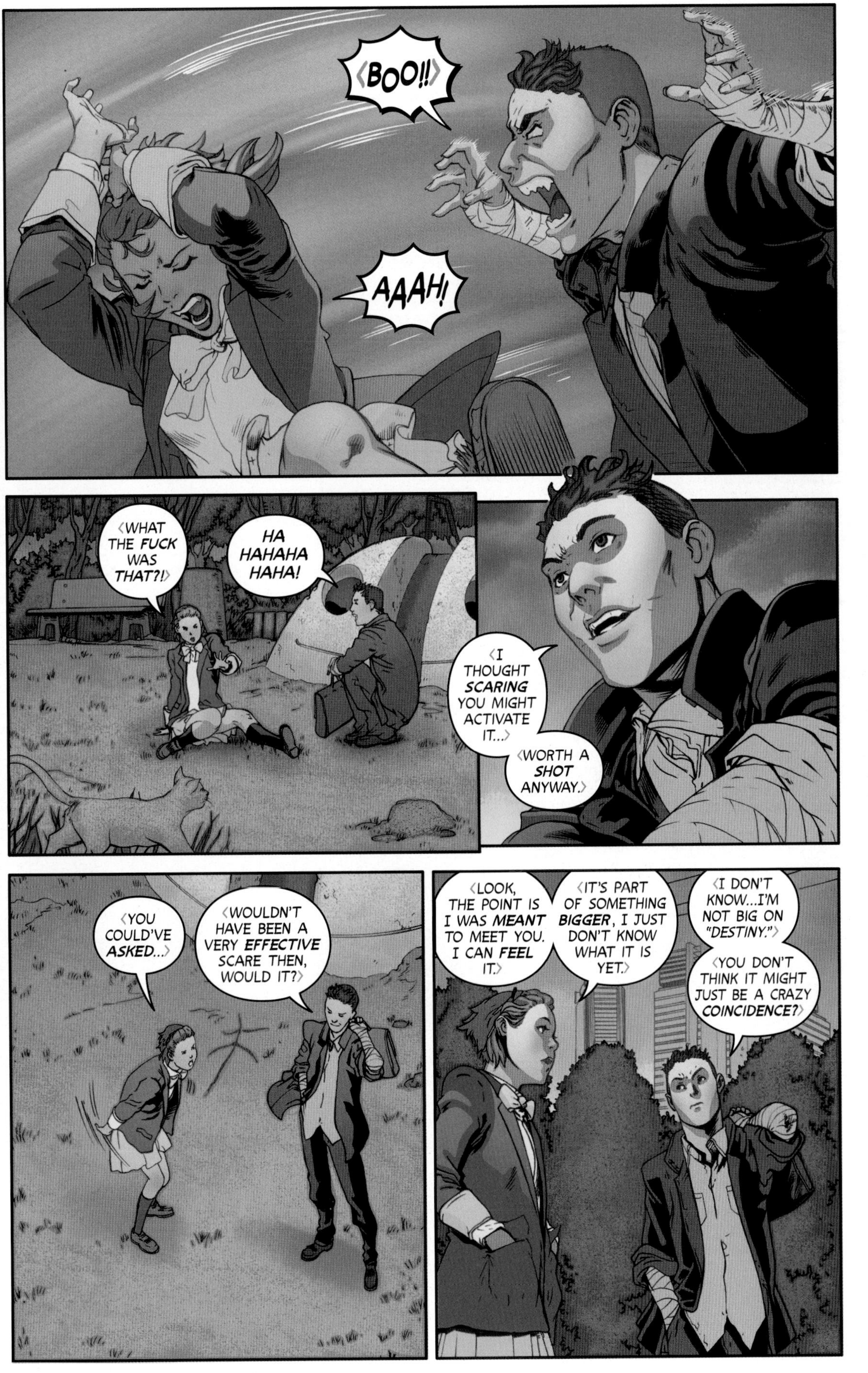
⟨BOO!!⟩
AAAH!
⟨WHAT THE *FUCK* WAS *THAT?!*⟩
*HA HAHAHA HAHA!*
⟨I THOUGHT *SCARING* YOU MIGHT ACTIVATE IT...⟩
⟨WORTH A *SHOT* ANYWAY.⟩
⟨YOU COULD'VE *ASKED*...⟩
⟨WOULDN'T HAVE BEEN A VERY *EFFECTIVE* SCARE THEN, WOULD IT?⟩
⟨LOOK, THE POINT IS I WAS *MEANT* TO MEET YOU. I CAN *FEEL* IT.⟩
⟨IT'S PART OF SOMETHING *BIGGER*, I JUST DON'T KNOW WHAT IT IS YET.⟩
⟨I DON'T KNOW...I'M NOT BIG ON "DESTINY."⟩
⟨YOU DON'T THINK IT MIGHT JUST BE A CRAZY *COINCIDENCE?*⟩

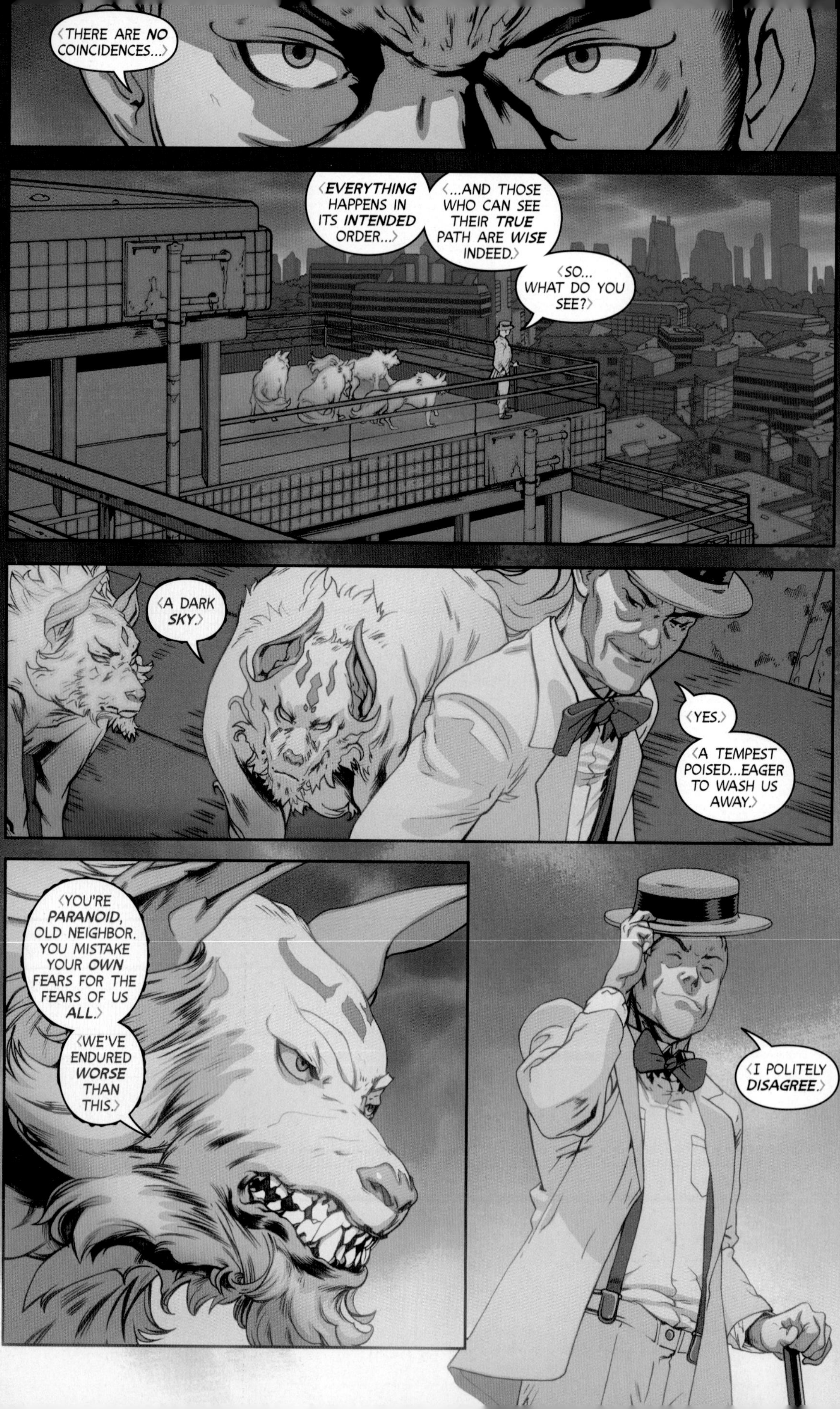

‹THERE ARE NO COINCIDENCES...›
‹EVERYTHING HAPPENS IN ITS INTENDED ORDER...›
‹...AND THOSE WHO CAN SEE THEIR TRUE PATH ARE WISE INDEED.›
‹SO... WHAT DO YOU SEE?›
‹A DARK SKY.›
‹YES.›
‹A TEMPEST POISED...EAGER TO WASH US AWAY.›
‹YOU'RE PARANOID, OLD NEIGHBOR. YOU MISTAKE YOUR OWN FEARS FOR THE FEARS OF US ALL.›
‹WE'VE ENDURED WORSE THAN THIS.›
‹I POLITELY DISAGREE.›

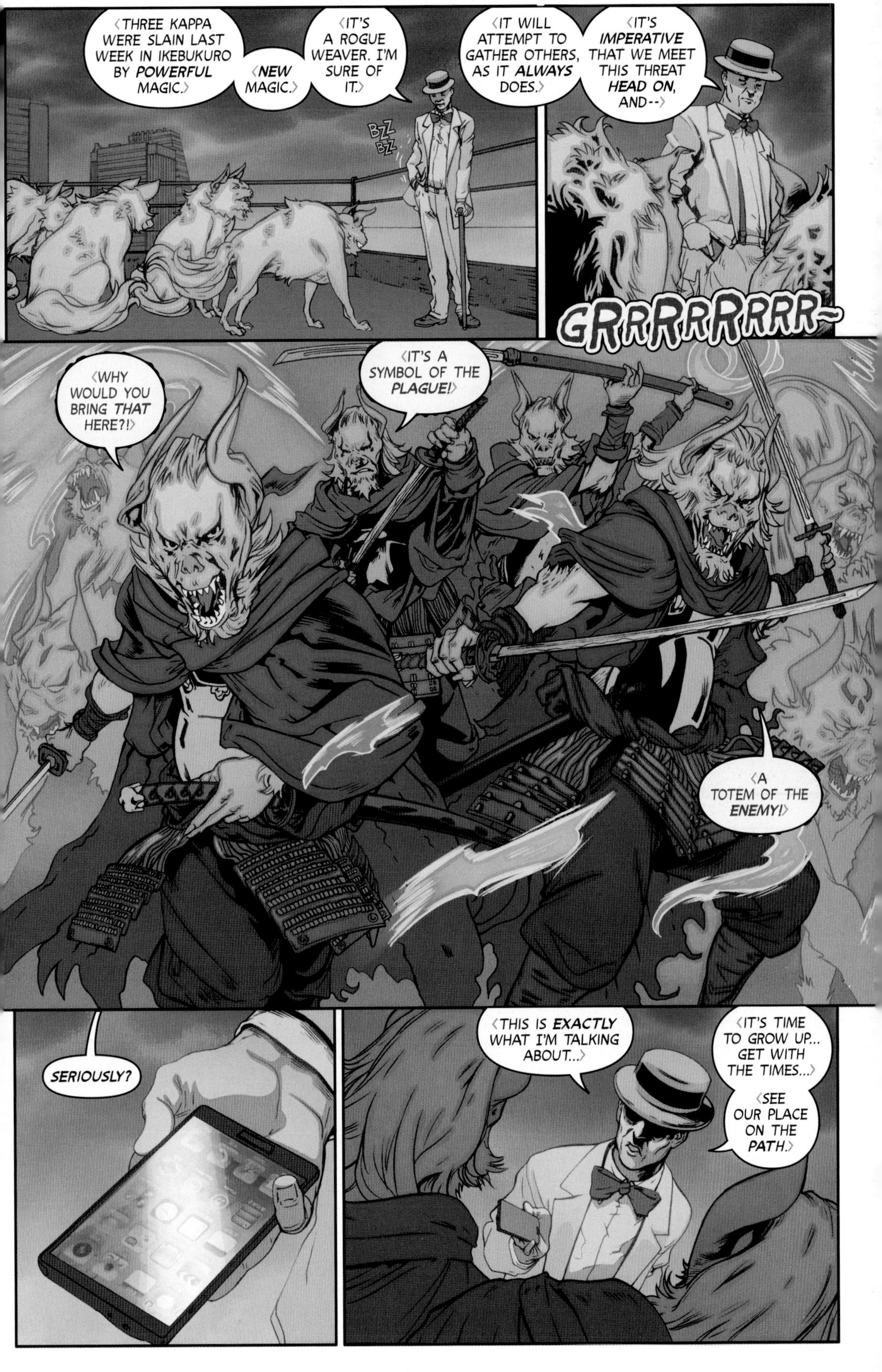
‹THREE KAPPA WERE SLAIN LAST WEEK IN IKEBUKURO BY *POWERFUL* MAGIC.›
‹*NEW* MAGIC.›
‹IT'S A ROGUE WEAVER. I'M SURE OF IT.›
BZZ BZZ
‹IT WILL ATTEMPT TO GATHER OTHERS, AS IT *ALWAYS* DOES.›
‹IT'S *IMPERATIVE* THAT WE MEET THIS THREAT *HEAD ON*, AND--›
GRRRRRRRR~
‹WHY WOULD YOU BRING *THAT* HERE?!›
‹IT'S A SYMBOL OF THE *PLAGUE!*›
‹A TOTEM OF THE *ENEMY!*›
*SERIOUSLY?*
‹THIS IS *EXACTLY* WHAT I'M TALKING ABOUT...›
‹IT'S TIME TO GROW UP... GET WITH THE TIMES...›
‹SEE OUR PLACE ON THE *PATH*.›

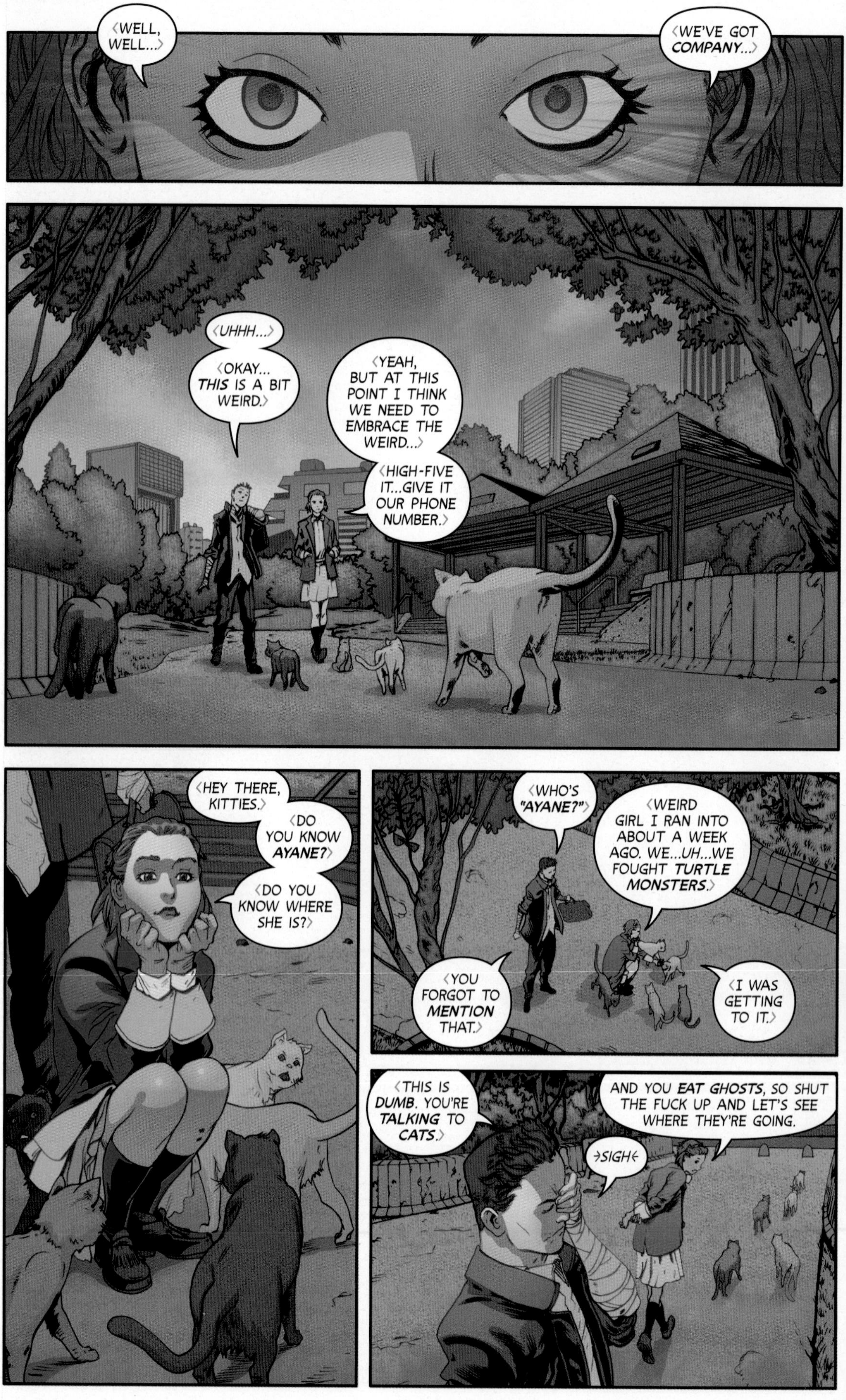

〈WELL, WELL...〉
〈WE'VE GOT COMPANY...〉
〈UHHH...〉
〈OKAY... THIS IS A BIT WEIRD.〉
〈YEAH, BUT AT THIS POINT I THINK WE NEED TO EMBRACE THE WEIRD...〉
〈HIGH-FIVE IT...GIVE IT OUR PHONE NUMBER.〉
〈HEY THERE, KITTIES.〉
〈DO YOU KNOW AYANE?〉
〈DO YOU KNOW WHERE SHE IS?〉
〈WHO'S "AYANE?"〉
〈WEIRD GIRL I RAN INTO ABOUT A WEEK AGO. WE...UH...WE FOUGHT TURTLE MONSTERS.〉
〈YOU FORGOT TO MENTION THAT.〉
〈I WAS GETTING TO IT.〉
〈THIS IS DUMB. YOU'RE TALKING TO CATS.〉
AND YOU EAT GHOSTS, SO SHUT THE FUCK UP AND LET'S SEE WHERE THEY'RE GOING.
›SIGH‹

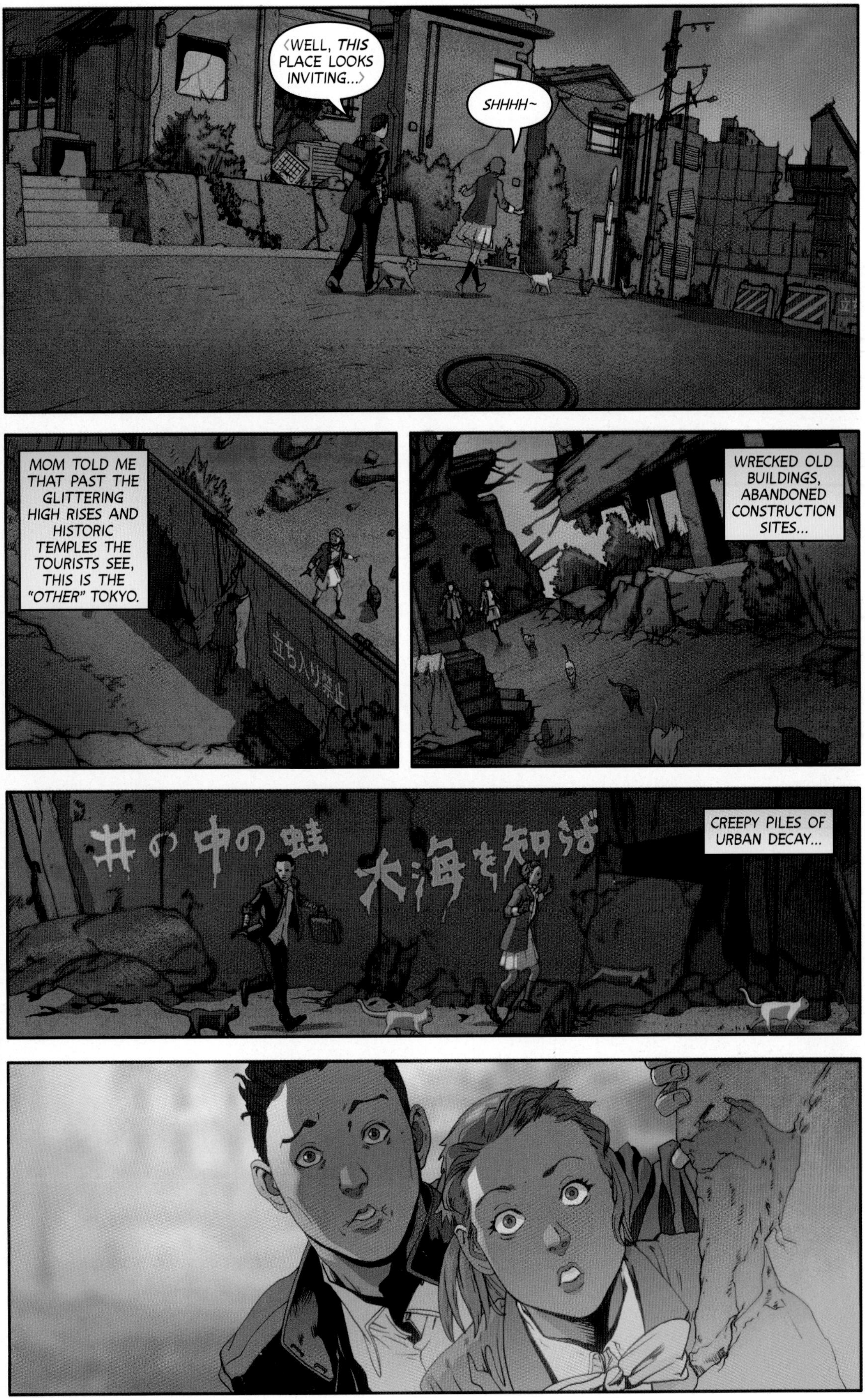
‹WELL, *THIS* PLACE LOOKS INVITING...›
*SHHHH~*
MOM TOLD ME THAT PAST THE GLITTERING HIGH RISES AND HISTORIC TEMPLES THE TOURISTS SEE, THIS IS THE *"OTHER"* TOKYO.
立ち入り禁止
WRECKED OLD BUILDINGS, ABANDONED CONSTRUCTION SITES...
井の中の蛙 大海を知らず
CREEPY PILES OF URBAN DECAY...

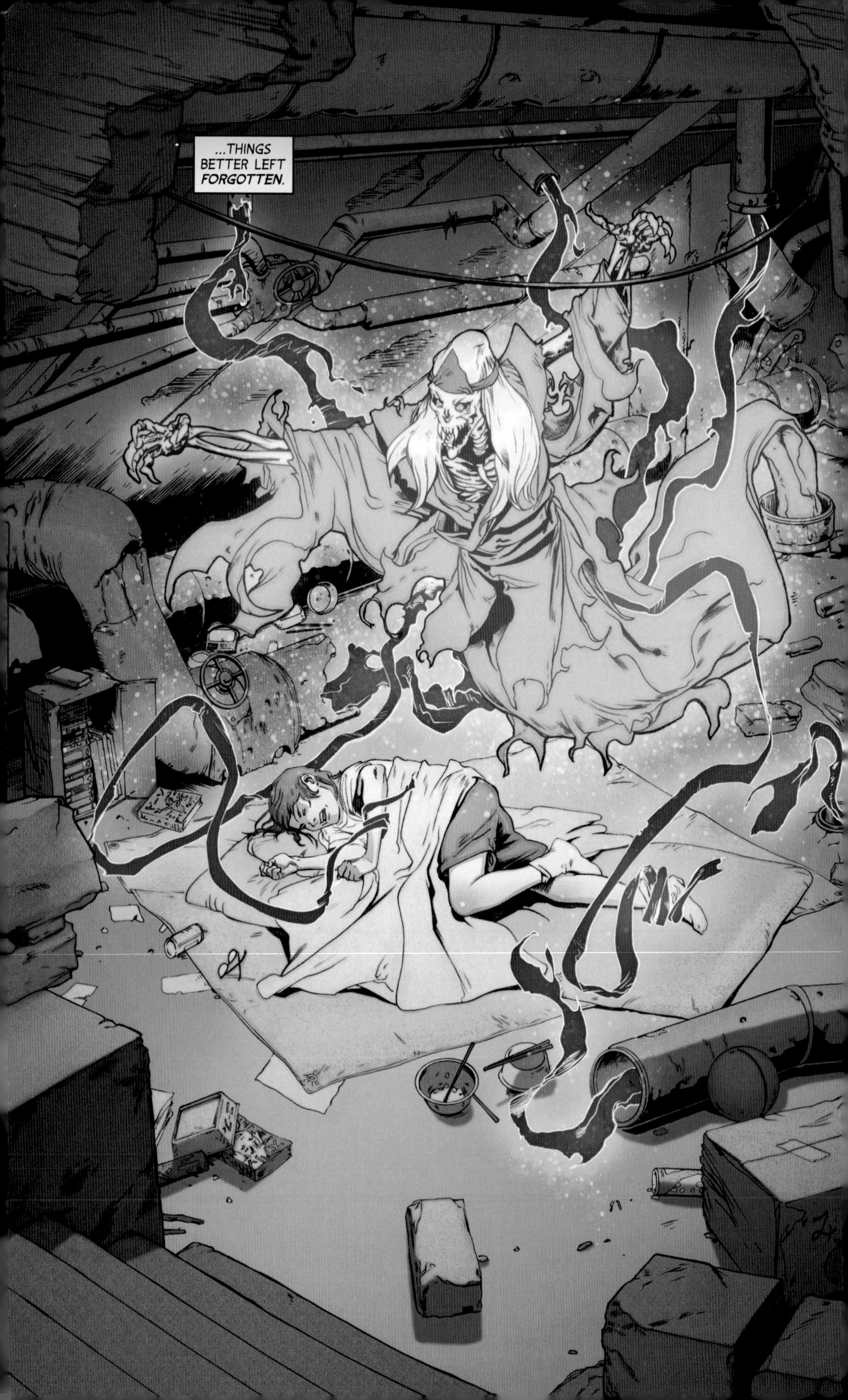
...THINGS
BETTER LEFT
FORGOTTEN.

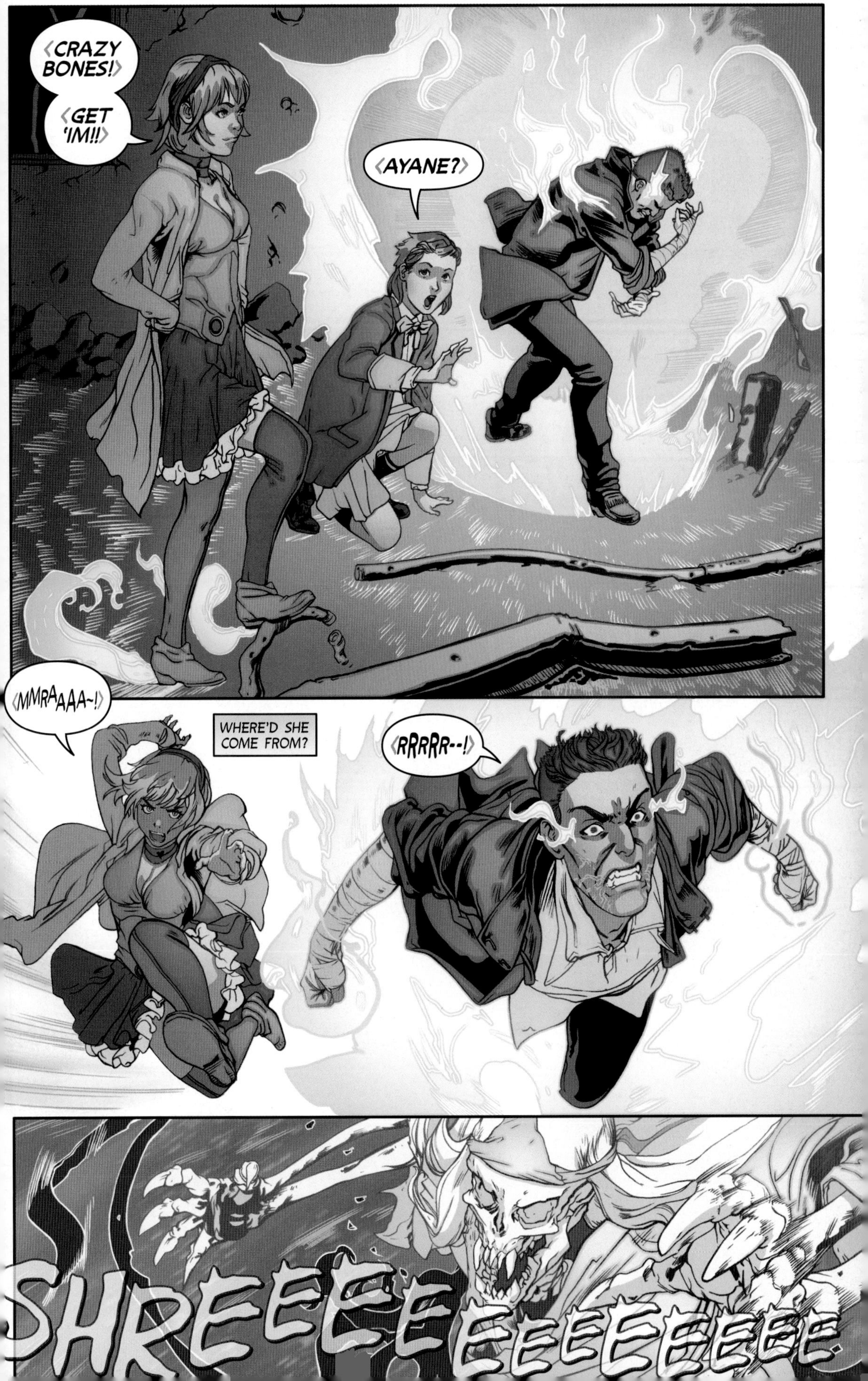
<CRAZY BONES!>
<GET 'IM!!>
<AYANE?>
<MMRAAAA~!>
WHERE'D SHE COME FROM?
<RRRRR--!>
SHREEEEEEEEEEEEEE

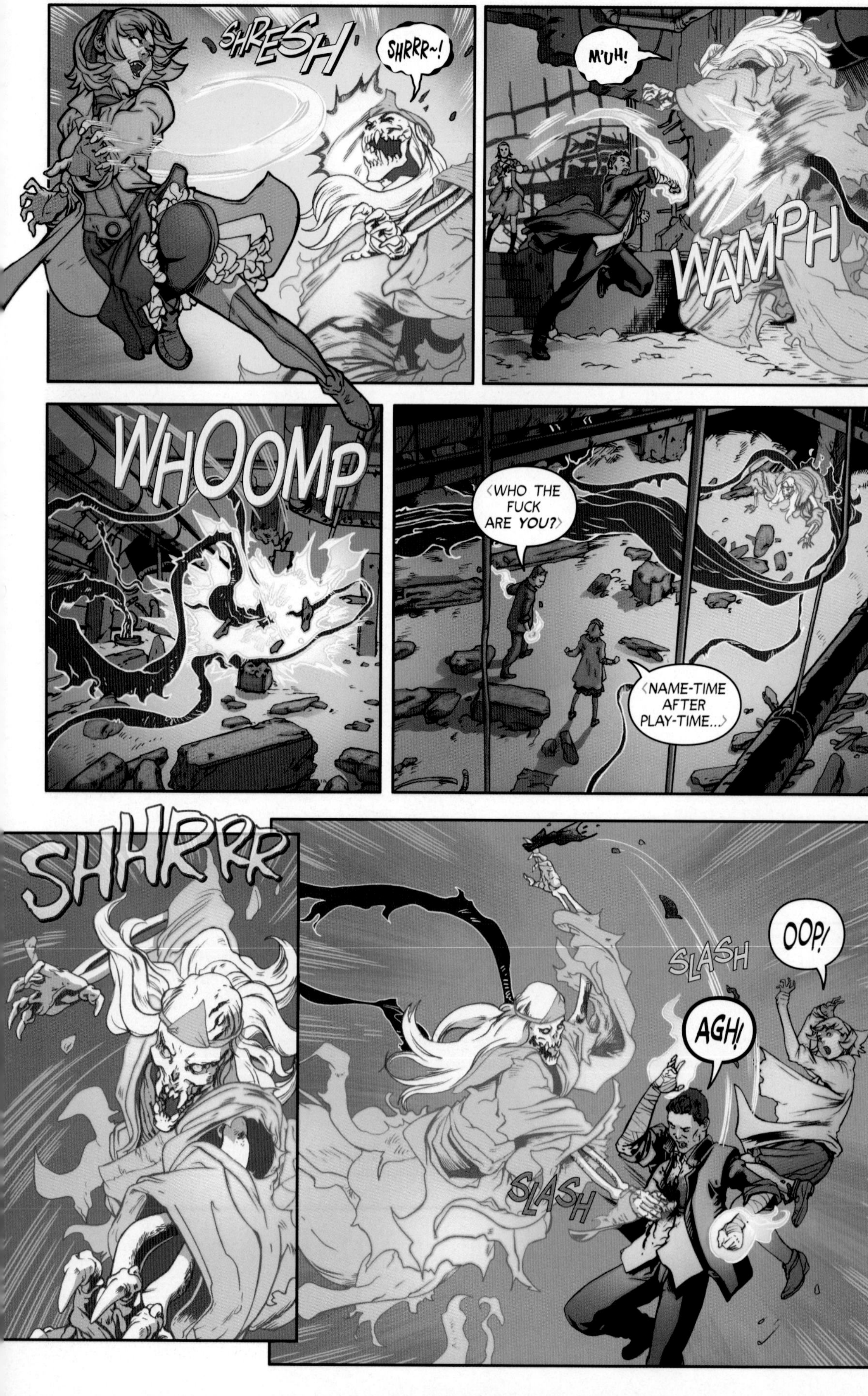
SHRESH
SHRRR~!
M'UH!
WAMPH
WHOOMP
<WHO THE FUCK ARE YOU?>
<NAME-TIME AFTER PLAY-TIME...>
SHHRRR
SLASH
OOP!
AGH!
SLASH

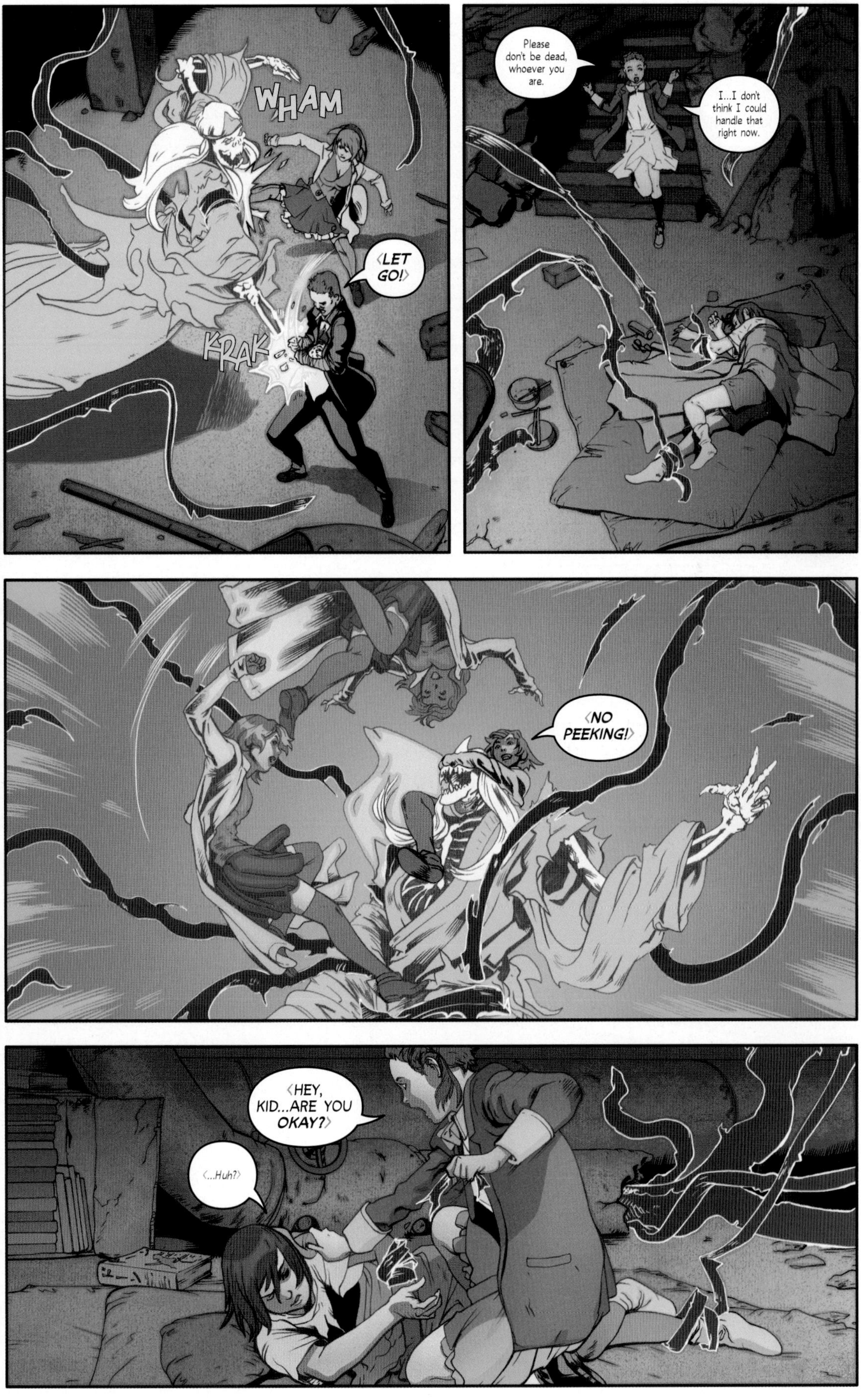
WHAM
⟨LET GO!⟩
KRAK
Please don't be dead, whoever you are.
I...I don't think I could handle that right now.
⟨NO PEEKING!⟩
⟨HEY, KID...ARE YOU OKAY?⟩
⟨...Huh?⟩

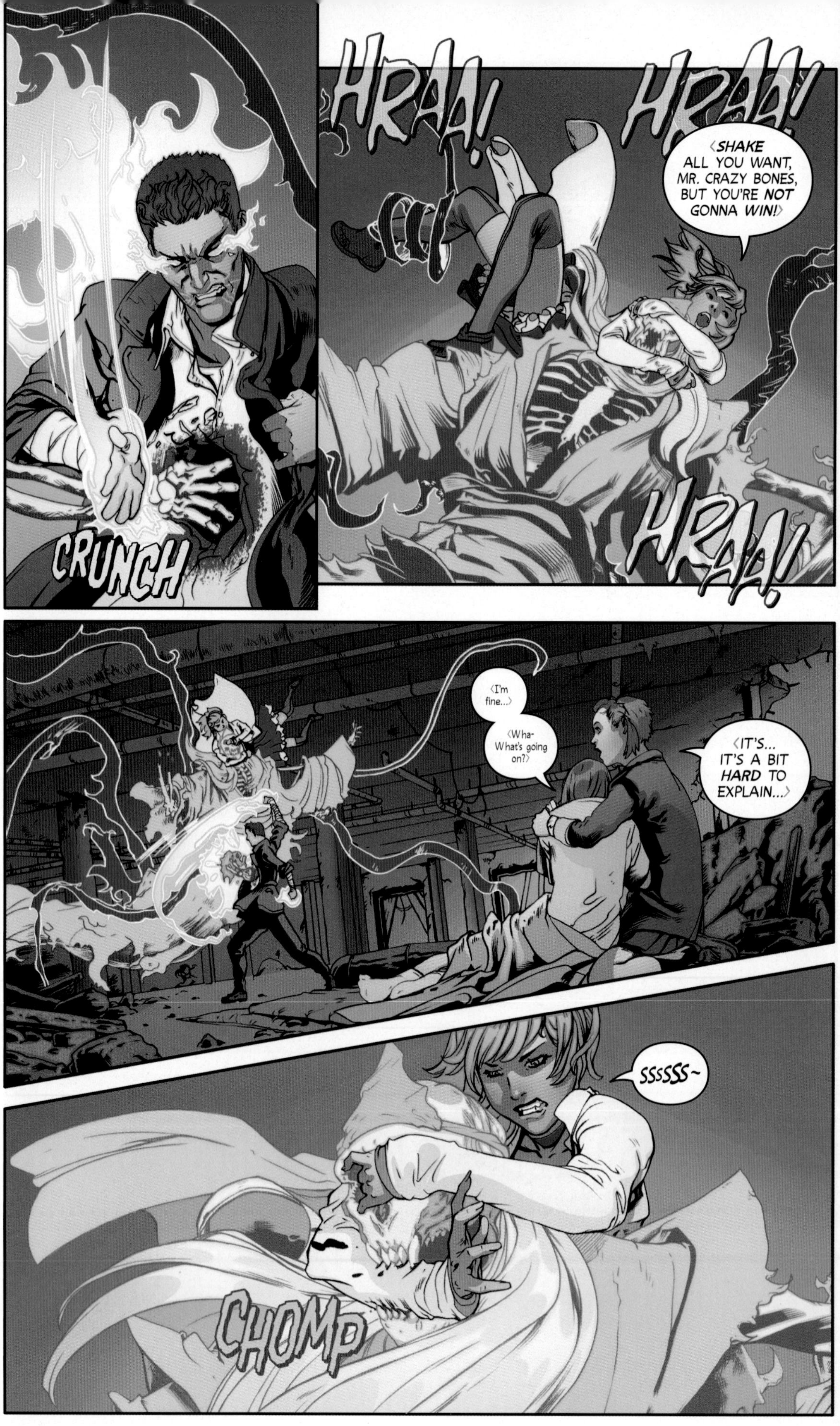
CRUNCH
HRAA!
HRAA!
⟨SHAKE ALL YOU WANT, MR. CRAZY BONES, BUT YOU'RE NOT GONNA WIN!⟩
HRAA!
⟨I'm fine...⟩
⟨Wha- What's going on?⟩
⟨IT'S... IT'S A BIT HARD TO EXPLAIN...⟩
SSSSSS~
CHOMP

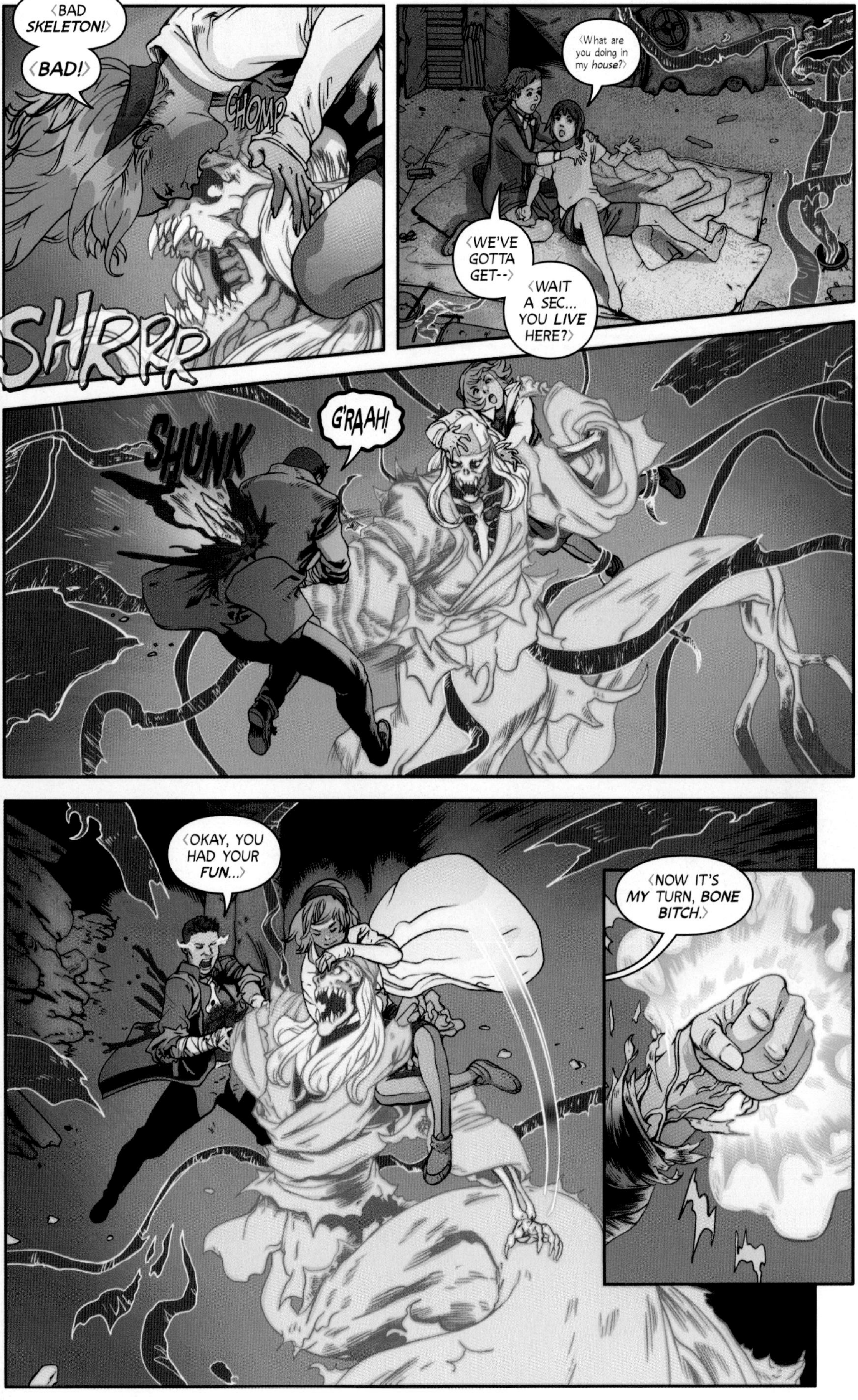

〈BAD SKELETON!〉
〈BAD!〉
CHOMP
SHRRR
〈What are you doing in my house?〉
〈WE'VE GOTTA GET--〉
〈WAIT A SEC... YOU LIVE HERE?〉
SHUNK
G'RAAH!
〈OKAY, YOU HAD YOUR FUN...〉
〈NOW IT'S MY TURN, BONE BITCH.〉

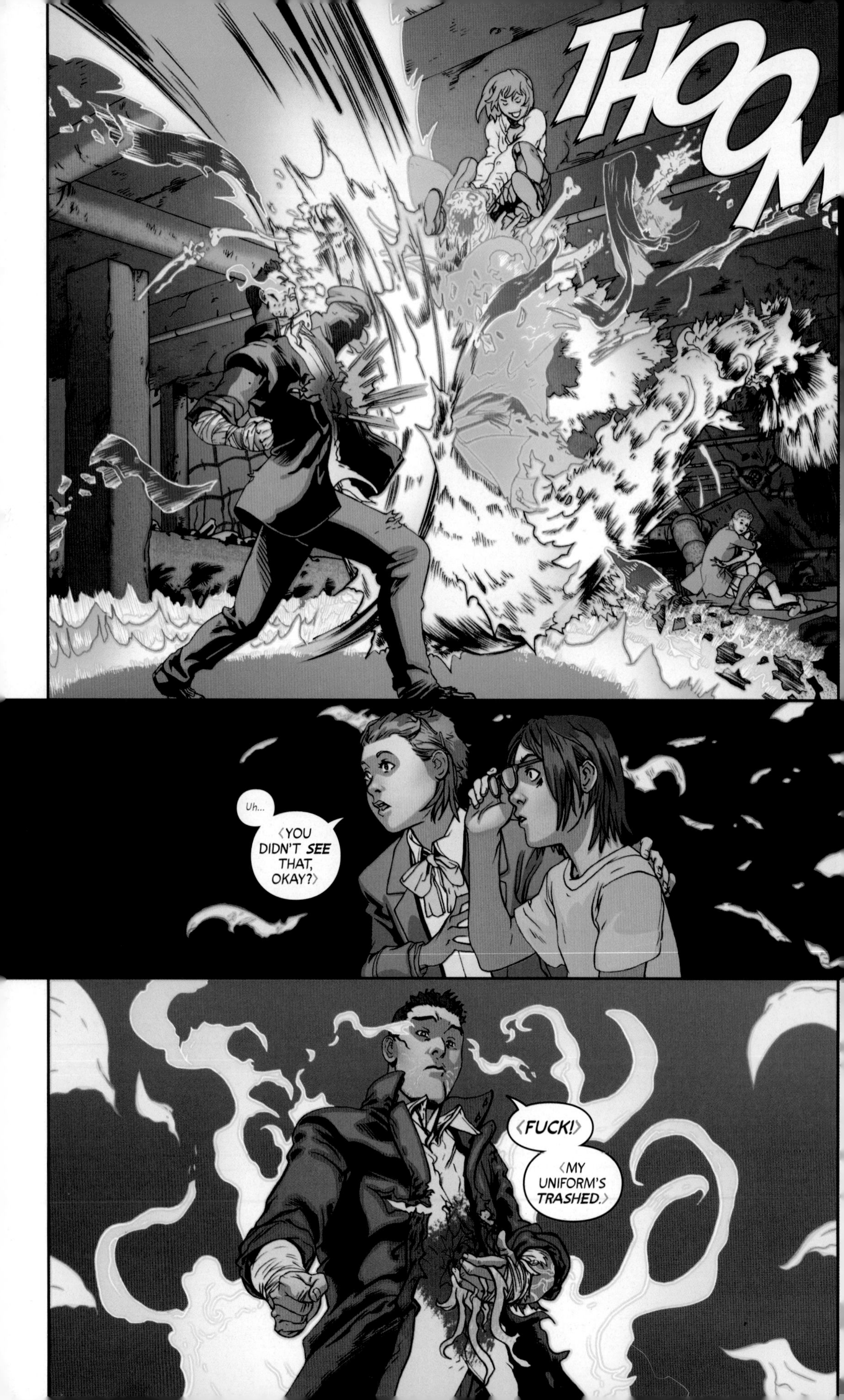
THOOM
Uh...
⟨YOU DIDN'T SEE THAT, OKAY?⟩
⟨FUCK!⟩
⟨MY UNIFORM'S TRASHED.⟩

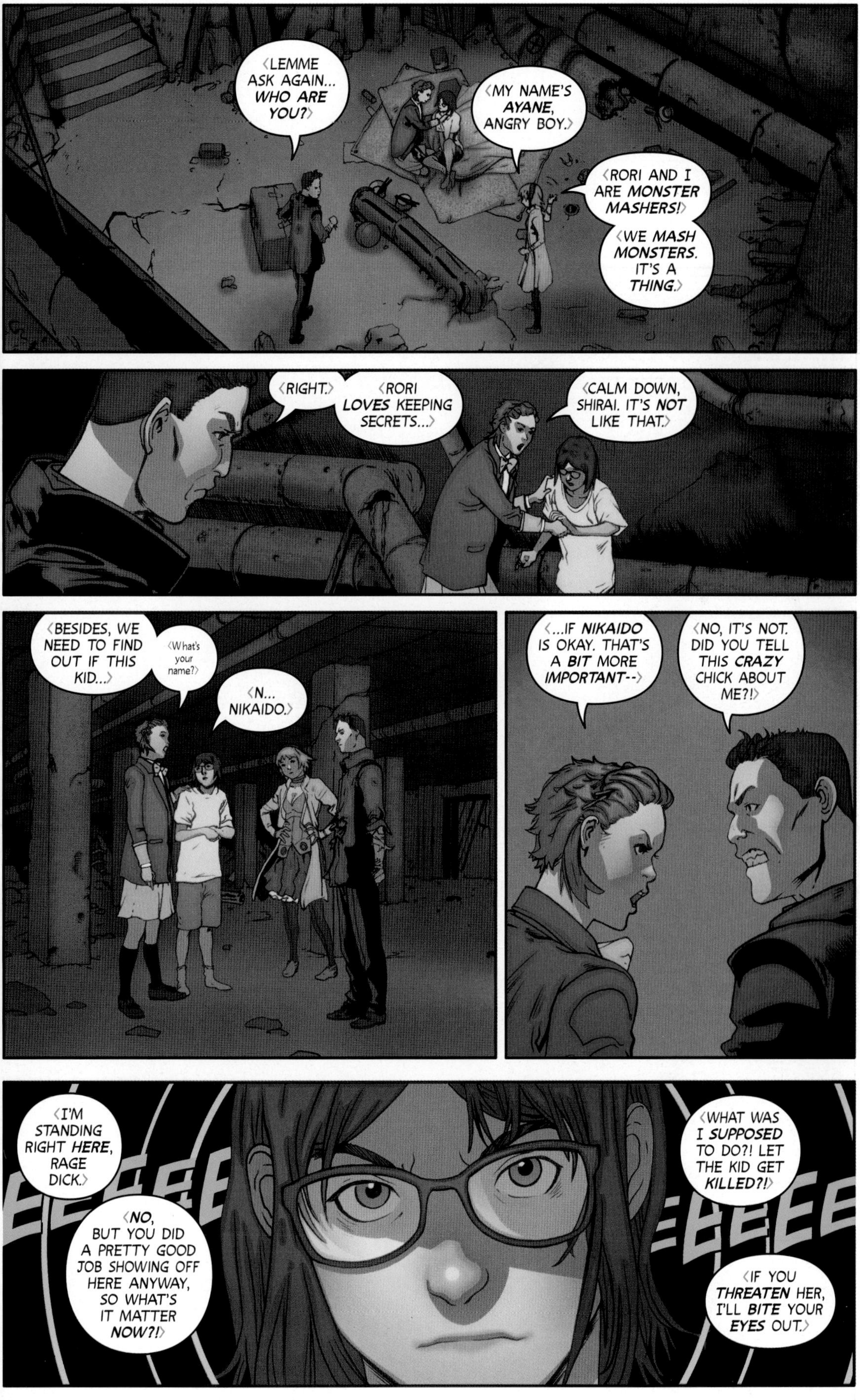
⟨LEMME ASK AGAIN... WHO ARE YOU?⟩
⟨MY NAME'S AYANE, ANGRY BOY.⟩
⟨RORI AND I ARE MONSTER MASHERS!⟩
⟨WE MASH MONSTERS. IT'S A THING.⟩
⟨RIGHT.⟩
⟨RORI LOVES KEEPING SECRETS...⟩
⟨CALM DOWN, SHIRAI. IT'S NOT LIKE THAT.⟩
⟨BESIDES, WE NEED TO FIND OUT IF THIS KID...⟩
⟨What's your name?⟩
⟨N... NIKAIDO.⟩
⟨...IF NIKAIDO IS OKAY. THAT'S A BIT MORE IMPORTANT--⟩
⟨NO, IT'S NOT. DID YOU TELL THIS CRAZY CHICK ABOUT ME?!⟩
⟨I'M STANDING RIGHT HERE, RAGE DICK.⟩
⟨WHAT WAS I SUPPOSED TO DO?! LET THE KID GET KILLED?!⟩
⟨NO, BUT YOU DID A PRETTY GOOD JOB SHOWING OFF HERE ANYWAY, SO WHAT'S IT MATTER NOW?!⟩
⟨IF YOU THREATEN HER, I'LL BITE YOUR EYES OUT.⟩

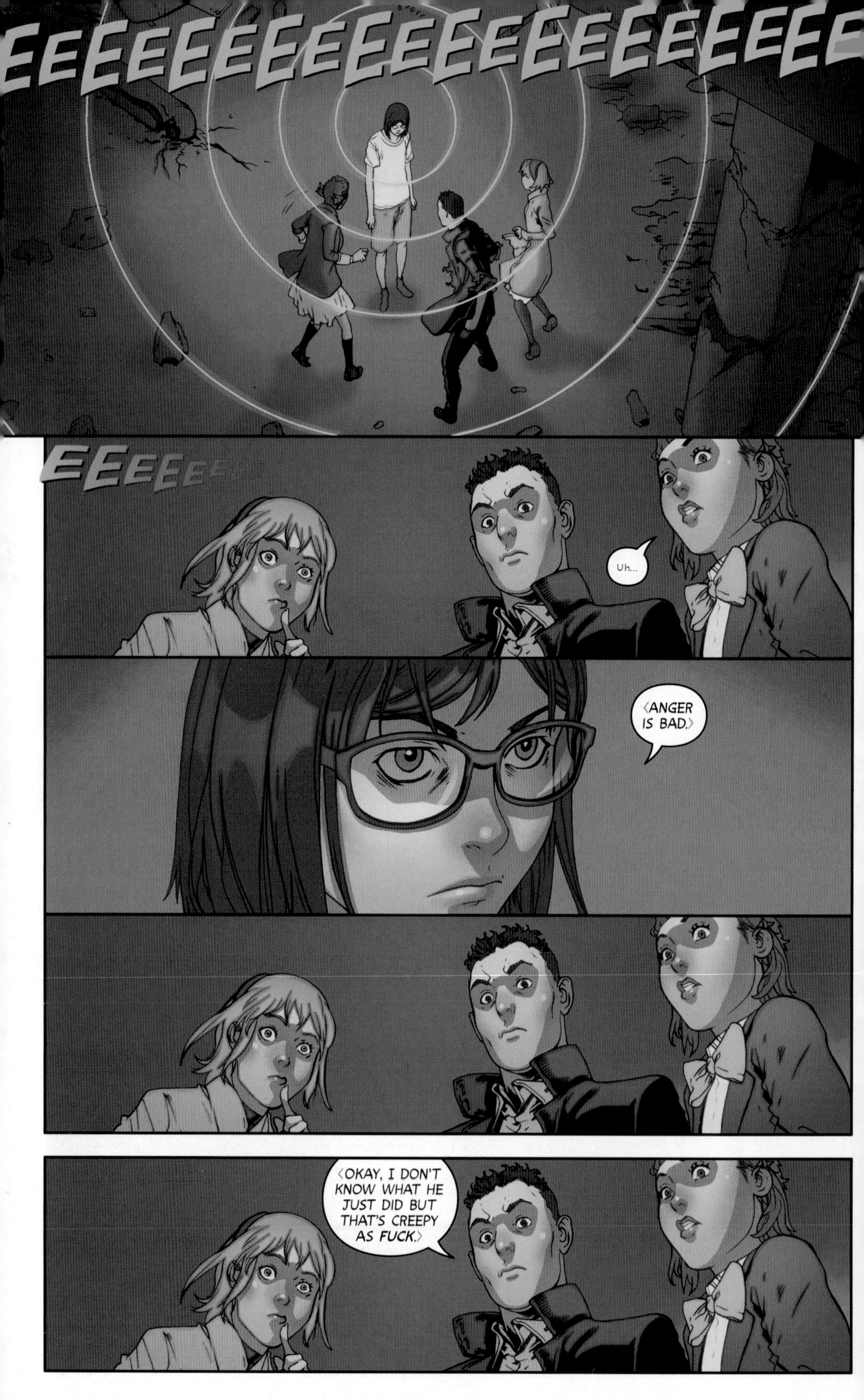
EEEEEEEEEEEEEEEEEEEE
EEEEEEE
Uh...
⟨ANGER IS BAD.⟩
⟨OKAY, I DON'T KNOW WHAT HE JUST DID BUT THAT'S CREEPY AS *FUCK*.⟩

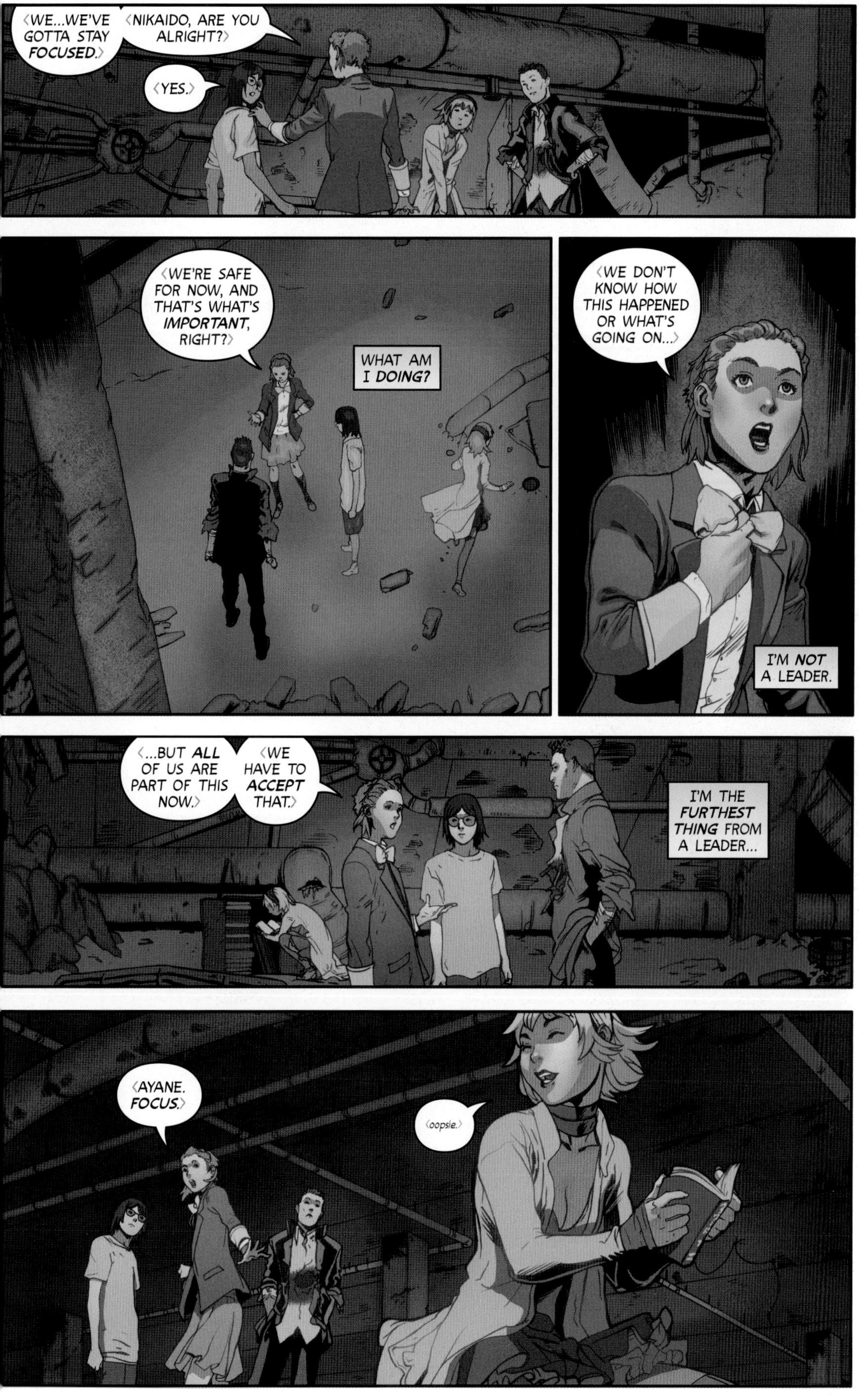

⟨WE...WE'VE GOTTA STAY FOCUSED.⟩
⟨NIKAIDO, ARE YOU ALRIGHT?⟩
⟨YES.⟩
⟨WE'RE SAFE FOR NOW, AND THAT'S WHAT'S IMPORTANT, RIGHT?⟩
WHAT AM I DOING?
⟨WE DON'T KNOW HOW THIS HAPPENED OR WHAT'S GOING ON...⟩
I'M NOT A LEADER.
⟨...BUT ALL OF US ARE PART OF THIS NOW.⟩
⟨WE HAVE TO ACCEPT THAT.⟩
I'M THE FURTHEST THING FROM A LEADER...
⟨AYANE. FOCUS.⟩
⟨oopsie.⟩

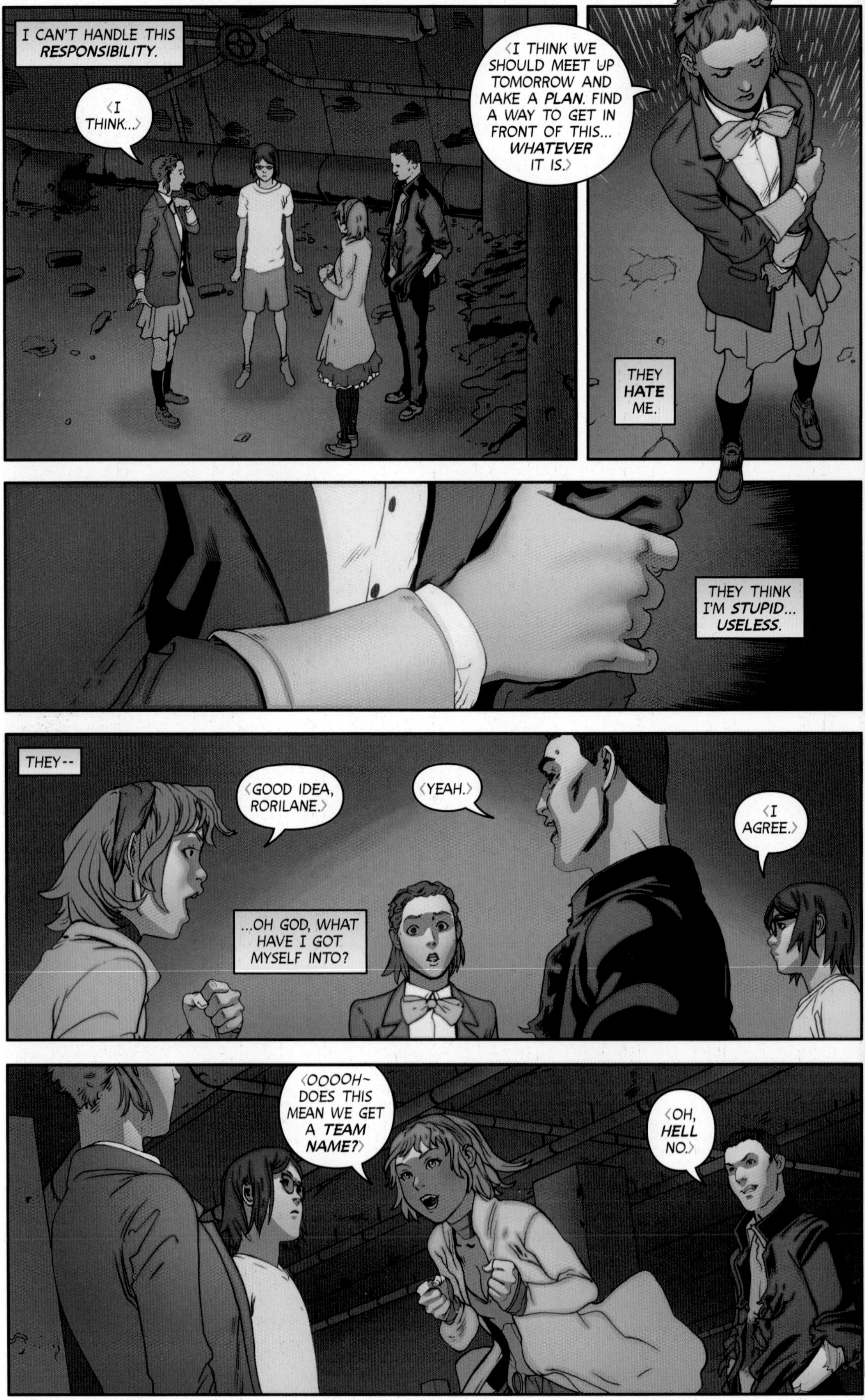
I CAN'T HANDLE THIS RESPONSIBILITY.
‹I THINK...›
‹I THINK WE SHOULD MEET UP TOMORROW AND MAKE A PLAN. FIND A WAY TO GET IN FRONT OF THIS... WHATEVER IT IS.›
THEY HATE ME.
THEY THINK I'M STUPID... USELESS.
THEY--
‹GOOD IDEA, RORILANE.›
‹YEAH.›
‹I AGREE.›
...OH GOD, WHAT HAVE I GOT MYSELF INTO?
‹OOOOH~ DOES THIS MEAN WE GET A TEAM NAME?›
‹OH, HELL NO.›

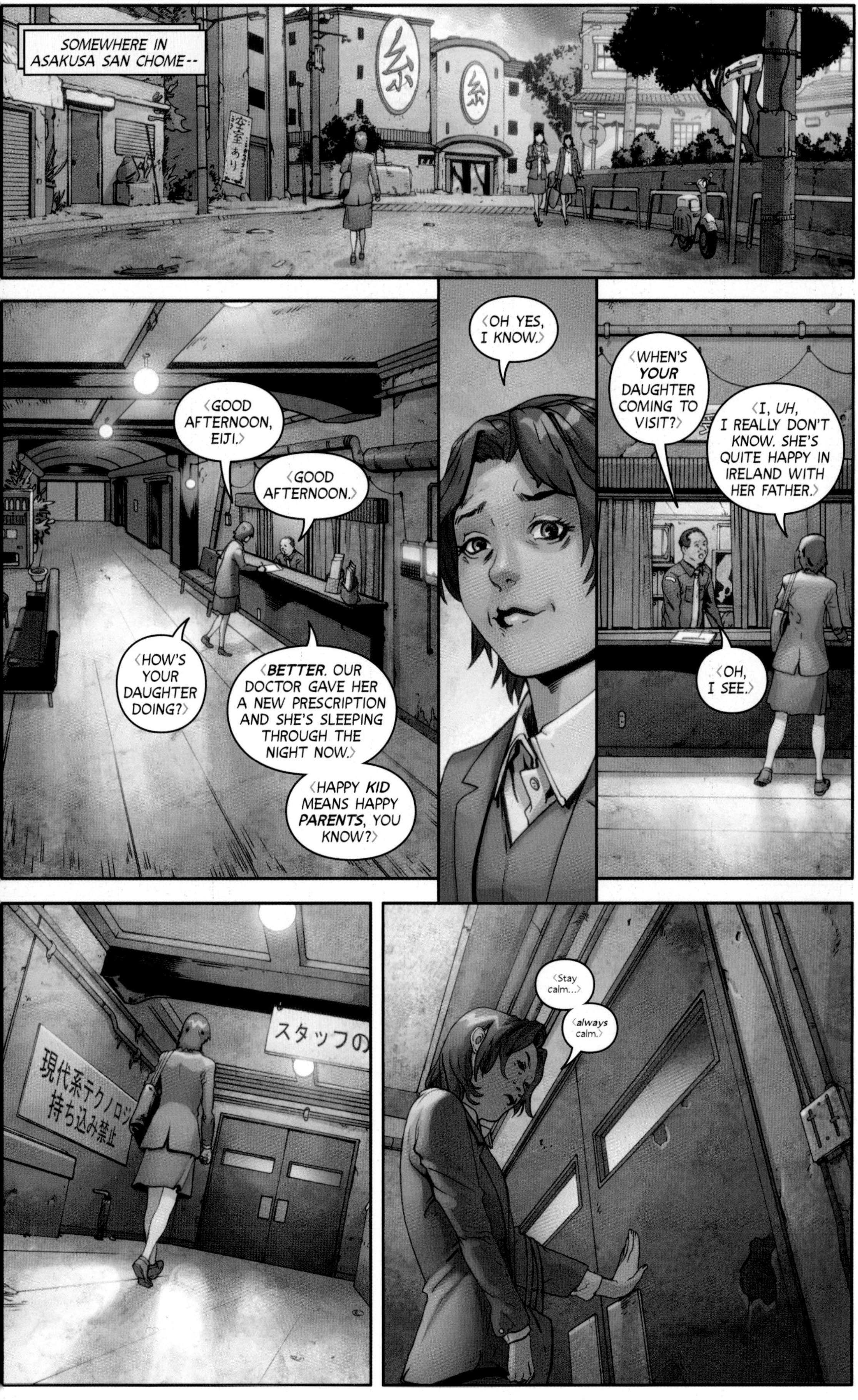
SOMEWHERE IN ASAKUSA SAN CHOME--
空室あり
⟨GOOD AFTERNOON, EIJI.⟩
⟨GOOD AFTERNOON.⟩
⟨HOW'S YOUR DAUGHTER DOING?⟩
⟨**BETTER**. OUR DOCTOR GAVE HER A NEW PRESCRIPTION AND SHE'S SLEEPING THROUGH THE NIGHT NOW.⟩
⟨HAPPY ***KID*** MEANS HAPPY ***PARENTS***, YOU KNOW?⟩
⟨OH YES, I KNOW.⟩
⟨WHEN'S ***YOUR*** DAUGHTER COMING TO VISIT?⟩
⟨I, *UH*, I REALLY DON'T KNOW. SHE'S QUITE HAPPY IN IRELAND WITH HER FATHER.⟩
⟨OH, I SEE.⟩
現代系テクノロジ
持ち込み禁止
スタッフの
⟨Stay calm...⟩
⟨*always* calm.⟩

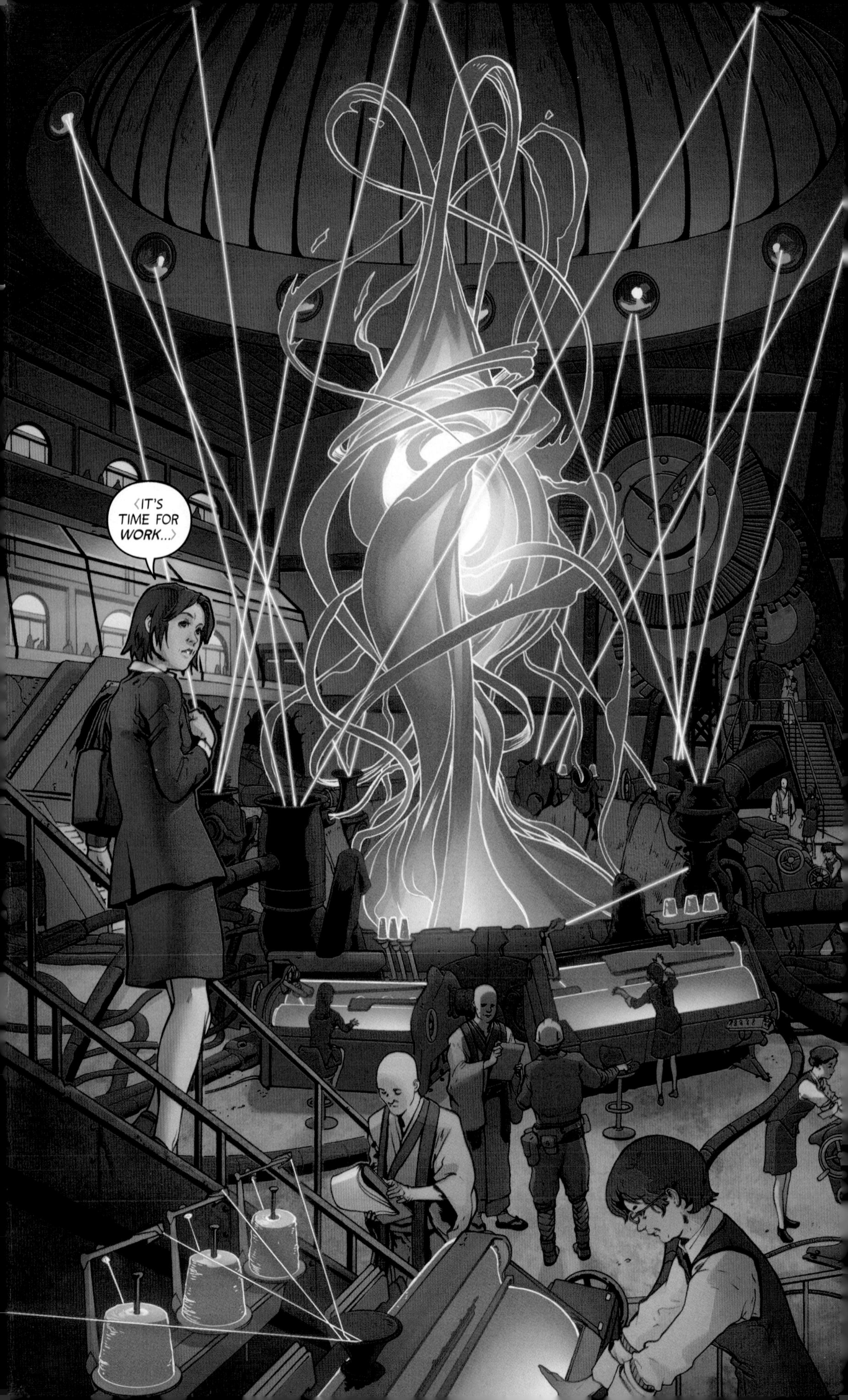
‹IT'S TIME FOR WORK...›

# Chapter Four

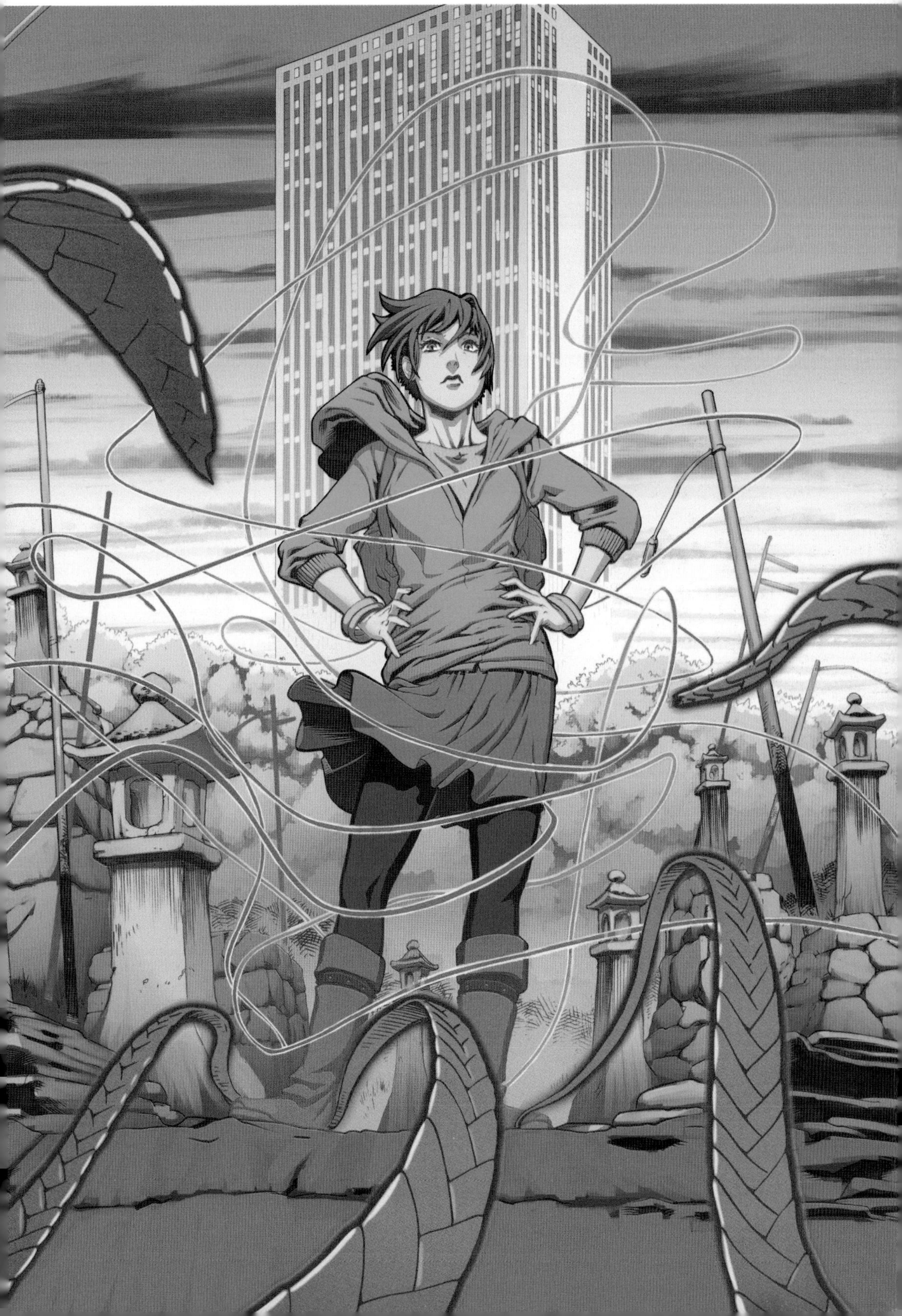

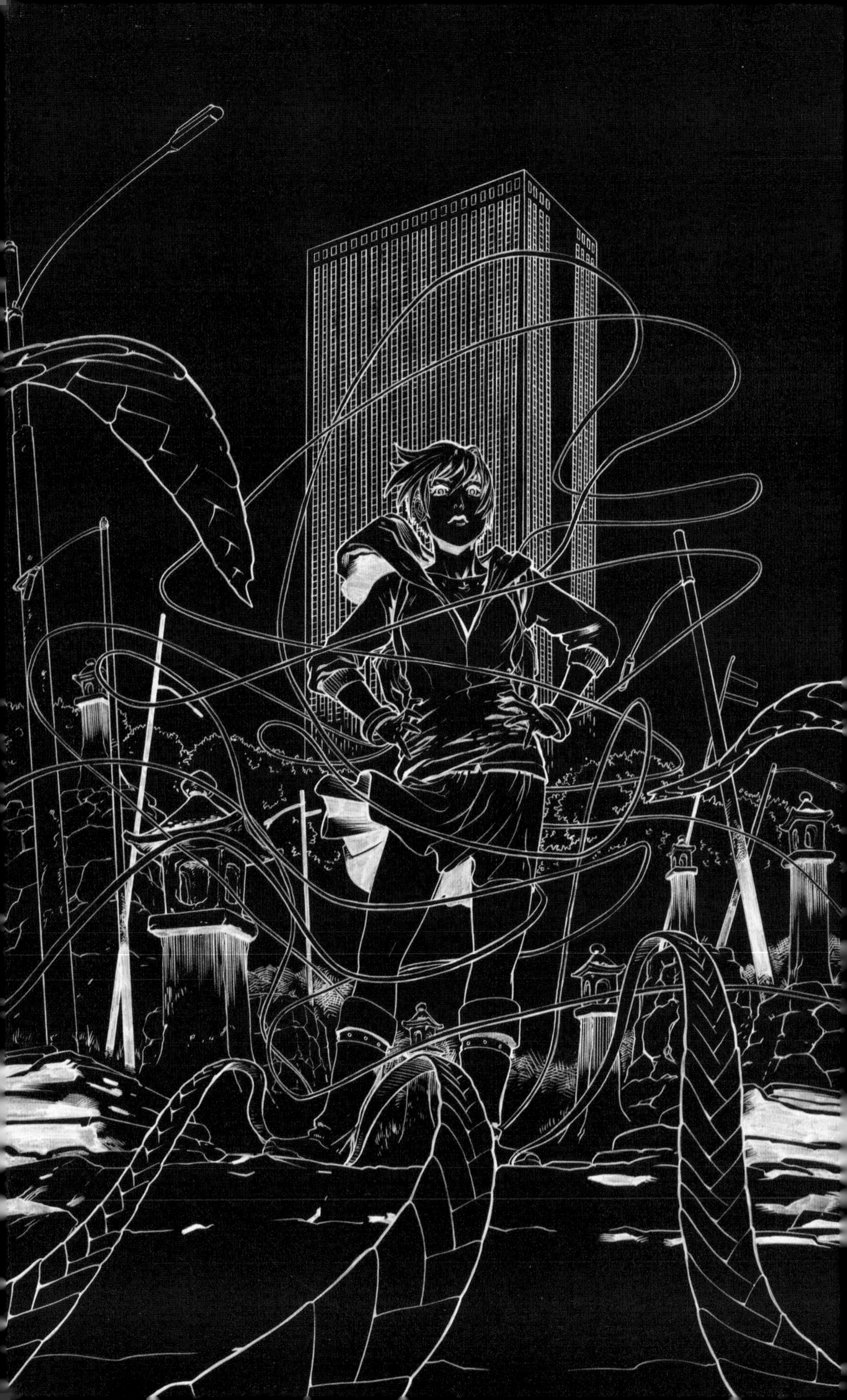

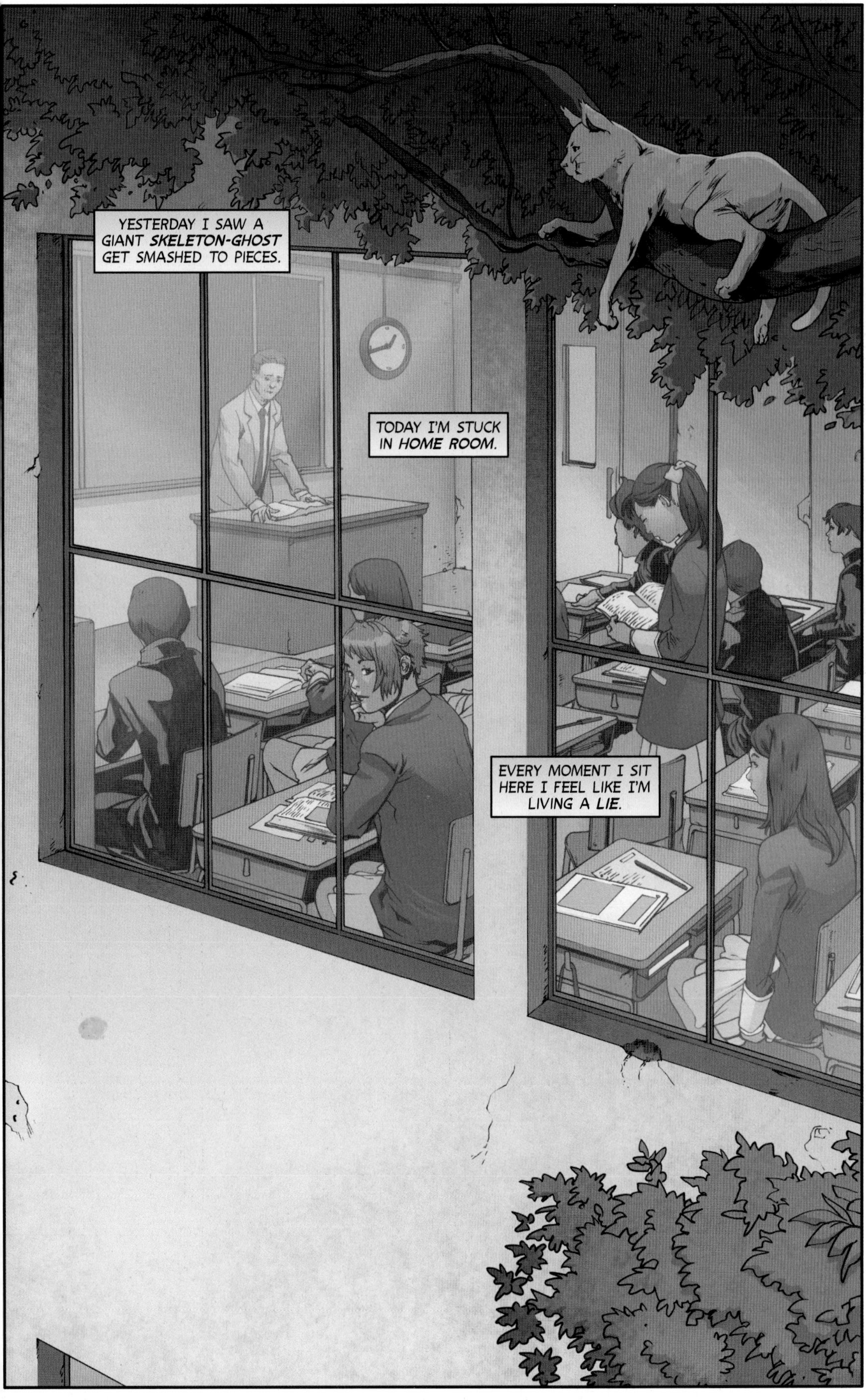
YESTERDAY I SAW A GIANT SKELETON-GHOST GET SMASHED TO PIECES.
TODAY I'M STUCK IN HOME ROOM.
EVERY MOMENT I SIT HERE I FEEL LIKE I'M LIVING A LIE.

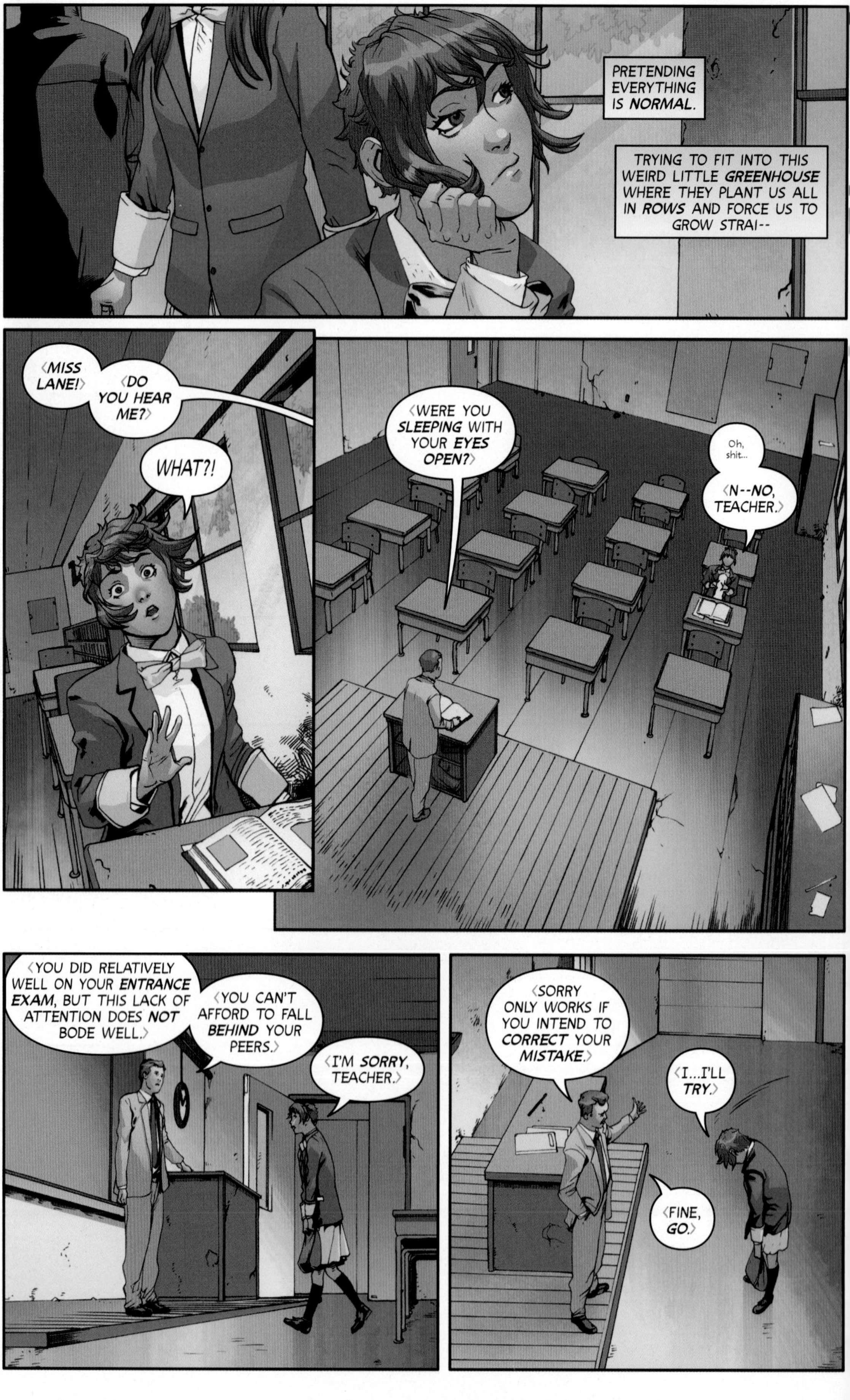
PRETENDING EVERYTHING IS NORMAL.
TRYING TO FIT INTO THIS WEIRD LITTLE GREENHOUSE WHERE THEY PLANT US ALL IN ROWS AND FORCE US TO GROW STRAI--
⟨MISS LANE!⟩
⟨DO YOU HEAR ME?⟩
WHAT?!
⟨WERE YOU SLEEPING WITH YOUR EYES OPEN?⟩
Oh, shit...
⟨N--NO, TEACHER.⟩
⟨YOU DID RELATIVELY WELL ON YOUR ENTRANCE EXAM, BUT THIS LACK OF ATTENTION DOES NOT BODE WELL.⟩
⟨YOU CAN'T AFFORD TO FALL BEHIND YOUR PEERS.⟩
⟨I'M SORRY, TEACHER.⟩
⟨SORRY ONLY WORKS IF YOU INTEND TO CORRECT YOUR MISTAKE.⟩
⟨I...I'LL TRY.⟩
⟨FINE, GO.⟩

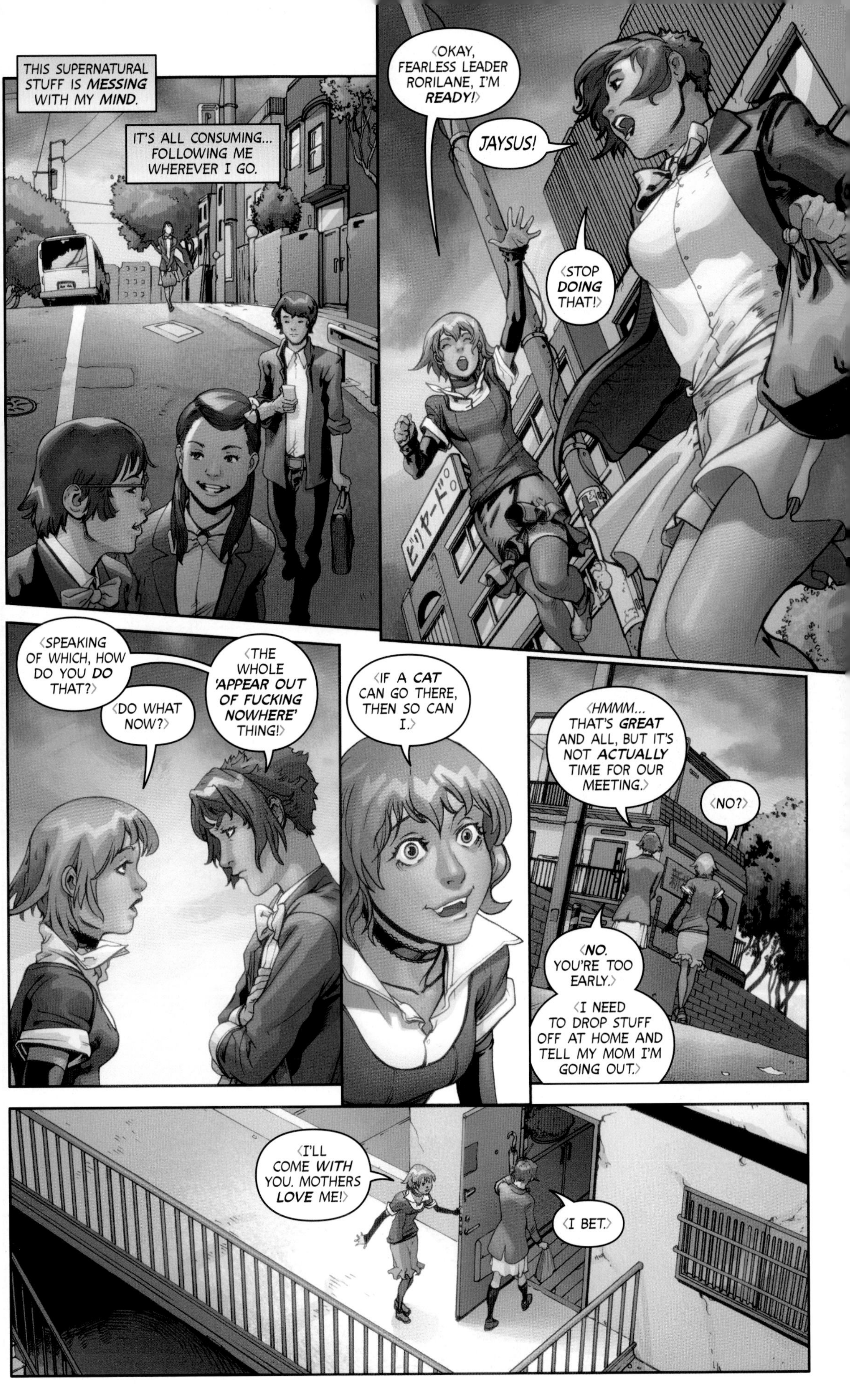
THIS SUPERNATURAL STUFF IS MESSING WITH MY MIND.
IT'S ALL CONSUMING... FOLLOWING ME WHEREVER I GO.
‹OKAY, FEARLESS LEADER RORILANE, I'M READY!›
JAYSUS!
‹STOP DOING THAT!›
ビリヤード
‹SPEAKING OF WHICH, HOW DO YOU DO THAT?›
‹DO WHAT NOW?›
‹THE WHOLE 'APPEAR OUT OF FUCKING NOWHERE' THING!›
‹IF A CAT CAN GO THERE, THEN SO CAN I.›
‹HMMM... THAT'S GREAT AND ALL, BUT IT'S NOT ACTUALLY TIME FOR OUR MEETING.›
‹NO?›
‹NO. YOU'RE TOO EARLY.›
‹I NEED TO DROP STUFF OFF AT HOME AND TELL MY MOM I'M GOING OUT.›
‹I'LL COME WITH YOU. MOTHERS LOVE ME!›
‹I BET.›

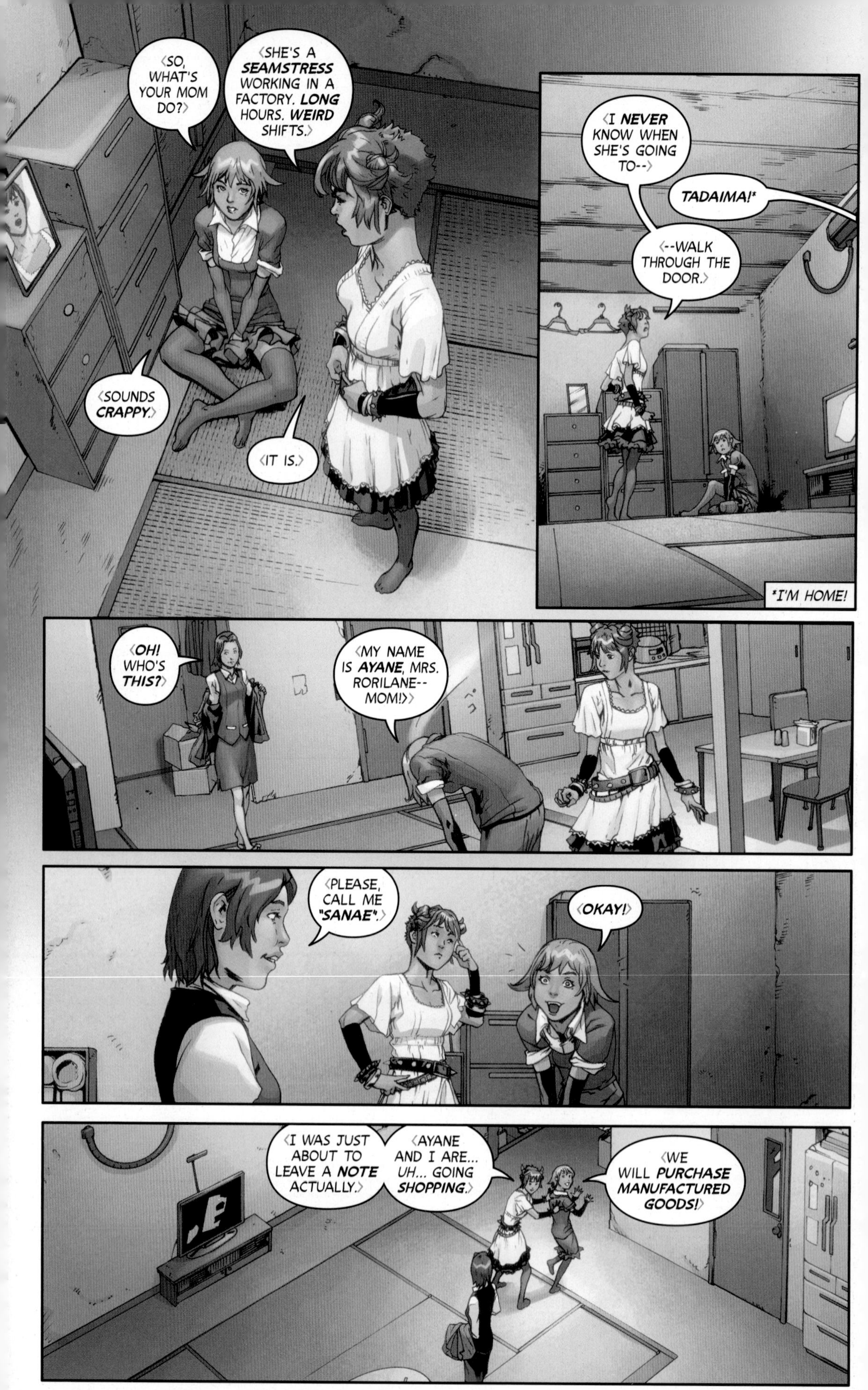

‹SO, WHAT'S YOUR MOM DO?›
‹SHE'S A SEAMSTRESS WORKING IN A FACTORY. LONG HOURS. WEIRD SHIFTS.›
‹SOUNDS CRAPPY.›
‹IT IS.›
‹I NEVER KNOW WHEN SHE'S GOING TO--›
TADAIMA!*
‹--WALK THROUGH THE DOOR.›
*I'M HOME!
‹OH! WHO'S THIS?›
‹MY NAME IS AYANE, MRS. RORILANE-- MOM!›
‹PLEASE, CALL ME "SANAE".›
‹OKAY!›
‹I WAS JUST ABOUT TO LEAVE A NOTE ACTUALLY.›
‹AYANE AND I ARE... UH... GOING SHOPPING.›
‹WE WILL PURCHASE MANUFACTURED GOODS!›

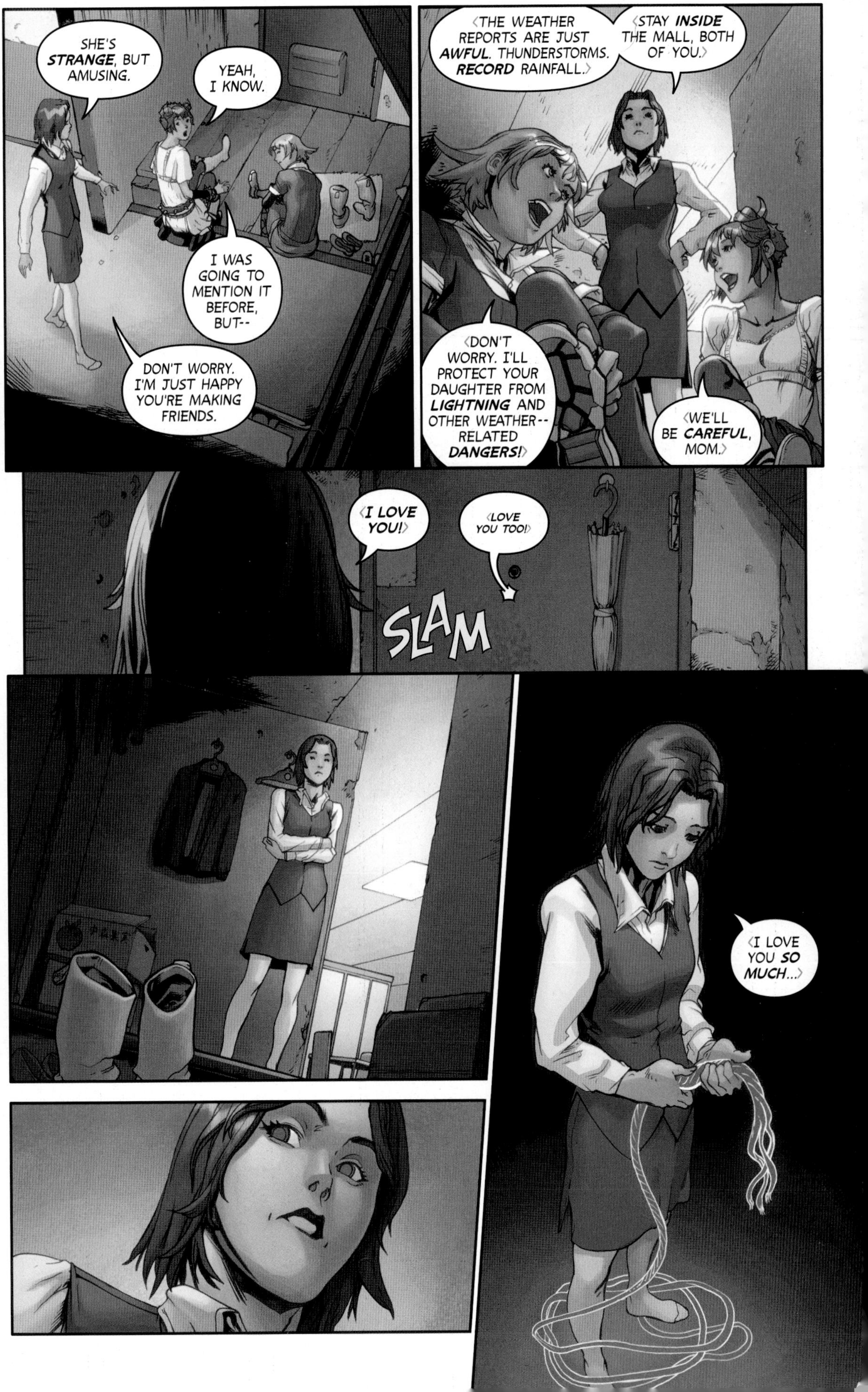
SHE'S STRANGE, BUT AMUSING.
YEAH, I KNOW.
I WAS GOING TO MENTION IT BEFORE, BUT--
DON'T WORRY. I'M JUST HAPPY YOU'RE MAKING FRIENDS.
〈THE WEATHER REPORTS ARE JUST AWFUL. THUNDERSTORMS. RECORD RAINFALL.〉
〈STAY INSIDE THE MALL, BOTH OF YOU.〉
〈DON'T WORRY. I'LL PROTECT YOUR DAUGHTER FROM LIGHTNING AND OTHER WEATHER--RELATED DANGERS!〉
〈WE'LL BE CAREFUL, MOM.〉
〈I LOVE YOU!〉
〈LOVE YOU TOO!〉
SLAM
〈I LOVE YOU SO MUCH...〉

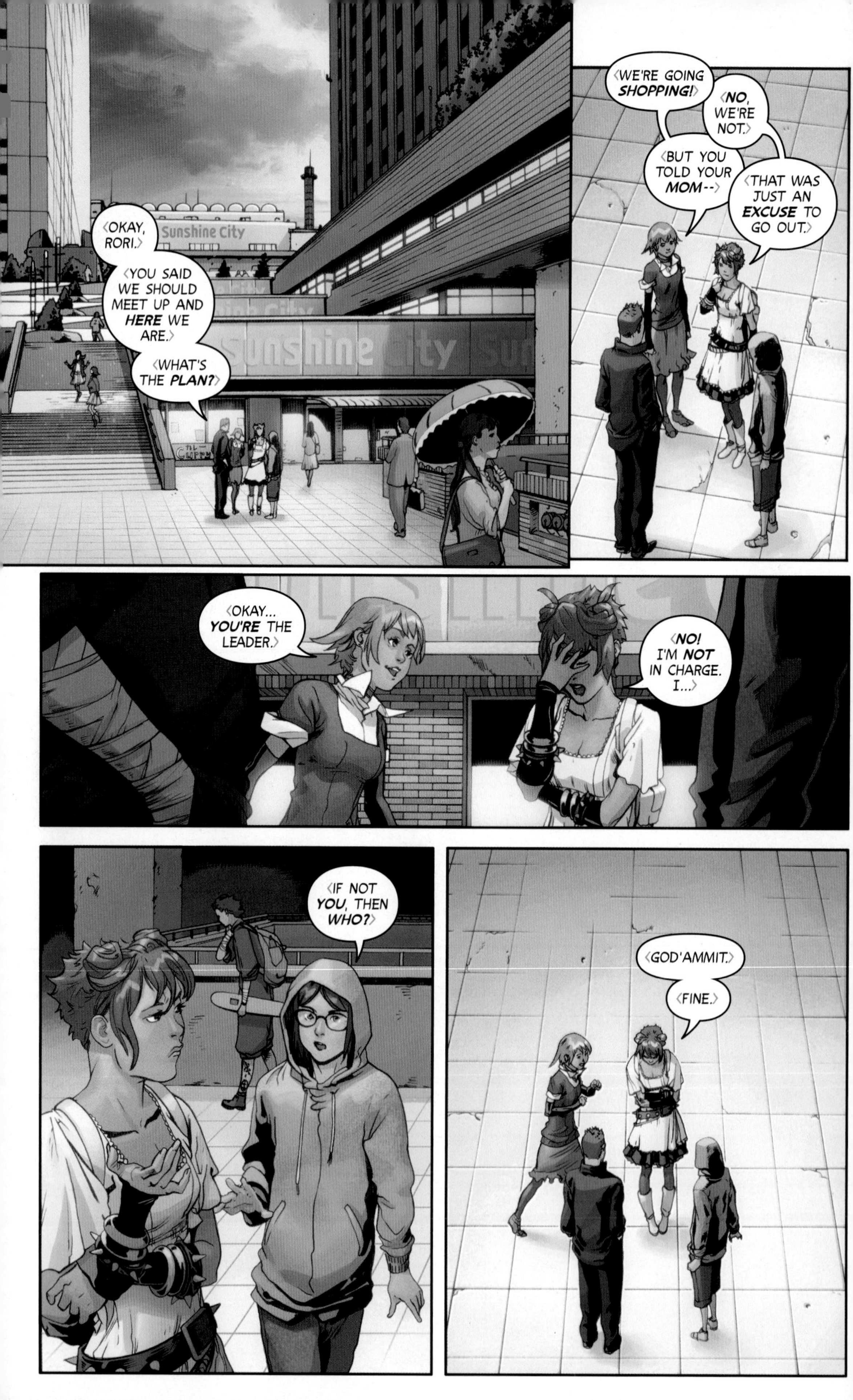

⟨OKAY, RORI.⟩
⟨YOU SAID WE SHOULD MEET UP AND HERE WE ARE.⟩
⟨WHAT'S THE PLAN?⟩
Sunshine City
⟨WE'RE GOING SHOPPING!⟩
⟨NO, WE'RE NOT.⟩
⟨BUT YOU TOLD YOUR MOM--⟩
⟨THAT WAS JUST AN EXCUSE TO GO OUT.⟩
⟨OKAY... YOU'RE THE LEADER.⟩
⟨NO! I'M NOT IN CHARGE. I...⟩
⟨IF NOT YOU, THEN WHO?⟩
⟨GOD'AMMIT.⟩
⟨FINE.⟩

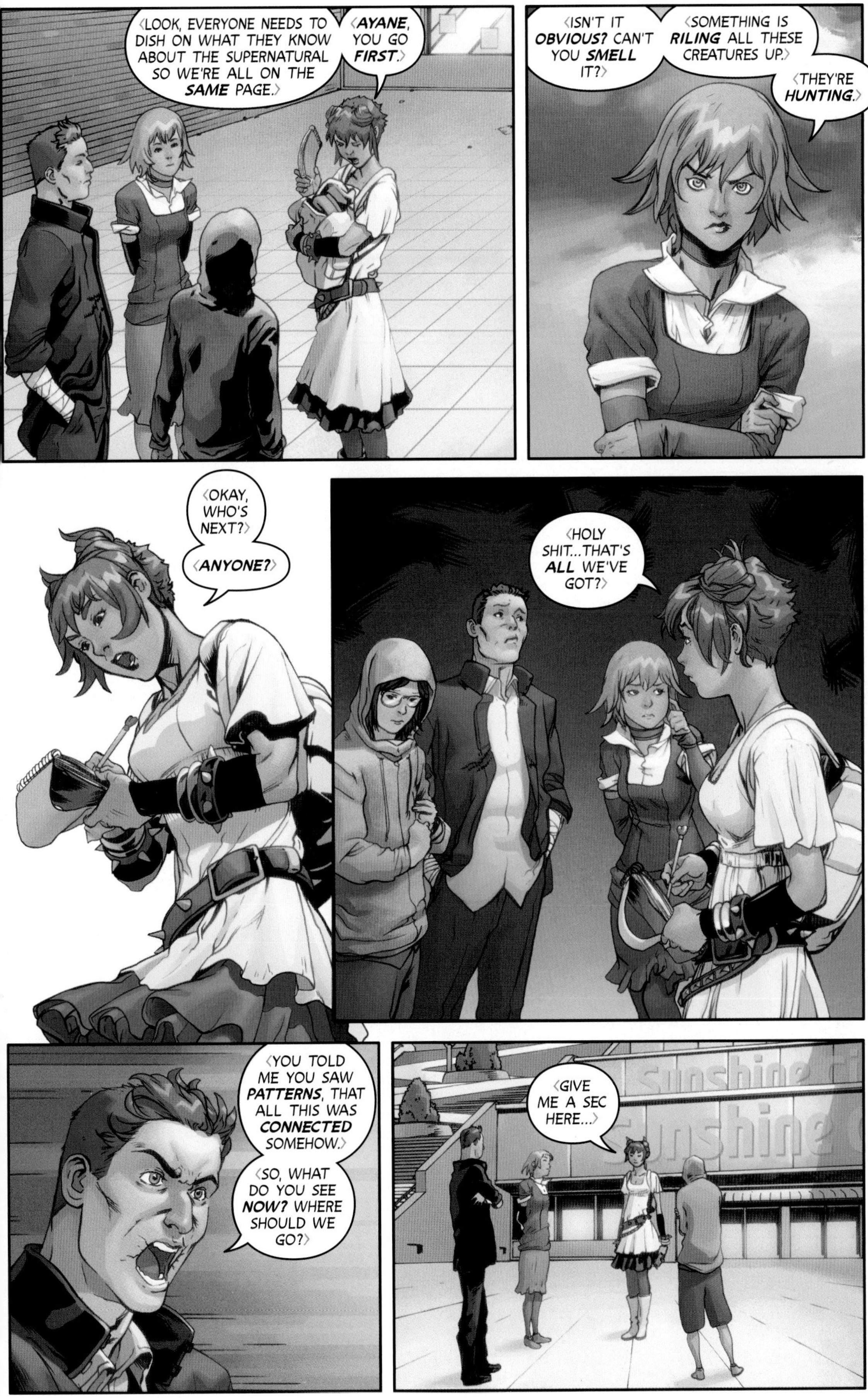
‹LOOK, EVERYONE NEEDS TO DISH ON WHAT THEY KNOW ABOUT THE SUPERNATURAL SO WE'RE ALL ON THE ***SAME*** PAGE.›
‹***AYANE***, YOU GO ***FIRST***.›
‹ISN'T IT ***OBVIOUS?*** CAN'T YOU ***SMELL*** IT?›
‹SOMETHING IS ***RILING*** ALL THESE CREATURES UP.›
‹THEY'RE ***HUNTING***.›
‹OKAY, WHO'S NEXT?›
‹***ANYONE?***›
‹HOLY SHIT...THAT'S ***ALL*** WE'VE GOT?›
‹YOU TOLD ME YOU SAW ***PATTERNS***, THAT ALL THIS WAS ***CONNECTED*** SOMEHOW.›
‹SO, WHAT DO YOU SEE ***NOW?*** WHERE SHOULD WE GO?›
Sunshine
‹GIVE ME A SEC HERE...›

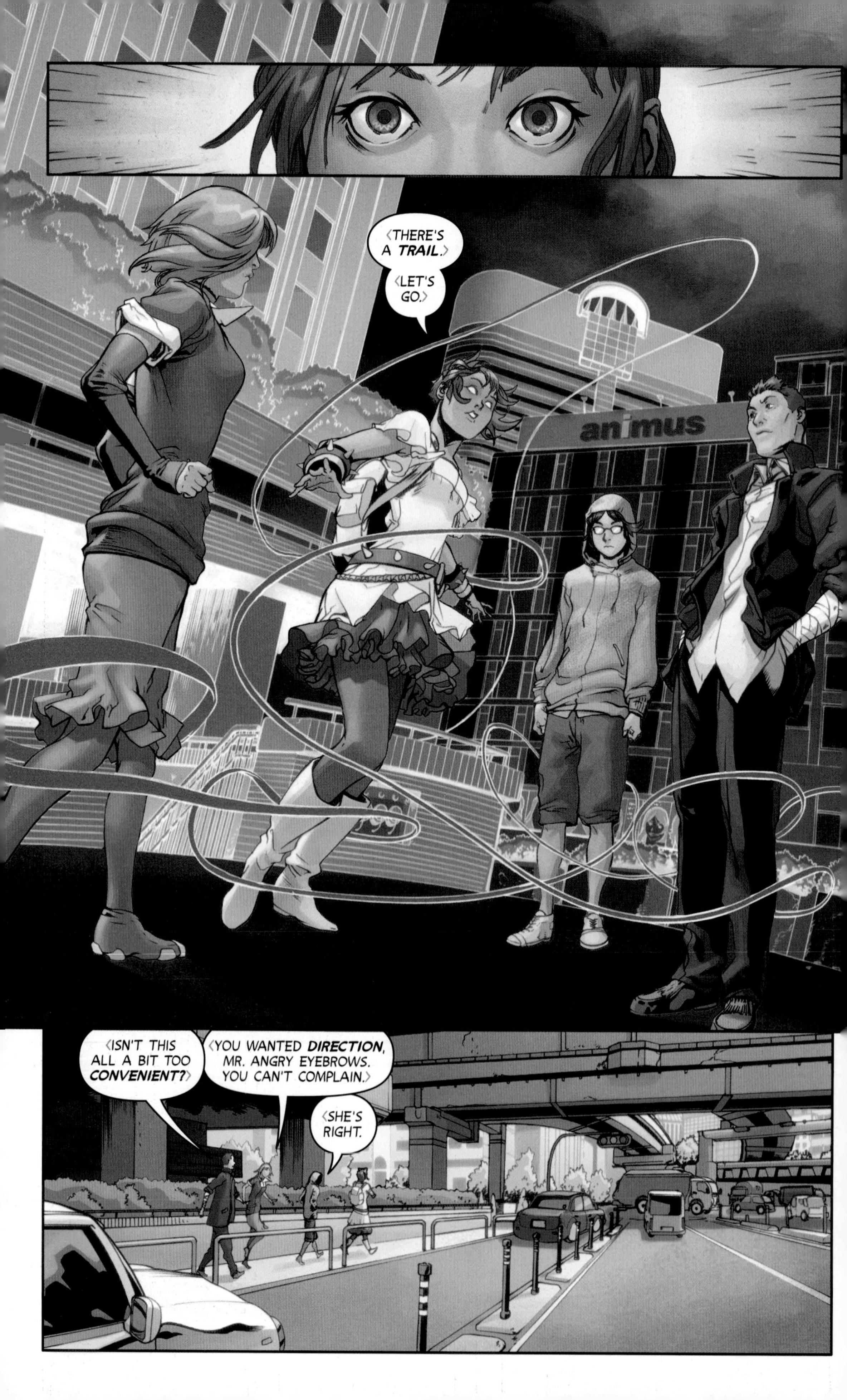
⟨THERE'S A TRAIL.⟩
⟨LET'S GO.⟩
animus
⟨ISN'T THIS ALL A BIT TOO CONVENIENT?⟩
⟨YOU WANTED DIRECTION, MR. ANGRY EYEBROWS. YOU CAN'T COMPLAIN.⟩
⟨SHE'S RIGHT.⟩

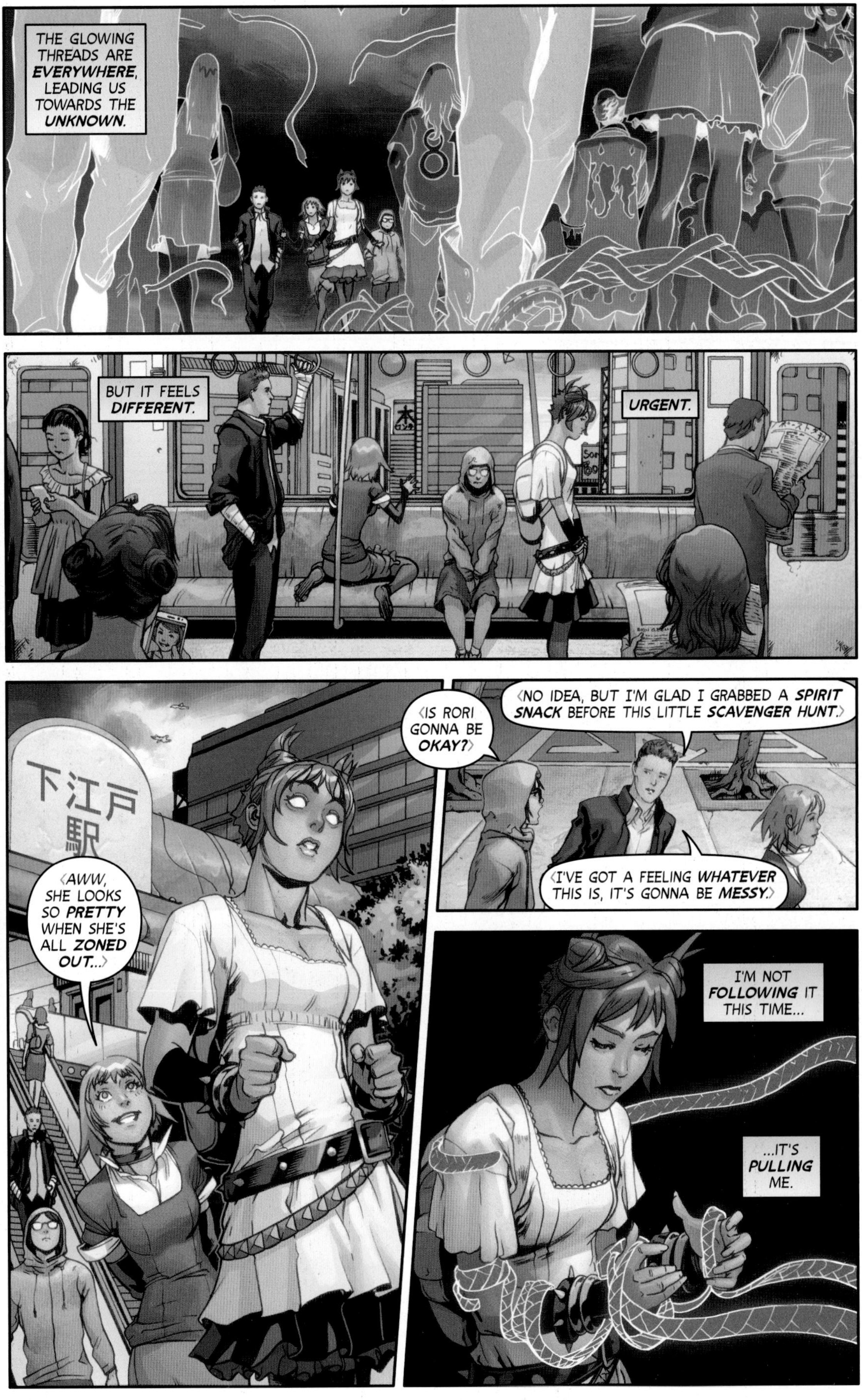
THE GLOWING THREADS ARE EVERYWHERE, LEADING US TOWARDS THE UNKNOWN.
BUT IT FEELS DIFFERENT.
URGENT.
下江戸駅
‹IS RORI GONNA BE OKAY?›
‹NO IDEA, BUT I'M GLAD I GRABBED A SPIRIT SNACK BEFORE THIS LITTLE SCAVENGER HUNT.›
‹I'VE GOT A FEELING WHATEVER THIS IS, IT'S GONNA BE MESSY.›
‹AWW, SHE LOOKS SO PRETTY WHEN SHE'S ALL ZONED OUT...›
I'M NOT FOLLOWING IT THIS TIME...
...IT'S PULLING ME.

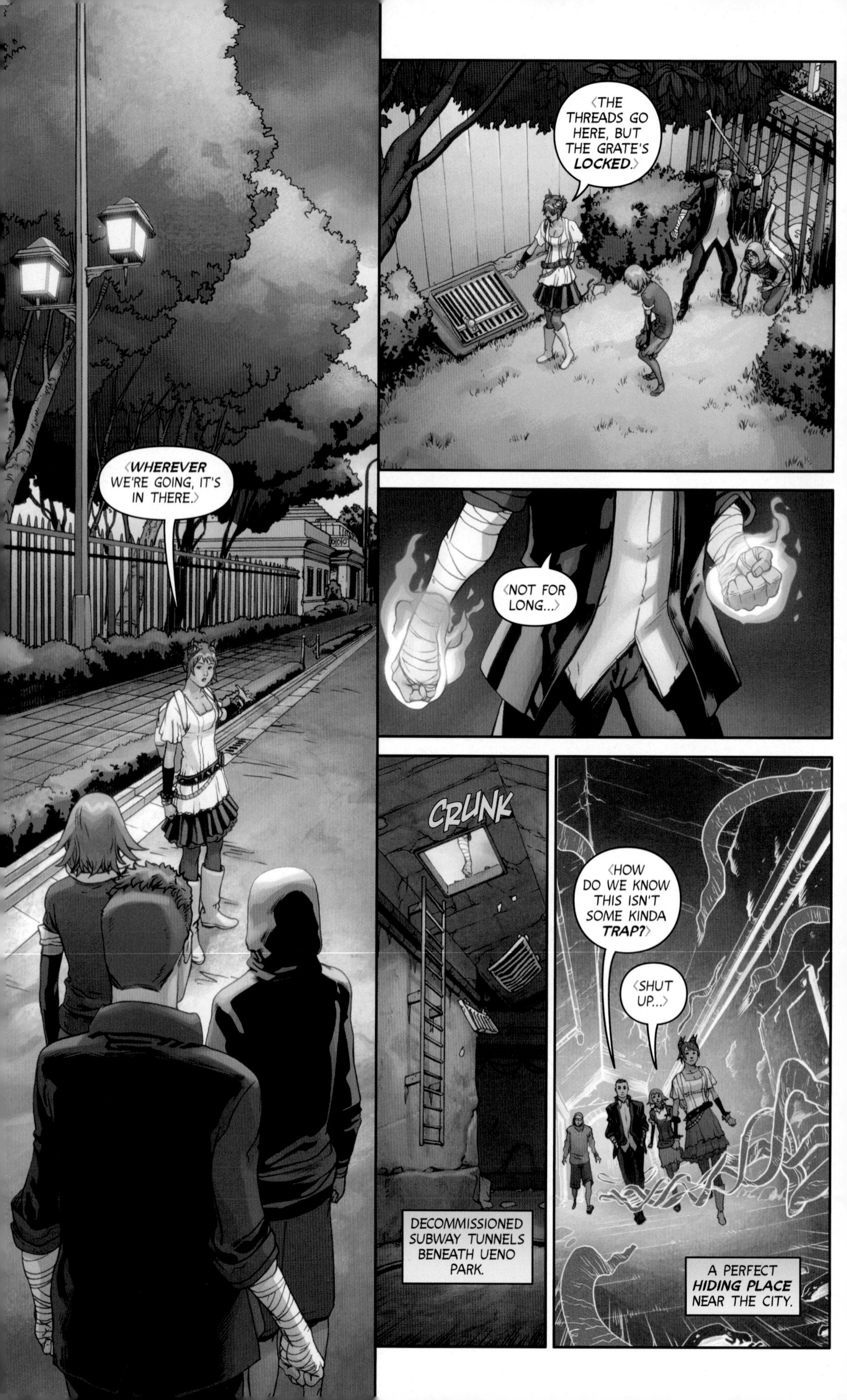

‹WHEREVER WE'RE GOING, IT'S IN THERE.›
‹THE THREADS GO HERE, BUT THE GRATE'S LOCKED.›
‹NOT FOR LONG...›
CRUNK
DECOMMISSIONED SUBWAY TUNNELS BENEATH UENO PARK.
‹HOW DO WE KNOW THIS ISN'T SOME KINDA TRAP?›
‹SHUT UP...›
A PERFECT HIDING PLACE NEAR THE CITY.

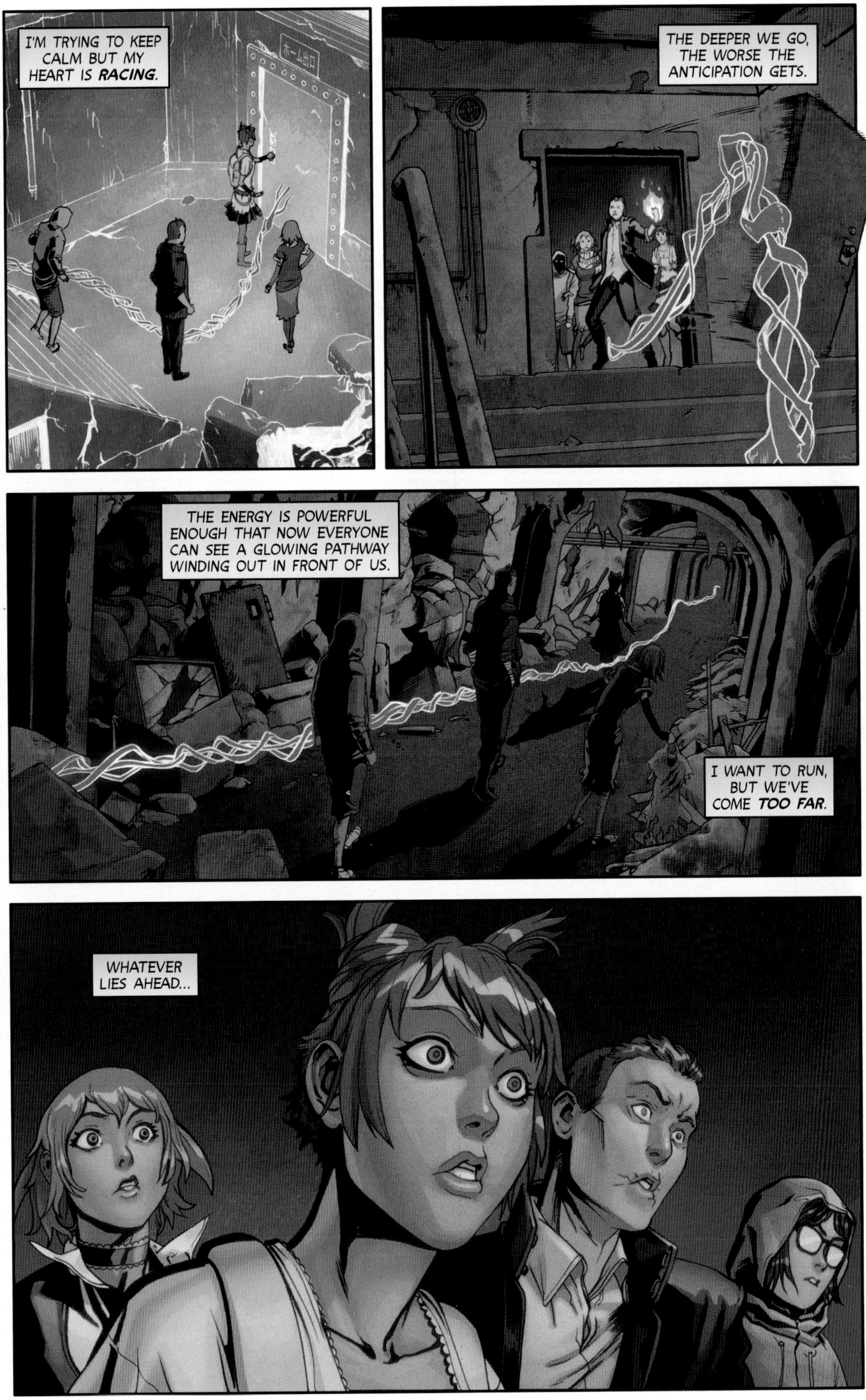
I'M TRYING TO KEEP CALM BUT MY HEART IS RACING.
THE DEEPER WE GO, THE WORSE THE ANTICIPATION GETS.
THE ENERGY IS POWERFUL ENOUGH THAT NOW EVERYONE CAN SEE A GLOWING PATHWAY WINDING OUT IN FRONT OF US.
I WANT TO RUN, BUT WE'VE COME TOO FAR.
WHATEVER LIES AHEAD...

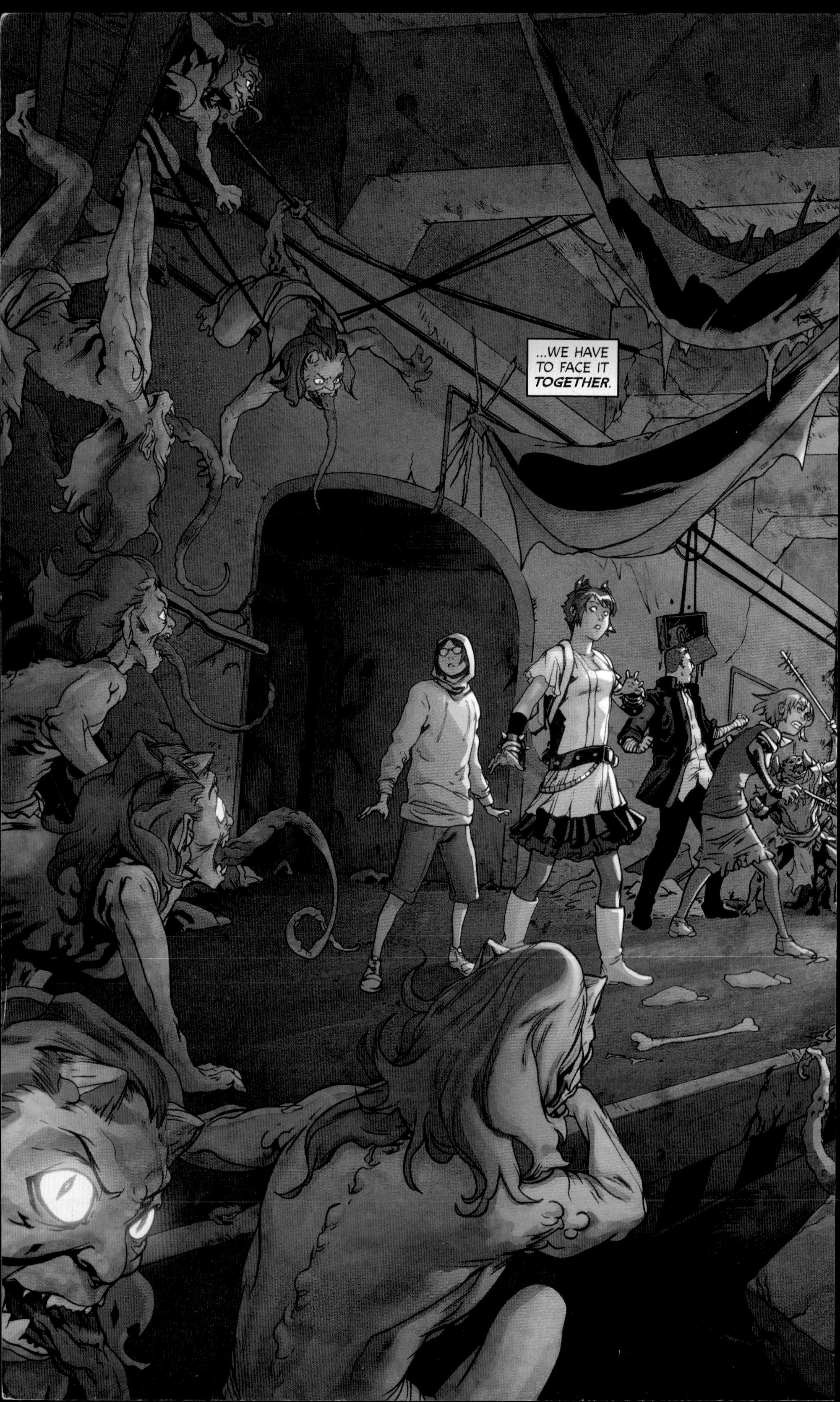
...WE HAVE TO FACE IT *TOGETHER*.

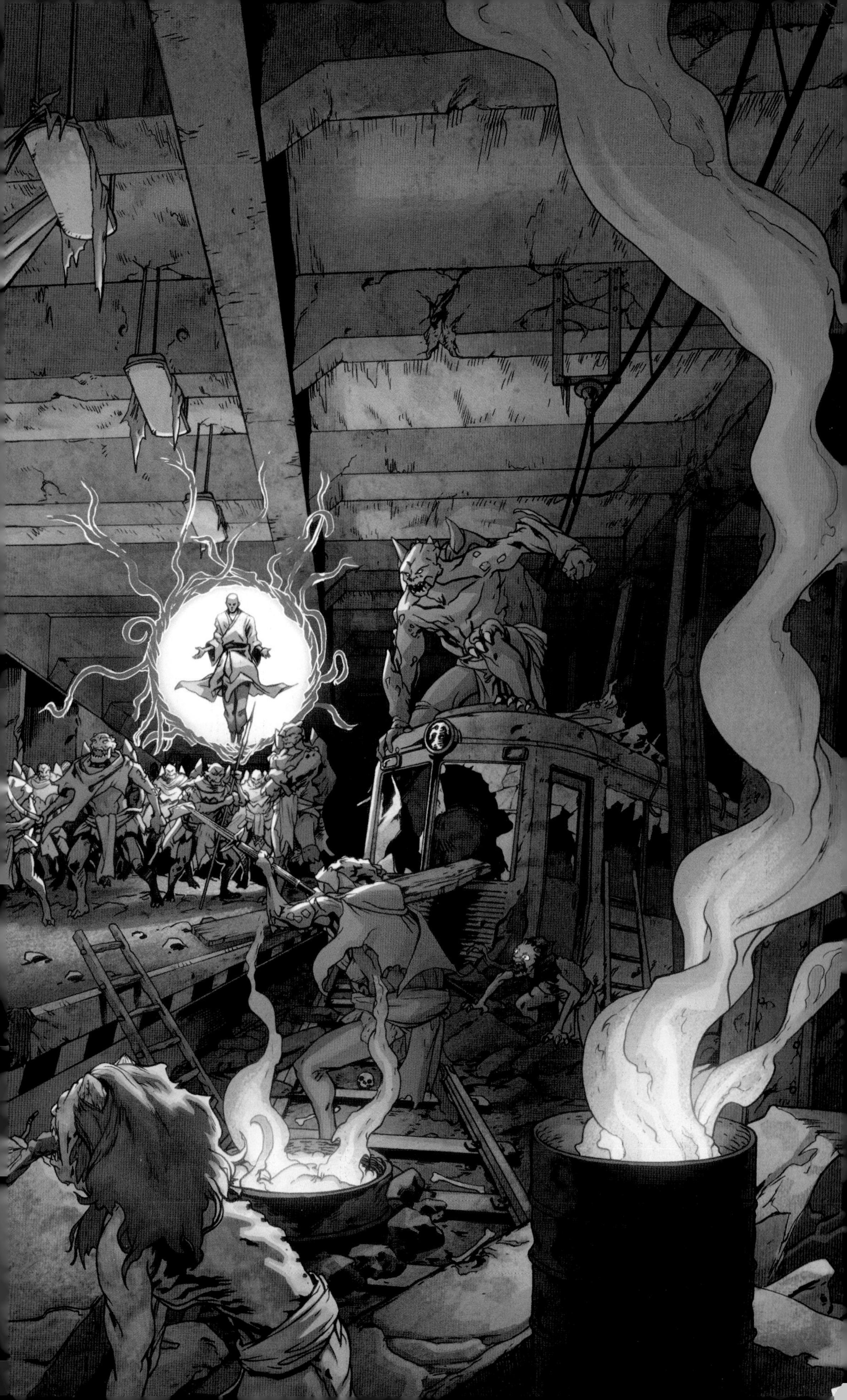

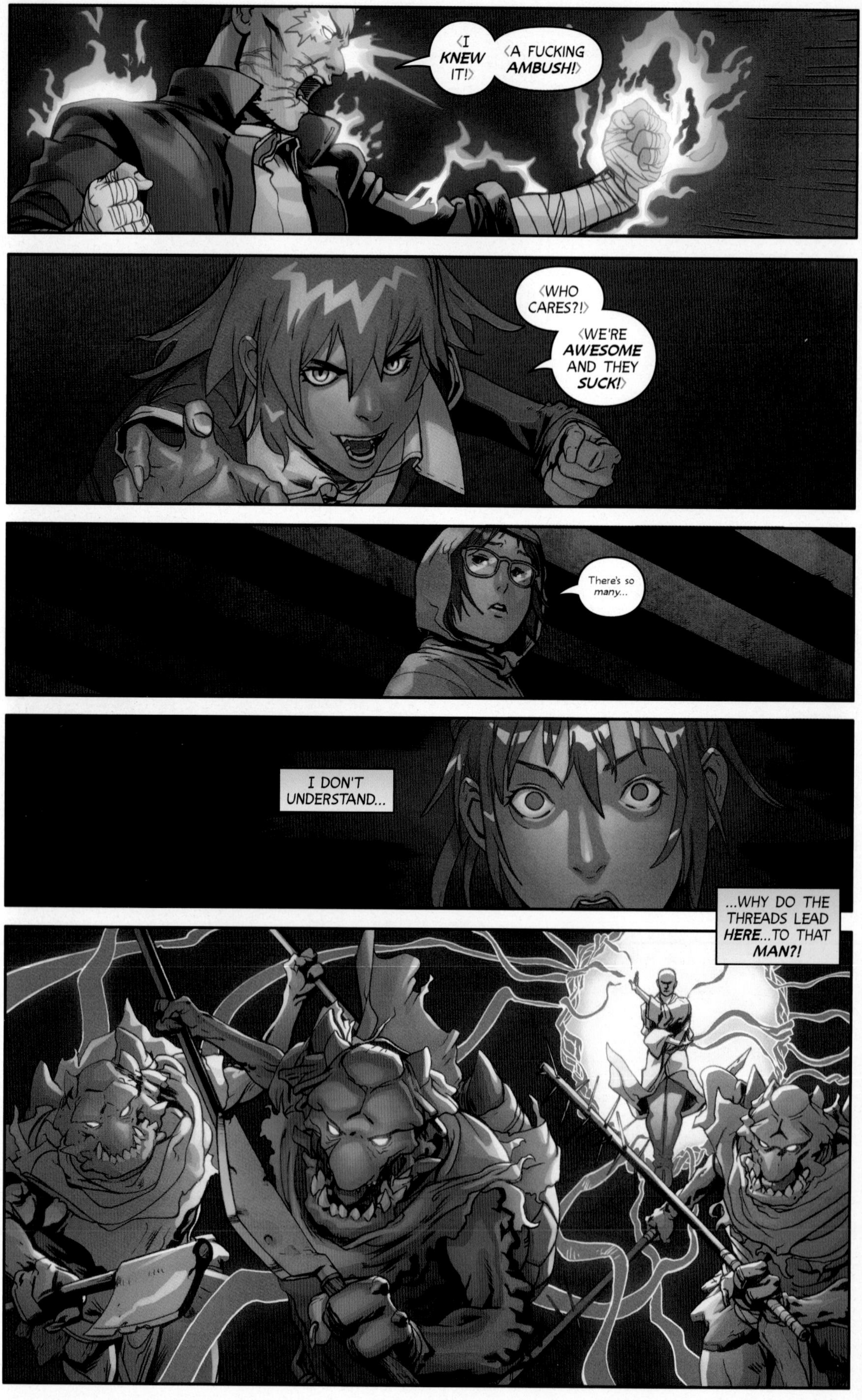

‹I KNEW IT!›
‹A FUCKING AMBUSH!›
‹WHO CARES?!›
‹WE'RE AWESOME AND THEY SUCK!›
There's so many...
I DON'T UNDERSTAND...
...WHY DO THE THREADS LEAD HERE...TO THAT MAN?!

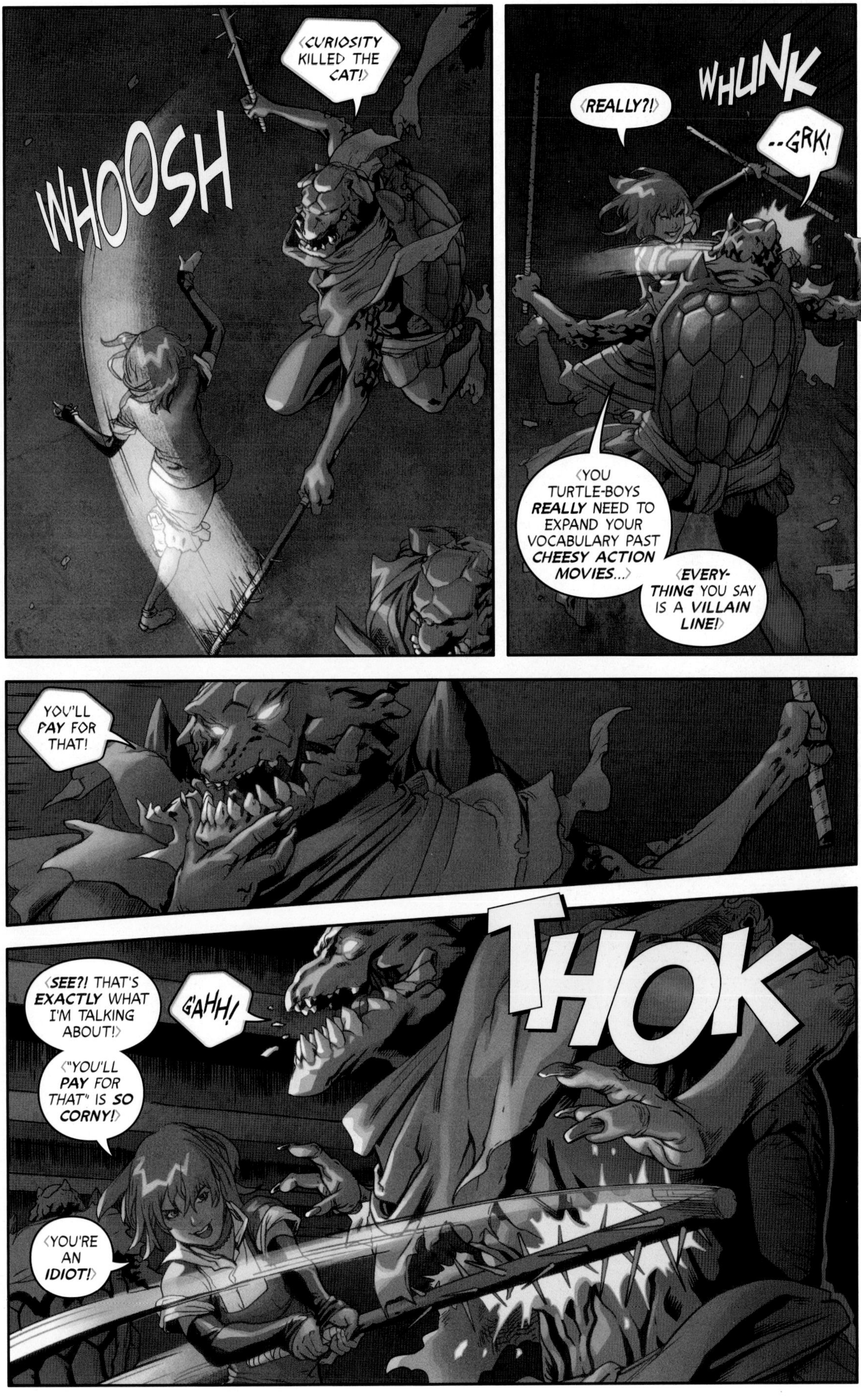

<CURIOSITY KILLED THE CAT!>
WHOOSH
WHUNK
<REALLY?!>
..GRK!
<YOU TURTLE-BOYS REALLY NEED TO EXPAND YOUR VOCABULARY PAST CHEESY ACTION MOVIES...>
<EVERY-THING YOU SAY IS A VILLAIN LINE!>
YOU'LL PAY FOR THAT!
THOK
<SEE?! THAT'S EXACTLY WHAT I'M TALKING ABOUT!>
G'AHH!
<"YOU'LL PAY FOR THAT" IS SO CORNY!>
<YOU'RE AN IDIOT!>

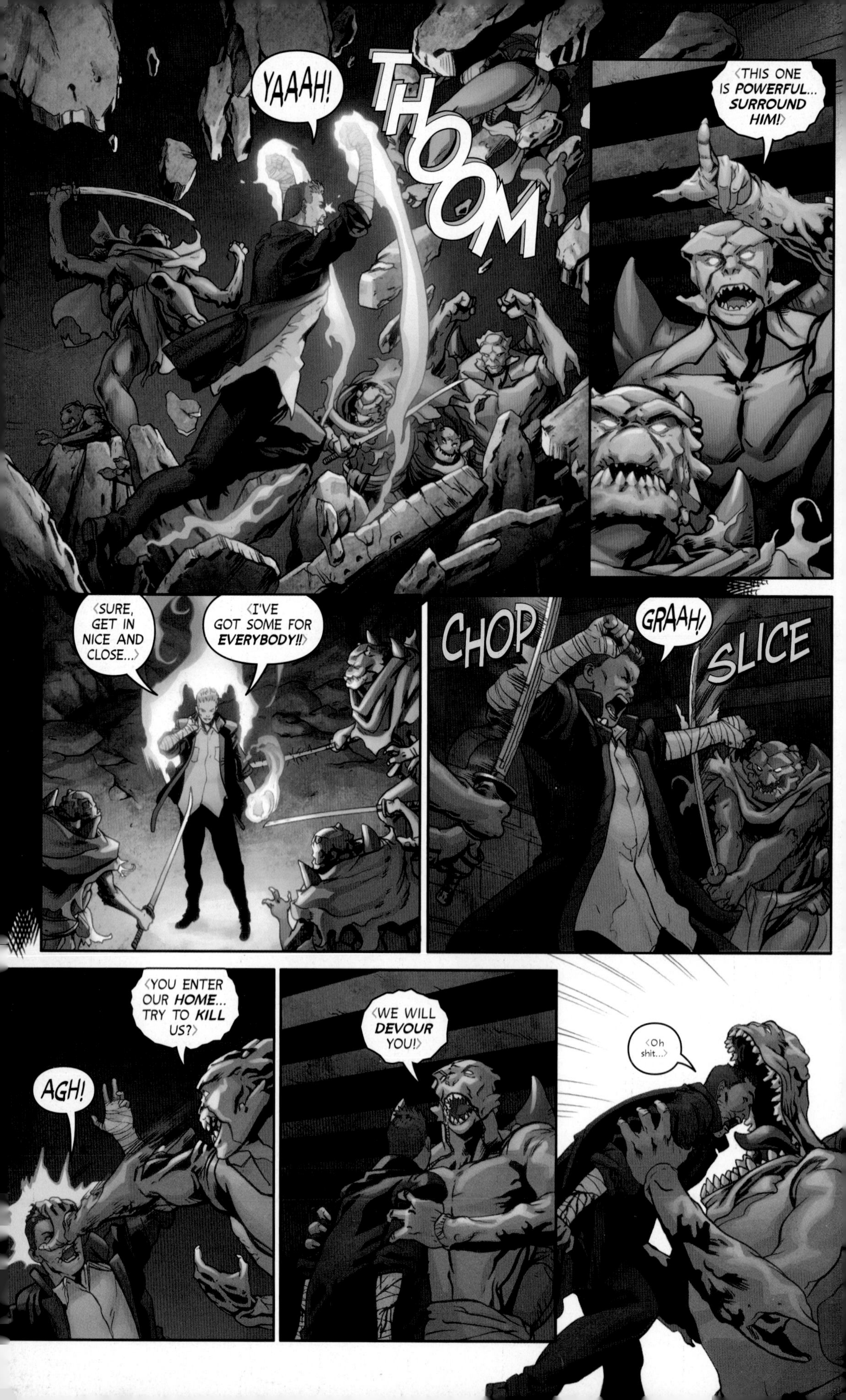
YAAAH!
THOOM
⟨THIS ONE IS POWERFUL... SURROUND HIM!⟩
⟨SURE, GET IN NICE AND CLOSE...⟩
⟨I'VE GOT SOME FOR EVERYBODY!!⟩
CHOP
GRAAH!
SLICE
⟨YOU ENTER OUR HOME... TRY TO KILL US?⟩
AGH!
⟨WE WILL DEVOUR YOU!⟩
⟨Oh shit...⟩

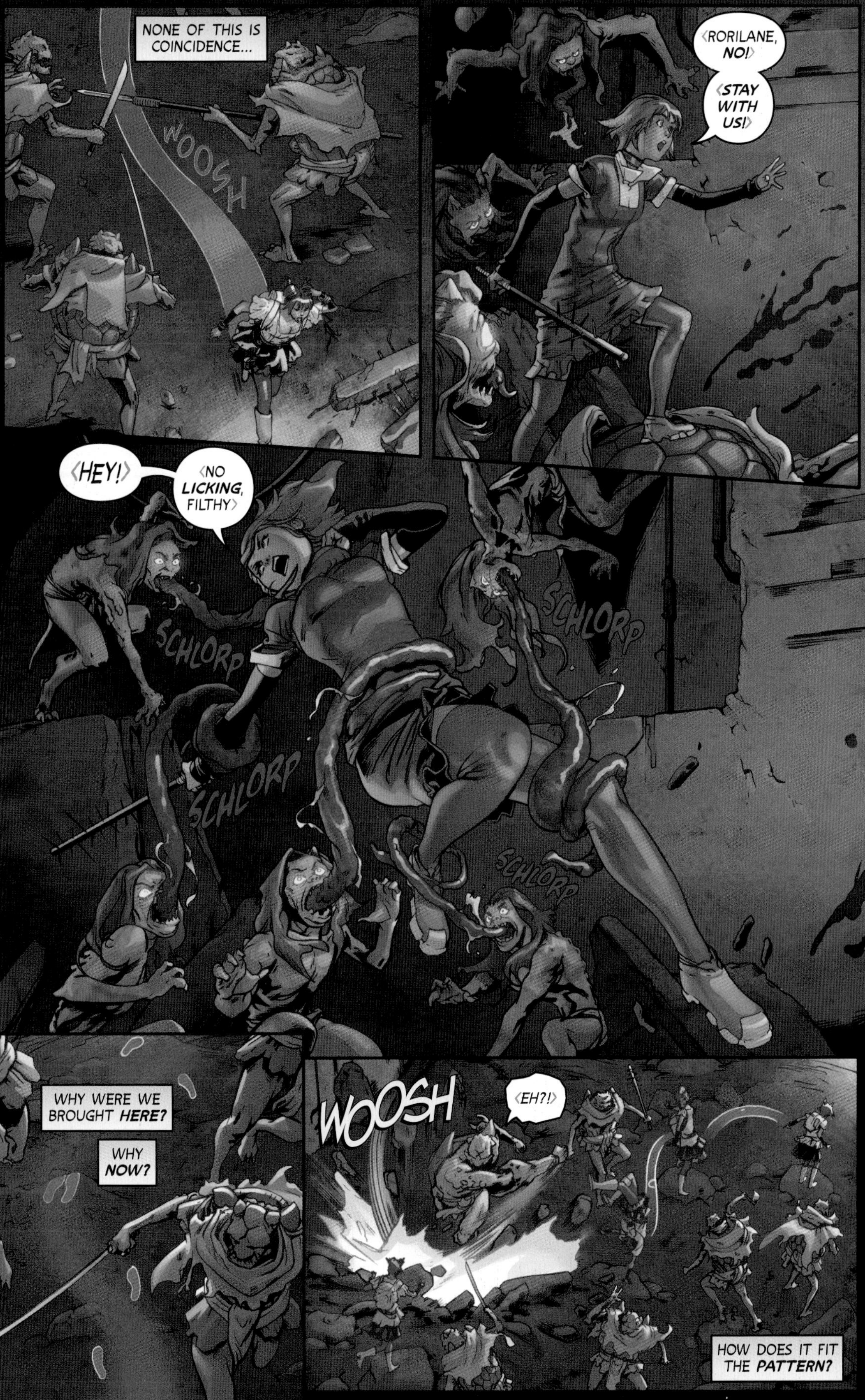
NONE OF THIS IS COINCIDENCE...
WOOSH
‹RORILANE, NO!›
‹STAY WITH US!›
‹HEY!›
‹NO LICKING, FILTHY›
SCHLORP
SCHLORP
SCHLORP
SCHLORP
WHY WERE WE BROUGHT HERE?
WHY NOW?
WOOSH
‹EH?!›
HOW DOES IT FIT THE PATTERN?

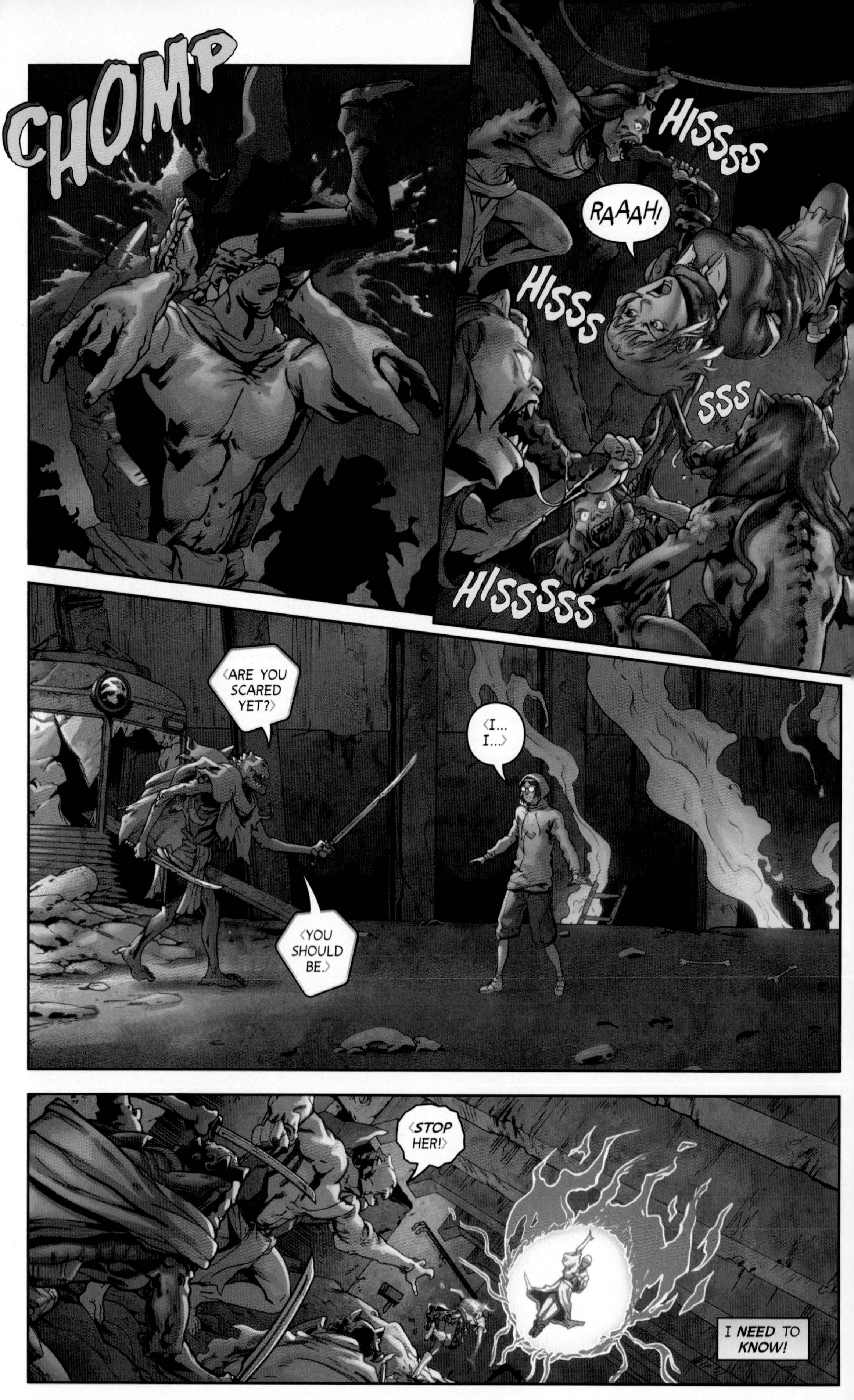
CHOMP
HISSSS
RAAAH!
HISSS
SSS
HISSSSS
‹ARE YOU SCARED YET?›
‹I... I...›
‹YOU SHOULD BE.›
‹STOP HER!›
I NEED TO KNOW!

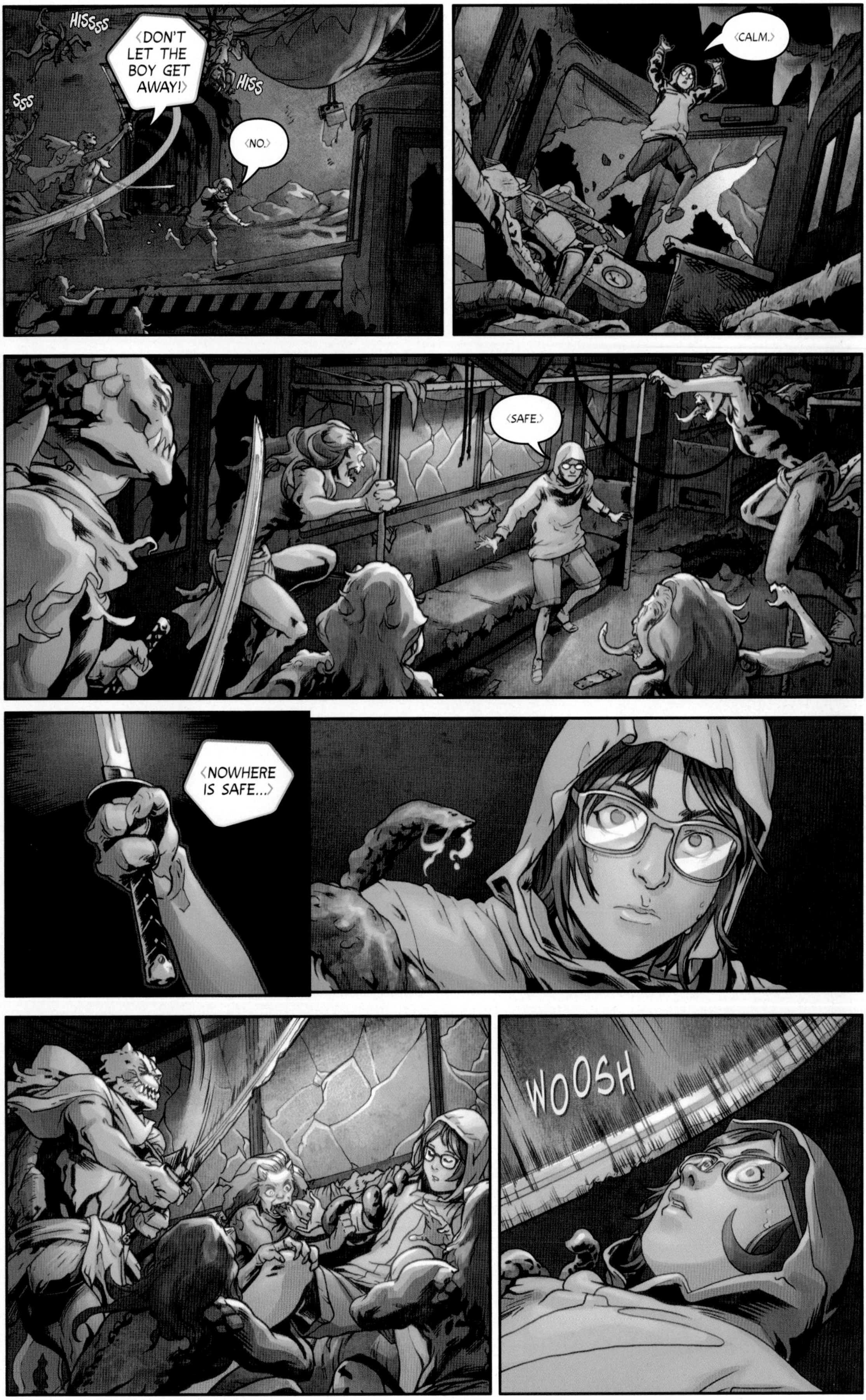
HISSSS
⟨DON'T LET THE BOY GET AWAY!⟩
HISS
SSS
⟨NO.⟩
⟨CALM.⟩
⟨SAFE.⟩
⟨NOWHERE IS SAFE...⟩
WOOSH

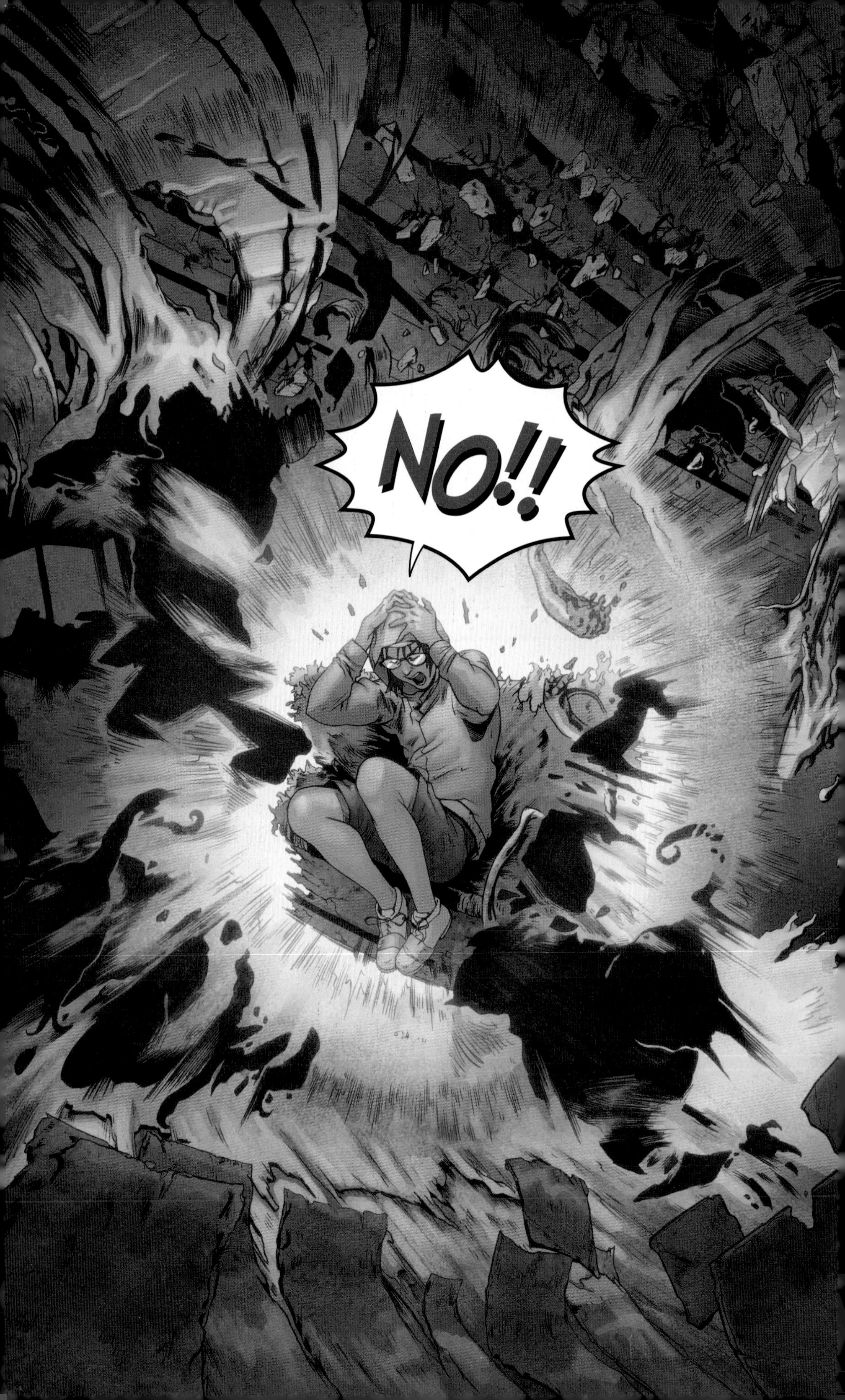
NO!!

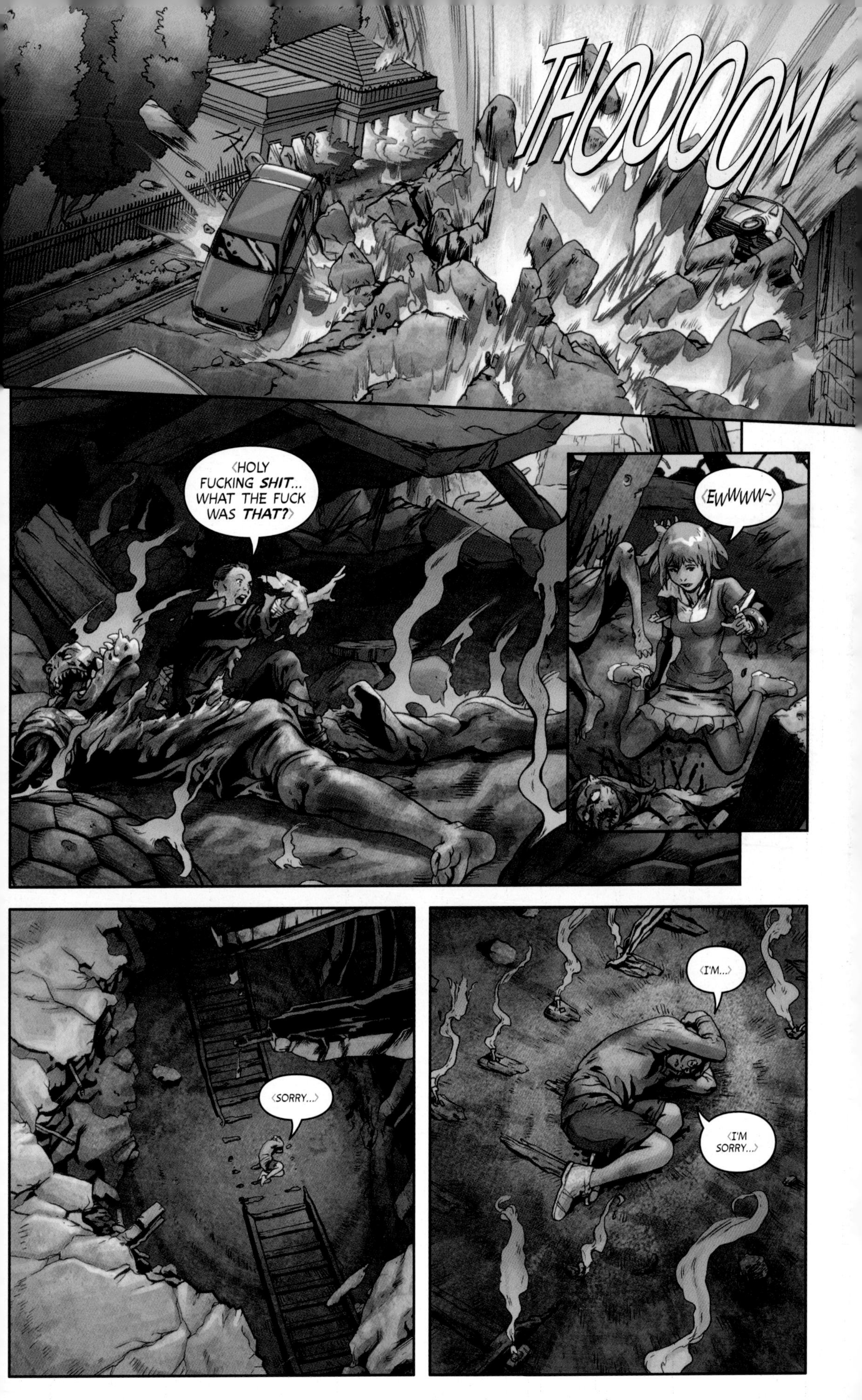
THOOOOM
‹HOLY FUCKING SHIT... WHAT THE FUCK WAS THAT?›
‹EWWWW~›
‹SORRY...›
‹I'M...›
‹I'M SORRY...›

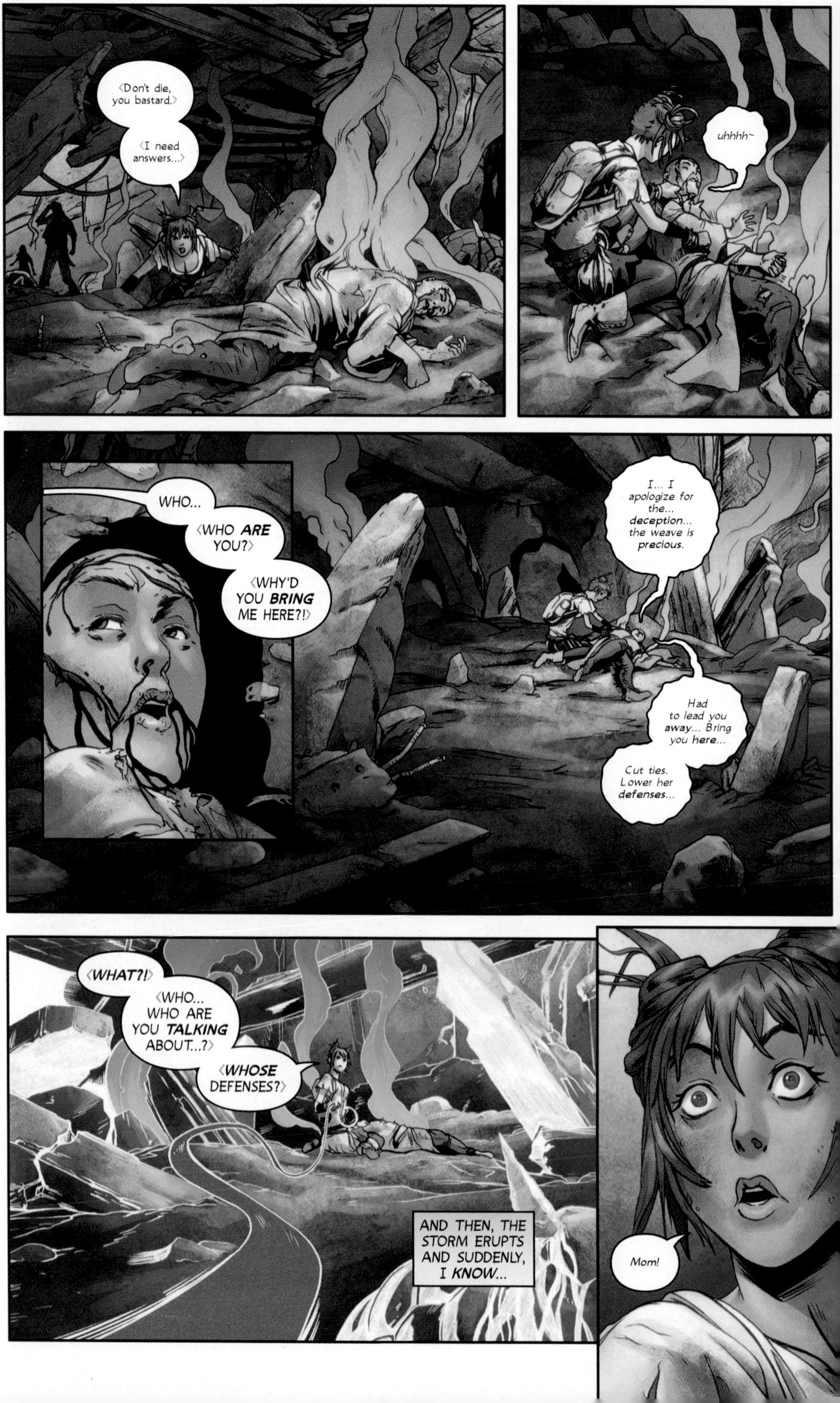
<Don't die, you bastard.>
<I need answers...>
uhhhh~
WHO...
<WHO **ARE** YOU?>
<WHY'D YOU **BRING** ME HERE?!>
I... I apologize for the... **deception**... the weave is **precious**.
Had to lead you **away**... Bring you **here**...
Cut ties. Lower her **defenses**...
<***WHAT?!***>
<WHO... WHO ARE YOU ***TALKING*** ABOUT...?>
<***WHOSE*** DEFENSES?>
AND THEN, THE STORM ERUPTS AND SUDDENLY, I ***KNOW***...
*Mom!*

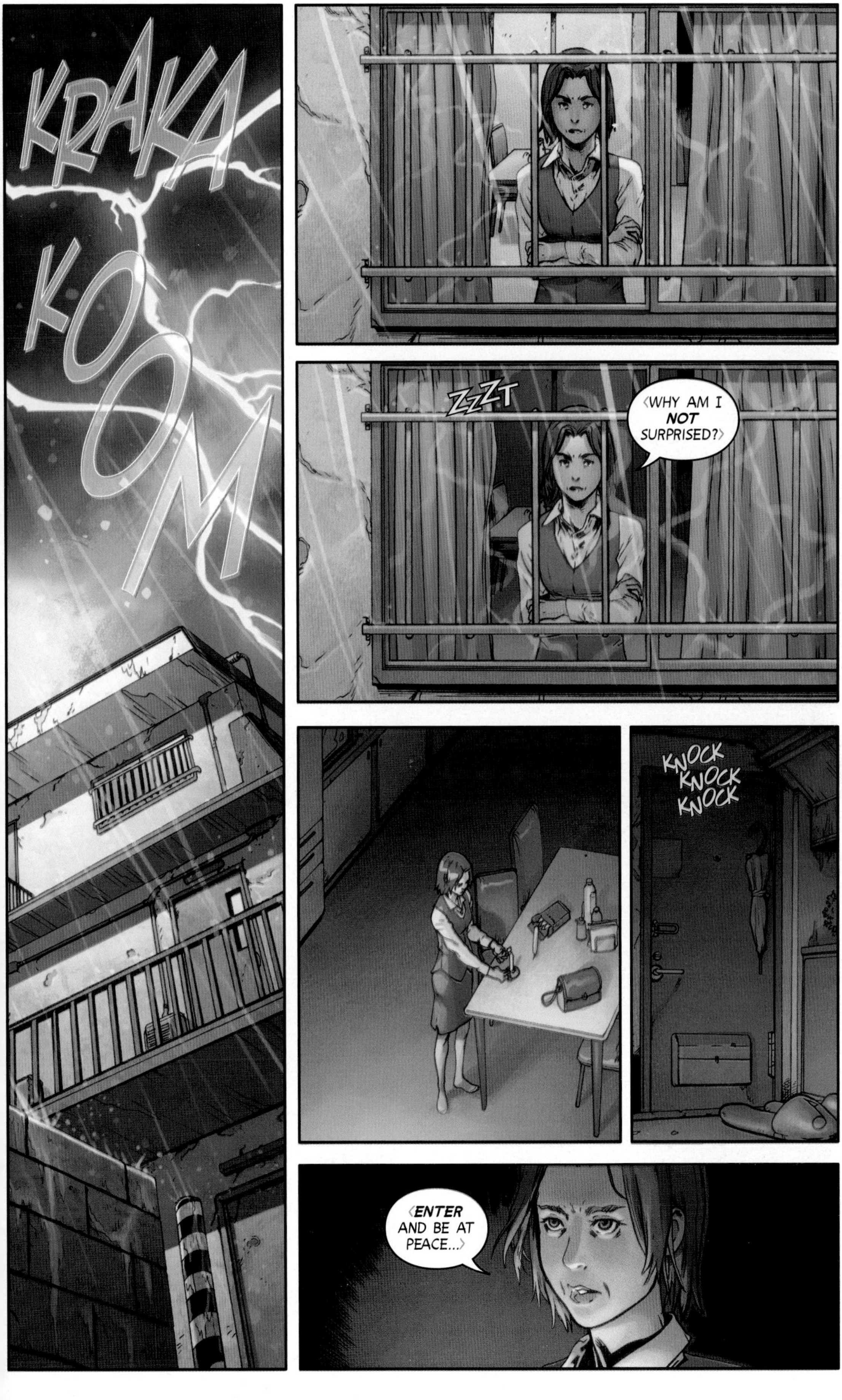
KRAKA KOOM
ZZZT
‹WHY AM I NOT SURPRISED?›
KNOCK KNOCK KNOCK
‹ENTER AND BE AT PEACE...›

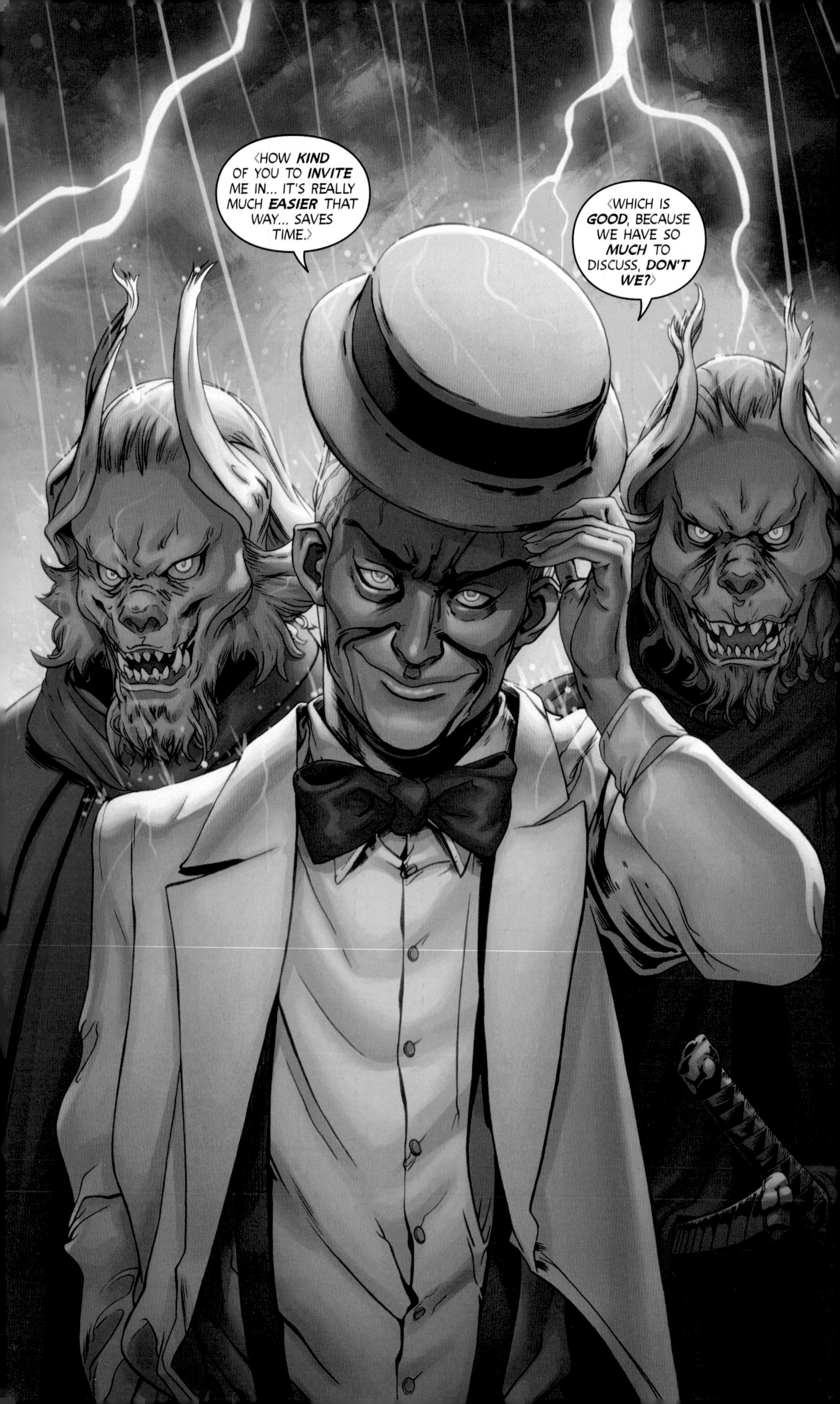

<HOW KIND OF YOU TO INVITE ME IN... IT'S REALLY MUCH EASIER THAT WAY... SAVES TIME.>
<WHICH IS GOOD, BECAUSE WE HAVE SO MUCH TO DISCUSS, DON'T WE?>

# Chapter Five

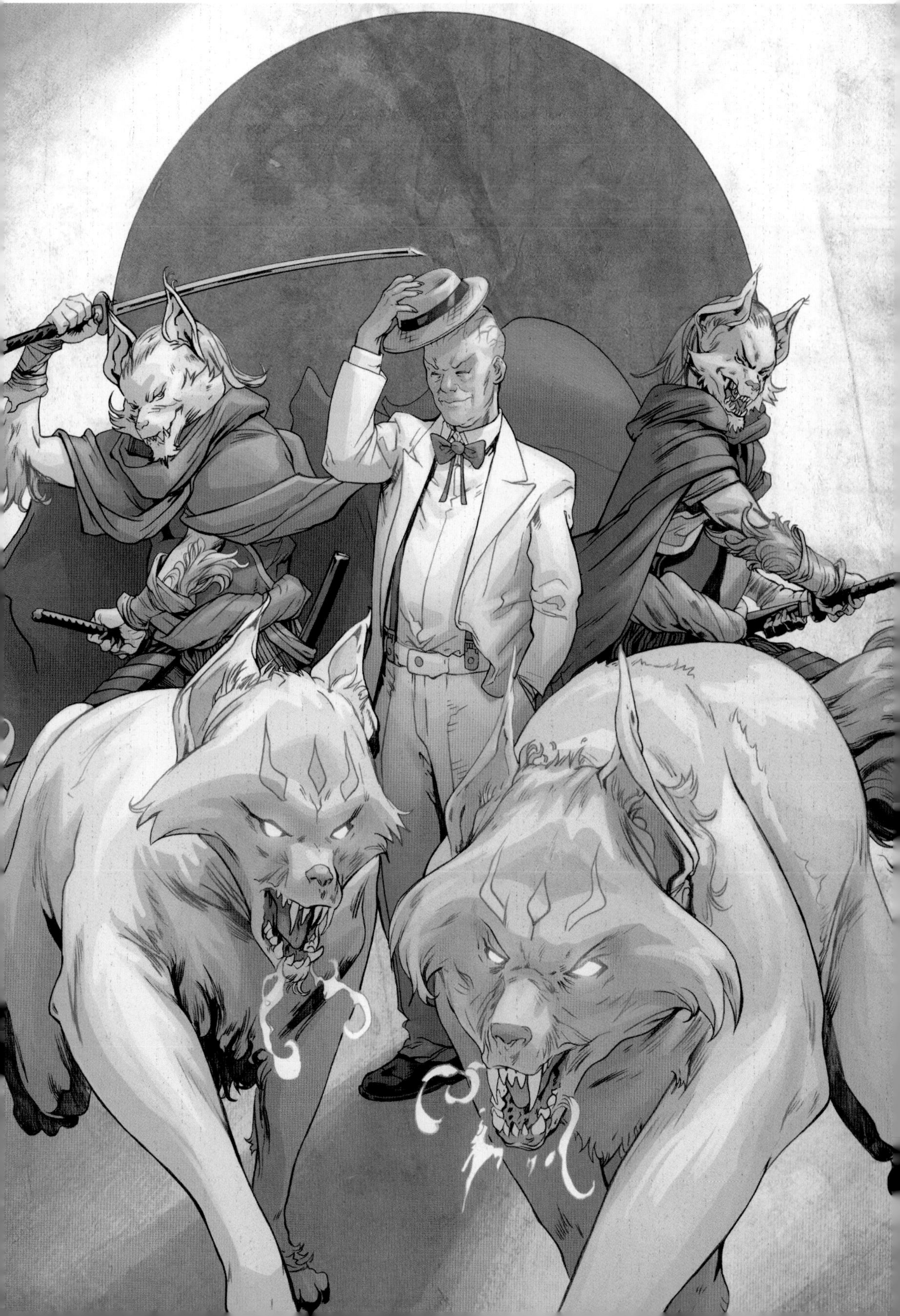

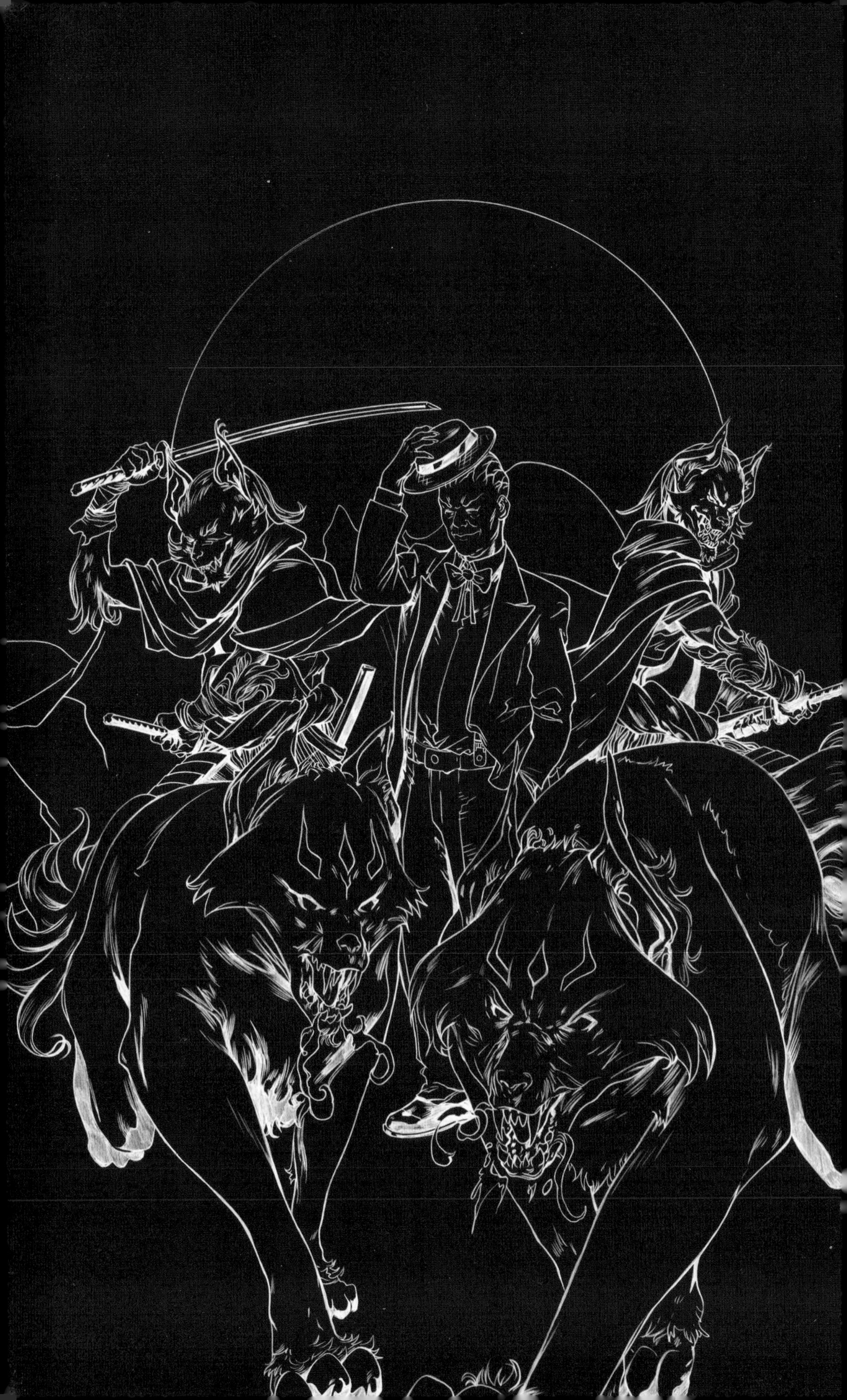

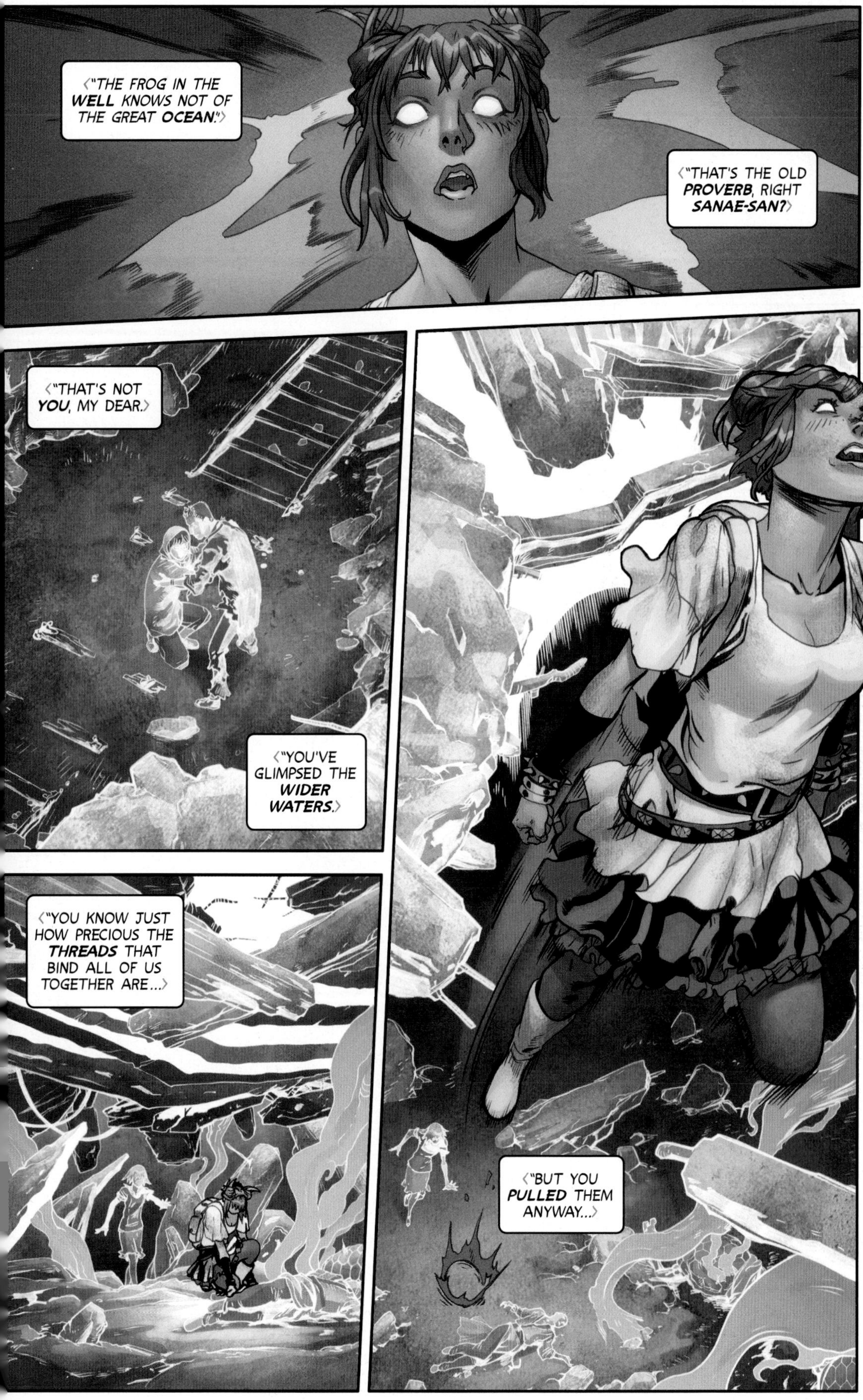

‹"THE FROG IN THE WELL KNOWS NOT OF THE GREAT OCEAN."›
‹"THAT'S THE OLD PROVERB, RIGHT SANAE-SAN?›
‹"THAT'S NOT YOU, MY DEAR.›
‹"YOU'VE GLIMPSED THE WIDER WATERS.›
‹"YOU KNOW JUST HOW PRECIOUS THE THREADS THAT BIND ALL OF US TOGETHER ARE...›
‹"BUT YOU PULLED THEM ANYWAY...›

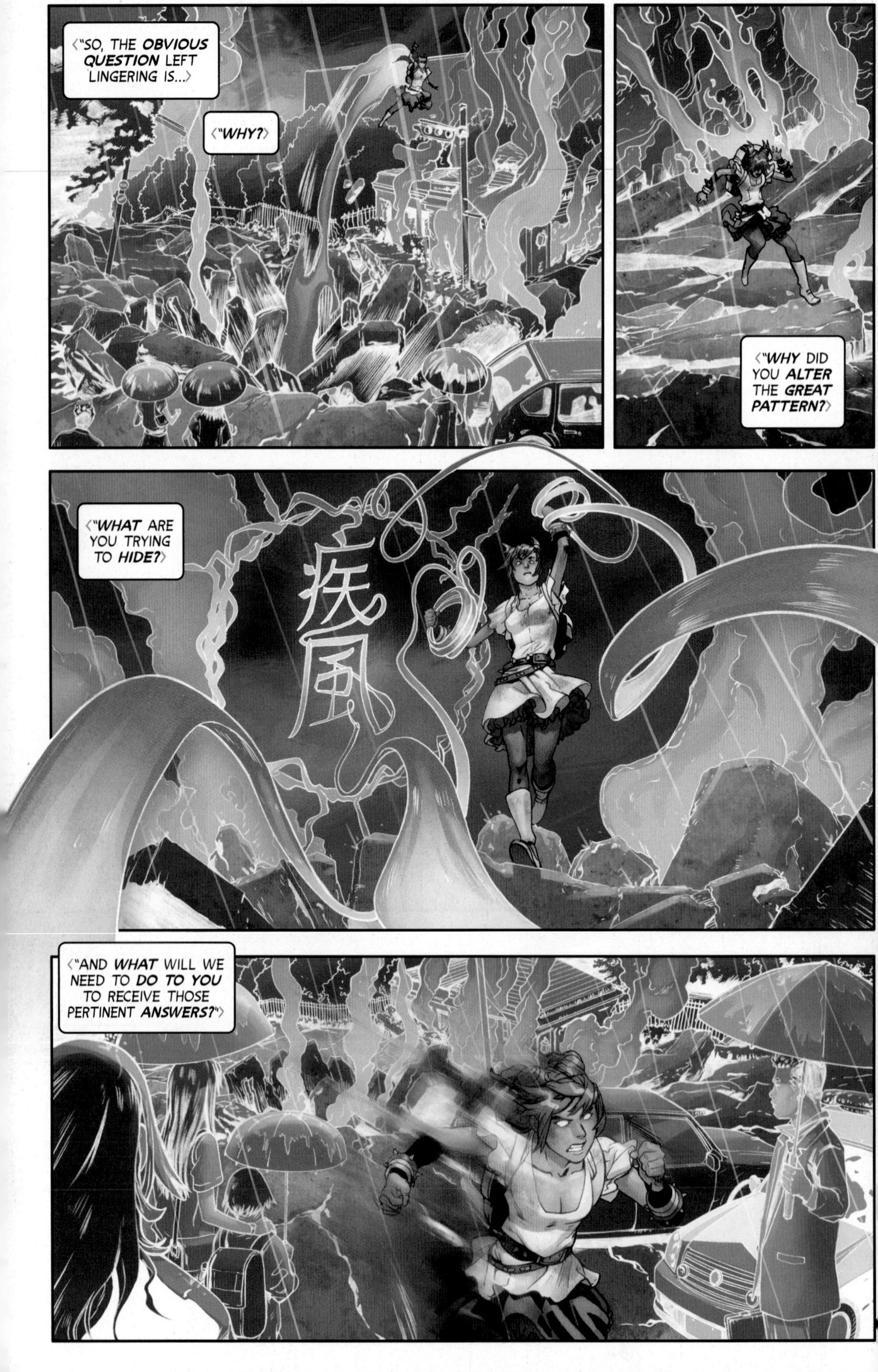

<"SO, THE OBVIOUS QUESTION LEFT LINGERING IS...>
<"WHY?>
<"WHY DID YOU ALTER THE GREAT PATTERN?>
<"WHAT ARE YOU TRYING TO HIDE?>
疾風
<"AND WHAT WILL WE NEED TO DO TO YOU TO RECEIVE THOSE PERTINENT ANSWERS?">

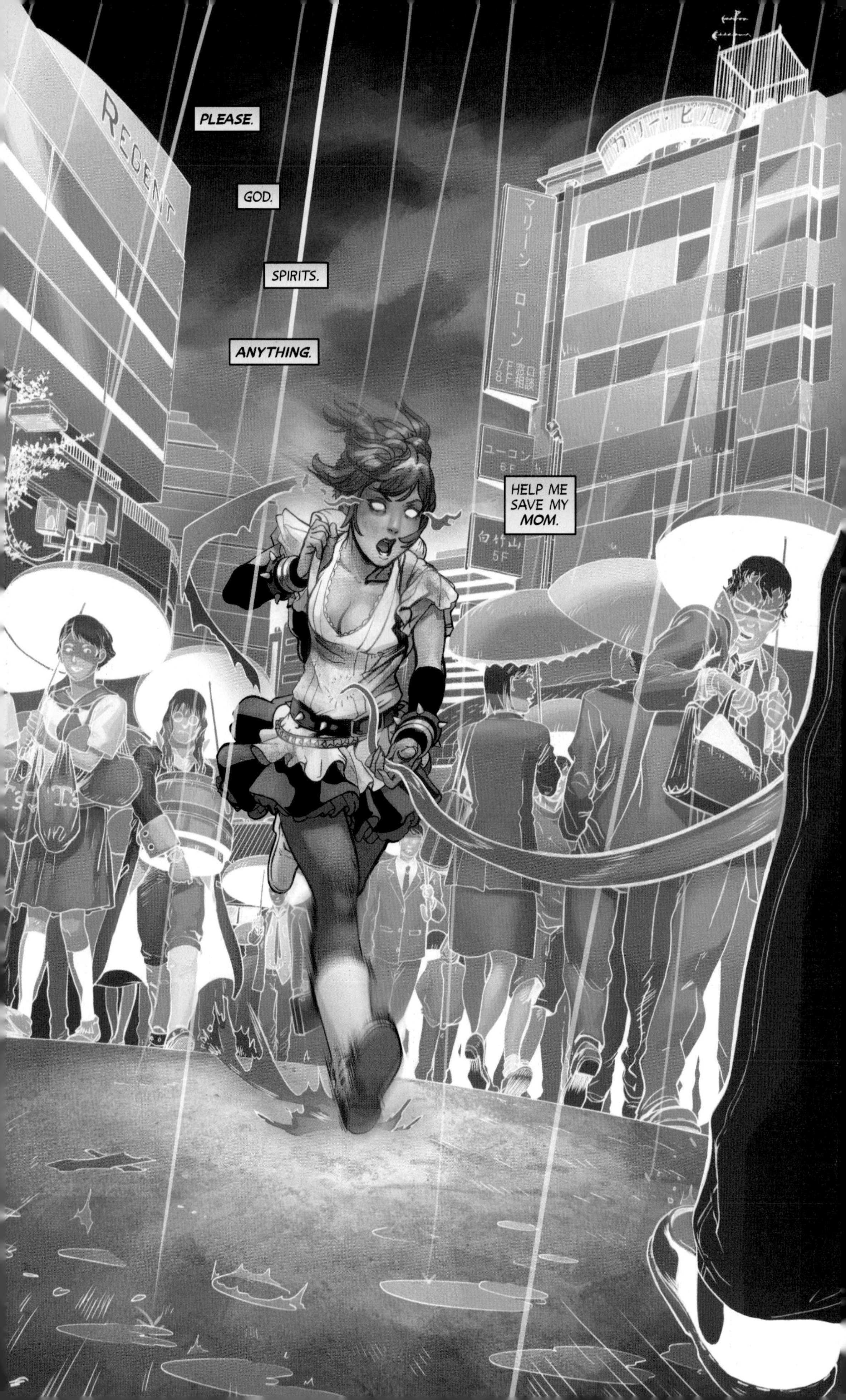
PLEASE.
GOD.
SPIRITS.
ANYTHING.
HELP ME SAVE MY MOM.
REGENT
マリーン ローン
7F窓口
8F相談
ユーコン
6F

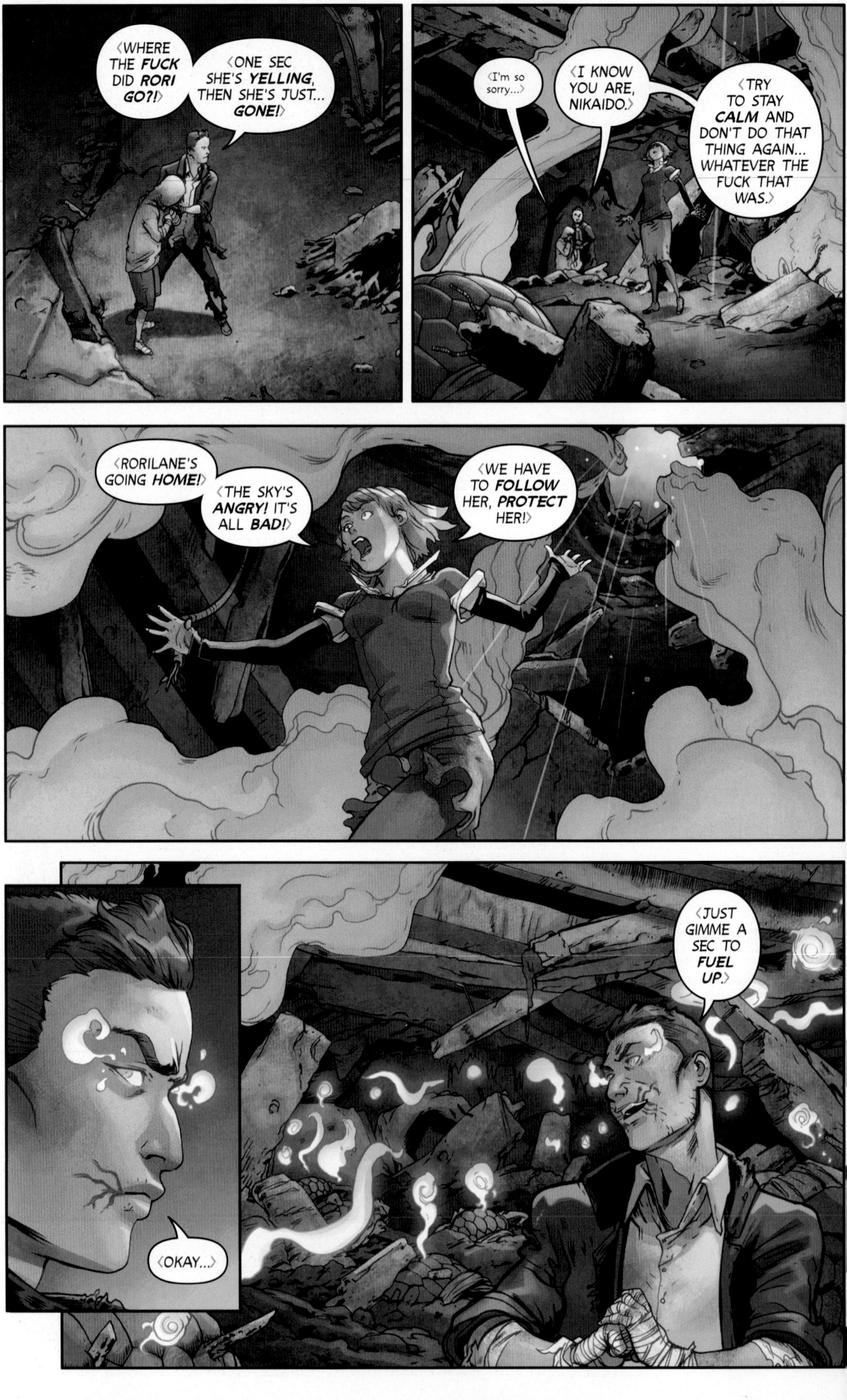

⟨WHERE THE FUCK DID RORI GO?!⟩
⟨ONE SEC SHE'S YELLING, THEN SHE'S JUST... GONE!⟩
⟨I'm so sorry...⟩
⟨I KNOW YOU ARE, NIKAIDO.⟩
⟨TRY TO STAY CALM AND DON'T DO THAT THING AGAIN... WHATEVER THE FUCK THAT WAS.⟩
⟨RORILANE'S GOING HOME!⟩
⟨THE SKY'S ANGRY! IT'S ALL BAD!⟩
⟨WE HAVE TO FOLLOW HER, PROTECT HER!⟩
⟨JUST GIMME A SEC TO FUEL UP.⟩
⟨OKAY...⟩

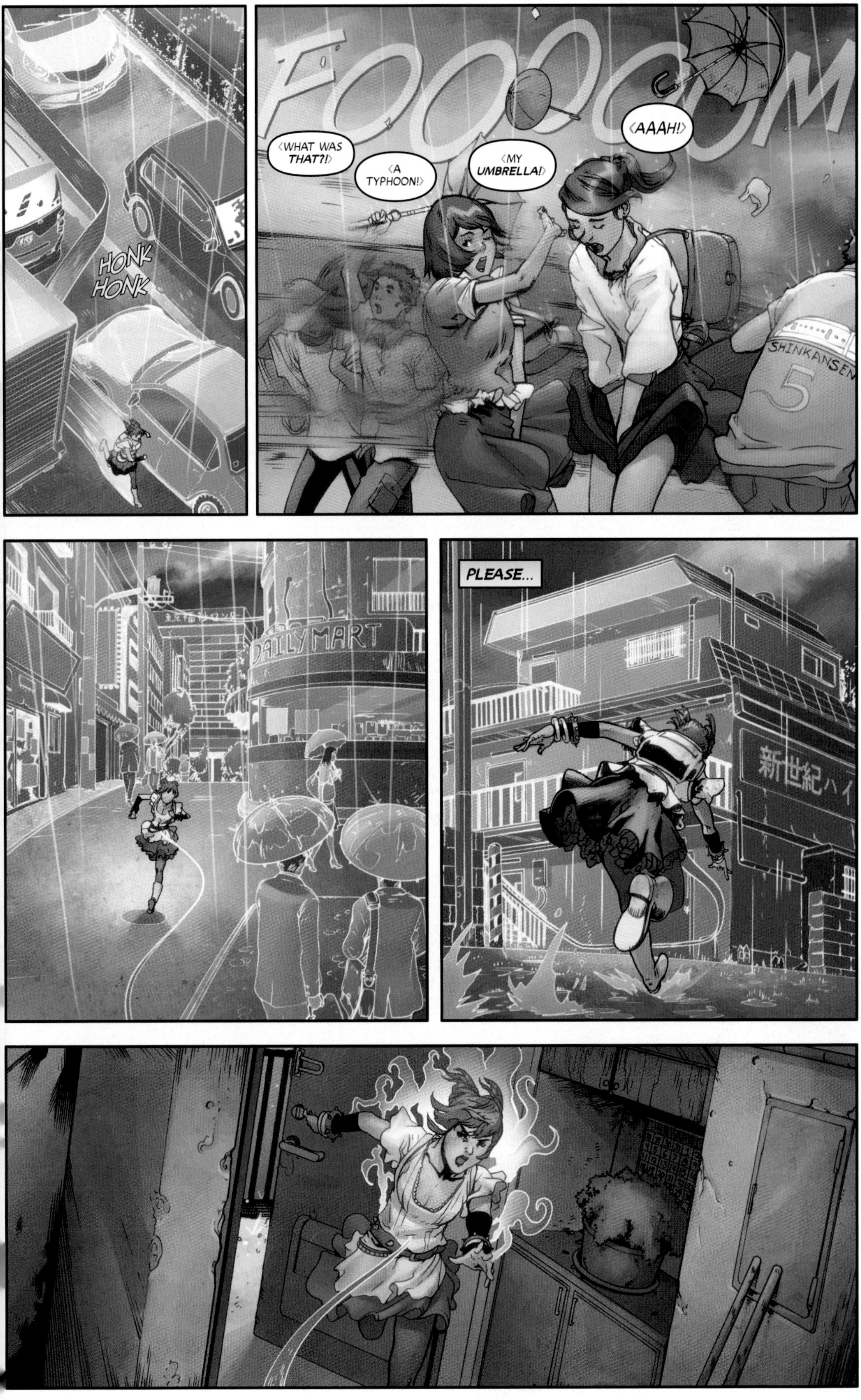
HONK
HONK
FOOOOOM
‹WHAT WAS THAT?!›
‹A TYPHOON!›
‹MY UMBRELLA!›
‹AAAH!›
SHINKANSEN
5
DAILY MART
PLEASE...
新世紀ハイ

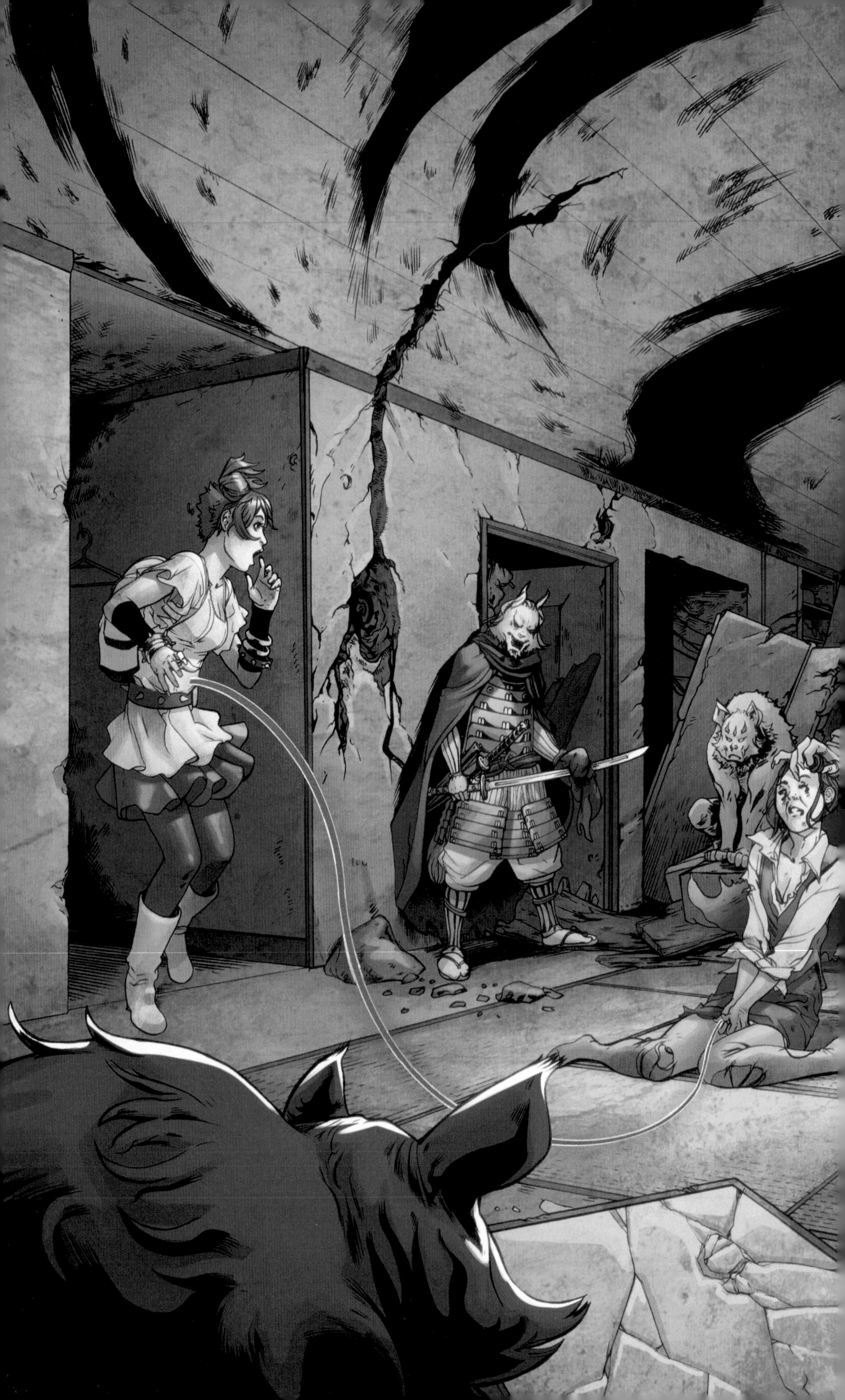

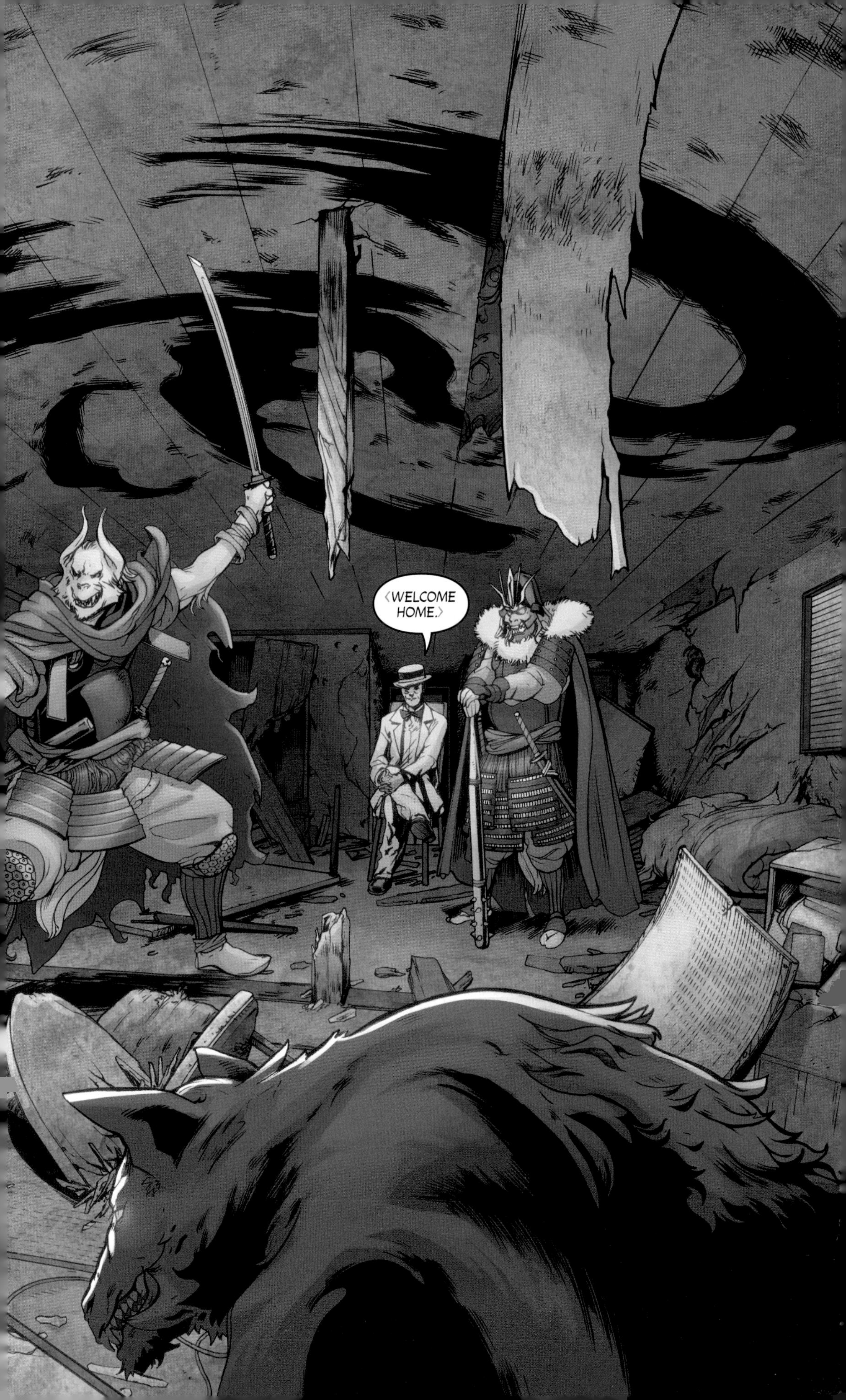
〈WELCOME HOME.〉

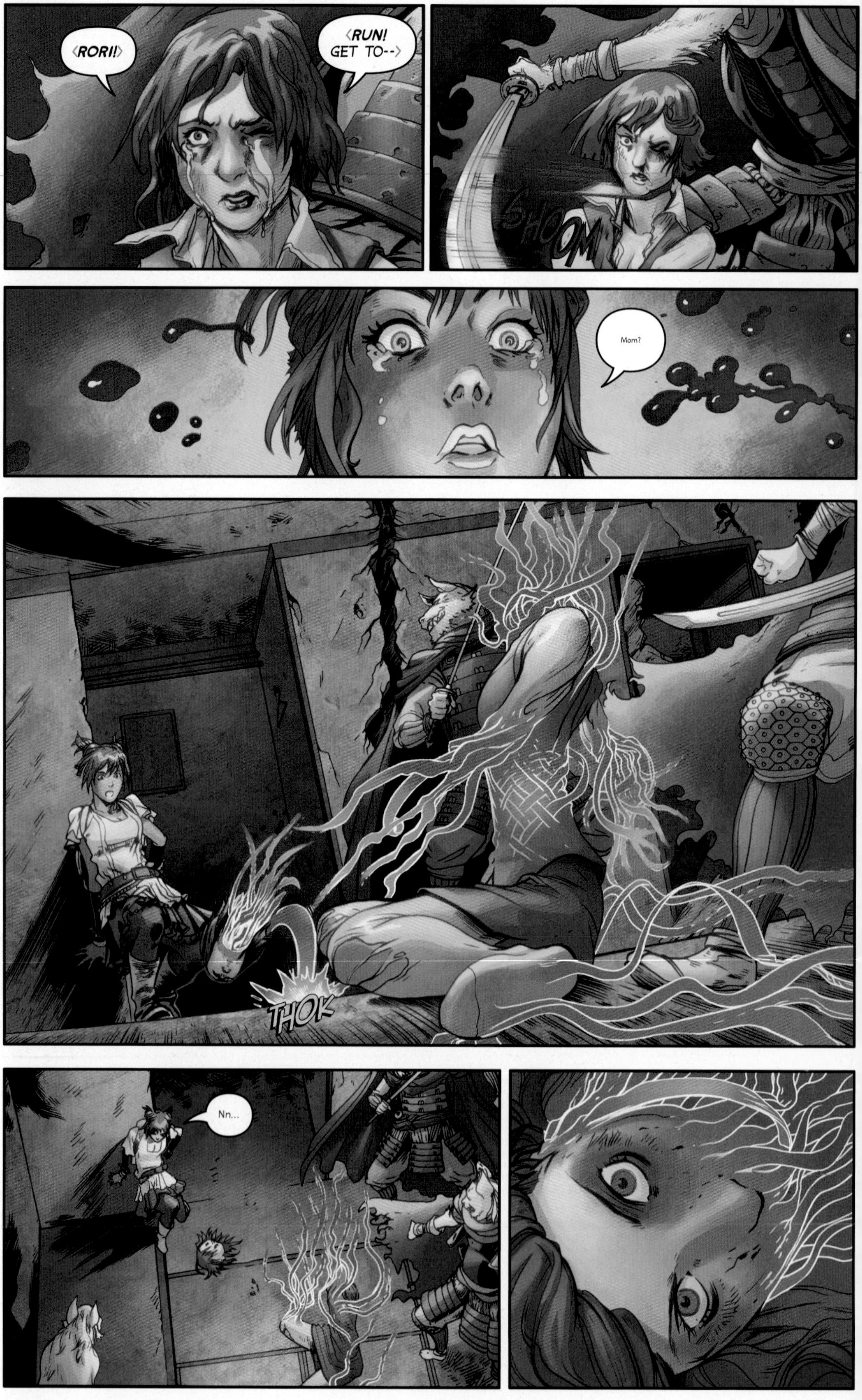
⟨RORI!⟩
⟨RUN! GET TO--⟩
SHOOM
Mom?
THOK
Nn...

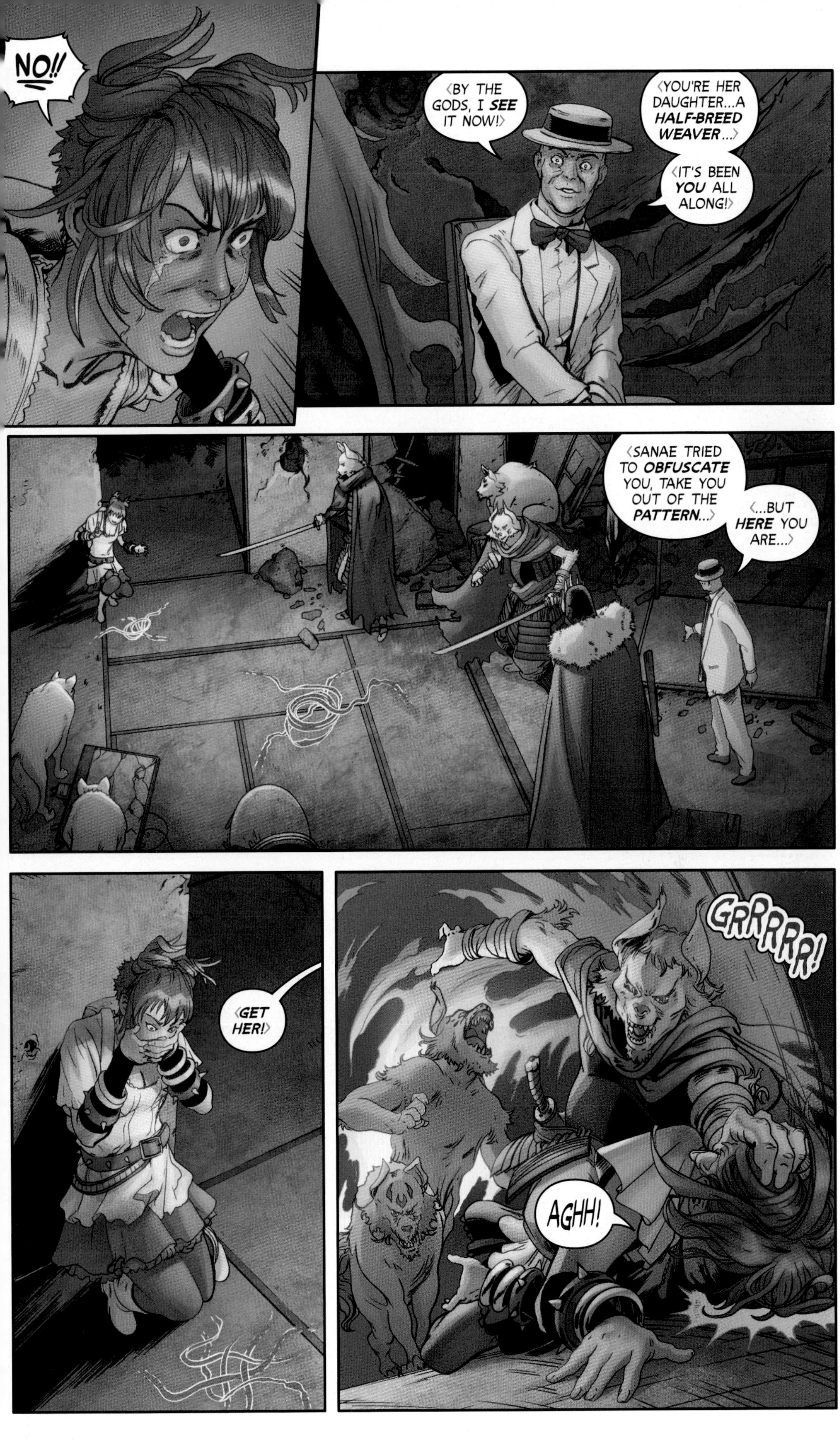
NO!!
‹BY THE GODS, I SEE IT NOW!›
‹YOU'RE HER DAUGHTER...A HALF-BREED WEAVER...›
‹IT'S BEEN YOU ALL ALONG!›
‹SANAE TRIED TO OBFUSCATE YOU, TAKE YOU OUT OF THE PATTERN...›
‹...BUT HERE YOU ARE...›
‹GET HER!›
GRRRRR!
AGHH!

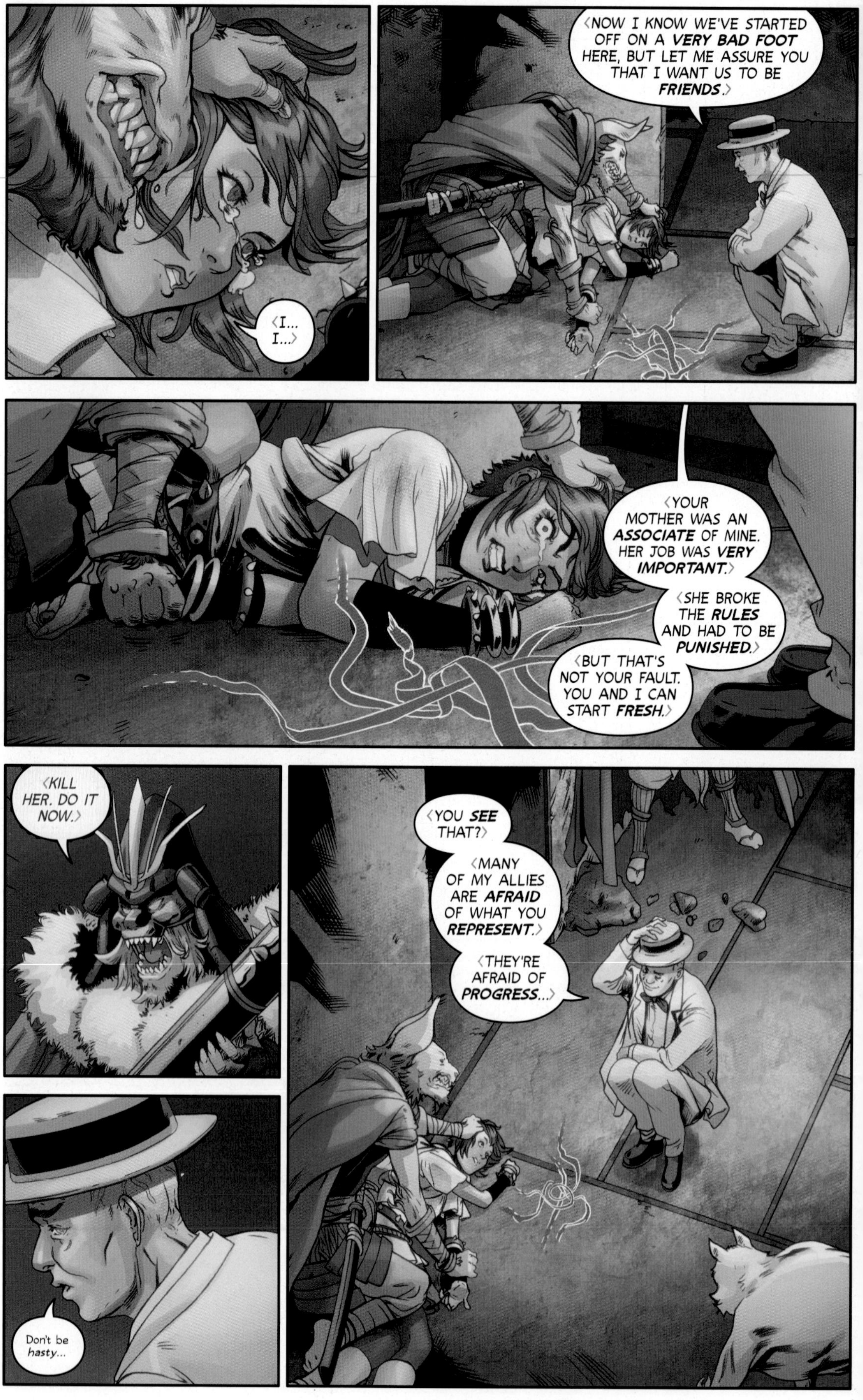

〈I... I...〉
〈NOW I KNOW WE'VE STARTED OFF ON A VERY BAD FOOT HERE, BUT LET ME ASSURE YOU THAT I WANT US TO BE FRIENDS.〉
〈YOUR MOTHER WAS AN ASSOCIATE OF MINE. HER JOB WAS VERY IMPORTANT.〉
〈SHE BROKE THE RULES AND HAD TO BE PUNISHED.〉
〈BUT THAT'S NOT YOUR FAULT. YOU AND I CAN START FRESH.〉
〈KILL HER. DO IT NOW.〉
Don't be hasty...
〈YOU SEE THAT?〉
〈MANY OF MY ALLIES ARE AFRAID OF WHAT YOU REPRESENT.〉
〈THEY'RE AFRAID OF PROGRESS...〉

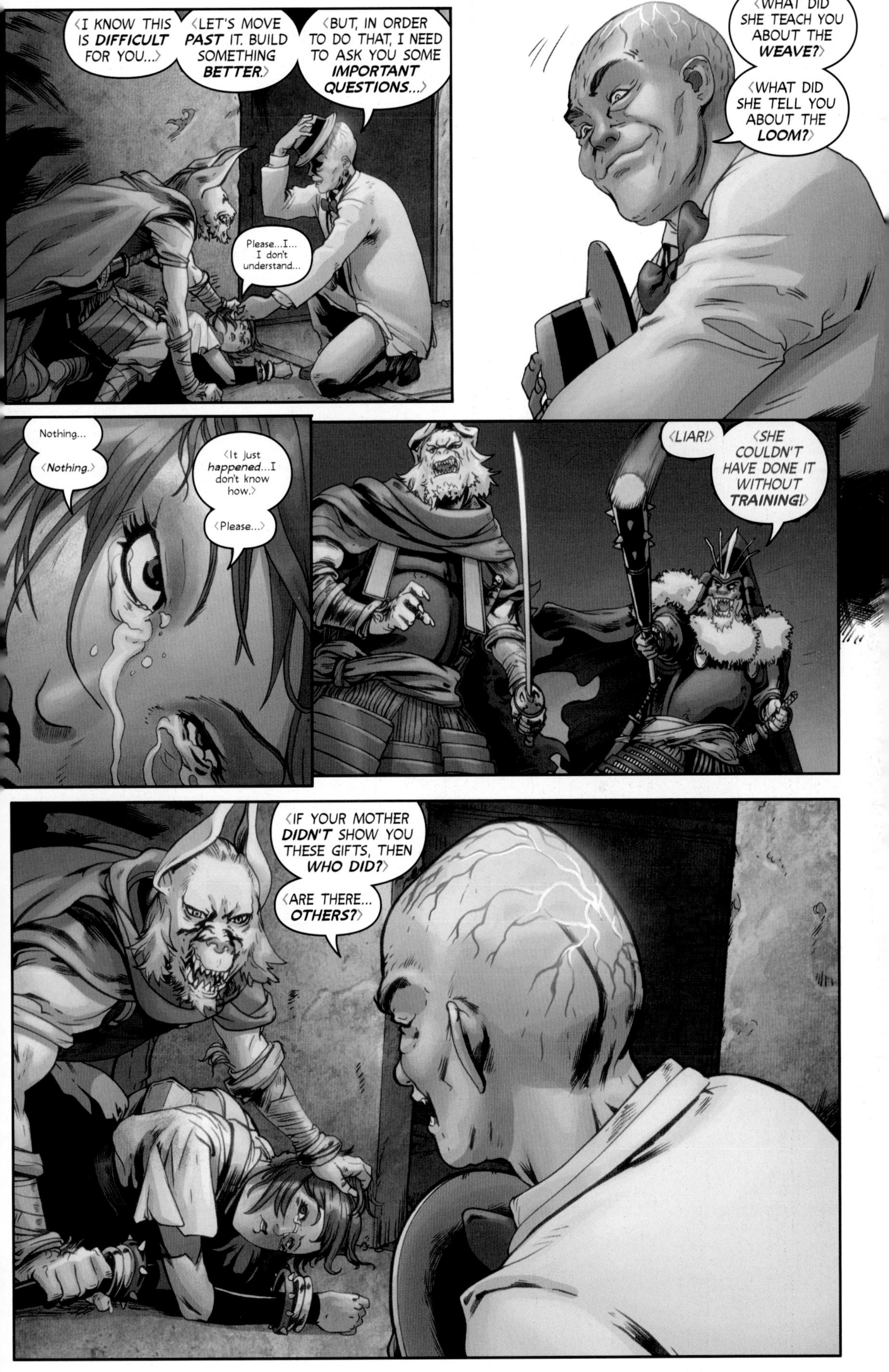

<I KNOW THIS IS DIFFICULT FOR YOU...>
<LET'S MOVE PAST IT. BUILD SOMETHING BETTER.>
<BUT, IN ORDER TO DO THAT, I NEED TO ASK YOU SOME IMPORTANT QUESTIONS...>
Please...I... I don't understand...
<WHAT DID SHE TEACH YOU ABOUT THE WEAVE?>
<WHAT DID SHE TELL YOU ABOUT THE LOOM?>
Nothing...
<Nothing.>
<It just happened...I don't know how.>
<Please...>
<LIAR!>
<SHE COULDN'T HAVE DONE IT WITHOUT TRAINING!>
<IF YOUR MOTHER DIDN'T SHOW YOU THESE GIFTS, THEN WHO DID?>
<ARE THERE... OTHERS?>

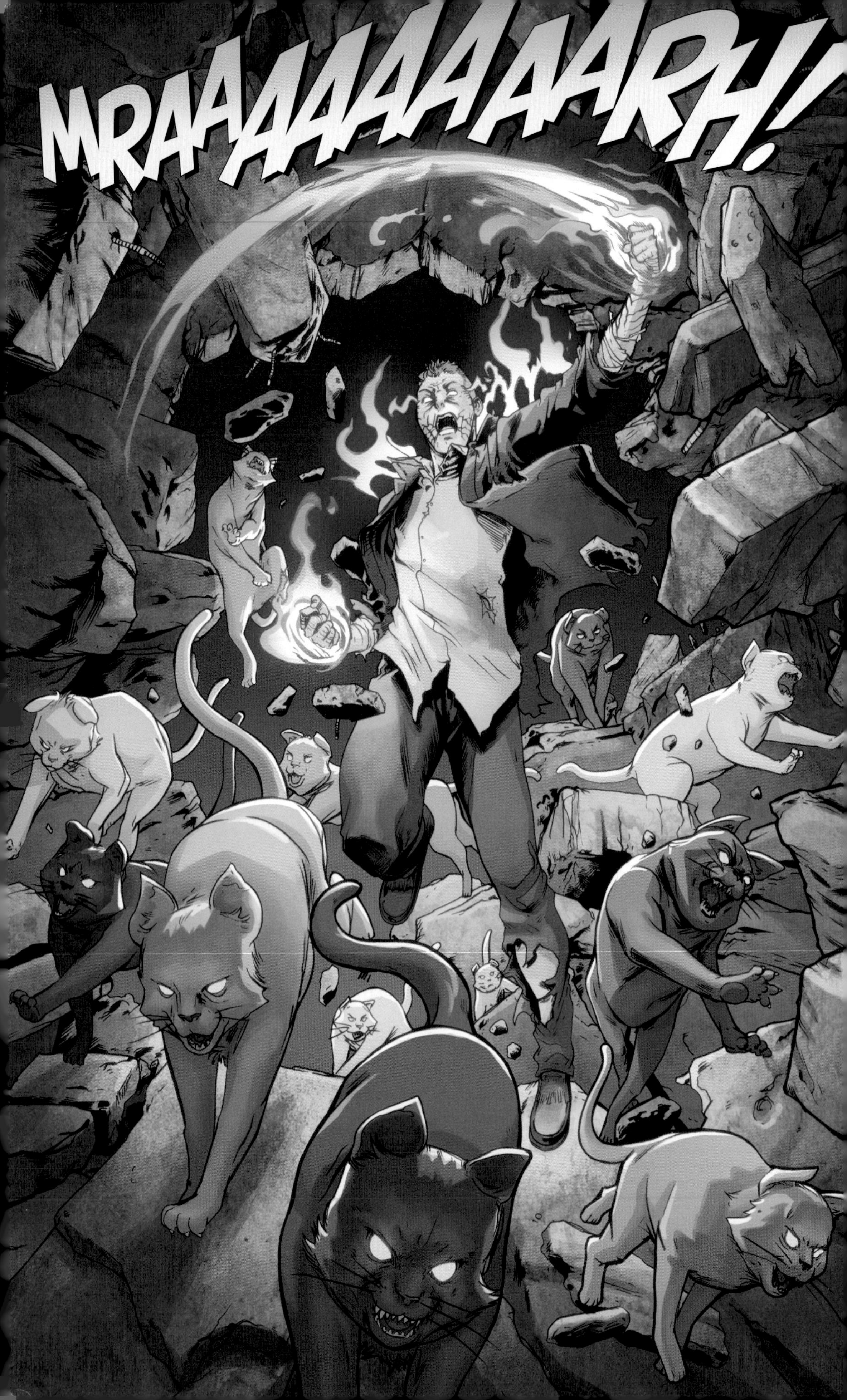
MRAAAAAAAARH!

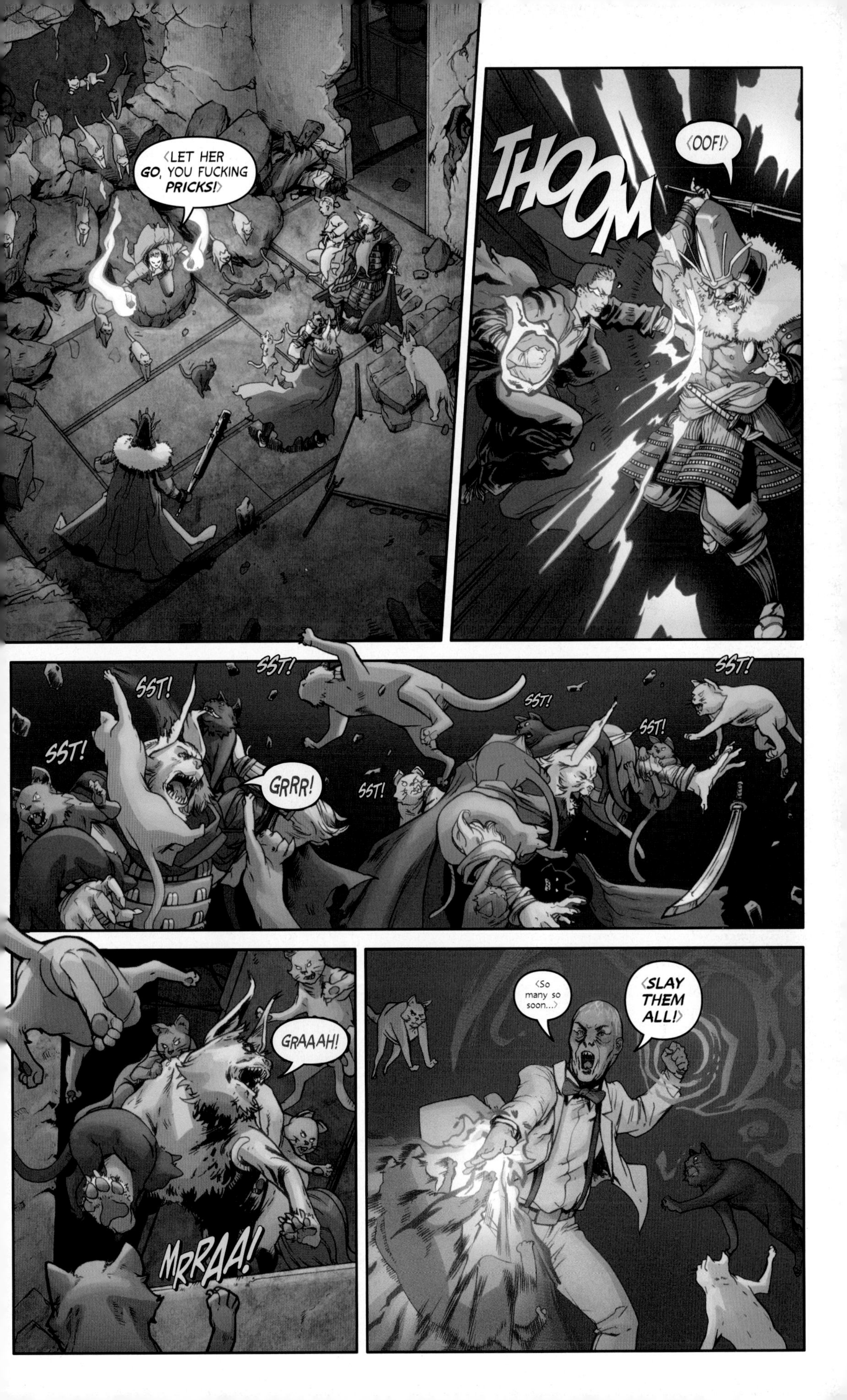

‹LET HER GO, YOU FUCKING PRICKS!›
THOOM
‹OOF!›
SST!
SST!
SST!
GRRR!
SST!
SST!
SST!
SST!
GRAAAH!
MRRAA!
‹So many so soon...›
‹SLAY THEM ALL!›

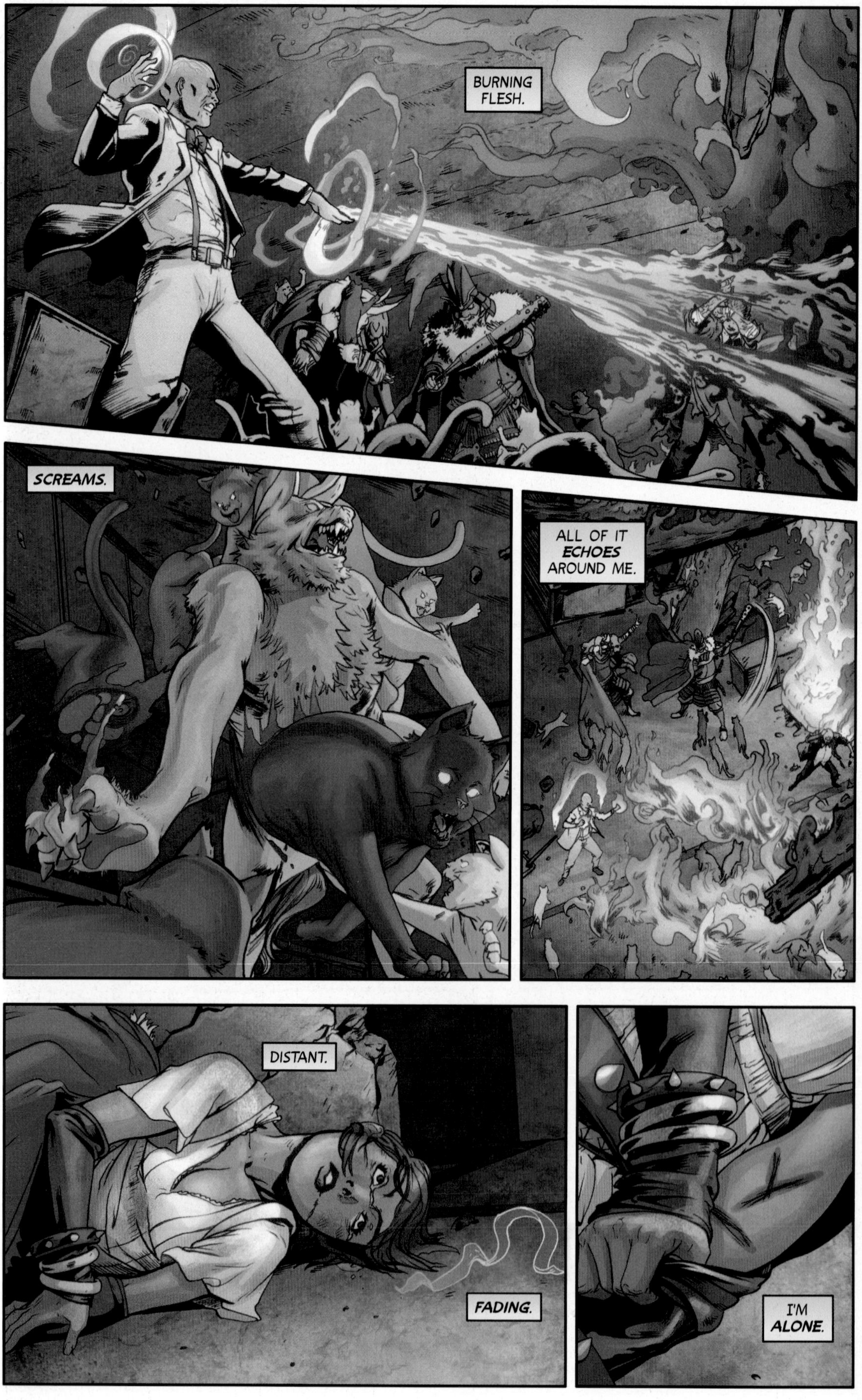
BURNING FLESH.
SCREAMS.
ALL OF IT ECHOES AROUND ME.
DISTANT.
FADING.
I'M ALONE.

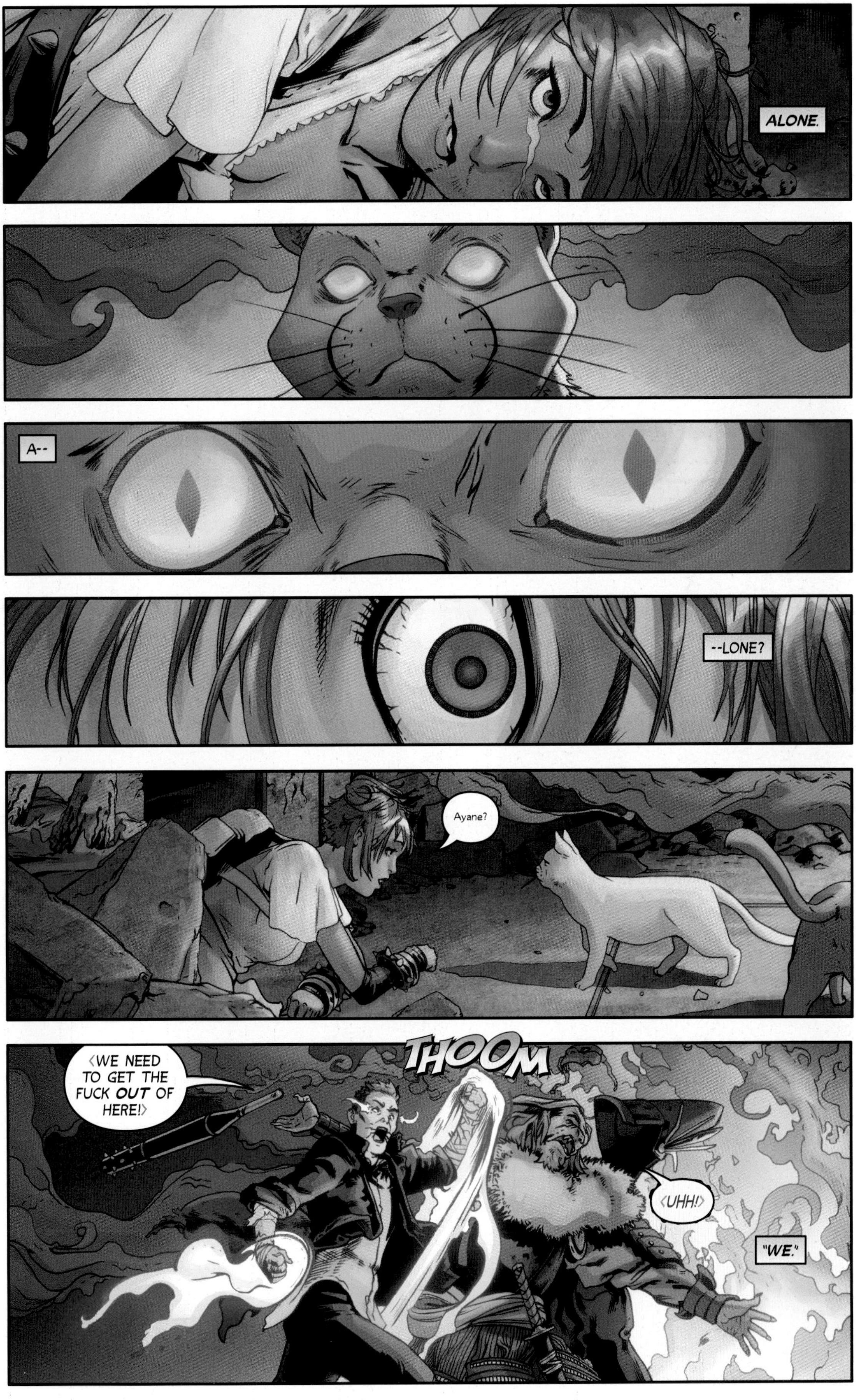
ALONE.
A--
--LONE?
Ayane?
THOOM
‹WE NEED TO GET THE FUCK OUT OF HERE!›
‹UHH!›
"WE."

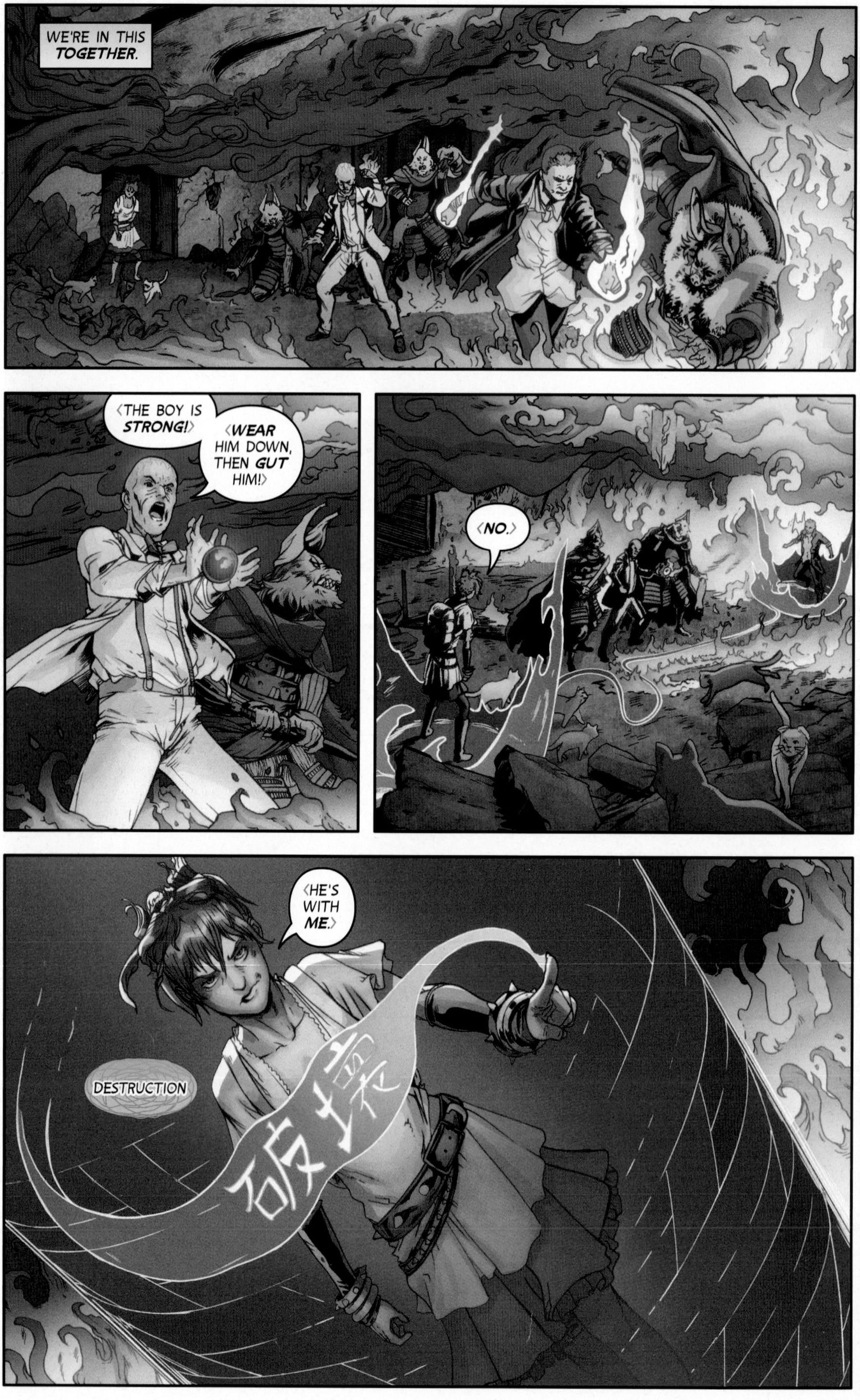
WE'RE IN THIS **TOGETHER.**
⟨THE BOY IS **STRONG!**⟩
⟨**WEAR** HIM DOWN, THEN **GUT** HIM!⟩
⟨**NO.**⟩
⟨HE'S WITH **ME.**⟩
DESTRUCTION
破壊

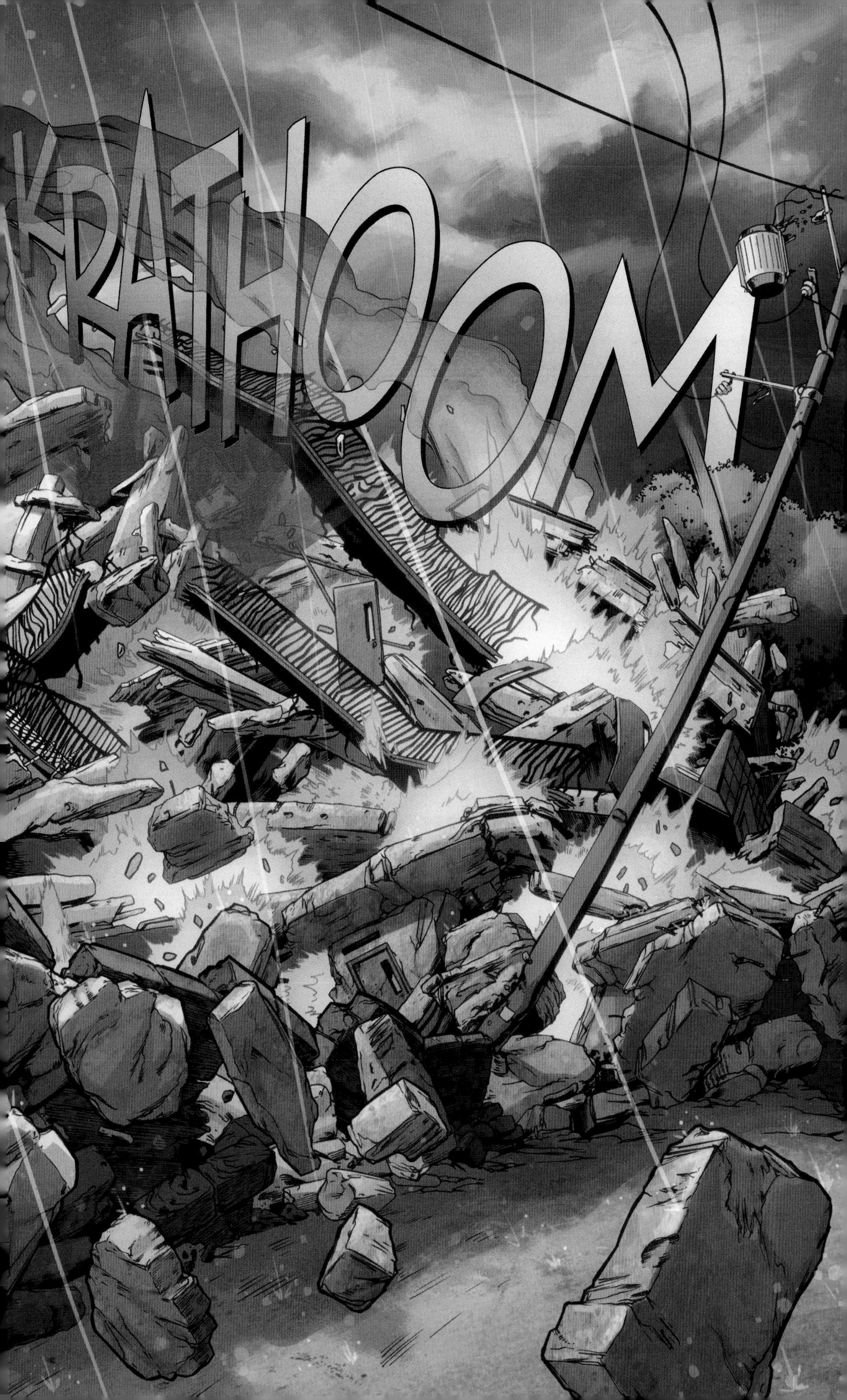
KRATHOOM

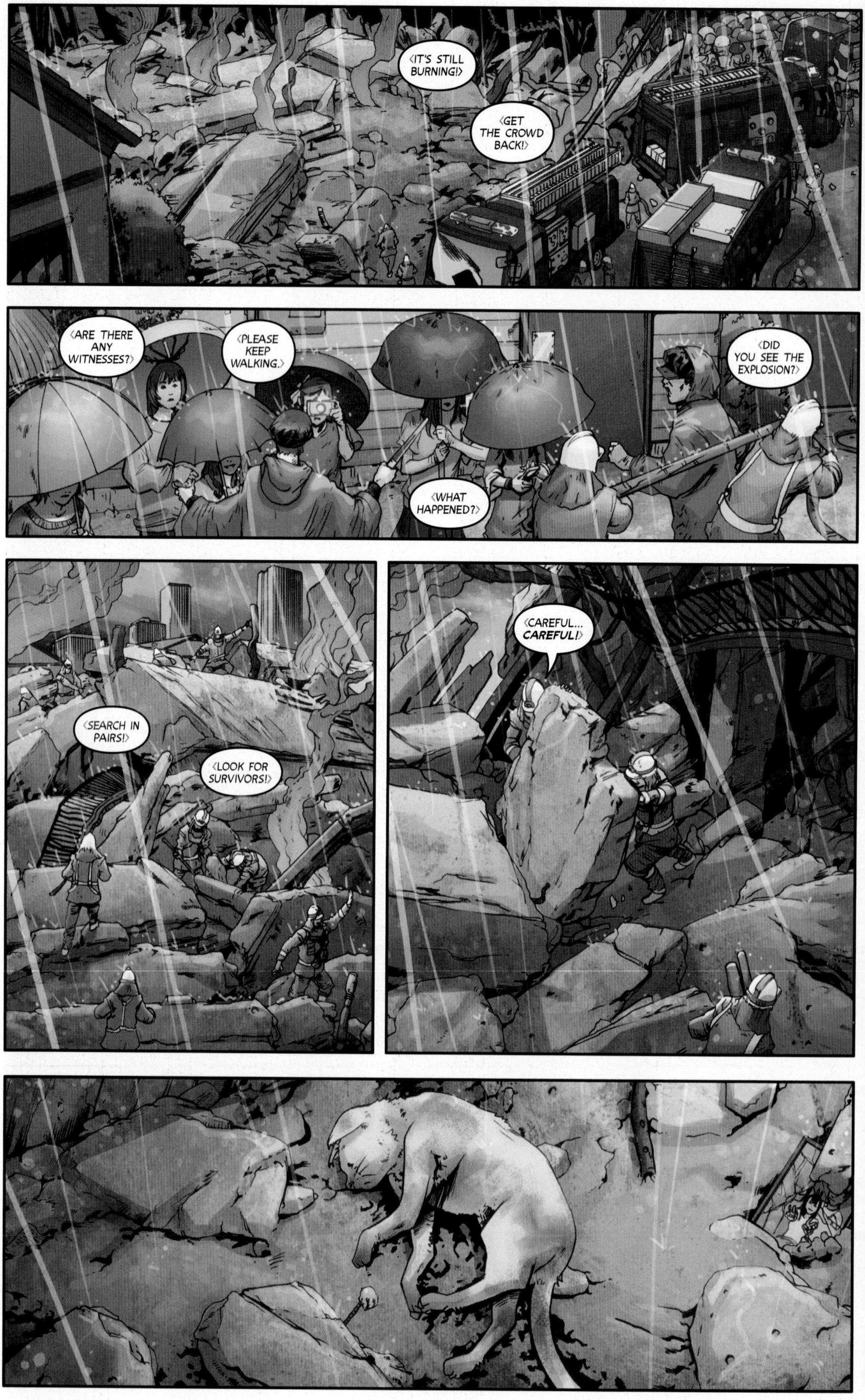

‹IT'S STILL BURNING!›
‹GET THE CROWD BACK!›
‹ARE THERE ANY WITNESSES?›
‹PLEASE KEEP WALKING.›
‹DID YOU SEE THE EXPLOSION?›
‹WHAT HAPPENED?›
‹SEARCH IN PAIRS!›
‹LOOK FOR SURVIVORS!›
‹CAREFUL... CAREFUL!›

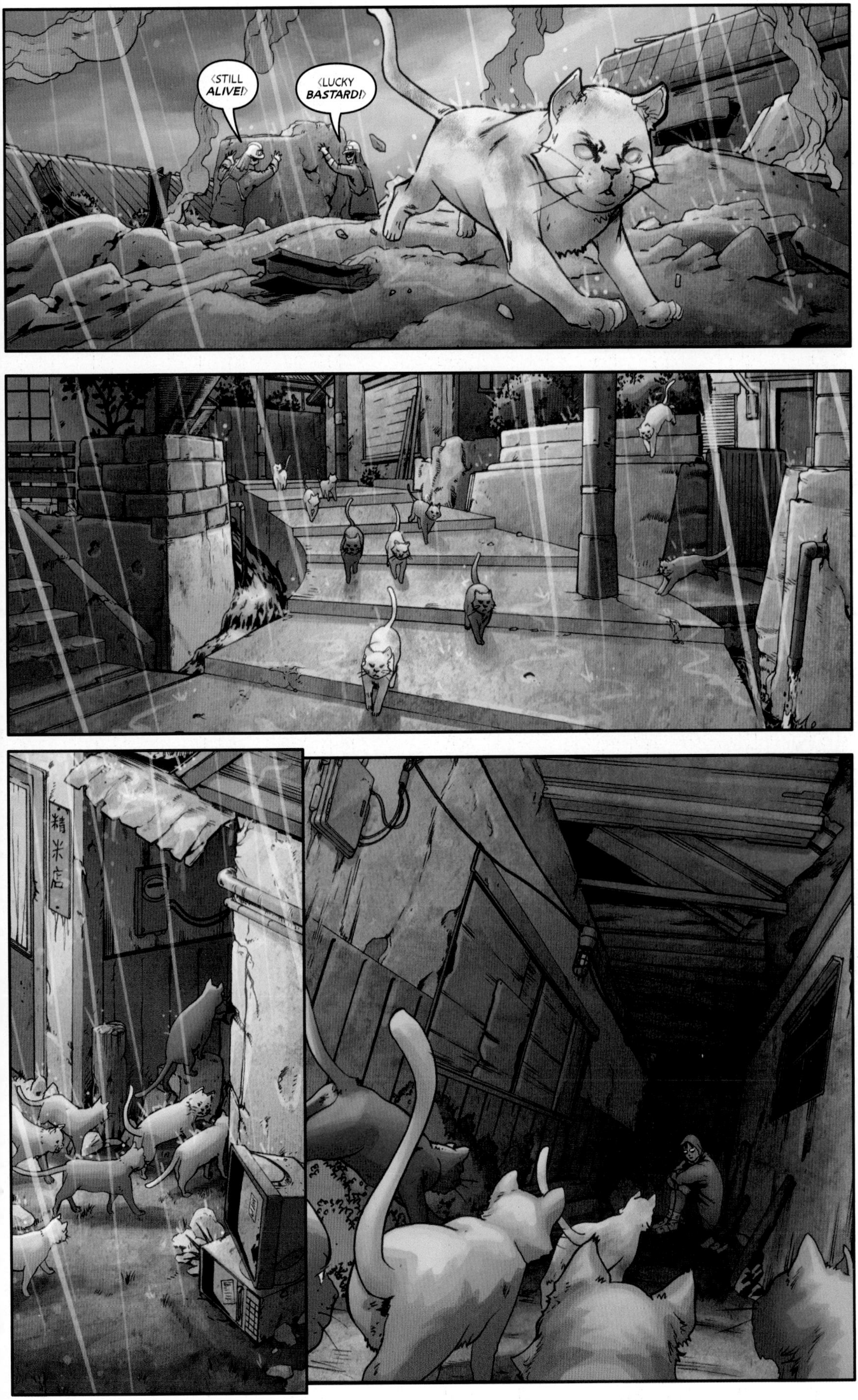
‹STILL ALIVE!›
‹LUCKY BASTARD!›
精米店

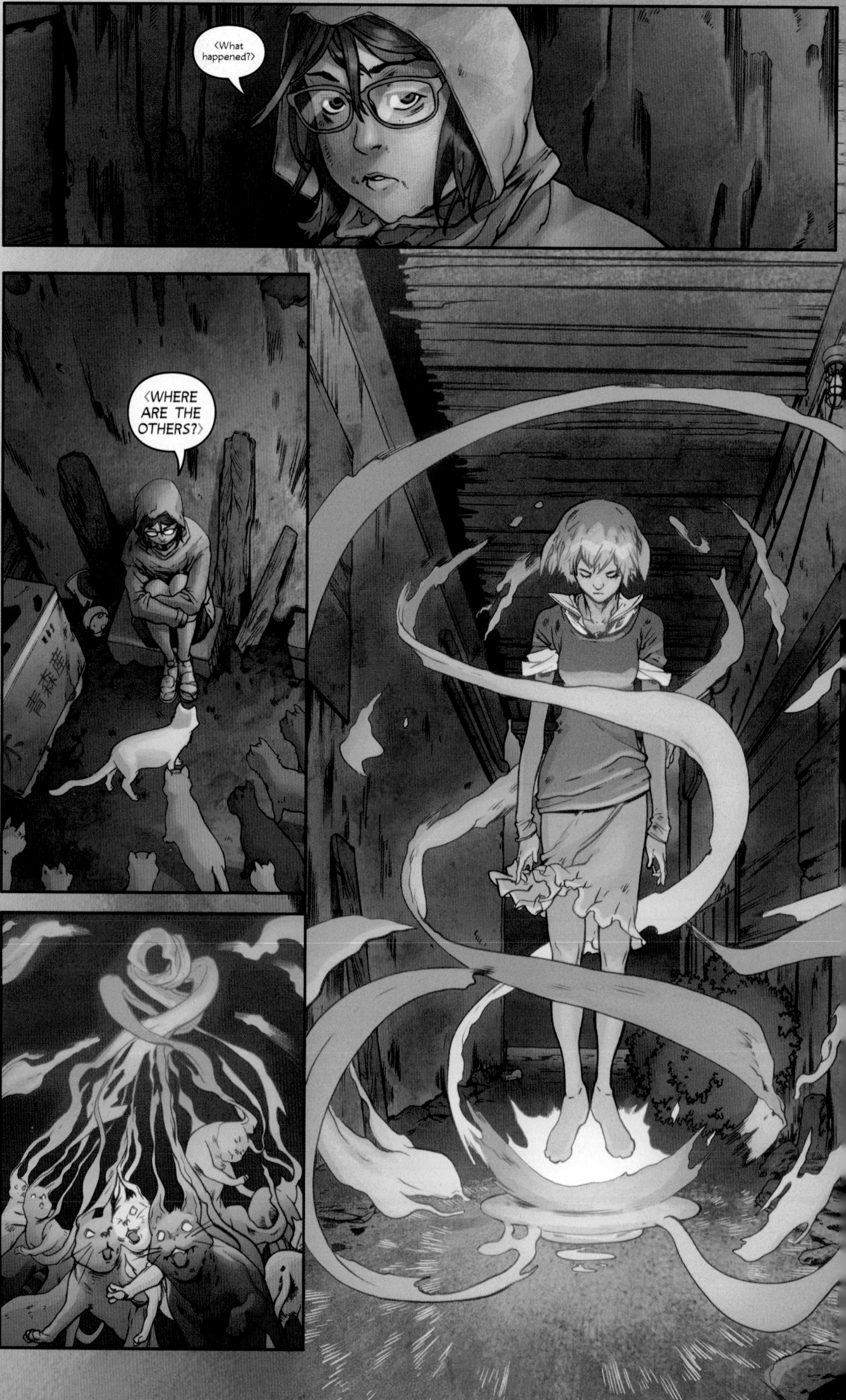
<What happened?>
<WHERE ARE THE OTHERS?>

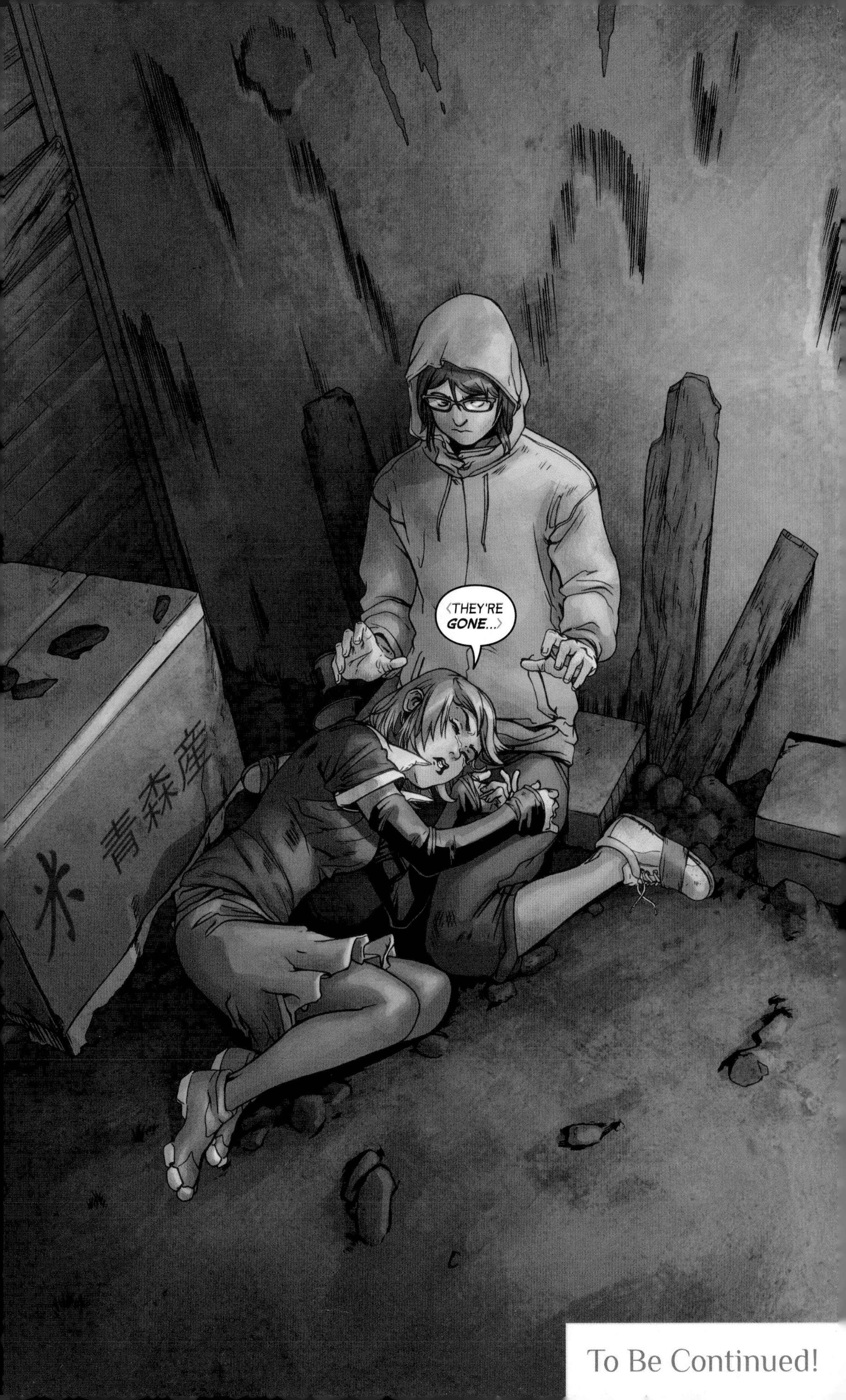
米
青森産
⟨THEY'RE GONE...⟩
To Be Continued!

# Character Design Sketches

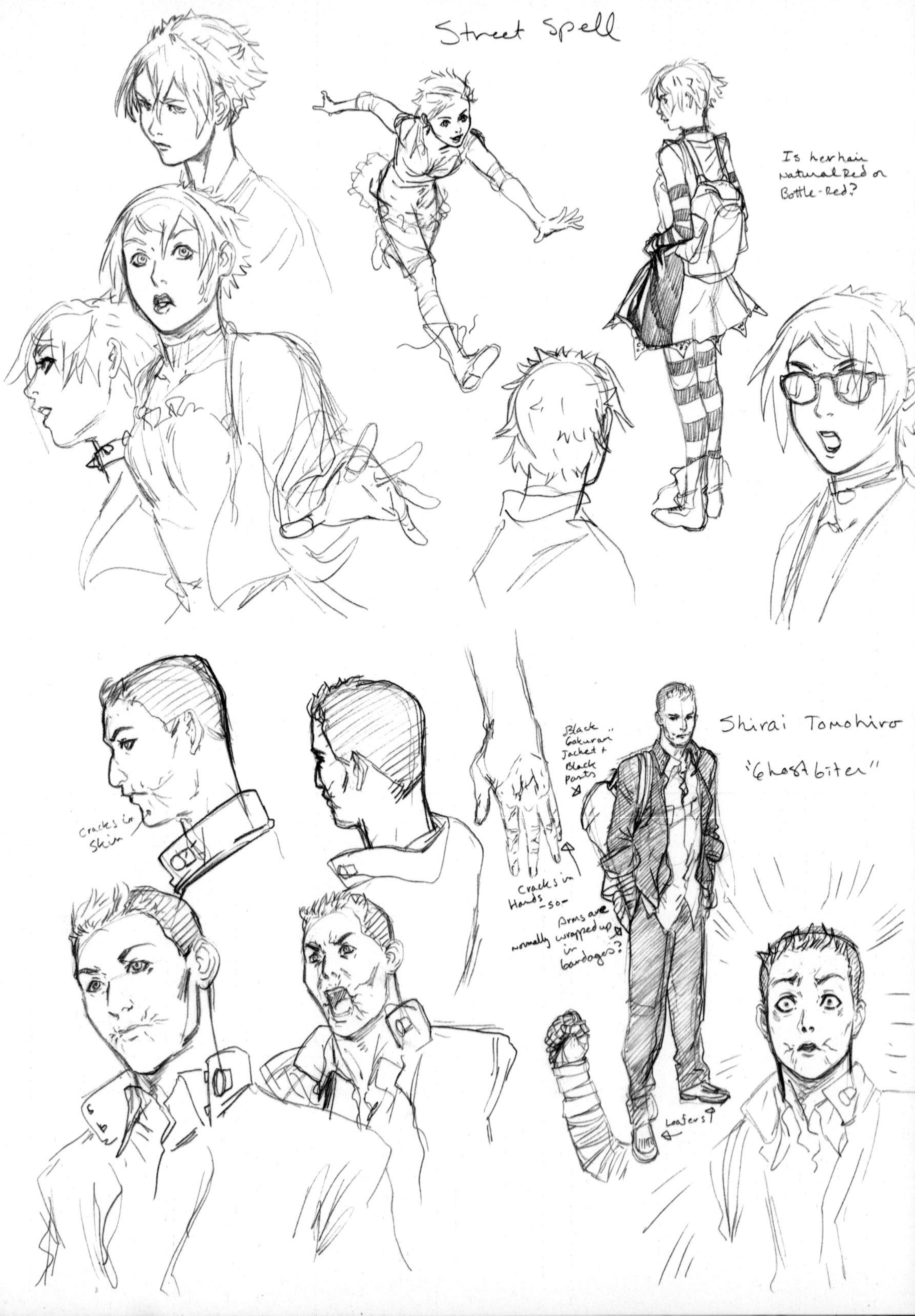
Street Spell
Is her hair natural Red or Bottle-Red?
Cracks in Skin
"Black" Gakuran Jacket + Black Pants
Shirai Tomohiro
"Ghostbiter"
Cracks in Hands -so-
Arms are normally wrapped up in bandages?
Loafers?

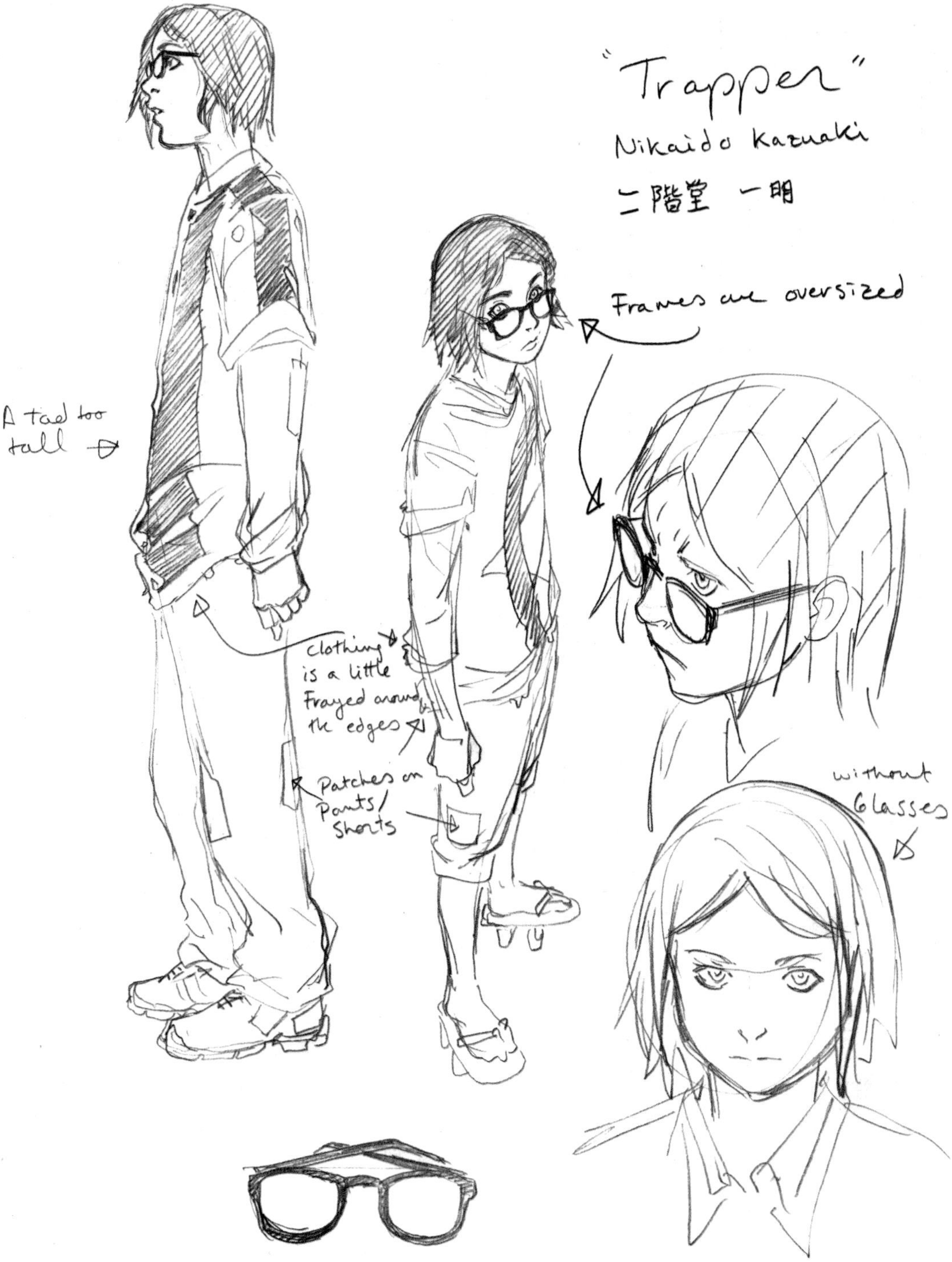
"Trapper"
Nikaido Kazuaki
二階堂 一明
Frames are oversized
A tad too tall
Clothing is a little Frayed around the edges
Patches on Pants/Shorts
without Glasses

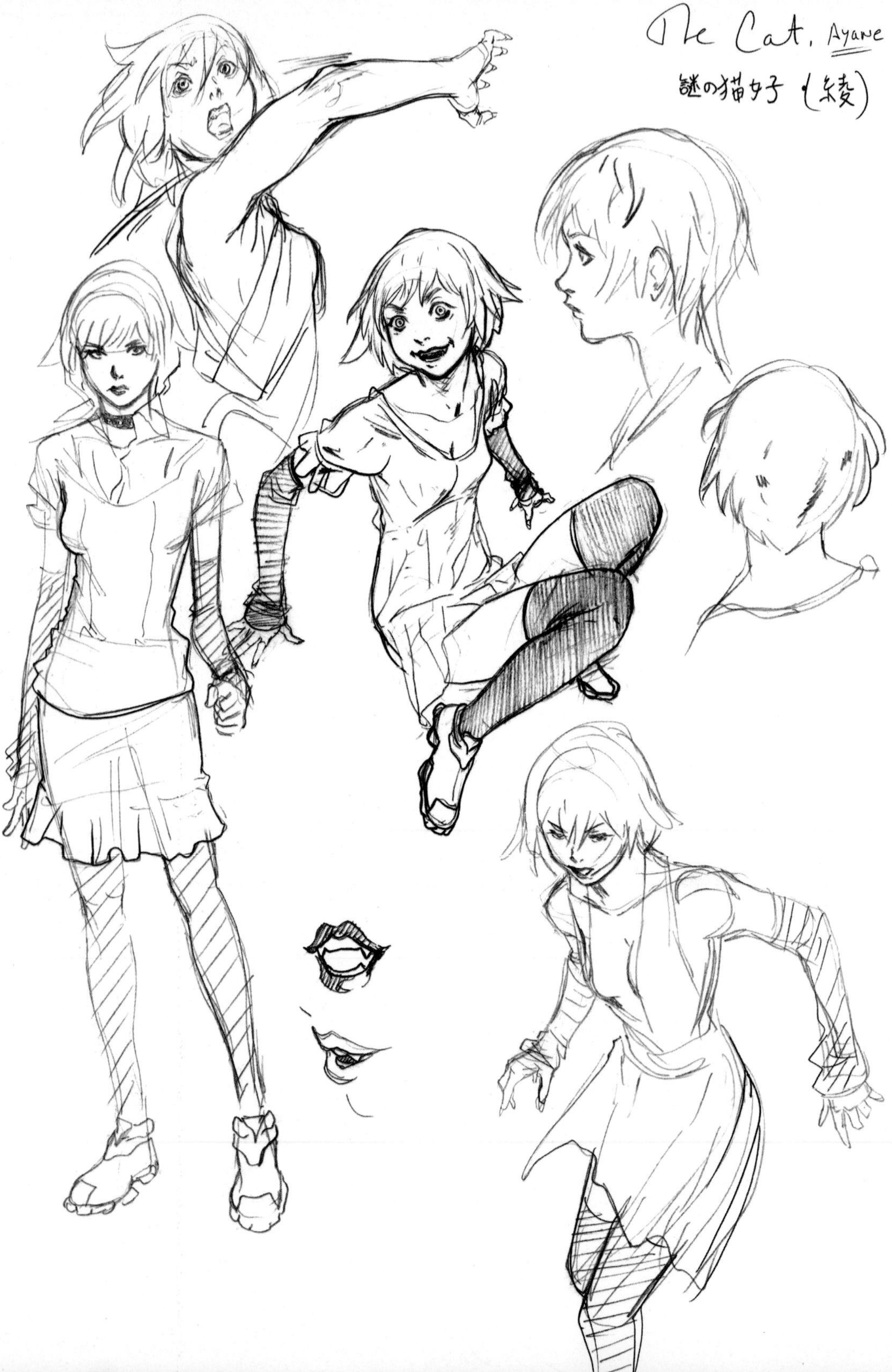
The Cat, Ayane
謎の猫女子・(綾)

# Akaname
## 垢嘗 (Lit: Filth Licker)

Yōkai come in many forms, from devolved deities like the kappa to visual puns like kyokotsu. Some even play a more traditional role, one found in every culture on earth—that of the bogeyman. Parents use these yōkai to frighten their children into good behavior. Do your chores, or a monster will come to get you. In the case of the *akaname*—the filth licker—they scare children into keeping the bathtub clean.

The bath is a venerated space in a Japanese home. More than just a place to get clean, the bath is where you relax and carve out some much-needed privacy in a packed house. Families wash outside of the tub, then climb in to soak. Everyone uses the same bathwater, and the bath is entered by order of Confucian precedence — the father first, then the mother, then the children by birth order. This means the tub gets progressively dirty (and the water more lukewarm) by the time the youngest child climbs in. As insult to injury, the youngest child is often responsible for cleaning the tub.

A dirty tub is a feast for akaname. The cockroaches of yōkai, they scutter in after dark and lick the remaining scum from the bathtub. While this may seem like a free cleaning service, they are pestilence bringers as well as just plain disgusting. Akaname come in an infinite variety; they can be any color from a filthy, moldy green to the bright pink of open sores. They can have one eye or two, and different counts of fingers and toes. The one characteristic all akaname share is their long, sticky tongue that they use to lap up the grease, hair, and filth left behind in the family bath.

4.5 Feet "Long" (not tall)

Hair forms a widow's peak around Horns

Loin cloth

Thick tadpole like tail.

Tongue is approx. 3 Feet Long + Studded with lumpy protrusions

Horns

Droopy Ears

Foot. Inside toe is Smallest, Outside is Largest.

# Hitodama

## 人魂 (Lit: Human Soul)

Will-o'-the-wisp. Foxfire. Corpse candles. There are many names in many cultures for the small balls of ghostly fire that appear during the twilight hours over bogs and swamps and graveyards. Scientists explain them away as the oxidation of hydrogen phosphide and methane gases produced by the decay of organic material—like rotting corpses. But they have long served a dual role in Japan as spirits of the dead as well as mysterious and spectral lanterns accompanying other supernatural creatures.

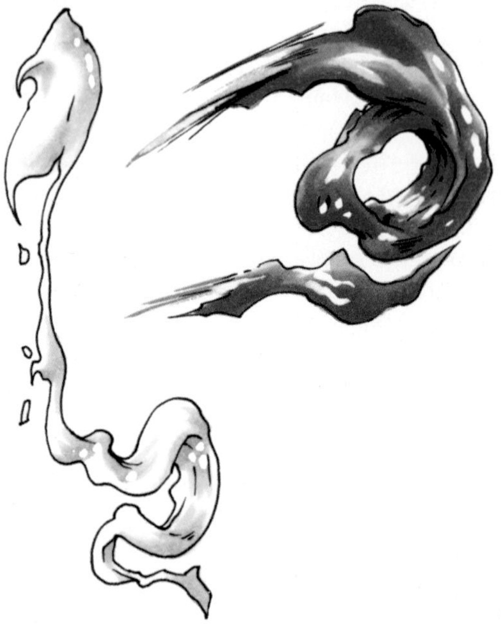

These balls of fire go by various names in Japan, each with its own nuance. *Onibi* (鬼火, demon fire) are dangerous evil spirits that can drain the life force from living things. *Kitsunebi* (狐火, foxfire) are manifestations of fox magic, summoned by magical foxes to light their processions. *Aosagibi* (青鷺火, blue heron fire) is the powdery breath of the magical blue heron, drifting lazily from treetop to treetop in the night.

And then there are *hitodama*, which translates as human soul. They usually accompany some sort of spirit, such as fully manifested ghosts—*yūrei*. Alone *hitodama* pose little danger, serving only as ill omens or to announce the presence of paranormal activity. They are often seen lingering around old shrines and ancient battlefields.

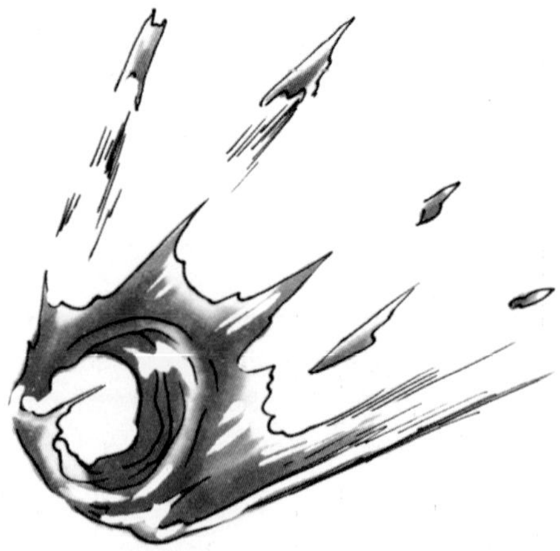

The exact nature of *hitodama* is a mystery. Are they souls of the dead, as the name implies? Could they be some lingering essence, not able to manifest as a full-blown *yūrei*, yet still not able to pass over complete to *anoyo*? Perhaps they are little more than whorls in the supernatural ether that surrounds Japan. Nobody knows.

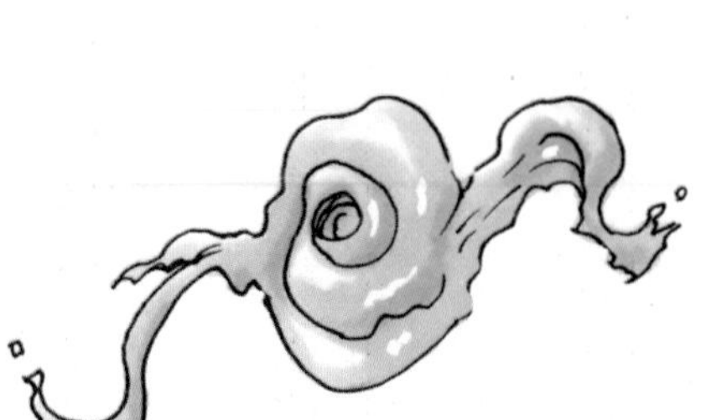

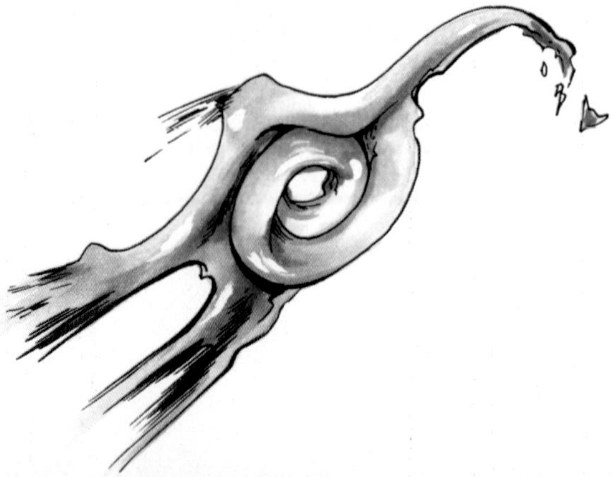

# Kappa

## 河童 (Lit: Water Child)

One of the most ubiquitous yōkai in Japan, kappa are found all across the Japanese islands, wherever there is fresh water. Once worshiped as gods of the rivers (and indeed you can still find shrines dedicated to kappa spread across Japan), they are now viewed as little more than mischievous imps — albeit dangerous.

Traditionally about the size of a small person, kappa appear as humanized turtles, complete with shell and beak. Even with their small size, they are stronger than normal humans. Their skin is green and mottled, their hands and feet are webbed and studded with claws, and they reek of fish. The kappas' most distinctive feature is the bowl-shaped indentation on their heads. This small bowl holds a reservoir of water that is said to be the source of their powers. If the water is spilled, they have to return to their river or die- although some kappa adapted to wear metal plates over their bowl for protection.

Myths about kappa are myriad, and show their changeable nature. Their arms are detached from their bodies—pulling on one arm shortens the other. Their favorite foods are cucumbers and the elusive *shirikodama* —a magical ball that resides in the human anus which kappa forcibly rip out in brutal attacks.

Their level of civilization is also fluid. The 1910 Tono Monogatari portrays kappa as barbarians who raid fishing villages and rape women. Other folklore describes them as civilized and intelligent; they are said to have taught medicine and bone-setting to humans, and are masters of the strategy game *shogi*. In Ryunosuke Akutagawa's 1927 book *Kappa*, they are portrayed as having a society based on radical capitalism, where poor kappa are slaughtered as food for the wealthy class.

In modern Japan, kappa experienced a renaissance lately, depicted as children's toys or cute, harmless mascots for sushi restaurants. But underneath the plastic smiles and friendly waves lie the brutal monsters of folklore.

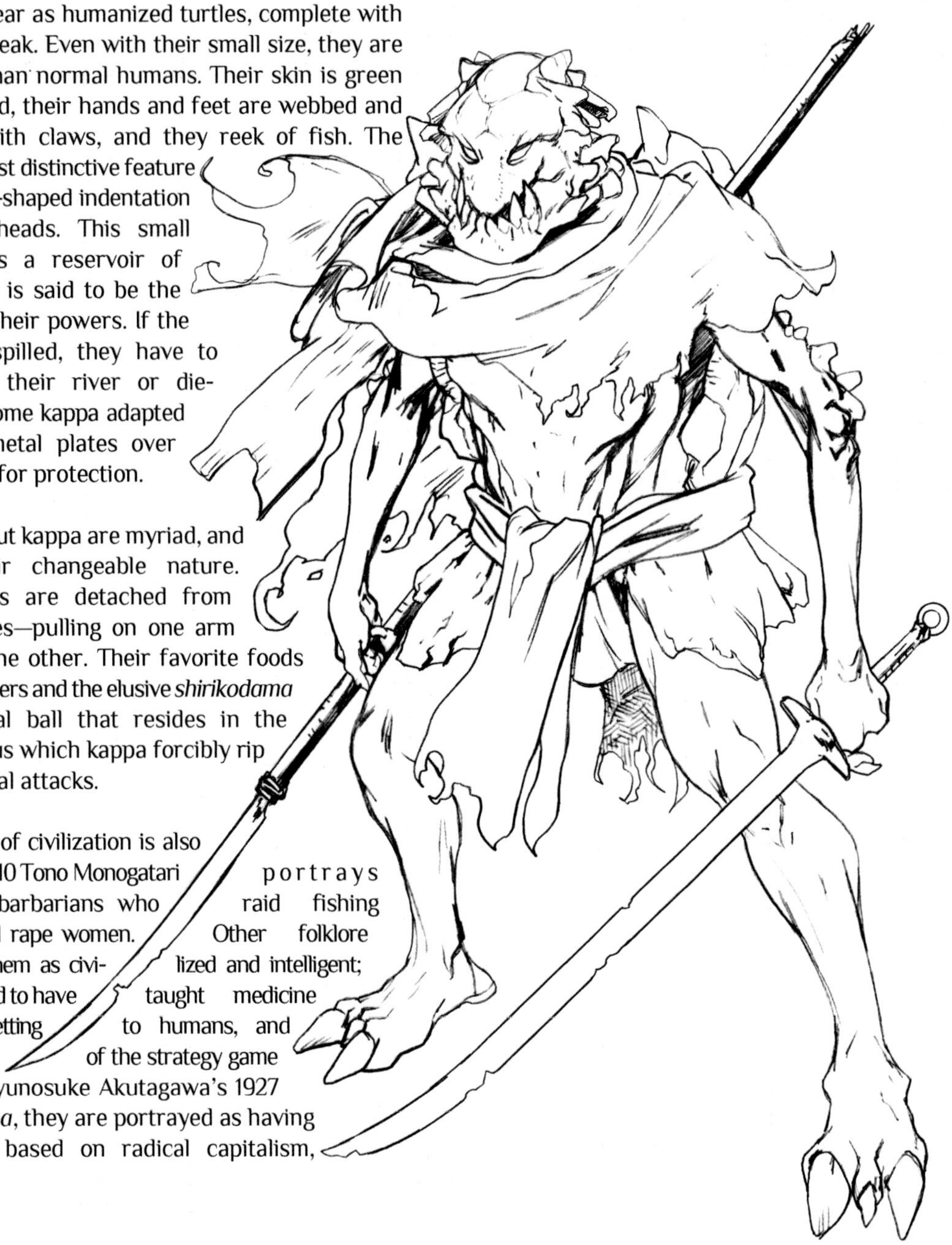

# Kitsune
## 狐 (Lit: Fox)

Wander off any beaten path in Japan, towards any shadow-haunted corner, and you will inevitably run into a pair of stone foxes, grim-faced and daunting, standing guard before a sequence of lonely red gates. The atmosphere of these shrines is different from other places—they are not for tourists. These are the fox shrines, dedicated to the kami Inari and her messengers the kitsune, the magical foxes of Japan.

Kitsune (狐) are the most complex and abstruse yokai in Japan's menagerie. Simultaneously sacred and profane, good and evil, celestial and earthbound, they are a study in contrasts. Kitsune are the servitors of gods, and worshipped as gods in their own right. They are also the husbands and wives of poor farmers, hiding their true natures with their shape-shifting abilities. Kitsune wield vast magical powers, and are sorcerers feared across the land. They are also vermin and troublemakers, who possess humans for no other reason than to get their hands on some tasty fried tofu. On days when rain falls from a blue sky, they hold their wedding ceremonies. On dark nights, balls of fire ignite from their tails. Their stories are as mercurial as the kitsune themselves.

Part of their wayward nature comes from the multiple sources for kitsune legends. While there is some dispute, most scholars agree that stories of magical foxes are not native to Japan. The majority of the oldest known Japanese kitsune stories come from the 12th century collection *Konjaku Monogatari-shu — Tales of Times Now Past*. This 33-volume series collected the magical tales of China, India, and Japan. It is thought that the kitsune stories were based on Chinese legends of the *huli jing*, mischievous, nine-tailed, shape-shifting fox spirits that behave similarly to European fairies. Whatever their origin, kitsune were adopted with gusto by Japan, which quickly adapted and expanded on the tales of the *huli jing*.

In Japan, kitsune belong to a class of yokai called henge, transformed animals who have gained supernatural powers through long life. The necessary longevity varies legend-by-legend, but in general kitsune must reach 50 years of age before they come into their powers. When they attain 100 years old, they gain an extra tail and more abilities, and then another tail and level-up each subsequent century until they reach their ultimate form, a glorious nine-tailed fox—immortal and immensely powerful—called a *kyubi no kitsune*.

Like all transformed animals, kitsune have the ability to shape-shift and cast illusions. While skilled, they are not the most powerful in either of these arts. In a classic tale, a kitsune challenged a tanuki to a contest of illusions, and paid with his life. According to a common saying kitsune are able to take seven forms, while tanuki can take

Mystical Markings on the Head ⟶

In fox form they are very Bulky.

eight, and itachi (weasels) are the most capable, with ten forms to flow between. The seven forms of the kitsune are enough, however. There are myriad tales of kitsune who assume human form, get married and have children, then are betrayed by a fox tail poking out of a kimono on a warm summer's night.

But the true terror of a kitsune was in possession. Just as in old Europe, where mental illness was blamed on demonic possession, in old Japan the finger was pointed at kitsune whenever someone started acting strangely or frothed at the mouth. Many was the story of a mother who murdered her own children in a fit of rage, or a man found wandering naked in the streets, bathed in the blood of his own horse. In cases like this, there could always be a den of foxes found nearby to take the blame. Sometimes this possession was intentional; sorcerers called kitsunetsukai (狐使い; fox users) commanded kitsune and used their abilities for nefarious purposes. Percival Lowell detailed cases of fox possession in his 1895 book Occult Japan, as did Lafcadio Hearn for his 1894 *Glimpses of Unfamiliar Japan*. During the Edo period, *kitsunetsuki* (狐憑き)—fox possession—was a very real problem.

At the same time that they were considered dark devils, the familiars of foul sorcerers, kitsune were also sacred messengers and avatars of the kami spirit Inari, the goddess of rice and fortune. The origin of the connection with Inari is uncertain; they first appeared as her messengers, and the stone statues of Inari shrines still carry document rolls in their mouths. Eventually, the myths of Inari and her fox guardians merged until the goddess herself was depicted as an immense white fox.

Myths of the white fox are as contradictory as the kitsune themselves. Some see two distinct species of kitsune; the pure white zenko (善狐), meaning good foxes, or the base-colored yako (野狐), meaning field foxes. However these zenko were not always as pure as their fur. In the 16th century, the warlord Takeda Shingen became obsessed with a 14-year-old girl, the Lady Koi. Rumor had it that Koi was a white fox in disguise, the spirit of the Suwa Shrine bewitching the mighty warlord.

Fox shrines are scattered all across Japan, usually kept apart from the main buildings in some sparse and gloomy place. Worship is conducted by buying a small red gate and placing it before the shrine. There are exceptions to Inari's solitary nature, most especially the famous Fushimi Inari outside of Kyoto city, with literal tunnels of red tori gates placed by petitioners. The spectacular vision of Fushimi Inari has led to its appearance in films like Memoirs of a Geisha. But the pretty scene belies a more sinister nature.

Good or bad, sacred or profane, kitsune are always dangerous and not to be dealt with lightly. They are honorable after their fashion, and will keep their bargains. But a warning at these shrines—kitsune are powerful and can make wishes come true, but they exact a heavy price. More than most people are willing to pay.

# Kyokotsu

## 狂骨 (Lit: Crazy Bones)

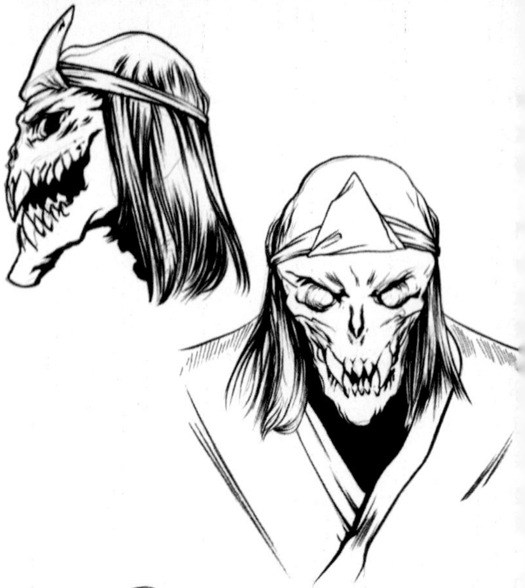

Be careful when you pull up a bucket of water from an ancient, abandoned well—you can get more than you bargained for. Draw from the wrong well and a kyokotsu might come popping up, like some skeletal Jack-in-the-Box eager to deliver its curse.

Clad in a white burial kimono, kyokotsu appear as little more than bones wrapped in a shroud. Shocks of white hair spring from their bleached-white skulls. They are thought to arise from people who were murdered and had their bodies stuffed into wells to hide the deed. Angry at being undiscovered and unburied, the bones reanimate and attack anyone unfortunate enough to come within their reach.

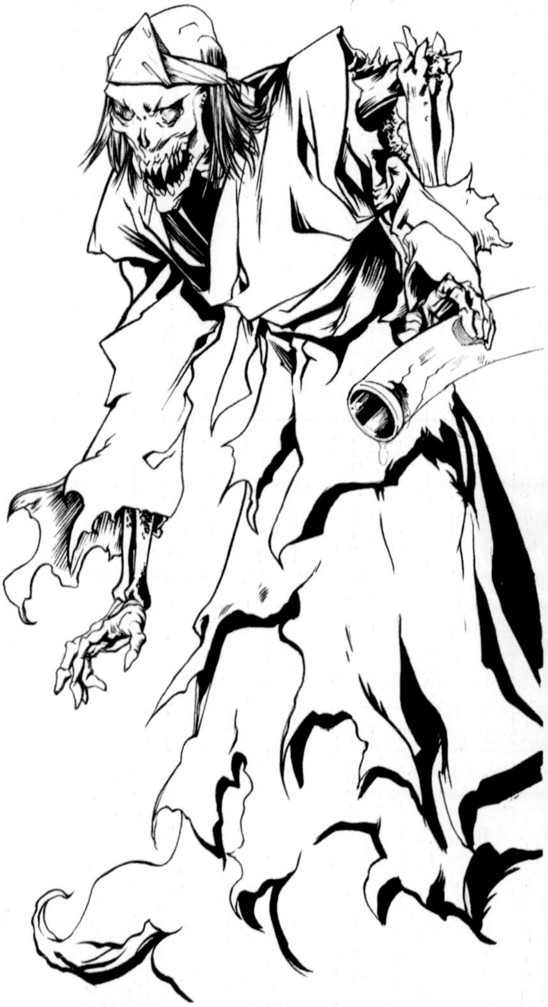

At least that's the theory. In reality, the kyokotsu was invented by artist Toriyama Sekien for his Edo period book *Supplement to the Hundred Demons of the Past*. Publishers were desperate for Toriyama to produce sequels to his popular Hundred Demons books, but the unfortunate truth was that he had run out of folkloric yokai to catalogue. So Toriyama did what any good artist would do—he made up new ones. Several of Toriyama's yokai, like kyokotsu, are based on puns and turns of phrases. The word "kyokotsu" literally translates as "crazy bones," which was a slang term for violent or aggressive men. Toriyama's "kyokotsu" was not unlike a modern monster artist creating his own "lazy bones" character.

Toriyama did have a basis for his creation. In Japanese folklore, water is a channel to the world of the dead, and the bottoms of wells are directly connected. Those who died in wells—by accident, suicide, or murder—were thought to be bound to it. Their curse was indiscriminate, attacking anyone who came too near. With his creation, Toriyama tapped into the old belief of an inexhaustible grudge that can come from water and the bottom of wells.

# Nurarihyon

## ぬらりひょん (Lit: Slippery Gourd)

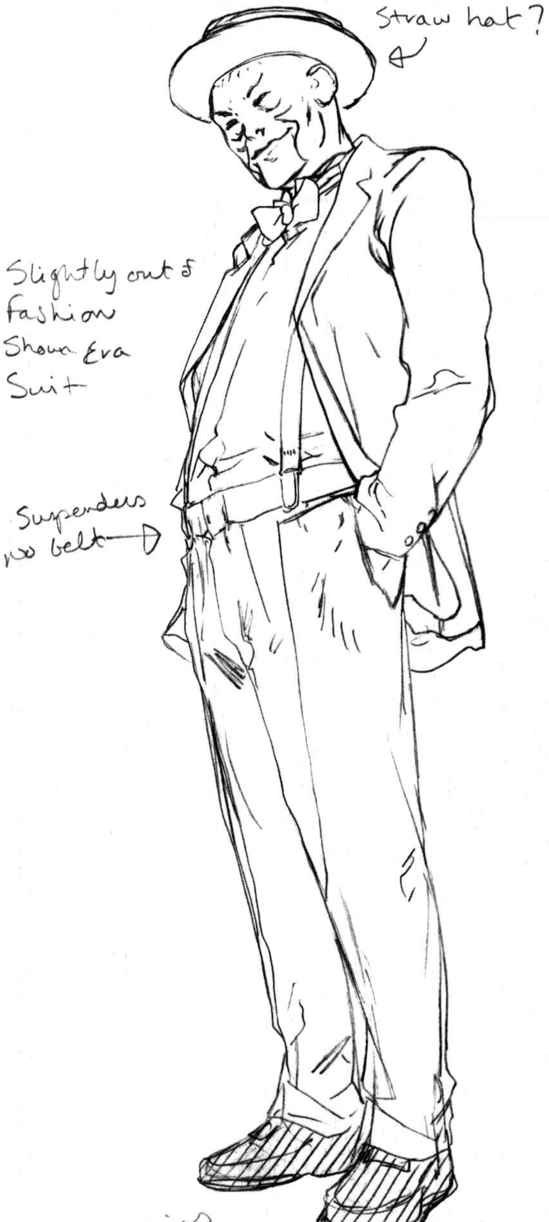

Straw hat?
Slightly out of fashion Showa Era Suit
Suspenders no belt


One of the most elusive of Japan's yōkai menagerie, the slippery spirit called Nurarihyon has evolved far beyond his humble origins.

In the oldest stories of Nurarihyon, he was a sea monster—his blobby head was the personification of the Portuguese Man-o-War jellyfish, floating in the Seto Inland Sea. In Okayama prefecture, he was considered an aspect of the massive Umibōzu sea monk. Yet when artists began illustrating the *Hyakki Yagyō-zu*, an odd man appeared dressed in a simple robe, balancing an enormous, veined, gourd-shaped head on a spindly neck. Somehow, this peculiar character was identified as Nurarihyon.

By the Edo period, Nurarihyon was a prominent member of the urban yōkai. Stories described his powers as a mysterious air of authority. Nurarihyon would find prosperous houses, then come in and start giving orders, eating and drinking delicacies, and acting like an important house guest. The people would feel so flustered at his imperious nature they began serving him without question. Only after Nurarihyon left would they realize they had been tricked.

In the late Showa period (1926-1989), Nurarihyon got a promotion. He gained the reputation as a commander of yōkai, leader of the Hyakki Yagyō. (All you have to do is look at the old scrolls to see this isn't true.) His elevated rank can be traced back to Shigeru Mizuki's seminal yōkai comic Kitaro, where Nurarihyon showed up and announced himself as the Yōkai Sōdaishō. This position was formerly held by the massive Mikoshi Nyudō. Whether the two fought some Great Yōkai War that saw Nurarihyon as the victor, or whether Nurarihyon used his slippery nature and air of authority to seize command is unknown. Either way, in modern Japan it is accepted that Nurarihyon is a leader of yōkai.

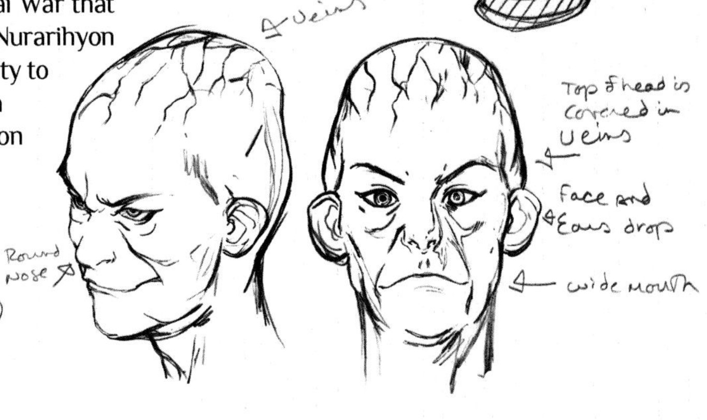

Veins
Top of head is covered in veins
Face and Ears drop
Round nose
wide mouth


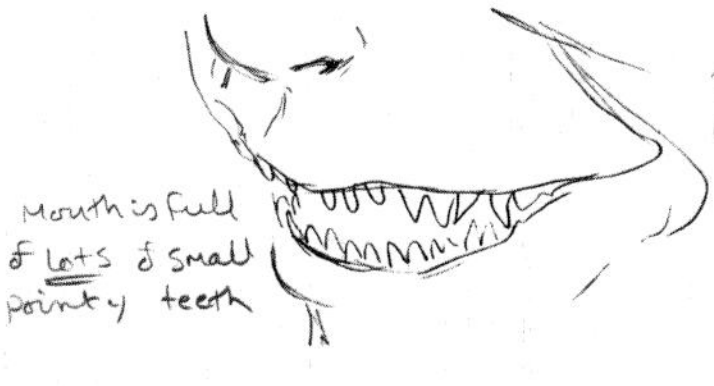

Mouth is full of lots of small pointy teeth

# Suiko

## 水虎 (Lit: Water Tiger)

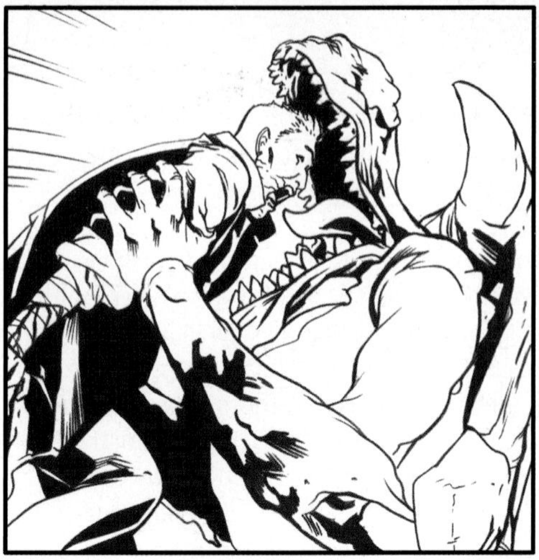

Kappa are the most ubiquitous of Japan's yōkai. While many monsters are found only in a particular region or environment, stories of kappa—or varieties of kappa–can be found almost anywhere across the Japanese archipelago. But this does not mean they are all the same.

The monsters called *suiko* —or water tigers—are massive and dangerous variants of the standard-issue kappa. Like vampires, suiko subsist on human blood. They are giants, covered in scales like a pangolin, and with hooked kneecaps and elbows that resemble a tiger's claws. Their skin is described as being mottled and patterned like a tiger's as well, which is all the more strange when you consider that suiko are invisible.

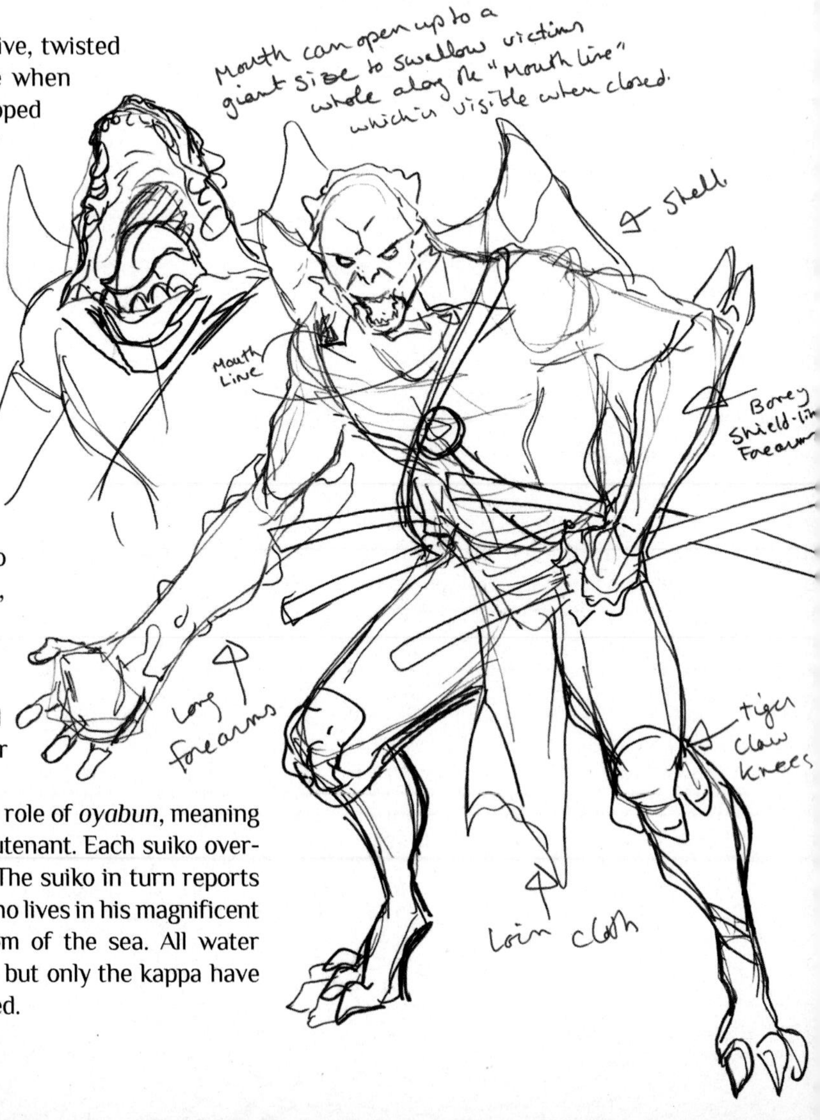

Mouth can open up to a giant size to swallow victims whole along the "Mouth Line" which is visible when closed.
Shell
Mouth Line
Boney
Long forearms
tiger claw knees
Loin cloth


It is said that suikos' massive, twisted bodies only become visible when they die. They can be trapped by using a dead body they have drained as a lure. Build a straw hut around the body, and the suiko will be inescapably drawn to it. They will run and run in circles around the hut. One trapped, the suiko will continue running as the corpse decays. Exhausted, they will die. And their horrible form will be revealed. For unknown reasons, they also fear scythes, flax seeds, and black-eyed peas.

There are some reports that kappa society is organized into gangs like the yakuza or the American Mafia.
In these tales, suiko play the role of *oyabun*, meaning something like a capo or lieutenant. Each suiko oversees 48 kappa in its squad. The suiko in turn reports to *Ryū-ō*, the dragon king, who lives in his magnificent palace *Ryū-gū* at the bottom of the sea. All water yōkai pay homage to *Ryū-ō*, but only the kappa have become organized and ranked.